DECEPTION
So
DEADLY

DECEPTION SO DEADLY

DECEPTION SO · BOOK ONE

Clara Kensie

Snowy Wings
PUBLISHING

To G:
T.P.O.L.

CHAPTER ONE

MY CELL PHONE rang, loud and shrill, shattering the classroom's silence.

He found us. He was coming.

The teacher scowled, reaching out her puffy hand to confiscate my phone as I slid it open and held it to my ear. Answer on the first ring—that was the rule.

One word, my mother's panicked command: *"Run."*

With trembling hands, I swept my American History notebook into my bag. Leave nothing personal behind—that was another rule.

Every second, he was getting closer. I stumbled toward the door.

"Maddie, where are you going?" Mrs. Landon demanded, then her voice softened. "Is something wrong?"

I rushed past her and out of the classroom, my breath coming in stuttery little gasps. Dennis Connelly was coming. How did he find us again?

I raced to my locker—the combination, what's the combination?—and cleaned it out, stuffing everything into my bag. Flew down the stairs. Dashed down the hall, almost colliding with a girl carrying an armful of books. Sprinted past the office, reached the exit—

"Hey!" A security guard, belly hanging over his belt, grabbed my arm. "Where's your pass?"

My brother darted over, lugging his bookbag and saxophone. "Let her go," he said, his calm and firm tone betrayed by the terror in his eyes. He pulled me away, and when I stumbled, he pushed me out the door. "Tessa, run!"

We were in public, but Logan used my real name. We no longer needed our aliases.

I glanced behind me. "Where's Jillian?"

The doors burst open and our sister shot outside, her blond hair flying behind her like a shiny cape.

Its engine running, our getaway car waited in the pickup lane with our dad holding the back door open. We ran and dove in. Dad jumped in the passenger seat, slamming his door closed as Mom stomped on the gas pedal and sped us away.

Night fell long before my mom pulled off the highway. She needed a break, the car needed gas, and we needed food. Weary, stiff, and achy, faces hidden under plain baseball caps, we filed into a twenty-four-hour diner and evaluated the late-night patrons: a couple of truck-driver types sitting at the counter drinking coffee and watching CNN on the grainy TV hanging in the corner; a table of teenagers goofing around, shoveling forkfuls of syrup-soaked waffles into their mouths.

A few of the boys, and one of the truck drivers, noticed Jillian. They always did. But their glances were appreciative, not suspicious. We could stay.

Normally Jillian would have given the boys a sly smile in return.

This time she tugged her cap lower and turned away.

At sixteen, I was only a year younger than my sister, but at four foot ten, I was almost a foot shorter. If the boys noticed anything about me at all, it was my lack of height. And that was fine with me.

When the gum-smacking hostess tried to lead us to a booth near the back, we asked for the table closest to the door. Always sit near the exit—that was another rule.

My parents took a newspaper from the counter and huddled over it while we waited for our food. Watching them closely, Jillian sipped ice water from a straw. Logan jotted musical notes on a napkin.

I slid my hands into the sleeves of my hoodie, poking my thumbs out of the holes I'd worn in the cuffs. "How did he find us this time?" We didn't use credit cards. We didn't use the internet. We didn't mail letters or borrow books from the library. Yet Dennis Connelly still managed to find us.

"We don't know, Tessa," Mom said, looking up from the newspaper and wiping the graying hair from her eyes. "Your dad saw him, so we ran."

Logan looked up from his napkin. "Where do we go now?"

"How about Louisiana?" Jillian said. "Or—ooh—California?"

"We're thinking Illinois this time," Dad said. "It'll work for our cover story."

She groaned. "But winter's just a couple months away! Illinois in winter will be no better than Nebraska was last year."

"Don't argue, Jillian." Mom rubbed her fingertips under her eyes. "Please. It's been a long day."

"You said our next place would be somewhere warm." Jillian's lip curled defiantly. "You promised."

Mom wrung her hands on the table. "I know. I'm sorry. We're just trying to keep everyone safe." With a low rumble, the coffee mugs started to vibrate.

Every muscle in my body went rigid. Logan's gaze darted to the kids in the back and the men at the counter. "Mom."

The napkin dispenser tipped over, hitting the table with a sharp slap.

"Wendy." My dad put his hand over hers, making a soft *clink* as their wedding rings touched. "Careful. You're losing control."

She gasped, and the mugs stopped rumbling. Keeping one hand on Mom's, Dad glowered at Jillian. "We're going to Illinois. That's it. No more discussion."

Jillian stared at the table and nodded. Mom set the napkin dispenser upright by hand, but only after she gave me a remorseful squeeze was I able to breathe again.

Our meals arrived, delivered by a bored waitress with lipstick on her teeth. No one ate much. This was our thirteenth run in eight years, but they never got easier. My father ate nothing. He scratched the stubble on his jaw, then rubbed his temples. Mom caressed his cheek. "Is your headache that bad, Andy?"

"I just need to sleep." He took her hand again, giving it a gentle kiss. "We all do."

We paid for our meal in cash. Logan pocketed his napkin. Later he would copy the new song into his composition book, which he always kept with him. Then we would burn the napkin. We could leave nothing personal behind.

Sometime in the middle of the night we stopped at a motel in a not-so-nice neighborhood where we could pay with cash and without answering questions. After reserving two adjoining rooms, we towed our only belongings, one getaway bag each, Logan's sax, and three heavy bags filled with cash, inside.

Not ready to separate for the night, Jillian, Logan, and I gathered in our parents' room. We spoke in whispers and kept most of the lights off. But even whispers were too loud for my dad tonight, so Mom eventually shooed us out. In their dark and silent room, she would rub his forehead until he fell asleep.

In our room, first thing I did was take a shower. I scrubbed myself clean, making the water hot, then hotter still, until the steam was thick as fog, thick enough to hide me from the world. I twisted the knob all the way up to wash my stomach. As I scrubbed the five jagged scars that ran from my sternum to my pelvis, I tried to ignore the memory of Dennis Connelly slicing me open eight years ago, with nothing more than his murderous glance.

When I was done, I turned off the water but stayed in the steam, breathing it in, filling my lungs with it, filling every cell with it, until it dissipated and the world came back into icy focus.

After putting on pajama bottoms and a T-shirt, I lugged my getaway bag back to the bedroom. Logan lay on one of the beds, eyes closed, listening to his old iPod and waving his index fingers like he was conducting an orchestra. Even after this long day, his conservative haircut was perfectly combed.

My mom sat with Jillian on the other bed, an issue of *Seventeen* open between them, their spat at the diner completely forgotten, or at least ignored. I crawled in on the other side and pulled the sheet up to my chin, using its sharp bleachy scent to conceal the stench of stale cigarettes from the mattress.

Mom shifted over to me. "I think," she said as she smoothed my hair, "this is the last time we'll have to run. He'll either give up, or he won't be able to find us."

I nodded, but she said that every time, her words generated only by wishful thinking. My mother was psychokinetic, not precognitive.

And Dennis Connelly would never stop hunting us. Not until he killed us.

A low moan came from the next room. Mom pushed herself off the bed. "Dad will be okay in a few days," she assured us. "Once we find our new place." She kissed us good-night, then, shoulders slumped, went to rub his forehead again.

Jillian slid under the covers next to me. Her getaway bag lay open on the floor, a jumble of clothes, cosmetics, and well-worn ballet shoes spilling out. She flicked her fingers at the magazine, and it rose from the bed, then set itself on top of the pile. "I wish we could've stayed in Vermont a little longer. I kind of liked it there."

"I thought Vermont was too cold for you," Logan said, pulling his earbuds out. With a dismissive wave, he sent his iPod floating over to the nightstand.

She sighed. "Kenny Fitch asked me to Homecoming this morning. I said yes."

"I wonder how long it'll take him to realize he'll have to find a new date," I said.

It wouldn't take Jillian long to find a new boyfriend. She would go on dates at our next location, too. Logan would probably start dating as well, now that he was in high school. They would make friends and go to dances and join clubs. I was the only one who couldn't pretend our lives were normal.

But tonight, my siblings couldn't pretend either. The door connecting to our parents' room swung open a bit wider after Logan's furtive glance. A tear slid down Jillian's cheek, and when she saw me looking, she swiped it away and turned her back to me. She flicked one finger at the lamp, and the room turned dark.

I lay awake for a long time, trying to imagine a life free from secrets and lies and Dennis Connelly. A life free from flinching at every horn beeping outside. A life free from jumping at every footstep passing by our door.

Wait. The door. Was it locked?

Jillian had come in behind me. She locked it. She must have.

But I didn't see her turn the bolt.

I whispered into the darkness. "Will one of you make sure the door is locked?"

Their only replies were the soft, even breaths of sleep.

Holding my breath for courage, I scrambled out of bed, scurried to the door. The bolt was locked. I tugged on the knob anyway, making sure. The door didn't budge. I rushed into my parents' room to check their door, too. We were all locked in.

Safe.

But not really. A locked door wouldn't keep Dennis Connelly out.

I crawled back in bed and stared at the shadows until a cloud of exhaustion finally carried me away.

The nightmare came and quickly brought me back.

Early the next morning, we waited silently on one of the beds while Dad searched for Dennis Connelly. He closed his eyes and sat motionless.

My father was a remote viewer. All he had to do was touch someone, and from then on he could see through their eyes and hear through their ears, no matter where they were. Dennis Connelly was one of the very few who could block himself from my dad's mobile eye.

Dad could never see him, except when he was close. That was how we knew it was time to run. That was how we stayed alive.

Dad slowly raised his hands to rub his temples. Jillian and I shot each other worried glances. His headaches were getting worse.

Finally, he opened his eyes and blinked, his gaze unfocused.

"Where is he?" I asked.

"I can't see him, which means he's far away. We're safe."

I added a silent "for now" at the end of his sentence.

It was getting late, and staying in one place too long between locations made us all jumpy. Time to pack up. With a few waves of her hand, Jillian's clothes stuffed themselves into her getaway bag. Logan directed his clothes to fold themselves up neatly. Our mom packed her things without even looking up from her crossword puzzle in the newspaper. A white washcloth scrubbed our fingerprints off every surface while our toiletry items floated out of the bathroom and tossed themselves into our getaway bags.

I collected my belongings and folded my clothes to put in my bag. "Relax, Babydoll," my mom said. "I'll do that for you." She returned to her crossword puzzle as my pajama bottoms floated over to the bag.

I plucked them from the air. "I got it, Mom." I might not be psychokinetic and move objects with my mind, or have remote vision and see through other people's eyes, but I could pack my own stuff. I didn't have much, anyway. A toothbrush, toothpaste, a hairbrush, jeans and hoodies and sneakers, pajamas, and my jogging clothes. That was all I needed.

Before we left to spend another day on the road, Mom made two last calls on her cell phone. First, she called our school and gave the secretary the same story she used every time we fled. All that ever changed were the names she used.

"Hi, this is Susan Monroe, I must apologize for not calling to excuse

Meredith, Maddie, and Michael from school yesterday. We had a death in the family and in my distress I simply forgot to call you. Thank you so much for your condolences. Actually, we're not coming back. Burt finished writing his book, so it was about time to move on anyway. You know, there is something you could do. The kids are still too upset to contact their friends. Will you please spread the word and tell everyone we'll be in touch soon?"

We wouldn't be in touch soon, or ever.

Next, she called the owner of the house we had rented with the same excuse. She told him to keep the security deposit, which we'd paid in cash when we moved in last April. The next time he came to the house, he'd find no sign that we had ever lived there. Before picking my siblings and me up at school, my parents had destroyed everything we'd brought into that house. We left nothing personal behind.

This was our thirteenth "death in the family," the thirteenth "book" my dad had written. A flimsy story, but if anyone cared enough to look into it, they wouldn't be able to find us. No one would be able to find us—not our classmates, not our landlord, not our neighbors.

Only Dennis Connelly. He found us every time.

My dad was still recovering from his headache, so Mom got behind the wheel of our getaway car again. We zigzagged from state to state, town to city to sprawling farmland, flying down highways and crawling down bumpy country roads, sometimes doubling back to cover our tracks. I stared out at the landscape as it zoomed by, not really seeing it. I'd seen it all before.

A few hours into our trip, we found a parking lot behind an abandoned building. We made sure there were no security cameras, then stuffed everything we could—our towels, sheets, and pillows from the motel, Jillian's magazine, Logan's napkin, our bookbags—into a metal garbage can. We stood back as a match lit itself upon Mom's silent command and floated into the can, burning everything to ashes.

In the next state, we stopped at a used car lot. My dad hopped out and paid the sticker price, in cash, for the first car he saw, a rusty maroon minivan. He followed us to our last stop, a junkyard. After ensuring there were no witnesses, Dad and I watched as Mom, Jillian, and Logan pulled and twisted our old getaway car into tiny pieces of unidentifiable metal.

Now the Monroe family no longer existed.

The Carson family existed, but no one knew we did. We were shadows.

CHAPTER TWO

WEEK LATER, our home in Vermont had already become a vague memory, its details fading and blending with all the other places we'd lived in the last eight years. The only house that stayed clear in my mind was our big red brick home in Kitteridge, Virginia, where I'd lived my whole life until Dennis Connelly took it all away. My mother had decorated our Virginia home herself: sleek and modern, black and white, glass and stainless steel. Our new hideout, in the northern Chicago suburb of Twelve Lakes, was a small rental house with green hail-damaged siding on the outside and mismatched thrift-store furniture on the inside.

A family that stayed hidden inside a house attracted curiosity, and worse, suspicion, so we were careful to appear as normal as possible. We came and went, mowed the lawn and pulled the weeds, acknowledged the neighbors with a polite wave when they passed by. But we never invited them in if they came over with a welcome-to-the-neighborhood platter of brownies. After a few days, the neighbors forgot about the new, quiet family on the block.

Now that we were relatively safe, I ached to go for a jog. It'd been over a week since my last one. I changed into my running gear and went to tell my dad I was leaving the house. I knew where I'd find him: in his office, eyes closed, sitting in a big leather armchair. He found the chair in the living room the day we moved in, and he had Logan float it into the dark paneled room at the back of the house.

Dad would spend most of his time sitting in that leather armchair, watching over us. He didn't have, or need, a real job. He used to be an investigative journalist for a prestigious newspaper in Washington, D.C. Between that, my mom's job as director of special events at a fancy hotel, and their stock market and business investments, they made a lot of money. We still lived off the cash they'd been able to withdraw before Dennis Connelly closed our bank accounts, because now my parents had a different occupation: ensuring our safety. It didn't pay anything, but it kept us alive.

I knocked on the doorframe. "Dad?"

He opened his eyes and blinked. "Hi, Tessa Blessa." His gaze fell to my stomach. My shirt hid my scars, but he never forgot they were there. My hand fluttered to cover my belly.

Dad blamed himself for those scars. If he hadn't written all those articles exposing the unethical and illegal practices of politicians and top military personnel, the government wouldn't have sent a killer to eliminate him and the rest of us.

But I never blamed my dad. I blamed myself, for trusting Dennis Connelly's warm smile and kind eyes, and for not running away to tell my parents that a stranger was in our yard.

Thin and pale, a tightness between his eyebrows and a dullness in his eyes, Dad seemed swallowed up by the armchair. And was that— "Dad, is your nose bleeding?"

"Hmm?" He blinked and sniffled, then pressed a tissue to his nose. "No. Just a shadow. It's dark in here." He crumpled the tissue in his palm, then rubbed his temples.

"Let me get you some Tylenol," I said.

"No, I'm f—" He sighed and sank farther into the chair, his head dipping as if he'd lost the strength to hold it up. "Okay. Thank you."

I dashed to the kitchen and returned with a glass of water and three pills. "Your headaches are getting worse," I said as he swallowed them.

"I'm just tired."

"Dad. It's obvious."

He took a slow sip of water, and another, then lowered the glass to the desk before finally meeting my gaze. "They are getting *a little* worse. But you don't have to worry. It's nothing I can't handle, and it's not affecting my mobile eye at all. I can still see Dennis Connelly when he gets close. We left Vermont a full half hour before he got there."

"In Nebraska it was an hour," I said. "In Montana we had ninety minutes. At least."

"The important thing, Blessa, is that we got away in time." He straightened his posture and plastered a smile on his lips. "Look at that. I'm feeling better already. What do you have planned for today?"

"I wanted to go for a run," I said, "but not if you're—"

"I'm fine. Go for your run. Do you have your new phone?"

"Yep." I tapped my new black cell phone, clipped to the waistband of my running pants. Our cell phone rules were simple: keep them charged, keep them on us at all times, and answer on the first ring. Our phones were the most basic of models—drugstore disposable flip phones with tiny keys, and no internet or social media or cool apps—and our parents had Logan program them so we could make and accept calls only from each other. Jillian liked to complain that normal kids had smartphones, but we had dumbphones.

Dad forced his smile even wider. "I'll peek in on you to make sure you're okay."

"Good. Thanks, Dad. I'll make it quick." I backed out of the office, watching him carefully. He turned on the television and clicked through the channels, humming a cheerful tune.

My parents insisted we were safe until Dad saw Dennis Connelly coming, but I still hated going anywhere alone. Logan, usually, was sympathetic about this, so I went to his room, where he was composing a song on his saxophone. "Want to help me find a new jogging trail?"I asked.

He sighed, then floated the sax into its case. "Let me change. I'll be down in a minute."

Our new house was near a park, so Logan and I headed that way. As we rounded the corner, a police officer rolled by in his shiny white cruiser as he patrolled our quiet neighborhood. I ached to flag him down. Ask him for help. Beg him for protection.

But I kept my hands at my sides and my mouth shut. Dennis Connelly worked for the government, and the two times my parents sought help from law enforcement—a police detective in Utah and an FBI agent in Pennsylvania—he had gotten wind of their investigations and learned where we were hiding. My dad saw him coming and we fled, but despite our warnings, each of our protectors was killed soon after. I would never forget my father's horrified expression as he used his mobile eye to watch Dennis Connelly slice those innocent men open, right down the middle. His message was clear: his reach was long. He would kill anyone who got in his way. And there was nowhere to turn for help.

Since then we depended solely on my family's powers to evade Dennis Connelly and stay alive.

The Twelve Lakes cop drove past Logan and me without a glance in our direction. I wouldn't ask him for help, and he would live to serve and protect the citizens of Twelve Lakes another day.

The park was another block down. Beyond the baseball diamond and playground, we found a jogging trail that wound around the tennis courts, into a small forest preserve and back again. Perfect. I turned onto the path and quickened my pace until I was in a full-out sprint. Logan kept up for a short while, then fell behind.

Trees and wildflowers blurred as I zoomed past them. My feet pounded rhythmically, left-right-left-right. Always on the lookout for anything suspicious, I kept an eye on the other runners as I zipped down the path. Ahead of me a woman speed-walked in black yoga pants, hips swinging and arms pumping. I passed her quickly. Running toward me on the other side of the path, a man pushed a little girl in a three-wheeled jogging stroller. Behind him ran a boy about my age, a royal blue T-shirt stretching across his broad shoulders, the cords of his earbuds bouncing with each step.

After the first lap my lungs started to burn, so I pushed myself for three hundred more steps, then slowed so my exercise-hating brother could catch up. Looking over my shoulder to find him, I stumbled. Before I fell, though, my arm was caught in a strong grip. The boy in the blue T-shirt steadied me, his blue-eyed gaze as warm as his smile.

I realized I was smiling back.

With a gasp, I yanked my arm away and fled.

Once I rounded the bend I waited for Logan. "Slow down a little, would you?" he grumbled. I didn't argue. I ran at his pace, keeping him close by my side. The broad-shouldered boy came up the path again and nodded at me. We ran the loop twice more, passing the boy each time. At the entrance to the path, we stopped, Logan panting and gasping with his hands on his knees while I stretched.

"Clockwise, huh?"

I turned to the voice, deep and confident. The boy in blue ran in place, his sandy-brown hair reflecting gold in the sun. "You were running in a clockwise direction on the path," he said. "I've always gone counterclockwise. I'll have to try it your way next time. You were going pretty fast."

I suppressed the urge to run again.

His feet slowed to a stop. "Sorry if I scared you back there."

Immediately Logan stiffened into bodyguard position, stepping between me and the boy. "He scared you?"

I started to nod but stopped. It wasn't the boy's fault I was scared. "I tripped and he caught me."

Logan relaxed, but when I said nothing else, the boy shrugged. "Okay, then, see you around." He put his earbuds back in and jogged off down the path.

From the corner of my eye I could see Logan watching me watching the boy. "Maybe," he said, "you'll actually make a friend this time."

The boy disappeared around the bend.

I blinked, then turned around and headed for home. "Don't count on it."

Two glasses of ice water hovered by the front door for Logan and me when we returned home. A pile of large shopping bags sat on the table. "Your new clothes," our mother greeted us from the linoleum floor, where she was on her knees with a bucket of sudsy water and a scrub brush, her hands covered in yellow rubber gloves. "Oh, and Tessa, look what I bought for us." Three glossy cookbooks rose from one of the shopping bags.

"Ooh!" I leaped over to inspect the recipes and plan the dinner menu, something we did together every week, but she held up her gloved palm.

"Study first, Babydoll. Classes have already started and you need to catch up."

She didn't tell Logan that *he* needed to catch up.

Our parents required us to get half B's and half C's: grades that weren't great, but not too bad, either. Good grades as well as poor grades attracted attention, and attention of any kind could be disastrous. Jillian and Logan purposely answered test questions wrong so their names wouldn't be published on the honor roll. I had to study hard to make those B's and C's.

Logan chugged his water, and with a wave of his hand, the empty glass zipped off to the kitchen, and his bags of clothes zoomed off to his bedroom. He followed behind them, thankfully not telling Mom about the boy at the park. Mom would get all excited and encourage me to be friends with him. Logan had probably forgotten all about that boy already. And now so would I.

I hooked my bags over my arms and plodded up the steps. Logan was already sitting at his desk with an open textbook, using his hypercognition to absorb a year's worth of education by swiping his palm over each page.

Jillian's textbooks were dumped on the bed in her room. She resented that she wasn't hypercognitive like Logan, but studying came easily to her anyway. This afternoon, instead of studying, she practiced ballet positions while directing her new clothes to hang themselves in the closet.

I put my clothes away by hand. Our wardrobes were high-quality, but simple and plain. No trendy fashions, no bright colors, no attention-grabbing labels. Just the way I liked it.

I also liked my new room. The closet door didn't stick the way the last one had, and this time I had a dresser *and* a desk, painted glossy white. My bed covered most of the old ink stain on the carpet, and the white eyelet bedspread matched the curtains over the window, which looked out over the front yard. Not that I'd ever risk opening the curtains.

My dad poked his head in. "I saw that you found a nice jogging trail," he said. "Nice of that boy to catch you before you tripped."

"Hmm?" I pretended I hadn't heard him as I stacked my new textbooks on the desk, then changed the subject. "How's your headache?"

"Gone," he said, and changed the subject again, to one we were both comfortable with. "I came up to help you study."

I chose a textbook at random and handed it to him. Dad helped me study every day. I needed it, and he liked it. Dad always said he and I needed to stick together. We were the only members of our family who had to move to put our things away or to get something from a shelf. Unlike the others, we actually had to use our hands to flip a light switch or open a drawer.

But my dad would never understand me completely. He had his mobile eye. No one in my family would ever understand what it was like to be the only one without any talents at all.

CHAPTER THREE

*W*E WERE HOMESCHOOLED the first few years on the run. I loved sitting at the kitchen table, safe at home between my brother and sister, while Mom and Dad acted as our teachers. But Logan absorbed his lessons in an instant, and Jillian didn't take much longer. The long days of boredom and isolation quickly weighed down on them, magnifying their misery until it grew into resentment and disobedience. Our parents were desperate to give us a childhood as happy and normal as possible, and to my mother, that meant school and all the things that came with it: football games, dances, and especially lots of friends. So as we got older, they sent us off to school. Follow the rules, they said, and we'd be safe.

Jillian and Logan flourished. I withered.

On Monday morning, Jillian, Logan, and I walked the half mile to our new school, Twelve Lakes Community High. A digital marquee at the entrance flashed red letters: *Welcome Thunderclouds! You'll find TLC at TLC!*

We paused, then stopped as we approached the building. Tan brick with dozens of narrow windows, it stood three stories tall. Students wandered from the buses, sprawled on benches, tossed footballs back and forth. Hundreds of students. More likely, thousands. TLC was, by far, the biggest school we'd ever gone to.

Jillian chewed her lip and scanned the crowd, the dark apprehension in her eyes slowly turning into bright excitement. New kids. New friends. New boys. Maybe even someone who would make her forget the Nebraska boy she'd fallen in love with. "Come on." She tugged me forward. "This place isn't that bad." She pulled me past a group of students lounging under a tree and scrolling on their phones, gracing one of them, a football-jerseyed boy with dark hair down to his jaw, with one of her silky smiles. He returned it with one of his own.

We hadn't even stepped foot in the building, and already Jillian was becoming everything our mother wanted us to be—everything she'd wanted to be herself but never was. Even Logan was nodding at a girl who was carrying a flute.

I concentrated on breathing, walking, and avoiding eye contact. As we climbed the front steps to the building, a shout rose from the crowd. "Hey! Clockwise!"

Oh no. The boy from the jogging path.

There he was in a khaki collared shirt, taking the steps two at a time until he reached us. My head only came up to his chest. "First day at TLC?"

"Yep," said Logan. "We just moved in last week."

"I'm kind of new too," the boy said. "Moved here last March. I'm Tristan, by the way. Tristan Walker."

"I'm Shelby Spencer," Jillian said, using her new alias for the first time. She gestured to Logan. "This is Scott. I guess you already know Sarah?"

"We jogged on the same path the other day, that's all." My voice came out all high and squeaky. Discreetly, I pulled her sleeve, urging her to move on. Indiscreetly, she shook me off.

Tristan squinted against the bright sunlight. "So what year are you guys?"

"I'm a freshman," Logan said, and when I didn't reply on my own, he answered for me. "Sarah's a junior."

"I'm a senior." Jillian tossed her hair, officially entering full flirt mode.

"I'm a senior too," Tristan said. "Hey, do you need to get your schedules? I can show you where the office is."

Before I could say no thanks, Jillian pinched me and gave him a brilliant smile. "That'd be great. Thanks."

He switched his books to his other hand and held the door open for us. He smelled like soap—fresh and light, like he'd never had a problem big enough to weigh him down. "Where are you guys from?" he asked.

Jillian and Logan answered at the same time. "Oklahoma." Our stock answer, and a complete lie. We'd never lived in Oklahoma.

"Why'd you move here?"

"Our dad's a writer. We can live anywhere," Jillian said. Another stock answer. "We've lived all over the country." That part wasn't a lie.

My siblings could chat with this boy all they wanted, but I was staying silent. Eventually people stopped seeing someone who never talked.

We reached the front office and Tristan opened the door for us again, then came in, waiting while the secretary printed out our schedules. Jillian handed hers to him. "Are we in any classes together?"

"Yeah. Physics and Trig. Cool." He took Logan's schedule and told him how to get to the band room, then he took mine. "You have Spanish right after American History," he said. "Those classes are on opposite ends of the building, but if you rush you should make it on time."

Our fingers brushed when he handed my schedule back. My pinkie on his index finger. Little and big. He seemed like he was waiting for me to say something, but I gave him only a nod.

His cheeks flushed. "Um, I should go meet up with my buddies. See you in Physics, Shelby." He left the office and disappeared into the crowded hallway.

Jillian watched him leave, and I could tell by her calculating look that Tristan would be her next conquest. Fine with me. Sure, Tristan was friendly. And nice. And okay, hot. But I wanted nothing to do with him, or with anyone at this school. All I wanted was to be invisible.

And I was. I had my routine: make no eye contact, speak as little as possible, hide behind a textbook. The only good thing about a school this big was that a new student was not exciting news. I did see Tristan a couple of times. He walked past my locker after third period, and once when I went down the wrong hall, he was chatting with a girl with curly brown hair. Both times his gaze skimmed over my head without landing on me. Good. I passed Jillian once, and even *she* didn't notice me, she was so busy batting her eyelashes at a boy as she asked him for directions to her Social Studies room.

Invisible.

At lunchtime, bookbag hanging on my shoulder and tray clutched in my hands, I scanned the cafeteria. The charred scent of burned beef and a thin layer of smoke hovered in the air. The room was packed wall-to-wall with tables, each jammed with rowdy students. Jillian and Logan had different lunch periods, so I was on my own. The only empty table was in the corner by the large window, showing the parking lot behind the school and the corn field beyond it. It was isolated, but I needed to sit near an exit.

There. Two boys, one wearing a blue Chicago Cubs shirt and the other wearing a red one, got up from a table semi-close to the exit, leaving it empty. I rushed over and claimed it, then opened my Spanish notes and pretended to study. Occasionally I'd peek at the other tables, but no one was looking at me. Perfect.

"It's Sarah, right?"

I looked up—broad chest and shoulders, confident smile, blue eyes. Tristan Walker. So much for invisibility. "Yeah," I said. "Sarah."

He didn't seem to notice the way my voice tightened when I said my fake name. Instead, he placed his lunch tray on the table and climbed into the seat across from me.

"I—" Before I could say anything to deter him from eating with me, he took a bite of his cheeseburger.

"I had Physics with your sister this morning," he said, swallowing his food. "She said you were a little overwhelmed. I don't blame you. This place is huge. She asked if I would show you around."

So. Instead of claiming Tristan for herself, Jillian had decided to play Cupid. She'd tried to set me up in Vermont, and in Nebraska and Montana, too. I did like the boy in Montana. He was sweet, and funny, and the most talented artist in the school. Jillian, remembering that I used to love painting, had made a good match. But it wasn't the boy—it was me. Everything I said to him was a lie. *I* was a lie.

It just wasn't worth it, getting involved with Tristan. I shouldn't even let him show me around the building. "That's really nice of you to offer," I told him, "but I'll figure it out."

A group from a center table called his name and waved him over. That girl with the curly brown hair was among them, along with a guy with bushy black eyebrows. He gestured to two empty seats.

"That guy's my tennis partner," Tristan said. "You want to go sit over there?"

My face must have turned bright red, or maybe horror was reflected in my eyes, because he chuckled. "Or, we could just stay here."

"Yes," I said, relieved. "Thank you."

He took a handful of fries, dipped them in a paper cup of ketchup, and ate them all at once. "Will you be in Twelve Lakes long?"

"Probably not." I picked the green peppers from my salad. "The longest we ever stayed in one place was fourteen months. The shortest was six days."

"Six days? What town was that?"

"I don't remember." That was true. "My mom registered us for school, but we didn't even get to start before we had to leave again." Dennis Connelly had tracked us down that time through our internet use, and we hadn't used the internet since.

I slid my hands into my sleeves. I had to stop talking. I'd already told him too much. But since he wouldn't leave me alone, I decided to ask him some questions of my own. "Where did you move from?"

"Wisconsin. Near Milwaukee."

"Why did you move here?"

"My dad was transferred to Malaysia." He took another big bite of his cheeseburger. "My mom and sister went with him, but I didn't want to. My uncle's the new facilities manager at TLC, so he and my aunt let me move in with them until I go to college next year. It's close enough that I can go home sometimes to see my friends."

Between bites of cheeseburger and fries, Tristan continued chatting, about his friends, his spot on the TLC tennis team, and deciding between Northwestern and Stanford. I wanted to respond, I wanted to ask him more questions, but all I could do was nod and give him weak smiles. The girls at the next table were watching us. Everyone in the lunchroom was watching us. Whispering. Pointing. Sitting with

Tristan was making me visible. The glow-in-the-dark kind of visible. The cafeteria seemed to become more crowded by the second. Was it smaller now than it was a few minutes ago? Everything became hazy, like a cloud had settled over the room.

"Are you feeling okay?" Tristan's brows furrowed.

I blinked to quell the dizziness and mumbled something about first-day jitters. When the bell rang I jumped up, almost tripping over my feet, and scurried out of the lunchroom.

Jillian and I walked home together without Logan, who'd stayed after school to audition for jazz band. He'd have to downplay his talent, of course, and he could never perform on stage, but he was happy enough just to play his sax. Jillian felt the same way about dancing. Our parents let her take all the dance classes she wanted, but like Logan, she could never participate in a performance. Band concerts and dance recitals were off-limits since we left Virginia. When performance day came along, they would miss it, claiming strep throat or a twisted ankle. They'd put on a private show for us, at home, instead. The last few years Jillian stayed in her room.

Jillian had her first class at the town's dance studio later that afternoon, and I had to hustle to keep up with her as she rushed home to change. When we got inside, all the lights were off—unusual, because we always kept the curtains drawn tight. In the dim sunlight that managed to seep through, we found our mother on the family room couch, stroking our dad's forehead as he slept.

I dropped my bookbag and rushed over. Dad's headaches had never been this bad so early in the day before. Mom held a finger to her lips, then gently slid out from under him, laying his head on a throw pillow. She followed us as we tiptoed through the kitchen into the dining room.

"I *knew* it!" Jillian snapped. The light bulbs in the brass chandelier over the table flickered on. "He overdid it, didn't he? He used his mobile eye all day today."

Our mother ran her fingers over the top edge of a framed painting on the wall. "We wanted to make sure the three of you were adjusting to your new school." With a frown, she inspected the dirt on her fingertips.

The light bulbs brightened as Jillian's eyes darkened. "Dad needs to watch for Dennis Connelly. Not us."

"Dad watched for him too, Jillian," I said. Never say Dennis Connelly's name out loud—that was another rule, one I had made for myself, a rule I had broken only once and will never, ever break again. "He always does."

A dishrag floated in from the kitchen, and Mom started polishing the frame with it. "Your safety is more important than your privacy."

"It's not just about privacy," Jillian spat. "Dad needs to save his strength."

Mom's grip tightened on the rag, and she spoke through clenched teeth. "We are not having this discussion again."

"But if you'd just try something new—"

"I said no." The rag dropped to the floor. My mother and sister glared straight into each other's eyes, mirror images but for their hair.

The light bulbs grew brighter.

"Jillian." I swallowed hard and tugged her sleeve. I had to get her out of here. "You have dance class, remember? Jill?"

But she didn't move, and neither did our mother. The room grew brighter and brighter, until the light bulbs exploded with a bang.

Trapping a scream behind my lips, I flew behind a chair as the room was sprayed with shattered glass.

The house was dark again, and silent.

"Wendy." Just a whisper, but it rang loudly as my dad hobbled over. "Jillian, take Tessa out for a run."

"But I have dance—"

"Jillian." Dad's expression was stone, his glare cutting. "Go."

White-faced, Jillian pulled me up, and we backed out of the room.

Jillian hated jogging even more than Logan did, but she had no problem keeping up with me on the trail that day. Leaves tore from branches, and twigs snapped off trees as she stormed past them. It wasn't long, though, before both the tree wreckage and her pace slowed, and when we reached the entrance to the path again, she stopped to catch her breath. She closed her eyes and became very still.

"You need to stop making Mom so mad," I said. "She's got enough to worry about."

"Shh. I'm trying something." She raised her hands to her temples. After a minute, she opened her eyes and dropped her arms with a defeated groan.

"What were you doing?"

"I was trying to see through Logan's eyes. You know, by remote vision."

I blinked at her. "You can do that? Since when?"

She kicked at the ground, ripping a patch of grass from the dirt. "Since never. I thought if I had a mobile eye, then I could take over watching you and Logan and Mom, and Dad could concentrate on watching for Dennis Connelly."

"But it's not working?"

"No. I thought it did, once, back in Vermont. I thought I saw through Mom's eyes when she was at the grocery store. Turns out she didn't even go to the store that day, but that's what gave me the idea. Since then I've tried seeing from your eyes, and Mom's and Dad's, and even my friends' from our old locations." She rotated a heart-shaped charm around the gold chain on her wrist, the one her boyfriend from Nebraska had given her. "But nothing's working. I may as well be *you*."

I flinched at that comment, but only internally. "Maybe Dad can help you."

"I asked, but Dad's scared that I'll get headaches too. And Mom doesn't want me to spend all my time keeping watch over everyone. She said it's their job to keep us safe, and my job to be a normal teenager." She snorted. "Like that's even possible."

"You're going to keep trying, aren't you," I said. It wasn't a question. Once Jillian decided she wanted something, she wouldn't quit until she got it. Even something as impossible as this.

"That's right. I don't care what Mom says, and I don't care if I get headaches. If something doesn't change, we're all going to die." She shot off down the path again and shouted over her shoulder. "But you don't have to worry. I won't let that happen."

Developing her own mobile eye wouldn't stop Dennis Connelly from coming, but if Jillian could take some of the pressure off Dad, his headaches would lessen or even stop altogether. Mom wouldn't have to take care of Dad all the time, and then she wouldn't be so stressed. Dad would be sharper, more alert, and maybe see Dennis Connelly coming sooner. We'd have more than a thirty-minute lead when we fled to our next place. We might be able to evade him forever.

Doubt, mixed with the tiniest bit of hope, pumped through my veins as we ran the loop once more before heading home. We cut across the park, where squealing preschoolers raced down the slide at the playground. Parents rooted for their Little Leaguers on the baseball field to the left, and on the soccer field to the right, a group of little kids surrounded a tall, broad-shouldered boy in a light yellow T-shirt.

Tristan.

He juggled a soccer ball from his feet to knees to ankles, up to his head and back again, to the delight of the kids watching him.

"Hey Tristan!" Across the park, the bushy-eyebrowed boy from the cafeteria whistled and waved a tennis racquet in the air. With a powerful kick, Tristan sent the ball soaring over the kids' heads and into the soccer net across the field. He gave each of the kids a high-five, then picked up a racquet from the grass and headed to the tennis court.

"How was lunch today?" Jillian said, blinking innocently at me.

"Horrible. Please stop trying to set me up."

"But you like him, right?" A little red leaf blew in front of me, making a heart shape in the air.

I swatted it away with the back of my hand. "Stop that. We're in public. And no, I don't like him. Not like that."

"He doesn't have to be your boyfriend. He can just be a friend." The leaf made a series of wide swoops before skidding onto the grass. "It would make Mom happy too. She's just sick that you won't make friends."

I picked the leaf up and held it by the stem. Crimson on one side, brown on the other. I twirled it between my fingertips until it became a colorless blur. "They can't be real friends when we can't even tell them our real names."

Then I crushed the leaf into tiny little pieces and let them flutter to the ground.

It was selfish, I knew, to keep my dad up late that night to help me study. He'd worn himself out that day, watching us on our first day of school. But he stayed up with me as long as he could. He knew what I was doing, because I did it every night. He knew I'd stay awake as late as possible, hoping that when I finally fell asleep, I'd be too exhausted to dream.

It never worked.

Mom's psychokinesis and Dad's remote vision protected us from Dennis Connelly. But no psychic ability could protect me from my dream. Partly nightmare but mostly memory, it came every night, for so many years now that I didn't remember which was which.

I sit under a tree in the yard, reading a book while nursing my injured knee with an ice pack. The sun is shining, then a shadow creeps over me. I look up and see a man, a man with thinning hair and a gentle smile beneath his graying mustache, and his blue eyes are kind and merry behind his round wire glasses. He smells kind of sweet, like a cherry cough drop. I like him, so I smile back. He tells me not to be scared, and I'm not. He holds a finger to his lips and says his name is Dennis Connelly and he is so happy to meet me. He asks me questions, and I don't have to answer out loud; this man somehow hears what I'm thinking.

It's a fun game, but then his face loses the smile and his eyes turn mean and he holds out his hand and tells me to come with him, come with him *right now,* and I am scared so I say no, out loud this time, and I know I should run run run away but I am frozen, and the man grabs me, carries me to a big black car and locks me inside. Up front, a lit cigar, smelling sickly sweet like burned cherries, fills the car with smoke. I cough and scream and pound on the window as the man dennisconnelly runs back to my house and sneaks inside. Distant, curdled screams pierce the smoky air, and I know dennisconnelly will kill my mom, kill my dad, kill my sister and brother, and he will take me away and kill me too. He will cut us all, he will slice us right down the middle, and we will bleed, and we may escape this time but it doesn't matter, we can run and run and run but he will find us, he will hunt us down, he will never stop until he kills us all, kills us all in a flood of blood.

And every night when the smoke cleared, I'd wake up sweaty and out of breath, heart pounding, biting my lips to keep from screaming.

Never, ever, *ever* scream. That was another rule, a rule just for me.

CHAPTER FOUR

PEEKING INTO THE lunchroom the next day, I spotted Tristan sitting at the table we'd shared the day before, his tray loaded with a saucy meatball sub and a slice of raspberry cobbler.

Jillian wasn't going to give up this time. Should I just go sit with him? Just walk over, sit down, and start talking?

No. Everyone would see us, and the room would shrink and run out of air.

And he'd call me *Sarah*.

I slipped away before he saw me and rushed outside. I found a spot on the concrete steps behind a pillar, sank down, and opened my bookbag. I'd forgotten to do my Civics homework last night, and it was due next period. It would be easier to do it out here anyway.

I couldn't find my Civics notebook, but I stayed out there in the shadows behind the pillar until the bell rang.

After that, I didn't bother with the cafeteria. Every day I returned to my safe, private little hiding spot on the steps.

Now that I sat outside for lunch, I saw Tristan at school only when he passed by my locker between classes. I saw him at the park most afternoons, though, when I went running with Logan. A few times he was jogging on the path, in my direction—clockwise. When he wasn't on the trail, he was usually on the tennis courts, lobbing the ball to the guy with the bushy eyebrows.

Today I stopped short at the sight of them playing tennis with two girls—the tall girl with curly brown hair, and an even taller girl from my Spanish class with straight black hair.

Drawing myself up to my full fifty-eight inches, I twisted my not-quite-blond, not-quite-brown, not-quite-curly, not-quite-straight hair around my finger. Logan caught up to me and stopped too. The curly-haired girl hit the tennis ball to Tristan. He returned it with a graceful swing, but instead of arcing elegantly over the net, the ball veered off his racquet at an unnatural angle, aiming straight at me.

I glared at Logan, who looked back with wide innocent eyes and a shrug, and I dashed away.

Logan went with me to the park the next afternoon too, but just before we reached the entrance to the jogging path, he detoured to a picnic table and sat down.

"What are you doing?" I asked.

He pulled a stack of index cards from the back pocket of his shorts. "I have a history test tomorrow and I need to study."

That couldn't be true. Logan never needed to study. He never even took notes.

"But don't worry," he said, shuffling through the cards. "I know you don't like to run alone, so I asked someone to go with you."

Oh no.

Logan raised his hand in a wave and shouted across the park. "Tristan, over here!"

And there he was, jogging over to us with an orange TLC shirt stretching over his chest, and his tousled brown hair turning gold in the sun, and his smile…

"This was Jillian's idea, wasn't it?" I muttered to Logan.

"Hers and mine." He grinned and tapped the index cards on the table. They were covered with musical notes and treble clefs.

My stomach tumbled, and it was all I could do to keep my feet from sprinting me away. "Why are you doing this?"

"Because I hate jogging, and you need a friend."

"But what if…" I lowered my voice. "What if *he* comes?"

"If *Dennis Connelly* comes anywhere close," Logan said, "Dad will see him. You have your phone. I'll be sitting right here. You'll be fine."

As Tristan approached, Logan slid the cards under his leg, and I tried to remember how to breathe.

"Hey, Scottie," Tristan said to Logan. "Big history test tomorrow?"

My brother pasted a miserable frown on his face. "I'm in Molinski's class."

"I hear she's brutal. I'm pretty good in history, so if you need help, let me know." He faced me next. "Ready to run, Clockwise?"

I was always ready to run. I darted off, for a moment considering running home rather than down the path. But… a small part of me *wanted* to run with Tristan. Just this once.

So I turned onto the path, clockwise of course, and ran alongside him. I could do this. Tristan and I were jogging together, that's all. Not even that—we were jogging *next* to each other. Despite what my siblings were trying to do, Tristan would never be my friend.

But I couldn't stop myself from sneaking glances up at him. Every so often I caught him peeking down at me too, and instead of running on concrete, I may as well have been soaring through the clouds.

Our shadows stretched far on the sidewalk as Logan and I walked home from the park. My shadow bobbed up and down, replicating the skip in my step. I'd run farther with Tristan than I'd ever run with my siblings, and was still going strong when Logan had appeared at the entrance to the loop to say it was getting late. I hoped my reluctance hadn't shown on my face when I said good-night to Tristan.

Maybe I had made a friend after all. A boy with blue eyes and broad shoulders named Tristan Walker.

As we walked up our driveway, Logan stopped short and stared at the house, head tilted, frowning. I followed his gaze but couldn't see anything. "What's wrong?"

"Look at the front window," he said. "What do you see?"

"White curtains. Closed."

"No. Look *at* the window. Not through it."

I looked again. When I tilted my head just the right way, the setting sun shone on the window—and in the bottom left corner, I saw it.

A handprint.

A little streaked, a little smeared, but definitely a handprint. And big—definitely a man's handprint. Like he'd been crouching in the bushes under the window. Watching. Listening.

I whirled around, suddenly noticing all the places someone could hide. In the bushes. Up in the trees. Across the street, behind the fence. In that car parked down the road.

I also noticed Logan's face. Usually so controlled, so strong, I sometimes forgot he was my *little* brother. But now his eyes were wide. Young. Scared.

Seeing him like that only heightened my own fear, but he must have realized that, because a moment later his usual stoicism wiped away his vulnerability. "I'm sure it's nothing."

"Don't say that just to make me feel better. It's not nothing."

"I'm serious. Look." He pointed to the house next door, its driveway cluttered with sports equipment. "That kid is always outside hitting baseballs with his dad. He probably hit one into our bushes." Each word was more forceful than the one before it, like he was trying to convince himself as well as me. "And then his dad leaned on the window to get it."

Far-fetched, but plausible. In any case, it couldn't be Dennis Connelly's handprint. Our father would see him before he could get close to us. "You're probably right."

Logan marched up to the window and, using the bottom of his T-shirt, wiped the handprint away. Then he reached into the bushes and pulled out an orange plastic hockey puck, which he held up triumphantly. "See? No reason to freak out." He pitched it into the next yard, where it bounced, then rolled, and finally came to rest next to the basketball hoop.

"Dad still should have known someone was that close to our house," I said.

Instead of heading to the front door, Logan returned to me on the driveway, this time not bothering to conceal the worry in his expression. "A few nights ago he had a bloody nose."

"I've seen that too."

Together, we trudged up to the porch. Logan stopped before opening the door. "You know, when Dennis Connelly finds us this time, we should stay. Stay and fight. Mom couldn't beat him on her own, but Jillian's PK is almost as strong as Mom's is now. And I'm getting there too. Between the three of us, we could beat one guy."

But then his gaze dropped to my stomach, and he sighed. It didn't matter how strong they were. They couldn't defeat someone who could slice a person open with just a glance.

Hands fluttering to my belly, I mumbled, "I wish you wouldn't say his name out loud."

Without using his PK, Logan opened the door and went inside without another word.

I squinted up at the darkening sky and shivered.

Late that night, after my nightmare woke me up, I heard furtive whispering coming from Jillian's bedroom. As my heart rate slowly returned to normal, I slipped out of bed and padded, barefoot, across the hall.

The desk lamp shed a dim light on Jillian as she reclined on her bed, fiddling anxiously with the heart charm on her bracelet. "I don't care," she muttered. "I'm not stopping."

"You're wasting your time." Logan's shadow loomed large on the wall as he paced. "And mine."

Were they talking about Tristan and me again? Logan was right: Jillian was wasting her time if she thought I'd do anything more than go jogging with him. "What's going on?" I asked.

They startled, then looked up. "Oh. It's only you," Jillian said, relieved. "We're just talking. Go back to bed."

"No." I crossed my arms. I was sick of these two plotting behind my back. "What are you talking about?"

"Nothing you can help with," she said, then added, "Sorry."

"Why not?" Maybe this wasn't about Tristan after all.

"I *was* trying to help Jillian with her stupid remote vision idea," Logan said. "But it's not working."

"I swear I'm getting close," Jillian insisted.

"You've been *getting close* for weeks," he said, "but really, you're no closer now than when you first started." He took my arm. "Seriously, Tessa. Go back to sleep. I'm going too. I'm not staying up all night anymore to help her with something that will never work." He pulled me from the room.

"Quitter," Jillian jeered at him, then her door closed itself behind us.

"You don't think she can do it?" I whispered to Logan in the dark hallway.

"No. She's just desperate," he said. "But you don't need to worry. I'll figure something out."

I didn't need to worry. Because *Logan* would figure something out. Because *Jillian* wouldn't let anything bad happen. Because *our parents* would keep us safe.

They never asked *me* to help, because they didn't think I *could* help.

I went back to bed, but instead of sleeping, I sat with my knees tucked under my chin, stared at a silver paperclip on my nightstand, and willed it to move.

It didn't.

CHAPTER FIVE

EVERY DAY AFTER school now, Tristan waited for Logan and me at the entrance to the running trail. Logan sat contentedly at the picnic table and studied his fake notes while Tristan and I ran through the park together, always in the clockwise direction. He easily matched my pace in a way Logan and Jillian never could, and sometimes quickened his, challenging me to run faster than ever before.

Our rapid pace saved me from long discussions with him, and when we did manage to pant out a conversation, I kept the topic neutral: school, teachers, TV. After our runs, I began to feel a strange new ache—not in my legs from running so hard, but in my cheeks, from smiling so much.

I had to admit, I liked having a friend.

One day on the jogging trail, he slowed to a stop and raked his hand through his hair. "I was supposed to go home to Milwaukee this weekend," he said. "My parents were coming back for a visit. But my mom got the flu, so they had to cancel the trip."

"That's too bad."

"Which means," he said, "I'll be here."

"Oh. Good." Now we could run together over the weekend. I started jogging again but he didn't, so I stopped.

"It's Homecoming," he said.

"It is?" I feigned ignorance, but it was impossible to be unaware of Homecoming. Posters on every wall, drumlines down every hall, school spirit activities every day. Jillian was going to the dance with a boy named Ethan. Our mom had taken her out to buy a fancy dress, and last night they'd studied the magazines to pick out a hairstyle. Even Logan was going to the dance, with a group of friends from jazz band. I had no interest in Homecoming, neither the game nor the dance.

"I never asked anyone to the dance," Tristan said, "because I wasn't going to be here. But now I will be. So…"

I stepped back. No. Please don't. Don't ruin this.

"I know it's last minute, but will you go—"

Another step. "I can't."

He blinked. "Are you going with someone else?"

And another step. "I'm not—I'm not going at all."

I heard him ask, "Why not?" But I'd already run away.

I had to squint to see through the haze of hairspray in Jillian's room. "Ouch!" She cried out as our mom pinned her hair up with a dozen rhinestone clips.

"Sorry," Mom said. "That's the last one." She stood back and covered her mouth with her hands as her eyes filled with tears. "You're so beautiful, Jillian."

And Jillian *was* beautiful, even more so than usual, standing gracefully in a violet taffeta dress, her hair pinned up regally with a few playful tendrils hanging past her shoulders. Mom had done her makeup, a bit heavier than usual, just enough to make Jillian's pink lips sparkle and her gray eyes smoky. Without question, she'd be the most stunning girl at the Homecoming dance tonight.

Mom had to stifle tears again when she saw Logan. Happy to finally have a chance to wear formal clothes rather than the tees and jeans he wore to blend in, he strutted into the room in his white dress shirt, navy sport coat and pressed Dockers. He was going as part of a group, but there was one girl in particular, a clarinet player, he wanted to dance with.

My mother gave me a pained look as I sat on the floor in my jeans and hoodie, knees tucked under my chin. "Are you sure you don't want to go, Babydoll? You can hang out with Jillian and her friends. I even bought you a dress. Green, to match your eyes." A kelly-green halter dress floated into the room and wiggled itself so its rhinestones sparkled.

"That's pretty, Mom," I said. "But I didn't buy a ticket." I'd never told her that someone had asked me to the dance and I'd turned him down. It would devastate her.

I slid my hands into my sleeves, knowing I was devastating her anyway.

"I thought you and I could cook something tonight," I said, to make it up to her. "You can teach me how to make a soufflé."

With a tight-lipped nod, Mom sent the dress from the room and adjusted a clip in Jillian's hair.

I hadn't seen Tristan at all since I'd run away from him. I sat on the steps at lunch, stopped at my locker when he wasn't around, stayed in my room after school. Jogging with him every day had given him the wrong idea. Now he thought we were more than friends.

Well, not anymore.

I'd done the right thing.

Downstairs by the front door, Dad went over the rules again, something he did each time Jillian or Logan went out with their friends. We divided our going-out rules into two categories: Rules for regular kids, and rules for kids who were hiding from a telepathic killer hired by the government. "No smoking, no drinking, no drugs, no sex." He counted off each rule on his fingers. "Do not get in a car with someone who's been drinking or doing drugs. Stay within a ten-minute drive of this house. Be home by midnight, not one minute later. Remember our cover story. If you slip up at all, run. If you see anyone or anything suspicious, run. If anyone looks like he's watching you… run."

Our parents also reminded them not to get their photos taken. "Not just formal portraits," Mom said. "Candid pictures too. You know what to do if your friends pull out their phones and take a photo of you."

My siblings gave a solemn and serious nod. They'd have to use their psychokinesis to break something in the phone, guaranteeing those photos would never turn out. Cruel, but necessary.

I had no way of stealthily breaking a phone. Another reason not to go to the dance. Now I was positive I'd done the right thing.

"Speaking of phones," Dad added, "keep yours with you at all times. The music will be loud, so put the ringer all the way up and keep it on vibrate."

Logan slid his phone in the inner pocket of his sport coat. Jillian slipped hers inside a secret pocket our mother had sewn under her skirt. She wouldn't feel the vibrations if it rang inside her little handbag.

A car pulled in the driveway. Jillian's date. My dad added one more thing right before the doorbell rang. "I'll be watching."

Instead of a solemn nod, Jillian bit her lips shut. Then they spread into a smile as she opened the door.

For a moment—just a millisecond, really—I wished it would be Tristan standing on the porch.

But it wasn't. The boy on the porch had black hair down to his jaw. The first boy Jillian had smiled at on the first day of school. We all held our breath as she led him a few steps into the foyer, as far as we'd ever allow anyone inside our house. "Mom, Dad," she said, "this is Ethan Mitchell."

A quick introduction, a brisk handshake, and Jillian pulled Ethan outside to his car. In and out in less than a minute. Perfect.

Mom drove Logan to the dance so he could meet his friends, and Dad and I stared at each other in the silence. "You didn't have to say no when that boy asked you to Homecoming," he said.

"You saw that?"

He nodded, pity clear in his eyes.

"I just…"My throat started to close up. "The lying, and—and the cameras—he was starting to think—"I had to force air into my lungs. "I can't, Dad. I just can't."

He sighed and drew me against his chest. "Oh, Blessa. I wish I could make you feel safe."

The cheese soufflé I made with my mother was a success: airy and scrumptious. Not successful enough to make her forget that I didn't go to the Homecoming dance, but at least her disappointment in my social life was replaced with pride in my cooking skills. I had more fun cooking with my mother than I would have had at that dance, lying to Tristan and avoiding cameras, anyway.

Just before curfew, Jillian slipped into my room, still in her dress. I was awake, staving off my inevitable nightmare by reading a book. "What happened to your hair?" I asked.

She shrugged and tucked her messy locks behind her ears. "Some clips fell out and I couldn't find them." She spun around the room, telling me every detail of the dresses, the decorations, the music. The Homecoming queen ripped her dress up the back. One girl got into a fight with her boyfriend and left the dance crying. Ethan was clumsy during the fast dances but smooth on the slow songs.

I hugged my knees to my chest and listened for a half hour, but she still hadn't told me the only thing I wanted to hear. Finally I had to ask. "Was Tristan there?"

She sank onto the bed. "Yeah. He was."

I swallowed hard, certain by the sympathetic look on her face that he hadn't gone alone.

"He went with Gianna," she said. "You know, that tall girl with the curly hair? I thought they were just friends, but I guess not anymore."

"Oh." I expelled my breath like I'd been hit in the chest, surprised at how hot the tears felt in my eyes. I blinked them away before they fell.

Maybe I hadn't done the right thing after all.

CHAPTER SIX

IND, COLD, AND drizzle wouldn't have driven me from my private lunchtime spot on the school steps, but the storm that blew in the following Monday came full-force. Thunder, lightning, even hail. I couldn't sit outside.

But I couldn't go to the cafeteria either, not with Tristan there. The girl with the curly brown hair, Gianna, would be there too, and they'd be together. I couldn't bear to see that.

I found a new hiding place, a storage area under the dim back stairwell. I sat between two folded-up tables and pulled my Civics homework from my bookbag, barely able to hear the rumbling thunder through the brick walls. This place was even better than the outside steps. Weatherproof. Quiet. Isolated.

Isolated, until the door swung open and two men in denim work shirts walked into the stairwell, pushing a cart of folding chairs. I jumped and maybe whimpered a little bit. The younger man, dark hair brushing his collar, smiled shyly, but the squat, older man with the shiny moon-face frowned. "Kids aren't allowed back here. Why aren't you in class?"

"Um." I forced myself to speak. "It's my lunch period?"

"Then go to lunch!" Like a warden escorting a dead man walking, he followed me down the long hallway to the cafeteria.

The lunchroom was darker, gloomier than it had been on the first day. Fog seemed to seep in through the windows, which showed a sky of black clouds, hail pelting the cars in the lot, and corn stalks struggling to remain upright against the wind. All of the students who usually went off-campus to eat must have decided to stay in, because the lunch line reached all the way across the cafeteria.

Holding my breath, I slunk in with my eyes and head down, praying no one would notice me.

And thanks to years of invisibility practice, no one did.

But I couldn't resist the urge to look for Tristan.

I found him immediately, standing on the far side of the lunchroom, talking to Gianna. The girl who *used* to be just his friend. In her high-heeled boots, she stood even taller than Jillian, and almost as tall as Tristan. He leaned in close and whispered something, making her laugh.

Good. I didn't want him to notice me anyway.

He must have felt me watching, though, because when he and Gianna walked to their table, she sat down, but he didn't. Instead he kept walking. Toward me. His steps were hesitant, like he was afraid I'd flee if he came too close. He reached me but kept his distance. "Hey, Sarah."

"Hi." I forced myself to look into his eyes. "Sorry." Sorry for running away when he asked me to the dance. Sorry I was wrong about not wanting any attachments. Sorry I missed my chance with him.

He nodded. "Me too. I thought… well. Anyway."

To avoid looking at him, I scanned the room for a seat. No empty tables, near an exit or otherwise. The table I used on my first day was occupied again, this time by six girls. Their plates still full, they wouldn't be leaving anytime soon.

"You'll never find a table today," Tristan said. "Why don't you sit with us?"

Us. How could such a tiny word sound so ugly? "Won't your girlfriend be mad?"

"My girlfriend?" He looked genuinely surprised that I knew about her.

"Gianna." I swirled my finger in my hair, indicating her curls. "You brought her to Homecoming."

"Gianna? She's not… When she heard I was staying in town, she asked me to go. As friends." He gave me a playful nudge. "She has a boyfriend who's away at college."

Warm relief swept over me, opening my lungs. "Oh." My face grew warm too. He grinned, and just like that, the awkwardness between us melted like ice in the sun.

We shuffled down the lunch line. All of the entrees had meat in them, so I chose a garden salad, an apple, and milk. He grabbed a fried chicken sandwich, a bag of Doritos, and a Coke. I wrinkled my nose and sneaked an apple on his tray. He stopped in front of the desserts, where he selected the largest piece of chocolate cake and put it on my tray. Then, before I could protest, he took my tray and headed toward the group of students sitting right in the middle of the room. His friends.

I tapped my cell phone. My feet twitched, aching to run, to find a new hiding spot. The girls' bathroom, maybe.

No. I could do this. I could sit with Tristan and his friends in the middle of the room. Just this once. I commanded my feet to follow him. Thank goodness he was holding my tray. My hands shook so badly I would have dropped it. I slid them inside my sleeves.

The fog thickened and thunder rumbled as we wove through the sea of tables. I imagined that fog wrapping itself around me like a blanket, dulling my anxiety as I followed Tristan to the table.

"Hey, guys, make room for us," he said as he climbed onto the bench. I changed my mind—*us* wasn't such an ugly word after all. He patted the empty spot next to him. Cheeks burning, insides churning, I climbed in and tried to fight the nausea as everyone stared at me. Tapping my phone again, I planned an escape route through the crowd in case it rang.

"This is Sarah," Tristan said, then introduced his friends. "This is Gianna, Chad, and Vanessa."

I gave Gianna an apologetic smile, which she returned with a polite one of her own. Chad was Tristan's tennis partner with the bushy eyebrows, and Vanessa was the girl from my Spanish class who'd played doubles with them. I nodded hello at everyone, then glanced at Tristan, silently begging him to take their attention off me. He obliged, steering the conversation to the Thunderclouds' football team. I relaxed a tiny bit and released the phone from my grip, then picked the green peppers from my salad.

"You did great," Tristan said to me once the football conversation was in full swing. His cool breath brushed my neck, under my ear. "It'll be easier tomorrow."

Tomorrow? No way. I'd be sitting outside, alone on the steps, tomorrow.

He looked at me, lighting up from the inside out: first his eyes, then his smile.

And that was it. No more solitary lunches on the steps for me. Tomorrow I'd be back here, sitting with Tristan and his friends. Maybe I'd even speak.

He polished off his sandwich and chips, then took an enthusiastic bite of the apple I'd put on his tray. Handing me a plastic fork, he slid the chocolate cake between us.

I hadn't thought about Dennis Connelly in at least ten minutes. No wonder Jillian was so boy-crazy.

I took a forkful of the cake and smiled at Tristan. He squeezed my knee under the table. Lightning flashed in the sky, and for a split second, everything was brighter.

CHAPTER SEVEN

ALTHOUGH IT WAS still storming, Mom, Logan, and I went to the town square that afternoon. Logan needed another composition book from the music store, and Mom and I had to go to the supermarket to pick up ingredients for dinner.

My mother shared her beauty with Jillian, her intelligence with Logan, and her psychokinesis with both of them. She shared her love of cooking with me. We made dinner together every night. I used to paint, oils on canvas, but stopped when my parents declared we didn't have room in our getaway car to bring my creations along. But like Logan's music and Jillian's dancing, cooking left nothing personal behind. Mom and I always made our meals from scratch. No mixes, frozen, or take-and-bake meals for us.

She was beaming this afternoon, and for the first time I could remember, those proud smiles were aimed at me. Dad had checked on me during my lunch period and reported to her that I was sitting at a table *with other kids*. Tonight's menu had originally called for veal—ugh—but Mom let me change it to something I would actually eat. I chose eggplant parmigiana.

"Maybe this Tristan boy will ask you on a date." She slipped her arm through mine in the produce aisle.

"It's not like that. We're just friends."

She and Logan exchanged knowing glances. I pretended to inspect the eggplants.

We stopped at the deli counter for the mozzarella, and as we passed the seafood section, Mom's face turned slightly green. Fish was *never* on the menu. It was the only thing she wouldn't teach me to cook. Logan and I quickly steered her to the bakery to pick out some fresh bread.

With our grocery bags hooked over our arms, we dashed through the rain to the minivan. I jumped into the front passenger seat, and Logan slid in behind Mom. She turned the key in the ignition, but nothing happened. She tried again. "That's odd. The car won't start." She took her hand away and stared at the key. It turned again on its own, but the engine only clicked, barely audible over the rain.

The color drained from her face. "He did this." Her panicked gaze darted around the darkening parking lot. "He's here."

"Who?" Logan asked.

There was only one *he*.

"It…it can't be him," I said. "Dad would've seen him coming. He would've called us." But I couldn't help looking out into the parking lot myself. Could Dennis Connelly have somehow slipped past my dad's mobile eye? There were dozens of cars in the lot, and he could be hiding in, under, or behind any one of them. I covered my stomach with my hands, already feeling him slashing it open again.

Mom let out a strangled cry. With a loud snap, the doors locked themselves. "If it's not him, then why won't the car start?" Her voice sounded like a child's. The key twisted itself in the ignition again, but nothing.

"It's an old car," Logan said. "Let me out and I'll check under the hood."

"No!" she cried. Rain pounded on the windows. The key turned in the ignition, over and over again, faster and faster. The gear stick jerked back and forth, and the glove box vibrated on its hinges.

"We can't sit in here forever." Logan's firm, quiet tone, so much like Dad's, helped to soothe her. "I'm sure it's just a problem with the engine. But come out with me to keep watch. If anything happens, anything at all…we'll fight."

She threw me a tormented glance. "What about Tessa?"

Logan frowned at me and pointed to the floor between the front seat and the dashboard. "Get down there."

"But—" There had to be some way I could help. "I can help Mom keep watch."

"Then she would have to watch you too." He shrugged out of his jacket and tossed it over. "Get down there and hide under this."

Logan thought I was a distraction, a hindrance. Holding back tears, I slid down and pulled the jacket over myself.

"On three," Logan said to Mom. "One, two…three." I heard them each take a deep breath and open the doors, then jump out into the pouring rain.

Dad slept through the whole thing.

He now sat in shamed silence on the sofa in our living room, grasping Mom's hand in his, as Logan described how they had locked the doors of the minivan to keep me safe as I huddled under the dashboard. How he'd opened the hood and waved his palm over the engine, learning how it worked with a single swipe. How Mom had paced around him, regarding everyone in the parking lot, even a young mother who dashed past with an umbrella in one hand and holding a toddler on her hip with the other, with suspicion. How he'd discovered the battery cables had come loose and how he'd simply tightened them to get our getaway car started again. How he had to steer from the backseat with his PK because Mom was too rattled to drive us home.

"It's an old car," Logan said. "That's all it was."

I couldn't let myself believe that until my dad confirmed, with a nod, that Logan's assessment was correct. An old car. Not Dennis Connelly.

But I would have felt better if Dad's nod wasn't so shaky.

It was no one's fault the getaway car hadn't started, but Dad blamed himself. "I shouldn't have let a little headache bother me. I should have been watching you." His voice was weak as Mom stroked his cheek. "I could have called. Told you Connelly was nowhere close."

Jillian, however, blamed Dennis Connelly. She stormed around the room, shoving end tables and armchairs out of her way with an angry glance. "He's nowhere close, but he still manages to terrorize us. It's not fair. When is it going to end?"

We all knew the answer to her question, but it was too horrible to say out loud.

CHAPTER EIGHT

TAPPED MY foot impatiently by Jillian's locker. I needed to go home, change, and get to the park. I'd been sitting with Tristan and his friends at lunch every day for two weeks now, and we'd resumed our Logan-chaperoned runs after school. We were supposed to meet on the path in half an hour. But Jillian had stopped packing her bookbag and was standing still, her gaze unfocused. Daydreaming.

"Come on!" I poked her.

"That's so cute," she murmured. "Logan's helping a girl open her jammed locker."

I peered down the hallway. Students chatted in groups as they dug textbooks and jackets from their shiny orange lockers. A few feet away, a girl applied lipstick in the mirror hanging inside her locker. At the other end of the hall, a boy leaned against his locker as he texted someone. But no girl with a jammed locker, and no Logan.

"Oh, good. He got it open," Jillian said, then snickered. "He probably used his PK and she never even knew it."

Logan was nowhere around. There was no way Jillian could see him, unless—

My whole body grew hot, then cold. I couldn't speak. Or move. "You did it?" I finally managed to squeak. "You have a mobile eye?"

With a smirk, she pulled me close. "Yeah. Kind of. It only works when Dad's doing it. Right now Dad's watching through Logan, and I'm piggybacking. We were watching through you earlier today." Then her tone fell flat. "Damn. He kicked me out again."

A group of chatty girls passed by, one of them calling Jillian over. "Shelby, over here!"

"I gotta go talk to them," she said, slamming her locker shut. "I told you that you didn't need to worry." I remained frozen as she shouldered her bookbag and sauntered off to join her friends.

Jillian had piggybacked on our father's mobile eye. One step closer, one monumental step closer, to developing a mobile eye of her own.

This was a *good* thing.

I was relieved. So relieved, in fact, that my knees shook, and I sank against the lockers.

Jillian was going to save us. With her new psychic ability. Logan had two abilities, psychokinesis and hypercognition, and now Jillian had two psychic abilities as well.

And I still had none.

"Everything okay, Sarah?"

I jumped at the voice, but it was just Tristan, walking by with Chad. He held his textbooks and notes in one large hand.

I managed to give him a weak smile. "Everything's great."

He frowned, clearly not believing me. "Still up for our run today?"

No way was I up for a run today. Not when Jillian had developed a new psychic power. Not when Logan could surreptitiously un-jam a girl's locker with his psychokinesis. Not when I couldn't even levitate a stupid paperclip.

But then I changed my mind. I had no psychic powers, but I had a friend. A friend who made me feel valued instead of inferior and useless. A friend who ran with me in the park because he wanted to, not because he was obligated to. A friend with broad shoulders and blue eyes and tousled brown hair that reflected gold in the light.

My weak smile became genuine. "I'll meet you at the park in half an hour."

Tristan was already at the entrance to the running path when I got there, swinging his arms to warm up his muscles and wearing an orange TLC baseball cap backwards. "Hey Clockwise. Where's Scottie?"

It took me a second to figure out he was talking about my brother. "I told him he could stay home." He didn't want to come anyway, and this time, I didn't argue.

Tristan brightened, first his eyes, then his smile. But his smile was softer this time, like he was honored I'd finally given him my trust. Together we sank to the grass to stretch. His gaze met mine, then lingered. "Wildflower eyes," he murmured.

"Hmm?"

"Your eyes. They're bright green with little flecks of color. Like wildflowers." He gestured to a small patch of violet, gold, and blue flowers, surrounded by green grass.

Like a butterfly, his words fluttered into my heart.

He hummed a little tune, soft and sweet.

"What's that?" I asked.

"An old song I heard the other day that made me think of you. 'Wildflowers.' By Tom Petty and the Heartbreakers. Do you know it?"

I shook my head. God, his eyes were so blue. Electric. Beautiful.

"Do you want to hear it?" he asked.

"Hear what?"

He chuckled. "'Wildflowers.' I saved it to my phone."

"Oh. Yes, please." I couldn't take my eyes from his face as he searched for the song on his phone. He hit play, and watched for my reaction as I listened. The lyrics sang of running away to find love and freedom. They were…

"…Perfect," I whispered. As the song played, I imagined Tristan holding me close, my head against his chest. *I turn my head up, he bends his down, and we…*

I pushed the image away right before we kissed.

I blinked and hopped up. "Let's run."

We ran side by side, matching each other step for step. Invisible strings kept the corners of my lips pulled up. My eyes were drawn to him like a magnet, to the way his pecs pulsed when his arms pumped, the way his hair bounced with each step—

"Eyes on the road, Sarah." He pulled me out of the way just before I would have crashed into a woman running in the opposite direction.

"Thanks," I said, feeling my face get hot.

"Good thing you have me to keep you safe."

I *did* feel safe with him. But no matter how safe I felt, he couldn't protect me from Dennis Connelly.

That thought stopped me short. What would I do if Dennis Connelly stepped out from behind a tree right now? What if my dad failed to see him coming? The smeared handprint on our front window. The loose battery cables in our getaway car. What if…

Oh God. I ran faster.

"Ready to pick up the pace?" Tristan asked as I shot past him. "You got it." A second later he was at my side, then he poked me. "Tag, you're it!" He darted off at full speed, then looked back at me with a goofy smile.

I forced myself to stop being so paranoid and have some fun. Jillian and Logan did it, maybe I could too. Quickening my steps until I was in a full-out sprint, I wove between the other joggers a few steps behind Tristan, trying to catch him. My feet pounded on the trail as I pumped my legs harder.

Tristan glanced behind him and slowed his pace. I leaped and grabbed the hat from his head. "Ha!" As I ran past him, I shoved the hat on my own head.

Oh—doing that slowed me down. Tristan was too close. I laughed and picked up speed again, determined to outrun him at least until we finished the lap.

I came close but didn't make it. He caught up with me just before the starting point. "Not bad, Sarah. But not good enough!" He grabbed his hat as he zoomed past and within seconds was far ahead of me. If I didn't run faster, he'd soon be around the bend, out of my sight.

I bore down, picturing my legs as pistons, pumping faster and faster. Tristan ran several paces ahead, but I kept him in sight. His lead was big enough that he could slow down and stop. He turned to face me, and with a teasing grin, adjusted the hat on his head before taking off again.

Big mistake. I shot myself forward like a cannon. A bullet. A few more steps and—yes! Just before we reached the starting point again, I caught up with him.

"Not good enough?" I jumped up and grabbed the hat back. "We'll see about that!" Sailing down the path for the third lap, I vowed to make it all the way around ahead of him this time. I jammed the hat on my head and ran. Sprinted. Flew. I heard him right behind me. He laughed, which slowed him down.

I managed to get a third of the way around before he caught up with me again. "I'm impressed," he said, and swiped the hat back. "If you beat me to the starting point, I'll let you keep this." He shot off again.

That was all the inspiration I needed. I soared down the path, dodging the other joggers. Soon I outpaced him. Five strides later, I ran right next to him. He whooped with surprise.

I didn't waste time grabbing the hat—that would just slow me down. We ran together. As he sped up, I matched his pace. My breath came easily. I was made for this. It was euphoric. I was flying.

The finish line approached. With a final burst of effort, I bolted ahead, finishing a full pace ahead of Tristan.

He had probably slowed at the last second to let me win, but I didn't care. I'd run faster than I'd ever run in my life. Together we collapsed to the grass, gulping in air. "It's all the…cheeseburgers…and junk food you eat," I gasped between breaths. "That was…your downfall."

He took his hat off as he caught his breath. "Your prize," he said, and slid it on my head. He was right on top of me, gazing into my eyes, his lips inches from mine.

I stopped breathing.

He leaned closer, another inch.

Yes, please.

He stopped. Smiled. Sat up.

"Come on, Clockwise." He stood and pulled me up. "One more time around. Slow. We need to cool off."

CHAPTER NINE

HE CLOCK TICKED past midnight, but I was wide awake as I lay in bed.

I'd almost kissed Tristan today.

Was Tristan awake too, thinking about our almost-kiss?

Even if he was, he'd be getting it wrong. He'd be thinking, *I almost kissed* Sarah *today.*

That was too painful to think about, so I encased the image in a cloud of fog and locked it up, and replaced it with something else: Jillian's new psychic ability.

Just as I was about to go across the hall to talk to her, she glided into my room and sat on my bed. "Pretty cool, huh? My remote vision? Aren't you excited?"

"Yeah." I slid my hands in my sleeves and rubbed my thumbnails into the cuffs. "How'd you do it?"

She glanced at my closet and directed my laundry to hang itself up. "A couple days ago I was in my room, trying to watch Mom while she was at the store. Dad was in his office. He was watching Mom at the same time I was trying to watch her, and we just..." She slid her palms together. "...connected."

"Oh. Cool." I watched my socks tuck themselves away in the bottom drawer of my dresser. "What's it like?"

"The images are warped and the sounds are garbled. Like everything is under water. But I can still see what he's seeing and hear what he's hearing. It's awesome. Mom and Dad are scared I'll get headaches, though."

"Do you?"

"Nope." She thrust out her chin. "And I don't care if I do. Piggybacking is a good first step, but it doesn't help us. Not at all. I'm going to keep at it until I can do it my own. Without Dad."

"You really think you'll be able to do it?" If anyone could, it would be Jillian. Through sheer force of will.

"I have to," she said, sliding the heart charm along her bracelet. "Ever since the car didn't start at the grocery store, Dad's been watching us more than ever. He used up a whole box of Kleenex this afternoon, his nose bled so much. He shouldn't be using his remote vision at all."

"But he'll never be able to stop completely," I said. "His mobile eye only works on people he's touched. You've never touched… *him*."

"No, but Mom and Dad have. And so have you."

The stench of cherry cigars filled my nose, and my hand fluttered to my belly. "So?"

"So, maybe between the three of you, it'll be enough for me to see him on my own." She took my hand from my stomach and held it between both of hers. "Maybe, if—*when*—I get strong enough, touching you will transfer his touch to me."

"That's ridiculous," I said. "It'll never work."

"It'll work." She tightened her jaw and her grip on my hand. "It'll work because I *want* it to work."

Then, quietly, she added, "It'll work because we *need* it to work. It's our only chance."

CHAPTER TEN

OGAN PEEKED INTO my room. "Star?"

I shook my head. "Waves."

He sighed and jotted a note in his notebook, then left to tell Jillian she was wrong again. Wiping all thoughts of Tristan from my mind, I pulled the next card from the deck and stared hard at it, not even daring to blink.

Logan returned a minute later. "She's positive this one is a cross."

I held up the card. "Circle."

"Try the next one."

The next card was a square. I stared it until my eyes dried out, and it became blurry. We'd gone through the deck three times already that night, and every night for the past week. Now that Jillian had a breakthrough, Logan was back on board. He set up a training program for her, involving quiet concentration, visualization, and Zener ESP flashcards.

They didn't ask me to help. They hadn't even considered asking me to help. But I'd insisted.

Now every night after our parents fell asleep—if they knew what we were doing, they'd put a stop to it immediately—I brought the flashcards to my room, picked one at random and stared at the symbol. Jillian would try to see the card from her room, through my eyes.

Logan kept a detailed record of her success rate, but it didn't take a math genius to know she was failing miserably. She was right only seventeen percent of the time. On average, non-psychic people like me scored twenty percent. Logan had tested me as the control, and I scored eighteen percent just by guessing.

This time Jillian stood in my doorway. "Waves?"

I showed her the square, and her fists clenched as she smothered a frustrated shriek. She'd never failed at anything before.

"You're trying too hard," I said. "You need to relax. Open your mind."

The deck shot from my hand, and she snatched it from the air. "I'm not taking advice from *you*. Switch with Logan. I need someone who's psychic."

Her words slapped me in the face.

"Jeez, Jill, she's just trying to help," Logan said. But he still took the cards.

Even with Logan concentrating on the cards and me as the go-between, Jillian was still wrong almost every time.

Tristan and I were so busy talking after our run Saturday morning that I didn't realize he'd walked me all the way home until we reached my driveway.

"What are you doing tonight?" He lifted his ankle up behind him to stretch his quad.

It was going to be a typical Saturday night for me: I'd stealthily watch my dad for nosebleeds while Mom and I planned next week's menu and waited for Jillian and Logan to get home, and after our parents fell asleep we'd have a clandestine training session.

But I couldn't tell Tristan that. "I'm going to the mall," I said instead. "They're having a sale on jeans."

Tristan switched legs. "Instead of shopping, would you like to go on a date with me?"

My breath hitched. "We're just friends, Tristan."

"We're more than just friends," he said. "And I want to make it official."

"Make what official?"

"Us. You and me."

Us. You and me. My heart echoed in rhythm: *Thump. Thump-th-thump.*

But I couldn't make *us* into anything more than what it was now. "We're officially friends," I said, digging my toe in the grass and squinting up at him. "That was a big step for me."

"Can't you take just one more step?" He held up his thumb and finger an inch apart. "A tiny baby step? Everyone already thinks we're dating."

"I—I don't want people to think about me at all."

"I think about you all the time. Want to know what I think?"

My answer was a whisper. "Yes."

"I think you're amazing. I think you're beautiful. And I think we should go on a date tonight."

Thump. Thump-th-thump.

Saying yes meant I'd have to lie to him.

And then one day, I'd have to leave him.

I had to say no.

But he was looking up at me with eyes bright and blue and full of hope. I thought about the past couple Saturday nights, how long and lonely they'd been, how I'd spent the whole time craving Tristan. If I didn't see him tonight, I'd have to wait until tomorrow. And suddenly tomorrow was too far away.

The word flew from my mouth without permission. "Yes."

Oh my goodness.

Oh my goodness!

"Yes?" His eyebrows rose a little in surprise. "You'll go out with me tonight?"

I couldn't stop myself from giggling. "Yes!"

He lit up from the inside out. "I'm leaving before you change your mind," he said, and started jogging away backwards. "Pick you up at seven."

In direct contradiction with the uproar of emotions I was feeling—anxious, excited, apprehensive, elated—my house was quiet and still when I went inside. I found Jillian sitting at the chipped kitchen table with an open textbook. "Where is everyone?" I asked.

"Dad's in his office. Logan thought he had one more saxophone reed left, but he couldn't find it, so Mom took him to buy more." She propped her chin in her hand and turned back to her homework.

"He lost it?" It wasn't like Logan to misplace things, even a saxophone reed.

"He probably just counted them wrong."

"Why are you home? I thought you had dance class."

"Mom and Dad grounded me for piggybacking again. I had to cancel my date with Ethan and everything." She looked up then, her eyes glinting with mischief. "At least one of us has a date tonight."

I froze. "You and Dad were watching me?"

"Just me. No psychic stuff either. I happened to open the door and saw you in the driveway with Tristan." The textbook slammed itself shut as she clapped her hands. "I'm so proud of you, Tessa, I could burst! I can't believe you said yes."

I couldn't believe it either. "I don't know if I can do it."

A chair slid out from under the table. "Sit," she said, and I sat. With a dreamy, faraway look in her eyes, she rotated the gold chain around her wrist. "Remember Gavin, from when we lived in Nebraska?"

Scrawny, serious, and studious, Gavin was nothing like the empty-headed pretty boys Jillian had dated before or since. "He gave you that bracelet."

"I was so in love with him," she sighed. "It hurt to lie to him. It physically hurt. In Nebraska, we had B names, remember? He thought my name was Brittany Billings."

I grimaced at the memory. I was Bethany, and Logan was Brandon.

"I hated that Gavin would never know my real name," she said. "I hated suppressing my PK around him. More than anything, I hated knowing the day would come when we'd have to run and I'd never see him again."

Jillian understood my problem after all. "So you hated everything about it."

"Not everything. I loved Gavin. I loved him more than I hated everything else."

"Do you still love him?"

She slid the heart charm around her chain again, then once more, before she answered. "No. I won't let myself."

"Why do you wear the bracelet, then?"

"I guess it reminds me that love is possible, even if it doesn't last forever."

We stared at each other for a long time, until I had to look away.

I had one more question, one that only my sister could answer. "I've never…what if Tristan wants to kiss me?"

"Do you want him to kiss you?"

"Yes." Absolutely. Desperately. Yes.

"Then let him kiss you." She hopped up and pulled me from the chair. "Now let's go upstairs, so I can figure out what you're going to wear."

After battling with Jillian over my outfit for the evening, we compromised on dark jeans, a silk tank and black ballet-style flats. Well, compromised was the wrong word. Every time I took something from my closet, it tore itself from my hands and flew into her room, where it locked itself away.

"No long sleeves for you tonight." She handed me an emerald tank, the brightest thing in my closet, and until now, unworn. "I don't want you spending all night rubbing holes in any cuffs. And the green brings out your eyes."

She painted my toenails Passion Pink and slid a headband in my hair, and even convinced me to wear a touch of makeup. As she painted my lips with strawberry-flavored gloss, I finally realized why Jillian wanted her privacy so much. "What about Dad? I don't want him to watch Tristan and me kissing."

But instead of getting pouty and going on a rant, she just folded a tissue for me to blot my lips. "Dad doesn't want to watch that either. But he knows that's not going to stop me. So he and I made a deal. I give him a signal," she said, crossing her fingers, middle over index. "And he stops watching. But only for five minutes. Then he checks back in to make sure I haven't gone too far."

By the spark in her eye, I was sure Tristan and I could have plenty of fun in those five minutes. I laughed out loud.

When Jillian was done, she pulled me into a hug so tight I couldn't breathe. "This was one of my favorite days, Tessa," she said. "I've always wanted to do sister things like this with you."

A lump appeared in my throat, and I hugged her back even tighter.

CHAPTER ELEVEN

*W*HEN MOM GOT home later that afternoon, Jillian presented me to her like an art project. "Tessa has a date with Tristan tonight!" she squealed, and Mom did too. Now, one fussed over my hair and the other inspected my makeup as we waited in the living room for Tristan to pick me up.

Mom pressed my face between her hands. "I'm so proud of you, Babydoll." She kissed my forehead, then laughed as she scrubbed off her lipstick-print with her thumb. She was so excited, I was surprised she didn't make the furniture dance around the room.

My dad shuffled in from his office, black hair disheveled, hazel eyes glazed. "We're good," he said, meaning we were still safe from Dennis Connelly. He blinked as his eyes cleared. "What's going on?"

"Tessa has a date tonight." Mom smoothed the waves in my hair, and I dodged a cloud of hairspray from the bottle hovering over my shoulder.

"A date?" His forehead scrunched. A date was different from a Homecoming dance, where we'd be surrounded by others, including my protective brother and sister. A date was…a *date*. "Is she old enough for that?"

Jillian growled. "She's sixteen, Dad."

Her eyes glittering, Mom gave him a patient nod. "She's ready for this."

"I told her about the signal," Jillian said, holding up her hand with her fingers crossed, mortifying both Dad and me. "So you'd better give her privacy if she uses it. *When* she uses it. Five minutes, just like me."

Jillian was excited, and Mom was ecstatic, but not me. My hands were shaking, and I was pretty sure one or both of them were using their PK to freeze my feet to the floor so I couldn't run and hide in my room.

But a few seconds later when the doorbell rang, I didn't need them to freeze me anymore. My nerves were doing that for them.

They glanced around the room, and the hair supplies and cosmetics zipped upstairs. My dad's face melted into an expression of worry and loss as an invisible push propelled me to the door. The knob twisted itself in my hand, and the door swung itself open.

Any apprehension I'd had dissipated into mist at the sight of Tristan, tall and gorgeous in a collared navy shirt, smelling of soap and strength and safety. We gazed at each other for a long moment.

Behind me, my dad cleared his throat.

"Oh. Yeah. Tristan, this is my dad, An—" I stopped as my heart stumbled over a beat. I'd almost introduced him as Andrew Carson, his real name. I looked at him in panic, unable to remember his alias.

He provided it for me. "Charles Spencer." He approached Tristan, hand extended.

Holding my breath, I watched as Tristan slid his hand into my father's.

There. That was it. A single touch was all it took. Now Dad would be able to watch Tristan, whenever he wanted, for the rest of his life. Guilt sliced through me like a knife.

"Nice to meet you, sir," Tristan said.

"This is my wife, Olivia," Dad replied, and Tristan gave my mother a charming smile. She returned it with one of her own—a smile of admiration and gratitude.

Jillian had moved to the stairway, probably to block it in case I decided to run. "Hey, Tristan." She flipped her hair behind her shoulders. "How'd you do on the Physics test?"

"Got an A. How about you?"

"Ninety-eight percent," she said. From the corner of my eye, I saw my mother frown.

"Nice," Tristan said. "You beat me by two percent."

"I just got lucky." She batted her eyelashes innocently. "I don't understand physics at all." That was a lie. She understood every subject. Science was her favorite, especially biology. She wanted to be a heart surgeon, if she lived long enough. But physics was a joke to Jillian because many of its rules didn't apply to her.

Mom gestured to the door. "Have fun, kids." Tristan had been inside for only a minute, but that was already too long. Time to go.

"Home by midnight, Sarah. Be good." My dad rubbed a spot under his eye. A message to me: he would be watching.

"Nice meeting you, Mr. and Mrs. Spencer," Tristan said, and to my dismay, enthusiastically shook my father's hand again.

Jillian had to cover her mouth to keep from laughing.

While Tristan drove to Twelve Lakes' town square he told me what he'd planned for our evening. He'd made reservations at Salutos, the nicest Italian restaurant in town, and afterward we could either play mini-golf or see a movie, my pick. I chose mini-golf. Movie theaters were dark and crowded, and you never knew who could come up behind you. Besides, I hadn't played mini-golf since Virginia.

Tristan circled the parking lot at Salutos twice before finding a spot. As we walked inside, he took my hand and glanced at me to see if I minded. I entwined my fingers with his to show him it was okay. I loved the feeling of his warm palm pressed to mine.

We pressed into the crowded lobby to wait for our table. Dark red brick peeked through the stucco, and strings of tiny white lights twinkled from the ceiling. A mural of Venice covered an entire wall. Tristan had picked a beautiful restaurant, except for the crowd and noise. The last restaurant I'd eaten in was that quiet twenty-four-hour diner after we'd fled Vermont. Only a handful of people had been in that place. Here, the mass of patrons shouted over each other and crushed us from all sides.

The hostess finally called Tristan's name, and after we pushed our way through the crowd, she seated us at a table.

The table was beautiful. A clean white tablecloth, a lit candle, three red carnations in an empty wine bottle. Napkins folded like fans.

But the table was in the middle of the room. I couldn't see the door or the people behind me.

I glanced around the restaurant, looking for anyone suspicious.

A well-dressed couple clinking their wine glasses together. A man with a sharp buzz cut wearing a crisply ironed shirt, ramrod straight in his chair, frowning as his frizzy-haired companion wiped marinara sauce from her sleeve. A bald man with a red beard sitting at the bar with two drinks, scowling at his watch. A harried busboy swiping dirty plates into a plastic bin.

Every single one of them looked suspicious.

"You okay?" Tristan raised his voice over the din.

I forced myself to smile. No one was watching me. No one had even noticed me. Dennis Connelly, with his kind eyes that turned sharp and mean, was not here.

I was safe.

Still, I tapped my cell phone to make sure it was there, and slipped my hands under my knees to keep them from trembling.

"Do you already know what you want to order?" Tristan asked.

I shook my head. I knew I should open the menu, but I couldn't move. Nausea and dizziness made the restaurant feel unreal and far away. I closed my eyes. Forced myself to breathe.

"Sarah?"

A hacking laugh cut through the din, and I opened my eyes. A man sitting in a corner booth was laughing, and he had something sticking out of his shirt pocket. A cigar. It wasn't lit, but I swore I could smell it. Burning cherries.

Run. *Run.* I had to leave. I had to get out of here. With clammy hands, I tried to push myself away from the table when another wave of nausea hit me.

The world began to fade into a cloud of fog.

"Tris..." Before I finished saying his name, he was at my side.

He took my arm and pulled me up. "I'm taking you out of here." He tossed some bills on the table and rushed me from the restaurant.

The fresh air cooled me, and now that we were away from the crowd, my lungs could expand again. Tristan helped me into his car, and we raced away. "You look a little better."

The dizziness and nausea faded with a few deep breaths, and after a few more, I couldn't even smell the cherry cigar anymore. "I feel okay now." Great, actually.

"What happened?"

"The crowd. The noise. It was too much."

"Want me to take you home?"

"No. I want to stay with you."Suddenly, surprisingly, sincerely. There was nothing I wanted more.

His lips twisted in doubt. "You sure?"

"Tristan." I put my hand on his forearm."I want to stay with you."

He did that thing again, where he lit up from the inside out. First his eyes, then his smile. "Then I have a great idea." He drove across the street to the supermarket. "Let's make our own dinner," he said as he led me inside. "I can't cook, but I can grill. We have a barbecue at home."

"I love to cook," I said shyly. "I can handle the stove."

With a satisfied sigh, he put his arm around me. "I'm liking you more and more every second, Clockwise."

The weight of his arm on my shoulders was heavy, and wonderful. I belonged there, under his arm. I pressed into him and breathed in his scent, feeling safe and cherished, like he could protect me from everything bad in the world.

He stopped in front of the meat counter. "Burgers? Steak?"

I crinkled my nose.

"Oh, I get it," he said. "You're a vegetarian, aren't you?"

"I haven't eaten meat in years." I didn't understand how anyone could kill something weak, defenseless, and innocent.

We turned away from the stacks of raw dead animals, and Tristan stopped and looked around the store like he couldn't fathom what to eat if it wasn't meat.

"We could make a pizza," I suggested. "Half veggie and half whatever you want."

"Perfect." We wandered around the store, picking out a pizza crust, sauce, and cheese, then headed to the produce section. "Hey Sarah. Catch."

I looked up just as he tossed a blue container of mushrooms at me. I caught it, and he immediately tossed me a bag of broccoli, then an onion right after that. I caught them all and tossed them back. He showed off by juggling plums, then apples, then cantaloupes. He tried to juggle watermelons until I begged with breathless laughter for him to stop.

My smile, and an occasional giggle, accompanied us all the way back to his house.

Tristan's house was in the same subdivision as mine, around the corner and a couple blocks away. Like mine, his house was older and a bit worn down. But inside, the afghans and throw pillows and knickknacks gave his house a relaxed hominess that mine would never have. The kitchen was cluttered but clean. We unloaded our groceries onto the counter.

"Helloooo!" A high-pitched voice called from the garage entry. A petite woman with a blond pixie cut walked into the kitchen, followed by a man with black hair that curled up at the collar of his plaid flannel shirt. I'd seen him before, but couldn't place him.

"Sarah, this is my aunt and uncle," Tristan said. "Melissa and Philip."

Melissa greeted me warmly, and Philip gave me a nod. I gave them the bashful smile I reserved for grown-ups and managed to squeak out a nice-to-meet-you.

"You've probably seen my uncle around school," Tristan said.

That's right; that's why he was familiar. His uncle was the facilities manager at TLC. He was one of the men who'd found me in the back stairwell on that rainy Monday, the nice one who *hadn't* marched me back to the cafeteria.

"What happened to Salutos?" Melissa asked.

"Too crowded." Tristan took my hand. "We're making dinner here."

Her gaze traveled to our clasped hands. "We'll stay out of your way," she said with an amused grin, and pulled Philip from the room.

"I'm starving," Tristan said as soon as we were alone again. "Let's make that pizza. What do we do first?"

"Preheat the oven," I directed, much more comfortable cooking in a kitchen than eating in a crowded restaurant. I was in charge here. No surprises. No danger. "And wash the veggies. I'll need a cutting board and a knife."

He followed my instructions, then spread sauce over the crust while I grated the cheese. I decided to ask him questions so he wouldn't ask me any. "Do your aunt and uncle have any kids?"

He plucked a mushroom from the container and tossed it in his mouth. "Not yet."

"You mentioned you have a sister. Older or younger?"

"She's fourteen. You two will get along really well. She's a vegetarian too."

"Too bad she's in Malaysia with your parents."

"Not forever. They're moving back in a year or so."

"Oh." He didn't realize it, but I would never meet his family. By the time they came back to the States, my family would have run again. Or we'd be dead. I changed the subject before my mood deflated. "Were you on the tennis team at your old school, too?"

"Tennis, ski, cross-country. And student council."

Now that we weren't surrounded by classmates, joggers, and

restaurant patrons, my apprehension evaporated, and questions came easily to me. I wanted to know everything about him. I grabbed a tomato and started dicing it. "Do you miss living at home?"

"Yeah." He scattered the mozzarella over the sauce. "But I like it here too. Especially now that I have you."

Our gazes met, and my face became hotter than the oven.

I wondered what his lips tasted like.

"Hey!" He grabbed the knife from my hand. "Careful. You almost cut yourself."

"Whoops. Thanks." I hid my burning face behind my hair as I wiped my slippery hands on a dishrag.

Tristan finished dicing the tomato for me. Not as neatly or precisely as I would have done it, but he had definite potential. We added more cheese and veggies to the pizza, then he slid it in the oven. He turned to face me, arms crossed and expression all business. "*My* turn to ask the questions."

Oh God. But I had just asked him a million questions; it was only fair that I had to answer a few. I tapped my cell phone, then thrust my chin out the way Jillian did when she was pretending not to be nervous or scared. "Go ahead."

"Hmm." He cocked his head with his eyes narrowed, studying me. "What's your favorite color?"

Turning my sigh of relief into a laugh, I said, "Periwinkle."

"What's that?"

"It's a shade of blue, but in certain lights it looks purple."

"A color that's two things at once. Interesting. And your favorite food?"

"Blueberries."

"Ah. Tiny, but lots of flavor." He grinned. "Like you."

I bit my lips to keep from smiling, but it wasn't working.

"Favorite subject in school?"

"Art," I said.

"Really? I didn't know you took art."

"I don't. We move too often. I can't haul my paintings with me all over the country." And we certainly couldn't leave them behind.

"What states have you lived in so far?"

Okay, time to lie. "Well, you know we just moved from Oklahoma. Before that we were in Colorado." We'd never been to either state, except to drive through them in our mad dash from Dennis Connelly. We covered our tracks in the states we had lived in by lying about states we hadn't. "We've lived in so many places they all blur together," I said. At least that part was true.

Tristan opened the fridge. "Lemonade or Coke?"

"Lemonade, please." I searched the cabinets and found the glasses, then placed them on the table.

"So your dad's a writer," he said as he poured the tea. "What about your mom? Does she work?"

"Nope. What about yours?" Maybe if I turned his questions around, he'd talk about himself again. "What do your parents do?"

"My mom's a preschool teacher, and my dad works for a company that manufactures computer hard drives. He transferred to Malaysia to oversee the construction of their new plant." He winked. "But it's my turn to ask the questions, remember?"

Darn. My plan didn't work. Tristan was determined to get to know Sarah Spencer. I tossed my hair in an effort to appear nonchalant. "Ask away."

"What does your dad write?"

"Books."

He guffawed. "I mean, what does he write about? Anything I've heard of?"

Oh. God, I was such an idiot. "I'm sure you haven't. He writes about the economy, things like that."

"Why did he come to Twelve Lakes?"

"He says Illinois has an interesting economic history." Another stock answer. I was doing okay. I could do this.

"I should read his books, now that I'm dating his daughter."

Panic zipped through me. I had *no* stock answer for this one. I gripped the counter, scrambling to think how Jillian would reply if Ethan said the same thing to her. "Don't waste your time," I said. "His books are long and boring and confusing, and anyway, he uses a pen name," I added, in case he decided to take a trip to the library or look up Charles Spencer on the internet.

"Oh, yeah?" He set two plates on the table, then slid a glance at me. "What's his pen name?"

How stupid of me to bring up a pen name! Of course he'd ask what it was. The only name that came to mind was Xander Xavier. But if he looked up that name, he'd learn Xander Xavier was the pseudonym of respected journalist Andrew Carson, who was killed eight years ago along with his wife Wendy and their young children, Jillian, Tessa, and Logan, in a tragic gas explosion at their home in Virginia.

"Um…" I needed to redirect him. "We need a pizza cutter."

He dug through a drawer, and I held my breath. "Aha! Found it. Here you go."

Wow. I was better at lying than I'd thought. That realization made me feel guiltier than ever.

The buzzer on the oven rang. Both Tristan and I sprung to take out the pizza. "Sit," I told him. "I'll get it." He obliged, and I sliced the round pizza into small triangles, then placed it between us on the table.

For the first time in a long time, I was ravenous. I served each of us a piece and took a big bite of mine.

We chatted casually about school and his friends—*our* friends—and before long we'd eaten almost the entire pizza. "Best pizza ever," he said, and patted his stomach. "What about mini-golf? It's still open if you want to go."

I'd forgotten about mini-golf. As long as I was able to deflect his questions about my family, I could stay at Tristan's house forever. I could tell by his tone that he didn't want to leave either. "I'd be happy staying here," I said. "We can watch a movie or something."

"That sounds perfect." He grinned.

In his family room, we scrolled through the movies on Netflix. He let me choose, so I selected one called *Say Anything,* because there were infinite things I wanted to say to Tristan, but would never be able to.

He turned down the lights, and we sank onto the couch, then he pulled my legs over his lap and put his arm around me. I loved sitting with him like this. Content. Comfortable. Safe. I snuggled in the crook of his arm.

The movie played on the television, but my gaze kept returning to Tristan. He kept glancing at me and smiling.

His eyes were so beautiful. So blue. So deep.

And his jaw—so strong. He had scruffy hair on his chin. I wanted to brush my fingertips on it.

And his hair. Neatly combed when he picked me up, it had since fallen out of place. I loved his hair tousled like that.

And his lips…

So soft, yet so strong. I wondered if his kisses would be gentle and slow, or passionate and urgent.

Could he hear my heart pounding?

His eyes locked onto mine, and he shifted so we were face-to-face.

Please kiss me. Please.

He leaned in, just an inch, then another.

For the quickest of moments, I glanced at my hand and crossed my fingers, middle over index. If my father had been watching, he wasn't anymore. I had five minutes.

Tristan moved in another inch, then stopped. He gazed at me, eyes endlessly deep. He took a lock of my hair and ran his fingers through it.

But no kiss. Why wasn't he kissing me?

I couldn't stand it anymore. Just as I reached to grab his shirt and pull him to me, he cupped his hand behind my head, threading his fingers in my hair, and pressed his lips onto mine.

Bliss.

I kissed him back, our lips crushed together, intense and eager, my arms snaking around him to press him closer to me, and I never, ever, ever wanted it to end.

Slowly, our kisses became tender and unhurried until we parted. I looked up at him, dazed. "Don't…you don't have to stop. We still have time." A few seconds, at least. I wanted every one of them.

The patter of light footsteps on the stairway reminded me that Tristan and I weren't alone in the house. He sat up just as we heard his aunt enter the kitchen. "I do have to stop," he whispered. "But I'll kiss you again tomorrow. And the next day. And every day."

I sighed at that thought and sat up, snuggling back into him. A few minutes ago, I'd wanted this evening to never end, but the thought of kissing him again tomorrow would make it easier to say good-night.

CHAPTER TWELVE

HAT NIGHT I floated on a cloud up to my room and slid into bed, certain dreams of Tristan's strong arms and tender kisses would keep the nightmare away.

A shadow slithered across my wall, and before I could bolt, something pounced on me. "So? How was the kiss?"

Jillian.

It was only Jillian. Waiting for me, practically bursting with squealy excitement.

Once I swallowed my scream, I told her everything about my date with Tristan. She was the only person in the world I could tell everything to, especially the kissing part. We talked in whispers, smothering our giggles behind our hands until the sun rose.

Mid-morning, I rushed to meet Tristan for our daily run. It'd been too many hours since I'd last seen him. We ran down the path at a slower pace than usual, smiling widely and stopping completely when he pulled me behind a tree for a long, delicious kiss. Finally we found a quiet place in the park and lay on the grass and watched the clouds. How odd that our first date was just last night. I felt like we'd been together for years, rather than only a few hours.

We were brand-new and forever at the same time.

He walked me home, holding my hand and sometimes raising it to his lips for a kiss, and when we reached my driveway, he gave my cheek a respectful peck.

I didn't want respectful. I didn't want a peck. Grabbing the collar of his T-shirt to pull him down, I sealed my lips to his. He slid his arms around me and lifted me to my toes. I slid my arms around his neck, bringing him even closer, never letting my lips part from his.

He tensed and pulled away just before I heard a deep cough from behind me.

"Hello, kids."

Oh God. My dad.

Tristan scraped his hand through his hair, his face reddening as I felt the blood drain from mine. I'd been so entranced with him that I'd forgotten to send my father the crossed-fingers signal.

He strode over with an open smile and an extended hand.

"Morning, Mr. Spencer," Tristan said as my dad gripped his hand and shook it up and down. Dad engaged him in a friendly discussion about the afternoon's NFL games.

My father didn't even like football. But he wasn't out here because of the kissing. He could have just given a stern tap on the front window to stop us from kissing.

Tristan said something and Dad laughed, then casually slid his hand onto Tristan's shoulder and kept it there.

And then I knew why Dad came out here: he needed to touch Tristan again. But one touch, the handshake from last night, was all it should have taken to connect Tristan to his mobile eye.

Something was wrong. I tried to keep my breath even, calm.

With a final squeeze of Tristan's shoulder, Dad released him. He caught my eye as he strolled back to the house. "Come see me when you get in," he said with a reassuring wink. "No rush."

"Whoops," Tristan said as soon as we were alone again. "I hope I didn't get you in trouble. He didn't seem too upset, though."

I couldn't speak. I gave him a noncommittal shrug instead.

"Want to come over and study later?" he said. "Maybe watch the games?"

"Um." I couldn't. I had to find out why Dad needed to shake Tristan's hand again. "I can't. Sorry."

"Meet me at the corner tomorrow morning then," he said. "I'll walk you to school."

"Okay." I glanced at the house. "I have to go."

He bent down to kiss me, then stopped. "Better not get caught doing that again." He chuckled and jogged away.

I remained frozen on the driveway until the front door opened again, and my dad shuffled over to me. "Come on, Tessa Blessa. Let's go in." With his arm around my shoulders, he guided me inside.

The moment the door closed, I stammered, "What's wrong?"

He stumbled to the living room, and with a huge exhale, collapsed on the couch. "I can't see through Tristan. I tried last night, and again this morning."

A burning heaviness like hot coals formed in my stomach, and I sank next to him. "Your mobile eye stopped working? This is it? It's over?"

"Nothing is over. My mobile eye is fine. I watched your sister's boyfriend this morning as a test. He was playing a video game. The problem isn't me, Tessa. It's Tristan."

"Why? What's wrong with him?"

"Nothing's wrong with him. There have always been people it simply doesn't work on. Tristan may be one of them. Sometimes it takes more than one handshake, and it doesn't ever work on about five percent of the people I touch. They have some kind of natural immunity to it. Remember your first-grade teacher, Mrs. Heinrich? It didn't work on her. There've been a few people over the years. And of course, it doesn't work all the time on Dennis Connelly. I can only see through him if he's close."

I flinched at the sound of his name.

"We can say his name out loud, Tessa," Dad said. "He won't hear us."

I shook my head, then had a thought that made me gasp. "You don't think Tristan—"

"If Connelly knew we were in Twelve Lakes, he'd come here himself. He wouldn't send a kid to do his dirty work." He patted my knee. "I'd check on your boyfriends even if we didn't have to worry about Connelly. Any parent would, if they had the same ability I have. Tristan seems like a great kid. But I simply can't trust someone who I can't watch."

I remembered my parents demanded I be transferred from Mrs. Heinrich's first-grade class, even though she was a sweet elderly woman and the closest thing to a grandmother I ever had. Now I knew why they didn't like her.

"I'll try to watch him again this afternoon," Dad said. "If it works, you can go out with him again."

"And if it doesn't?"

He didn't reply.

I spent the afternoon in my room, staring at my homework but unable to concentrate on any of it. After resisting Tristan for weeks, I had finally faced my fears and gone out with him. And I loved it. But now, less than twenty-four hours later, I could lose him.

Dad didn't come up to help me study. He was holed up in his office, concentrating on Tristan.

Please let his mobile eye work on Tristan this time. Please.

Mom called me down to make dinner, but I was more of a hindrance than a help. I put a tablespoon, instead of a teaspoon, of dill into the salad dressing, and I forgot to set the timer on the oven, and the pork chops burned. We had to toss everything and make spaghetti instead.

When it was time to eat, I sat down but didn't pick up my fork. "Did it work?" I asked my dad.

His stony face showed me my answer. "I tried twice. It didn't work either time."

Logan spooned tomato sauce over his pasta. "What didn't work?"

"Dad still can't watch Tristan," Jillian said.

I stared hard at my plate. "So that's it? I have to stop seeing him?"

"I'm afraid so, Blessa," Dad said. "I don't like being blind to him. I'm sorry."

I had to break up with Tristan. I blinked, trying to make the idea sink in.

"That's not fair!" Jillian said. "If you didn't have your mobile eye you would trust him."

Logan slurped a long noodle into his mouth. "He's a great guy, Dad. He always stops by my locker to say hi. He even offered to tutor me."

"Jillian, Logan, thank you for your input, but this is the way it has to be," Mom said. She looked like she was about to cry. "I'm so sorry, Babydoll."

Jillian pounded her fist on the table, making Mom flinch as if she'd been slapped. "You two have always been overprotective of her. We all have. And not just since Dennis Connelly tried to take her. We've always treated her like she's breakable. But you know what? Tessa is not breakable. She's normal. She's the only normal person in this freak show of a family. So let her be normal. Let her be with Tristan."

"It's not just Tessa." Dad nodded regally, like a judge. "We'd make the same decision about you if I couldn't watch Ethan. Tessa can have a boyfriend. But it has to be someone I can watch."

I didn't want a boyfriend just to have a boyfriend. I wanted *Tristan*. But I couldn't say that out loud. I couldn't go against my parents' demands.

But Jillian could.

"No. It *has* to be Tristan," she said. Her utensils rose from the table and spun around like a tornado. "Tessa has friends for the first time in years, and it's all because of him. If you take him away, she'll just go back to the way she was before."

"We are trying to keep her safe," Mom said, spine straight, lips straight, eyes boring straight at Jillian. A low rumbling noise came from the table. The bowl of spaghetti was vibrating.

"Mom, it's okay," I said. "I'll do it. I'll break up with him." I shot Jillian a look. *Stop.*

"Five percent, Dad!" Jillian cried. "Your mobile eye doesn't work on one out of every twenty people. That's a lot. Tristan happens to be that one in twenty. You just don't like it that he makes Tessa happy, and *you* can't."

"Enough!" Mom roared, and the bowl of spaghetti flew into the air, then hurled itself against the wall.

Trapping a scream behind my lips, I bolted, ducking behind my chair. Jillian's utensils dropped like stones, clattering to the table.

Dad pushed himself up from the table and put his arms around Mom. "Jillian, go to your room," he said without looking at her.

White-faced, Jillian scrambled away.

As our father comforted our mother, soothing her with his firm, calm voice, and Logan helped me to stand, I stared at the tomato sauce on the wall. It slowly dripped down, thick and pulpy and red, like blood.

Normally I would have cleaned it up. But this time, I just walked out of the room.

After our parents fell asleep that night, I went to Jillian's room for her mobile eye training session. Logan wasn't there yet. Good. I needed to thank my sister for defending me, even though it hadn't worked. And then I needed to ask how to break up with Tristan when my heart felt like it had been hacked into thousands of tiny pieces.

She lay on her bed with a scowl on her lips and earbuds in her ears, ripping through pages of a magazine. Several items—a hairbrush, a hand mirror, a bottle of lotion—floated in the air, angrily pulsing to the beat of music I couldn't hear.

I knocked on the doorframe. "Jill?"

She looked up and pulled the earbuds out, and the items zipped to the dresser as she bounded across the room. "It doesn't have to be over just because Mom and Dad say it is," she hissed, dragging me to sit on the bed. "You don't have to break up with Tristan. I can help you keep seeing him."

"How?"

"I've been thinking about this all night. All you have to do is tell them you're going to a friend's house, like that girl Vanessa from your Spanish class. But really, you'll go to Tristan's."

"But Dad watches us all the time," I said.

"Don't worry about that. I can tell when he's doing it now. I get this little pull in my head. So every time he starts, I'll text you." She hopped up and pirouetted across the floor, her hairbrush flip-flopping behind her. "You can leave the room and go hide in the bathroom or something. He won't watch you there."

Jillian's plan could work. For the first time in our lives, we could lie to our parents.

But we were already lying to everyone else. Home was the only place in the world I didn't have to lie. It was bad enough we weren't telling our parents about Jillian's training sessions. But that was to protect them, so our dad could eventually rest. Sneaking around to see Tristan was completely different. It would be worse than a lie. It would be a betrayal.

I swallowed hard. "I won't lie to Mom and Dad."

She stopped mid-twirl and the hairbrush fell to the floor with a dull thump. She gave a long, slow sigh. "I know. Just thought I'd try."

"It's better if I end it now anyway," I said, thrusting out my chin. "It won't hurt to leave him when we have to run again."

She raised one perfectly plucked eyebrow. "Now you're just lying to yourself."

There was a knock on the doorframe, and Logan entered, carrying the Zener ESP cards. He slid them from the case and made them shuffle themselves in the air. "Ready to practice?"

Jillian's face tightened. "Not tonight."

"Why not?" he asked.

"I don't feel like it. I'm tired."

"You're not getting headaches, are you?" I asked.

"No, I am not getting headaches. Can't I just be tired for once?" She waved a finger at the light switch, and the room darkened. "Get out. Both of you. I need to sleep."

I thanked Jillian again and left with Logan. The Zener cards zipped after us just before the door swung shut, and he caught them in his palm. "That sucks about Tristan," he said.

"Yeah." One of the framed pictures on the wall was crooked. Perhaps at one time the yellow flowers in the picture were bright and cheery, but now they were faded and dingy.

Logan wiggled his index finger, and the frame straightened itself. "I'll go jogging with you again if you want."

"Thanks, Logan."

When sleep finally came for me, my nightly dream came with it, Dennis Connelly's eyes feverish with victory as he sliced me open with just a glance. I awoke shaking and breathless, biting my lips to stifle the scream clawing out of my throat, and I had to run my hands over my stomach to make sure my wounds were still closed.

He was coming for us anyway, whether my parents forbade me to date Tristan or not.

CHAPTER THIRTEEN

RISTAN LEANED AGAINST the thick oak tree at the corner the next morning, thumbs flying over his phone. When he saw me he tucked the phone in his pocket and gave me a cheerful wave. I had to force my feet to move toward him, when all I wanted to do was run back home and hide from what I had to do.

I studied him as I approached. What made him immune to my father's mobile eye? What made him different from almost everyone else in the world?

Probably the same thing that made me different from everyone else in my family: chance. Random, arbitrary, heartless chance.

We really did belong together. And now I had to break up with him.

"Hi," he said. "Was your dad upset about that kiss on your driveway yesterday?"

"He didn't say anything about it."

"Good. Then I can do this." Dipping me backwards, he planted an enthusiastic kiss on my lips. He tasted like mint and smelled like soap. I wanted to slide my arms around his neck and press him closer and never let him go.

Instead I pushed him away. Closed my eyes. Took a breath. Licked my lips, swallowed.

"Tristan, I—"

But I couldn't say it.

"There's something I need to do at home," I said instead, then turned and ran back to the house.

My parents were still in the kitchen, eating breakfast and looking at papers spread over the table. When Mom saw me, she held her arms out. "Oh, Babydoll. That must have been so hard. Was he crushed? Come here."

I didn't step into her hug. I stayed where I was, gripping the strap of my bookbag with both hands to keep them from trembling. "I won't do it."

They said nothing. They didn't move at all except for raising their eyebrows in confusion, or maybe disbelief. Finally my mom's arms dropped to her sides. "Tessa, don't tell me—"

"There are a million reasons why you should trust Tristan," I said, "and only one reason you don't. A reason you wouldn't even have if you didn't have a mobile eye. But even if you never trust him, you can trust me." I drew myself up as tall as I could. "Tristan thinks I'm Sarah Spencer, daughter of an author of economic books. He will never know the truth."

With each word I spoke, I grew stronger. My hands stopped trembling, and I held my chin high. "I'm not going to lie to you. I'm not going to sneak around. I will follow the rules. But I am not breaking up with Tristan."

I waited for them to respond, or for Mom's eyes to harden and the plates to start vibrating, but they just stared at me in stunned silence. So, keeping my chin high, I pivoted and marched out the door.

Tristan was walking up my driveway, tall and strong with concern visible in his eyes. "Everything okay?"

Laughing, I ran to him and jumped, wrapping my arms around his neck and my legs around his waist, and crushed my lips to his."Everything's perfect." Not really, but *he* was perfect. And he was mine.

He spun me around, returning my kiss with one of his own before setting me down again. He took my bookbag and put it over his shoulder, then tucked me under his arm as we headed for school.

I slid my arms tightly around him, determined to never let go until Dennis Connelly tore me away.

Mom was already in the kitchen when I went to help make dinner that night. Waiting for me, leaning against the table, wringing her hands. Rice, mushrooms, cheese, and several cartons of organic chicken stock were set on the table behind her.

"I thought we were making chicken tetrazzini," I said. Chicken tetrazzini was on the menu we'd planned for tonight. Simple, *quick* chicken tetrazzini.

"I changed my mind," she said, her voice forcibly bright. "Tonight we're making mushroom risotto."

Making risotto meant standing over the stove, adding the stock into the rice, a small amount at a time, and stirring, stirring, stirring until it absorbed.

She had me trapped.

Twenty minutes later, I'd grated the Parmesan, sliced and sautéed the mushrooms, and coated the rice in oil in the pan. But she never said a word about Tristan or about my refusal to break up with him. She never moved from the table.

She just stood there. Watching.

Only when I was at the stove, stirring the first half-cup of stock into the rice, did she say something. "I never wanted this life for you, Tessa," she said. "I promised myself your childhood would be better than mine. And it was, at first. You had the biggest smile and these amazing green eyes that just sparkled." She gave a mournful sigh. "But then everything…fell apart…and you lost your smile, and all I saw was the fear and loneliness in your eyes."

Then she was behind me, lifting my hair and smoothing it behind my shoulders. "I probably looked the same way when I was growing up."

Mom hardly ever talked about her childhood. When she did, it was only in clipped hints of food banks and thrift stores, and of living in a broken-down mobile home with her mother, who worked the night shift in a factory and died when Mom was a senior in high school. The other kids, she said, treated her like a contagious disease. The only other thing I knew was that she'd first discovered she was psychokinetic when she was twelve and was so afraid of it she'd told no one, until she met my father nine years later and realized she wasn't alone.

She'd been as lonely as I was. Lonelier. At least I had Jillian and Logan.

Overwhelmed with the need to comfort her, I started to turn around. But she flicked her fingers and the carton of stock rose from the counter, then poured a bit of itself into the rice. I turned back to the stove and stirred.

"Tristan is bringing that sparkle back into your eyes," she said. Her hands trembled as she weaved my hair into a loose braid. "Dad and I are so grateful to him for that. And we do trust you. We know you'd never tell him anything. But Babydoll, we are not changing our minds about this."

I thrust out my chin. "Neither am I," I said. "I'm not breaking up with him."

Her hands froze, still holding my hair, and the cutting board vibrated on the counter. With a whimper, I dropped the wooden spoon and gripped the handle on the oven door so tightly my knuckles turned white. Dad wasn't here, he wasn't here to calm her down—

A fissure snaked down the measuring cup.

"Please," I whispered, squeezing my eyes shut. "Please please please don't."

With a pained, horrified gasp, she dropped my hair. Then she was gone, but only when I smelled the burning rice was I able to uncurl my hands from the handle and breathe again.

I tried again the next morning, and every morning after that, to break up with Tristan. But when he put his arms around me and looked down at me with such warm affection in those blue eyes, I just couldn't. The words simply would not form on my tongue. My whole body relaxed, every muscle, every cell, when I was with him. Breathing was easy. I belonged in his arms. I belonged with him.

So I belonged with him, against my parents' wishes.

We met every morning at the corner to walk to school together. We'd stop at his locker first, then mine, where we'd chat and he'd give me little kisses until the last possible second. At lunch we sat with our friends, and they'd laugh at his efforts to eat while keeping one arm around me. After school we'd go for a run, then hang out in the park until I had to go home.

At home, it was becoming hard to breathe.

Reluctantly accepting that I was not going to bend, my parents never again ordered me to break up with Tristan. But my mother's control over her psychokinesis, already tenuous when she became upset, became more and more fragile every day. When I helped her make dinner, her hands would start to tremble, then a bowl would vibrate, until eventually the entire kitchen buzzed and hummed and rattled. Sometimes a bottle or glass would suddenly shatter on its own.

Then my dad would rush in and take her hand, shooing me out with a jerk of his head. I'd scuttle off, unable to meet his disappointed gaze.

Worst of all, Mom had stopped calling me Babydoll. I don't think she even realized it.

CHAPTER FOURTEEN

HE NEXT WEEKEND brought rain, and because we couldn't go running, I asked Tristan to take me to the little bookstore in the town square. He chose a couple bestselling crime novels for himself. I knew exactly which book I wanted and easily found it in the children's section. "*Anne of Green Gables* is my favorite book," I told Tristan. "I've read it at least ten times."

He thumbed through it and skimmed a few paragraphs as we waited in line. At the register I pulled some cash from my handbag, but he told me to put my money away. "You love this book," he said, "so I want to give it to you." Explaining that his parents transferred a few bucks into his bank account each month, he bought all three of our books.

We went back to his house for lunch. Melissa was leaving for her shift at the acute care center, wearing thick white nurses' shoes and pink scrubs printed with a Scooby-Doo pattern. Philip gave me a nod and his shy smile, then headed to his garage workshop. A few minutes later, the staccato sound of hammering filled the house.

After a lunch of grilled cheese and tomato soup, Tristan and I brought our books and two mugs of hot chocolate up to his bedroom.

We could barely hear the sound of Philip's drilling and pounding in here, even with the door open. Much better for a cozy afternoon of reading.

Tristan had a navy comforter on his hastily made bed, a laptop on his desk, and his shelves were cluttered with books and a trophy from a tennis tournament. Completely masculine, completely him.

He plugged his phone into the speakers on his nightstand. Then he looked at me, unsure. There was only one chair.

Reading while sitting at the desk would be uncomfortable. I felt safe here with Tristan, alone in his room. Feeling safe made me feel brave, and feeling brave made me feel slightly wicked. I sat on his bed and patted the space next to me. Neither of us would have to sit at the desk. We'll read, together, on the bed.

Surprised, then delighted, Tristan fluffed up the pillows for support. I snuggled in his arms and opened my book. "This is nice," I murmured.

He kissed the top of my head. "Best rainy day ever," he said, and opened his own book.

We breathed in rhythm.

His heart beat along with mine. *Thump. Thump-th-thump.*

Our bodies were so close. So warm.

I realized I'd read one paragraph three times and still didn't comprehend it.

He closed his book, then took mine. "Lay down."

I glanced at my hand and crossed my fingers, then lay my head on a pillow. The hypnotic pitter-patter of the rain tapped on his window. The rest of the world was far away. The only things that existed were Tristan and me, in his room, on his bed.

He brought his lips to mine, and we kissed. Sweetly. Lazily. He brought his lips to the hollow of my neck. He slid one hand around my waist, the other behind my head, threading his fingers in my hair. My hands wandered down to his hips, and I hooked my fingers through his belt loops, pulling him even closer.

Holding me against him with one hand, his other glided slowly up, up my side, up to my ribs, up to my breast…

And then he stopped.

With a frustrated growl he tore himself away and lay on his back, breathing heavily. We still had time, so I reached for him. But he shook his head. "You don't have to stop," I whispered. I didn't want him to stop. I wanted him. I'd even let him see the scars on my stomach. I wouldn't explain how they got there, but I didn't care if he saw them.

He turned on his side, supporting his head with his hand. "I'm not going to stop. But this," he said, tracing my collarbone with his finger, "is the Borderline. There is no crossing the Borderline."

Before I could protest, he explained. "We shouldn't do anything we'll regret later."

"I'd never regret doing anything with you."

"From what you and your brother and sister have told me, your parents are strict. You can't use the internet. You can't even use your phones except to call each other in emergencies. And they aren't exactly thrilled that we're together. If they ever found out we did… *anything*, they'd never let you see me again. I have you now, and I'll do whatever it takes to keep you. Even—" he paused to kiss my collarbone "—if it means never crossing the Borderline."

With sinking disappointment, I realized Tristan was right, though for more reasons than my parents' rules. The further I went with him physically, the harder it would be for me when it came time to leave.

Maybe he was right about the regret, too.

"Okay," I whispered. "No crossing the Borderline."

Tristan drove me home just in time for dinner, but before I left the car, he slipped the *Anne of Green Gables* book from my hand again.

Expecting another kiss, I glanced at my hand and crossed my fingers, then leaned in. But he had opened the book and was writing an inscription on the front page:

To Sarah, and rainy days
-Tristan

He handed it back, and *that's* when he slid his hand behind my head, caressed my cheek with his thumb, and kissed me.

Legs jellified from the kiss, I dashed through the rain inside, then went straight to our garage and lifted the hatch of our minivan. My getaway bag was crushed at the bottom, under everyone else's. Anything we wanted to take with us to the next location we kept in our getaway bags, ready for our next run. Jillian had her pointe shoes, Logan had his sheet music. My parents had their cash and a stack of fake IDs. I never had anything important enough to keep. Until now.

I pulled out my bag and slipped my new book inside. I wouldn't leave this copy behind when we fled Twelve Lakes. I now had something to remind me of Tristan, something irreplaceable.

A few evenings later I knocked on the door to my dad's office. He sat in his big leather chair behind the desk, watching the news on the television across the room. He snapped off the TV and waved me in. "What's on the agenda tonight?"

I held up my American History book. "I have an essay due tomorrow." Tristan had offered to help me with it, but I turned him down. My dad looked forward to our study sessions, and he was already so disappointed in me. I didn't want to take away even more of our time together.

We discussed the assignment, then I wrote my paper and handed it to him. "I've been watching Tristan," he said, his gaze never leaving the sheet. "Through your eyes, of course."

"So you see how nice he is," I said. "And respectful," I added, thinking of the Borderline, and every kiss he'd planted above it.

"He treats you very well," he admitted. "But your mother and I still disapprove."

I slid my hands into my sleeves and poked my thumbs through the holes I'd worn in the cuffs.

"We've considered moving again," Dad said. "Leaving Illinois."

"We'd run again? To keep me away from Tristan?"

"But we can't bring ourselves to do something that extreme. Not unless you slip up."

"Thank you, Dad." My shoulders sagged with relief.

"Tessa." No longer hiding behind my paper, he was looking at me, his hazel eyes stone, his expression stern. "Do *not* slip up."

I swallowed hard. "I won't. I promise." I meant it more than ever now. One slip, and I'd lose Tristan. My family would run again, not because of Dennis Connelly, but because of me.

Dad nodded and went back to my paper.

"Are your headaches getting better?" I asked.

"A little."

"And your bloody noses?"

He handed my homework back to me. "Haven't had one in over a week."

But when I left I saw the bloody tissues in his garbage can.

Late that night, I reported to Jillian's room to practice her remote viewing. Her light was off, and she lay on her bed with her arm over her eyes. Logan sat next to her. As I stepped in, the Zener ESP cards flew out of her room and into Logan's. "We're not training tonight?" I asked.

Logan shook his head.

"I know you're discouraged, Jill, but you haven't given it enough time," I said. "You'll get it eventually."

She raised her arm enough to glower at me.

"We're quitting," Logan said.

She aimed her cold stare at him. "Not me. I never quit."

"What's going on?" I asked.

"I found this in the bathroom." Logan held up a large bottle of Extra Strength Tylenol. He shook it, and it made no noise. Empty.

"You're getting headaches?" I asked Jillian.

She nodded behind her arm. "They weren't bad at first, but they keep getting worse. The one I had last night was so bad I wanted to die."

"But you told us you were fine."

She lifted her arm to glare at me again. "I'm very, very good at lying."

"Did your nose bleed?"

"Just a little."

I collapsed onto her desk chair with a huff. "You have to quit, Jillian."

"*Never*," she growled. With the heels of her hand, she swiped her tears away. "I'll think of something else. I will not just sit here and wait for Dennis Connelly to kill us."

But her eyes had the same helpless, hopeless look our parents' eyes always had. When I looked at Logan, his eyes looked the same way.

I was sure mine did too.

CHAPTER FIFTEEN

BEEF TENDERLOIN AND roasted vegetables were on the dinner menu the next night. All week long I'd been the helpful, obedient daughter, volunteering to do the boring grudge work my mother didn't like—the washing, the measuring, the chopping. Tonight I ended up making the entire meal, because she was on her hands and knees, frantically scrubbing the floor.

She still hadn't called me Babydoll.

When dinner was on the table, Mom called everyone in to eat. Logan and Jillian came, but Dad didn't come out of his office.

"Someone go get your dad." Mom said from the sink, where she was washing her hands. "He probably fell asleep watching TV again."

I hopped up from the table before Jillian or Logan could and padded down the hall. Mom was right—he'd fallen asleep in his leather chair behind his desk. "Dad," I whispered, not wanting to startle him. "Dinner's ready. Come have a few bites, and then you can go to bed."

He didn't stir, so I gently shook his arm. "Daddy?"

With a groan, he fell forward, his head hitting the desk with a loud, hollow thump. Something wet and warm spattered me, and it took me a moment to realize it was blood.

I would have screamed, but screaming was against the rules. It came out as a strangled whimper instead.

The room swirled. Dizzy and numb, I watched through a curtain of fog as Jillian and Logan rushed in. I wasn't allowed to scream, but my mother was, and when she saw my dad she screamed with such horror the television screen shattered.

Jillian's gaze darted around the room. "Dennis Connelly's here. He's here, isn't he? Tessa, did you see him? Where is he?" The office door slammed itself shut.

I stumbled to the wall, the room narrowing, tilting. He could be anywhere. He could have been hiding in the living room, watching Mom and me make dinner. He could have been upstairs, watching Logan play his saxophone or Jillian do her homework. I could have passed him in the hall, walked right by him, when I came to get my dad. What if he was standing outside the office, right now? What if—

What if he was in *here*?

The closet. He could be in the closet. Or crouching behind the desk. With a single murderous glance, all five of us would be sliced open.

My knees trembled, and I sank to the floor, hands over my belly. The air became hazy, shadowed, dim.

"He's not here." Logan's low, calm voice, juxtaposed with our mother's wailing and Jillian's panicked cries, made the fog lift a bit. He had dragged our father to the floor and was now pointing to his stomach. "Look."

I swallowed a sob. Forced myself to breathe. I blinked, then peered through the fog at my dad. His shirt was saturated, soaked, drenched, with red. But there were no cuts, no gaping wounds, no violent slices across his body.

All of that blood was coming from his nose.

It took an hour for Dad's nose to stop bleeding. An hour more before he could sit up without support and give us a weak wave. Another hour after that for me to stop shaking and for the fog to clear.

We camped out in the family room overnight, all five of us, taking turns pressing icepacks to Dad's head because he said they helped his headache. As the sun came up, he lay on the couch, his head on my mother's lap while she stroked his forehead with a trembling hand. Clots of dried blood were embedded in the stubble along his jaw, but with her red, puffy eyes, she looked more bedraggled than he did.

"Dad?" Logan, wearing that young, vulnerable expression again, whispered the question I'd been afraid to ask. "What about your mobile eye? Does it still work?"

Dad struggled to sit up. "I don't know. I'll have to try it."

"Don't," I said. "What if you pass out again?"

"We have to know if it still works," he said. "If it doesn't..."

The rest of that sentence was too horrible to finish. Nodding reluctantly, I slid my hands into my sleeves. We all held our breath as he closed his eyes.

"Wait," Logan said.

Dad opened his eyes again. "What?"

"Don't waste your strength trying to see Connelly yet." Returning to his usual stoic, rational self, he straightened his posture. "If you don't see him, and hopefully you won't, you won't know if your mobile eye is working or not."

Our father nodded. "Good point."

Jillian was on the floor, slumped at the coffee table. She lifted her head. "You can watch through me." She gave him a subdued smile. "Bet you never thought I'd *offer* to let you do that." We all snickered, and she rose and left the room.

With Mom grasping his hand and Logan and me holding our breath, Dad closed his eyes. After a few moments he winced, but held up his palm when I told him to stop.

Eyes squeezed shut, he sat motionless, except his face became tighter and tighter. Just as a spot of blood trickled from his nose, he opened his eyes. "She's in Tessa's room, peeking out the window."

Mom, Logan and I let out a collective sigh of relief, then sucked it back in as he moaned and sank back into the couch cushions. "I'm fine," he said, his voice strained. "Just give me a minute."

Jillian returned. "Did it work? I didn't feel you watching this time."

"The connection was weak, but I could still see through your eyes. I heard you say 'Hey, Dad, look at the pretty sunrise.'"

"That's right." Her legs shook as she lowered herself to the couch.

Mom covered her face with her hands. She whimpered, but when she lowered her hands her eyes were focused and strong. She spoke for the first time in hours. "We can't put your father through any more pain," she said. "And we can't risk losing his remote vision. So. He will watch for Dennis Connelly only. A few times a day, a few seconds at a time, and that's it." Her gaze landed pointedly on Jillian, then Logan, then me. "Which means we have to trust the three of you now more than ever."

Fear and vulnerability weighed me down, turned my lungs to stone. My father could no longer watch us to make sure we were safe. Our lives balanced on the edge of a canyon, and at any moment, Dennis Connelly could sneak up behind us and push us over the edge.

My parents and siblings might be able to save themselves. They had built-in defense weapons.

I had nothing. And now there would be no safety net to catch me.

We promised solemnly to follow the rules, to be on our best behavior. Our lives depended on it.

Jillian stood to get ready for school, and no one but me saw the tiny smirk on her lips.

Tristan paced under the tree at the corner that morning, watching for me. I rushed over and buried my face in his chest. The tighter he held me, the easier it was to breathe. I inhaled his fresh, soapy scent until he pulled away, cupping my chin in his fingers and studying me with a frown. "Something's wrong," he said. "What happened?"

I swallowed hard. "Nothing's wrong."

"You look…scared. Tired. Like you didn't sleep all night."

"I was up late writing a paper."

The concerned, sympathetic look in his eyes told me he knew I was lying. "Do you ever sleep well, Sarah?"

I told him the truth this time. "No."

"Is there anything I can do?"

The truth again. "No."

He sighed, then put his arm around my shoulders. We walked all the way to school with me tucked under his arm, and even though my father couldn't watch me anymore, I'd never felt safer in my life.

CHAPTER SIXTEEN

*F*LASHING LIGHTS, THUMPING bass and a thick cloud of cigarette smoke assaulted me as Tristan and I stepped into Ethan's house. Jillian had told us that he was having a few people over and had invited us to stop by, but half the senior class was here, along with many of the juniors.

I spotted my sister across the room, chatting with her friends. I started to wave but stopped. Blinked. She'd left our house wearing a plain blue top, much like my plain peach top, and jeans and sneakers. Now she wore a bright yellow halter that tied behind her neck and a black miniskirt with black platform heels. She held a cigarette in one hand and a red plastic cup in the other. I knew, without a doubt, what was in that cup. Beer. It's bitter, stale stench permeated the air, even through the stink of cigarette smoke.

My father couldn't watch over us anymore. To me, that meant danger. To my sister, it meant freedom.

"Is it too crowded in here for you?" Tristan shouted over the music. "Do you want to leave?"

This party *was* too crowded for me, but I pushed inside anyway. I had to get Jillian out before a neighbor called the cops. No police.

Dennis Connelly would get wind of it. "I have to get my sister first. Our parents will go ballistic if they find out we're at this kind of party."

With Tristan behind me, I wiggled through the crowd to where Jillian had been standing a minute ago. By the time I got there, she was gone. I craned my neck to see over the crowd, but I was too short.

Red plastic cups passed from hand to hand, lights dimmed, music pulsated. Vanessa and Chad swirled over, then Gianna, shouting at us over the music before disappearing again to refill their cups.

Like a dam bursting, more kids poured into the party. The layer of smoke thickened, coating my lungs with sickly sweet fumes. I went rigid.

Tristan grabbed my arm. "What's wrong?"

"A cigar," I said, my voice high. "A cherry cigar. I can smell it. Someone's smoking a cherry cigar." I had to get out of here.

Just before panic set in, Tristan put his arm around me and pushed through the crowd. Instead of going outside, he whisked me into a den and shut the door behind us. "I saw the football team passing around a few cigars. On our first date at Salutos, someone had a cigar too. That smell must really bother you, huh?"

The air was fresh in here. Clean. No smoke. No burning cherries. I took a deep breath, clearing my lungs, clearing my mind. I gave Tristan a shaky laugh. "I hate cigars. They're disgusting."

The bass still pumped through the bookcase-lined walls, but it was muffled. And we were alone.

We sank onto the leather sofa, and he put his arm back around me. I leaned into him and rested my head on his shoulder. "Better?" he asked.

"Yeah. Thanks." To thank him properly, I kissed him, on that soft spot right under his jaw. He returned the kiss by nuzzling my neck.

I shot a glance at my hand and crossed my fingers, then stopped. No need to send Dad a signal. He wasn't watching me.

Freedom and desire filled me like air in a balloon. I slid my hands behind Tristan's head, teasing him with tiny kisses, my lips wandering over his temples. His cheeks. His neck.

His breath was heavy, catching each time he inhaled.

He ran kisses up and down my collarbone, so soft and slow, then kissed me hard on the mouth before stopping completely to gaze at me. "The girl with wildflower eyes," he murmured, cupping my head and stroking my cheek with his thumb. "I need to tell you something."

I nodded, not really hearing him, feeling only the heat from his body and mine. Hot, hotter. His gentle breath, his lips close to mine. I kissed his lower lip, then his upper lip.

He kissed me back, then pulled away. "When I came to Twelve Lakes…"

I kissed his neck, resting my lips there, his pulse beating so fast against them.

"I never thought…" he said.

I kissed his left shoulder. His right shoulder. Lifted his hand and kissed his palm. The inside of his wrist.

"This wasn't what I expected," he said.

I pressed my lips to his neck, right under his ear. He moaned.

"But I can't…hold it back anymore," he whispered. "I need to tell you. Tonight. Now. I want you to know."

He took both my hands, stopping me from kissing him again. He kissed my fingertips, one by one. Then, still holding my hands, he stared straight into my eyes. Took a deep breath.

When he exhaled, he spoke along with it. "I love you."

And just like that, our shiny, beautiful moment was shattered into a million tarnished pieces. "Wh-what?"

"I love you." A warped, hopeful smile appeared on his face. "I'm in love with you."

Tristan loved me.

Tristan was *in love* with me.

But he didn't really love me. He loved Sarah Spencer. He was in love with a girl who would cease to exist the moment her cell phone rang.

I had only cared how hard it would be for *me* to leave him. I had never, not once, considered how hard it would be for *him*. How could I have been so selfish?

His smile faded, his eyes widening with confusion, as I pushed him away and scrambled off the couch. "Sarah—"

"Don't," I choked, and ran off, desperate to get out of the room, away from him.

I yanked open the door and ran out, back into the loud music and hazy air. Stumbling over an overturned chair, I pushed my way back into the party in search of Jillian. She would know what to do. She would take care of this, and then she'd take me home. We shouldn't be here anyway.

Tristan shouted for me—shouted for *Sarah*, but I'd disappeared into the crowd, grateful, for once, for my lack of height. Ducking between the party-goers, I caught a glimpse of swirling yellow—Jillian's top. She was standing with Ethan, and I could hear her laughter over the music. She tilted her head up and kissed him, then laughed again, as if headaches and bloody noses and Dennis Connelly were the furthest things from her mind.

I was already ruining Tristan's night. I couldn't ruin hers, too, by asking her to break up with my boyfriend for me.

That was something I should do myself.

Turning around, I made my way back through the mass of partiers, this time searching for Tristan.

We sat on an iron bench in Ethan's backyard, under a tree that had lost all its leaves. The stars struggled to shine through a thin layer of clouds in the inky November sky. Tristan slid off his hoodie and held it out to me. "Put this on," he said. "You're cold."

I didn't want it. I didn't want him to be so nice to me right now. But I put it on anyway. He was right; I was cold.

In just a white T-shirt now, he sat with his elbows on his knees and stared off at some point in the distance. I slid my hands into the sleeves of his hoodie and rubbed my thumbs in the cuffs.

"I don't want to see you anymore," I said finally, trying to make him hate me for breaking up with him with such abrupt cruelty.

He didn't move. Didn't look at me. "I scared you off. I should have waited to tell you."

"Even if you'd waited a week, a month, a year, it wouldn't matter," I said. "I don't want you to love me."

With a scoff, he said, "Too late."

"You don't know me enough to love me. You'll never know me enough to love me."

"I started falling in love with you the day we met on the jogging path, and all I wanted to do was make that scared, sad look in your eyes go away." His own eyes showed a mixture of pain and confusion. "I knew nothing at all about you then, not even your name."

"My *name* isn't important." I winced at my own lie. "The only thing you need to know about me is that one day I'm going to leave. My family always leaves."

"That won't stop me from loving you."

"But it should! If you didn't love me, you would just forget about me after I leave. But now you think you love me. And when that day comes, and I don't show up at the corner, or meet you on the jogging path, or answer my door, your heart is going to break."

He put his hand over his heart, as if it was already broken. It took every ounce of strength I had not to take that hand in mine and kiss it. "I don't want to be the cause of that much pain. I can't stand the thought of hurting you like that. Because I love you, Tristan."

I gasped a squeaky little *oh!* and my hands flew to cover my mouth. Hearing myself say those words revealed what my subconscious had been hiding from me all along, maybe even since the first time I saw him, with his confident smile and his broad shoulders, jogging on that path in the park.

I loved him.

I *loved* him.

But it didn't change anything.

He lowered my hands and held them. "You love me?"

I looked into his eyes. "I do. I love you."

"Then we can find a way to be together."

"You're hoping for a future than can never happen."

"It *can* happen. We belong together." He squeezed my hands. "We love each other, Sarah."

And there it was. He'd just proven I was doing the right thing, by saying one awful, terrible word.

Sarah.

"I love you, Tristan." I pulled my hands away and turned, unable to look at him. "But I can't be your girlfriend anymore."

Forcing myself to stand on trembling legs, I walked away.

I'd almost reached the back door to the house before Tristan called out. "When you're nervous or scared," he said, "you slide your hands up into your sleeves and rub little holes in the cuffs for your thumbs."

His words froze me; I stopped walking and stopped rubbing my thumbs.

"You tap your phone when you're unsure how to answer my questions." He rose from the bench. "You like vegetables, except for green peppers. You love to cook but you're never hungry."

"That's—"

He reached me in four strides. "Attention makes you uncomfortable. The clothes you wear, the way you walk with your eyes on the ground, it's all so people won't notice you."

I stepped back.

He stepped forward. "You started jogging because it was something you could do alone, but you're scared to be alone. You let your brother and sister take care of you because for some stupid reason they don't think you can take care of yourself, and neither do you."

He took my arm and drew me close, so close our heads were inches from each other. "Every time you walk into a room, you look around to make sure it's safe. You look for the exits. You sit where you can see the doors."

Unable to breathe, I nodded.

"The first reaction you have to anything is fear."

A tear rolled down my cheek.

He wiped it away with the back of his finger. "You try to solve all your problems by running away."

I stared into his eyes, wide and soft and full of love.

"See? I do know you well enough to love you." He tucked my hair behind my ear. "But the only thing I need to know… is that the only time you're happy, is when you're with me."

It was all true. Every word.

"I also know there's a lot I *don't* know about you." He kissed my cheek, right by my ear, and whispered. "I know you have secrets, Sarah."

I gasped, then tried to scramble away, but he held tight to my arm. "I don't know what they are and I won't ask you to tell me." He gazed at me until my breathing slowed. "But if you want to tell me, you can trust me. I'll do whatever I can to help you."

I was unable to speak until the lump in my throat dissolved. "There's nothing you can do to help me," I said, burying my head in his chest. "I want to be with you. But I can't tell you the truth about so many things. I hate lying to you."

He lifted my chin so I looked at him. "I don't know what you're lying about, but I know it scares you. I promise, whatever it is, I'll keep you safe."

But Tristan couldn't keep me safe. Running and hiding were the only things keeping my family from Dennis Connelly. There was no way to fight him. He had the support of the government. He was almost invulnerable to my father's mobile eye. He had the power to read minds. He had the power to slice people open with a glance.

All Tristan Walker had was naïve hope.

"You shouldn't make promises you can't keep," I said, and shivered despite his warm hoodie. I wasn't cold on the outside. Just the inside.

Sighing, he rubbed my arms. "Let's go finish this at my house." He started to lead me away.

"Wait."

He stopped. Waited.

"Will you...I need you..." Inside my ribcage, my heart trembled, flip-flopped. "I need to hear you say something. One word. Just once, then never again."

"What word?"

I closed my eyes. Took a breath.

Licked my lips, swallowed.

Then I opened my eyes, looked into his, and said it. "Tessa."

CHAPTER SEVENTEEN

I ASKED TRISTAN to say one word. One word, one time. I told him the word to say, and it shot up like a bullet into the cold November air, then came careening back to earth.

But it didn't explode upon impact.

Tristan only gazed at me, then caressed my cheek with such tenderness I barely felt it. And then he whispered, "Tessa."

He said my name. My real name. He said *Tessa.* Except for my family, no one had said my name in over eight years. It sounded so right, so perfect, coming from his lips.

But that was it. Once would have to be enough.

"Who is T—" he started.

Taking his face in my hands, I silenced him with a kiss. "It's freezing," I said. "Let's get out of here."

With me tucked safely under Tristan's arm, we squeezed our way back through the party. It had become even more crowded, and Ethan's entire house vibrated with the booming bass. I needed to find Jillian and get her out, now, before the cops came, and before I left with Tristan.

We finally found her teetering in the kitchen near the keg and surrounded by a small group, her blond hair and yellow top making her the sun in the center of the planets. A teaspoon rested in her open palm. "Shelby," I shouted. "We have to go."

A girl who was wearing a skirt even shorter than Jillian's waved us away. "Hold on. She says she can move things with her mind. She's gonna show us with that spoon."

Stone. That's what my body turned into. A block of solid stone. Muscles immobilized. Lungs paralyzed. I tried to speak, to shout, to do anything to stop her, but when I opened my mouth nothing came out but a panicked little squeak.

Tristan tensed up beside me. "How much has she had to drink?"

My sister stared at the teaspoon in her palm.

It didn't move.

She shifted and stared again at the spoon, furrowing her brow.

Nothing.

"Ji—" I stammered, until some tiny part of my brain reminded me to use her alias. "Shelby!"

Face contorting, she grunted with effort, and when the spoon didn't float or wiggle or even vibrate, she squealed in frustration and flung it to the ground as her friends burst out laughing.

I could have fallen to the floor right along with that spoon. It was the beer. My parents never drank alcohol, not even on holidays or their anniversary. Alcohol inhibited their powers. Thank God. "Tristan, I have to get her home."

Chuckling, Tristan scooped up the teaspoon. "I think your career as a magician is over before it began, Shelby," he said. "Time to go." She laughed along with her friends but glanced at me as Tristan pulled her away, with just enough sobriety behind those unfocused eyes to show me her horrified guilt.

Tristan and I drove Jillian home, then he waited in the driveway while I helped her from the car. "I'm sorry," she cried over and over. "I'm so sorry. Please, please, you can't tell Mom and Dad."

She was right. If our parents found out she was drunk, Dad would start watching us again, making his headaches worse and probably blowing out his mobile eye completely. And if they found out she'd tried to show her friends that little magic trick, our time in Twelve Lakes, and my time with Tristan—the boy I loved, the boy who loved me—would be only a memory by morning.

I helped Jillian inside and brought her up to her room, where she fell asleep before I even shut the door. As I told our parents she must be sick with some kind of stomach virus, I stared at an old stain on the carpet. I couldn't look them in the eye.

I hated how easy it was to lie to them.

An hour later Tristan and I lay curled up together in the back seat of his car. Not wanting his aunt and uncle to disturb us, we'd parked at the end of the road under a streetlight that didn't work, the darkness broken only by the glow of the dashboard and the occasional passing vehicle. Our fiery kisses had slowed to grazing lips and gentle caresses. The car windows were steamy, and he'd never even crossed the Borderline. We didn't need the heat on anymore, but he left the battery running so his phone would play music through the speakers.

Eyes closed, I snuggled into him, sated and sleepy. I loved him, and he loved me. One day my family was going to leave, which made it even more important to enjoy the time we had left together. One month, one week, one day. However long we had, we would love each other until the end.

He stroked my arm with one hand, and with the other he played with my hair. "Clockwise."

"Hmm."

"Who is Tessa?"

My eyes opened, and I was no longer sleepy. But I didn't gasp, I didn't run. My lungs stayed open. I'd expected this. I wouldn't have asked him to say it if I didn't want him to know.

So I whispered, "Me."

Tristan froze, didn't even breathe.

"Sarah Spencer is an alias," I said.

He swallowed. "An alias."

"That's right."

"Tessa," he said deliberately, listening to himself say it. "Why?"

"I can't tell you why."

"Then why are you telling me your real name is Tessa?"

I caressed his cheek, rough with stubble. I loved it. I loved him. "Tonight at the party you said you know I have secrets. Yet you never confronted me, you never tried to trick me or force me into telling you anything. You love me even though you know I'm lying."

I gave him a kiss, then continued. "Tonight at the party you also told me you know the only time I'm happy is when I'm with you. That's true too. But every time you call me Sarah, I hate it. That one word reminds me I'm deceiving you. I want you to love Tessa. Not Sarah."

Using the dim lights of the dashboard to see, I studied him to make sure he understood. His eyebrows drew together, but he said nothing.

"I love you, Tristan. And I trust you. I trust you'll accept this secret and not ask me to explain it. I also trust you won't tell anyone."

He remained silent.

"You must think I'm crazy, or playing some sort of game," I said. "And if that's what you want to believe, that's okay."

"No, I believe you, Sarah…Tessa."

I loved hearing him say my name.

"Do you want me to call you Sarah or Tessa?" he asked.

"I'd be so happy if you'd call me Tessa when we're alone together," I said. "But you can't mess up when we're around other people. Including my family. Especially my family. If you don't think you can keep it straight, you'd better just stick with Sarah. Now that you know the truth, it won't bother me as much."

He took a deep breath. "Tessa." As he said it a car approached, its headlights shining directly on us.

"Shh!" I said, even though, logically, I knew no one in that car could hear him.

He waited for the car to pass. "Tessa," he said again, this time in a whisper.

I smiled at the sound, then frowned. "This is a big deal, Tristan. If my family finds out I told you, we'll leave town."

"So Shelby, Scott…those are fake names too? Everyone in your family has an alias?"

"Yes."

"What are their real names?"

My only answer was a cryptic smile.

"Is Spencer your last name?"

"No."

"What's your last name?"

I shrugged in reply.

He stroked my cheek with his thumb. "Is your family in trouble?" It didn't sound like a question.

It hit me, right then, that I had made a mistake. I should never, ever have told him my real name.

Of course he would assume my family was in trouble. He would ask questions, and he would probably tell someone we needed help, maybe even law enforcement. I had to get out of here. I started to scramble away, to fling open the door and run, but he grabbed my arm. "It's okay," he said. "Whatever it is, I can help you."

A vise clamped around my chest, and I pushed against him. "I have to go home. I have to tell my parents I slipped up. We have to run. Right now."

He held me effortlessly. He slid his free hand behind my head and kissed me, hard, crushing my lips, until I stopped struggling and kissed him back, with the same desperation and urgency as he kissed me.

He pulled away but didn't release his grip on me. "Sarah—Tessa, look at me. Breathe."

I inhaled, then exhaled.

"Again."

I inhaled again, then exhaled again.

"Just tell me," he said, "are you in *immediate* danger?"

I swallowed. "No." I resisted an impulse to reach for my cell phone. I wouldn't be in immediate danger until it rang.

"Then we have time to figure this out. There's no need for you to leave tonight."

I started to object, but he interrupted me. "All you did was tell me you want me to call you Tessa. I still don't know anything, and as long as I'm sure you're not in immediate danger, I won't pressure you to tell me anything else."

I looked into his eyes, trying to read him. I saw he was worried; I saw he loved me. I knew he would do anything to keep me with him. "You won't tell anyone?"

"No. Will you?"

"No."

The vise unclamped from my chest as we both sighed with relief.

"So we'll be Tristan and Tessa whenever we're alone together," he said. "And we'll be Tristan and Sarah everywhere else." He grinned. "Tristan and Tessa. That sounds nice."

I smiled too. "I know. It does." Much better than *Tristan and Sarah.*

"I'm going to kiss you now, Tessa."

He kissed me until 11:55, then drove me home in time for my midnight curfew. "Tessa, Tessa, Tessa, I love you, Tessa," he whispered, before I hurried into the house and shivered with delight up to my room.

It was just a tiny secret.

Minuscule, really.

I hadn't even told him my last name. And hearing him call me Tessa instead of Sarah would make being with him so much easier.

I pictured a scale in my mind, a scale of lies instead of a scale of justice. Each lie I told was a spherical silver weight. These were the secrets I was keeping from the people I loved. The scale on Tristan's side was weighed almost all the way down, burdened with all of the secrets I was keeping from him. Tonight, his side was lightened a bit when I told him my real name. That weight moved to the other side of the scale, representing the secret I was now keeping from my family.

The teeny tiny, itty-bitty, infinitesimal secret.

CHAPTER EIGHTEEN

"TESSA, TESSA, TESSA," Tristan sang softly the next day. Our textbooks lay unopened on the coffee table as we lounged on the couch in his living room. Philip was hammering away in his garage workshop, and Melissa was upstairs reading a book.

"I love hearing you say my name," I said with a contented sigh.

"I've been practicing all night. Tessa, Tessa, Tessa, I have something for you."

Expecting a kiss, I puckered my lips. Instead he pressed something into my hand. A flat, shiny white rectangle.

I sat up straight. "A cell phone?"

"Yep. I've already activated it. It's on my account, so don't worry about paying for it."

I shoved it back to him. "But you know my parents won't let me use a cell phone."

"You told me your entire family has fake names, and even though it's killing me, I won't ask you about it. But in return, you have to do something for me." He stared at me until I nodded. "I want you to keep this phone with you. Always. At night, keep it under your pillow." He pressed the phone back into my palm and wrapped my fingers around it. "If anything happens—anything—I want you to call me. I've already set it up for speed dial. Just hold down the one for my number."

Though thin and sleek, the phone felt heavy in my hand.

"Whatever is going on with your family, Tessa, I will not let you just disappear into the night." He stared at me with such fierce intensity, I had to look away.

I ran my fingers over the phone's smooth glass. Tristan obviously realized my family was in trouble. If agreeing to hold on to this phone would give him some peace of mind—and keep him from investigating further—then I would do it.

I would carry this white phone with me and sleep with it at night, and when we had to leave Twelve Lakes, I would use it to call him. But not until we were hours away. I would call him from the road, before we reached our next location, before we even decided where it would be. I would thank him for giving me the happiest days of my life. I would tell him how much I loved him. Then I would tell him goodbye. And finally, I would give the phone to Jillian and tell her to destroy it.

I pressed the One on the keyboard of my new cell phone and held it down. A second later, Tristan's phone rang. The ringtone was the chorus from 'Wildflowers.'

That night, I waited in Jillian's room while she brushed her teeth in the bathroom. While I'd spent the day with Tristan, she'd spent the day at home recovering from her so-called stomach virus.

I tried, but I couldn't be upset with Jillian for what she'd done at Ethan's party. What I had done was much, much worse. And I couldn't even tell her. I couldn't tell her that Tristan knew my real name. I couldn't tell her that in addition to my clunky black flip phone, I was also carrying a sleek white smartphone.

But I could tell her that Tristan loved me, and that I loved him. Maybe if she knew that, she'd realize that I needed to stay in Twelve Lakes for as long as possible. She'd realize that she needed to stay out of trouble.

As I waited for her, I paged through a college catalog she'd left on her bed. College. A waste of time. Why prepare for a career we'd never live to have? But it was another thing my mother wanted for us because she never had it for herself. Jillian wanted it too. Lately she'd been taking catalogs from TLC for colleges all over the country, though we'd never be able to go away. To stay safe, we'd have to live at home. Arlington Community College was one town over from Twelve Lakes, and if we were still here next year, Jillian would have to go there.

That didn't stop her from wishing otherwise, though. This catalog was from Hoffman University, a small, private college in eastern Iowa. She'd circled the pre-med courses, as well as some dance classes: African, Indian, kabuki. Arlington Community College probably didn't offer any of those.

With a sigh, I flipped through the pages. My eyes landed on a word, and I had to blink and focus on it again to make sure I'd read it right.

I had.

Oh my God.

I knew how to find help. I knew how to save my family.

I knew how to stop Dennis Connelly.

CHAPTER NINETEEN

"WHAT'S THE BIG secret?" Logan asked. He and Jillian stood before me in the school's computer lab. I'd slipped a note into their book bags last night, telling them to meet me here right after school.

I held out the Hoffman University catalog, opened to the course title that had caught my eye: *Parapsychology.* I'd circled it in red ink.

Logan made a swiping motion with his palm and read the course description without touching the page, but Jillian snatched the catalog and read aloud. "Parapsychology is the branch of psychology that studies psychic phenomena. Professor Pruitt Fielding offers a survey of paranormal occurrences and theories, including the ability to move objects without touching them, mind-reading, ESP, predicting the future, and more. Students will conduct experiments to prove, or disprove, the existence of psychic phenomena."

She wiggled her fingers at the door, which slowly swung itself shut. "So? We don't need a college course to prove psychic phenomena exists."

"It's not about the class," I said. "It's the professor. Maybe he can help us. I need you to fix a computer so we can send him an untraceable email."

"No way," Logan said sharply. "Connelly's killed everyone we've asked for help."

"Because we asked the police and the FBI, and he found out about it," I said. "This is different. Professor Fielding doesn't work for the government."

"Right. So what makes you think this guy could possibly help us?"

"He teaches a class about paranormal abilities," I said. "He's got to believe in them. He might have one of his own. Even if he doesn't, he'll have connections. Maybe he'll know other psychics, psychics who can protect us."

Logan scowled. Jillian stared at the catalog and traced the red circle with her finger.

I tried again, but lost confidence with each word. "Dad's headaches aren't getting better. And now Jillian's getting them too. We need to find someone who can help."

They still didn't respond. Maybe my plan wasn't so brilliant after all. "I'm sorry. It was a dumb idea."

"It's a great idea," Jillian said. She looked at me with astonishment mixed with a touch of admiration. "It's perfect."

"It is?" Logan and I said at the same time. My tone was hopeful. His was doubtful.

She slapped the catalog on the desk. "This is even better than trying to develop my own mobile eye. That would just help Dad watch for him, and watching him won't stop him from coming. But Tessa's plan will get help, so we *can* stop him. So we can destroy him."

"Mom and Dad will never let us do this," Logan said. "It's too risky. We shouldn't even be using the internet."

Jillian switched on the computer monitor. "We can't tell Mom and Dad. They're too scared to do anything but hide. Maybe they can spend the rest of their lives hiding, but I can't." Her gaze bored into me, and I'd never seen her look so serious. "I'd rather he kill us right now than spend one more day living like this."

She opened a browser and searched for Hoffman University, then searched for Professor Fielding's page. A portrait of a portly gentleman appeared on the screen, smiling behind a white mustache and beard. I could imagine him playing Santa Claus for his grandchildren. "He looks nice," I said.

"You said Connelly was nice too," Logan said. "Until he dragged you into his car and tried to kill everyone."

The stench of cherry cigars filled my nose as my hands fluttered to my stomach. "We have to take a chance, Logan." I'd taken a chance on Tristan, and it paid off. Maybe this one would too.

Jillian tapped her Rebel Red fingernail on the mouse. "Logan. Leave her alone and tell us how to send an untraceable email."

He didn't move.

"Tessa and I can figure it out on our own," she said, "but you can do it faster."

His gaze dashed back and forth between Jillian and me.

"Just imagine, Logan." She whirled around in her chair to face him. "We can live our lives the way we were meant to live them. No more running. No more aliases."

"Dad can write his column again," I said. "Mom can plan parties for a fancy hotel again."

"We can go away to college," Jillian said. "I can be a cardiologist. You can be a composer and conduct orchestras at Carnegie Hall. Tessa can be…well, whatever it is she wants to be."

I'd never thought about a career before. If my plan worked, I could be anything. A chef, maybe, with my own little bistro. Or a party planner, like my mom. We could work together at a hotel, or start our own business. Or I could be an artist. A painter. I could paint murals that covered entire walls. Entire buildings, even. Suddenly the possibilities seemed endless.

And I would never have to leave Tristan.

Joy bubbled up inside of me until it spilled over with a laugh. "Carnegie Hall, Logan! I can just see you conducting a huge orchestra, waving that stick in the air!"

"It's called a baton." He covered his smile with his hand.

"Come on, Maestro," Jillian said. "If Tessa has the guts to do this, you should too."

He let out a slow breath. "Okay. Let's do it before I change my mind."

It only took a few minutes. Logan scanned some websites with his palm and quickly learned how to send an untraceable email. Then Jillian wrote the message. Four simple sentences, and an image of a red star.

Professor Fielding,

Our family has psychic abilities and we are in trouble. If you can help us, copy and paste this star onto your webpage and we'll contact you with more details. Please, Professor. You're our last hope.

She glanced up at me, and I realized she was waiting for my approval.

I gave it to her with a nod.

We all held our breath as she clicked Send.

We knew Professor Fielding wouldn't respond right away, but we were still disappointed when we clicked on his webpage the next day and there was no red star.

No red star the following day either.

Or the next.

We each checked every day that week, and the week after that.

There was never a red star.

By November's end the trees in Twelve Lakes had shed all their leaves, leaving their branches bare and gray like gnarled claws. In our yard, the dry brown leaves littered the lawn and clumped under the bushes. To keep us from waking our napping father one Saturday afternoon, Mom sent Jillian, Logan, and me to clean up the yard while she busied herself inside, scrubbing the floor under the kitchen appliances.

Logan grabbed a rake, and Jillian followed him around with a yard waste bag. I pulled the dead leaves from under the bushes lining the front of the house. Jillian brought the waste bag over and held it open, shivering as I dumped an armful of leaves in. She dropped the bag and zipped her jacket up to the top.

"Where's your scarf?" I asked. Our mother had bought us winter gear just the week before.

She shrugged. "Left it somewhere, maybe." When I wouldn't stop staring at her, she snapped, "What?"

"It's weird, that's all. I lost my Civics notebook. You lost your hair clips at Homecoming. Logan lost his reeds. And now your scarf."

"So? People lose things."

"Not us. We don't leave anything personal behind."

She gave a forced chuckle. "Don't be so paranoid."

I glanced at the front window. A tiny bit of the handprint Logan and I had seen a few weeks ago was still there, smeared in the bottom corner. "Maybe we should tell Mom and Dad."

Stepping toward me, she spoke from behind clenched teeth. "You kept your mouth shut about my Zener card training sessions, and Ethan's party, and Professor Fielding. But now you want to ruin everything by telling them we *lost* stuff?"

A clump of leaves at her feet shot up like a geyser. "If you say anything, you know what'll happen? We'll run. Is that what you want? To leave Twelve Lakes? You want to leave Tristan?"

Swallowing hard, I gripped my white cell phone through my sweater. "No."

"Professor Fielding will put that red star on his website any day now, and soon you won't have to worry that a lost scarf is anything more than a lost scarf."

We turned at the sound of crunching leaves. A grinning Logan made his way over with the rake. "Remember how Mom and Dad would make a big pile of leaves for us to jump in?"

The memory made both Jillian and me smile. The yard of our house in Kitteridge, Virginia had over a dozen maple trees. Every autumn, their leaves turned a brilliant scarlet and tumble-fluttered to the ground. Like millions of red stars.

Now we only needed one.

CHAPTER TWENTY

UNDLED UP IN my thick white mittens and blue jacket, I kept my eyes on the path as I hustled home through the park to avoid any branches that had fallen from the trees. A heavy wind had been blowing since yesterday, bringing in the first snow of the season later this evening.

I'd spent the afternoon across the park at Vanessa's house, studying for a Spanish test. Tristan was watching a basketball game at Chad's. Tonight the four of us were going out for dinner at a non-crowded restaurant, followed by bowling. Vanessa and I had wrapped up early so we'd have extra time to get ready.

Tiny snowflakes whipped through the air, stinging my cheeks. From far away, I heard a low shout, but the wind carried the sound away. I hoped it would snow a lot tonight. Then tomorrow—if I was still in town—I could take Tristan to the park for a winter rendezvous. We'd bring a Thermos of hot chocolate and build a snowman.

A rhythmic plodding came from behind me. Footsteps, echoing my own. A die-hard runner, maybe. I loved jogging too, though not on a day as cold as this one. Bracing myself against the wind, I accelerated, enjoying the icy air frosting my lungs.

A groaning creak came from the trees, and suddenly that runner was right behind me, his steps urgent. Frantic. Shouting. Before I could move out of his way he grabbed me, pushed me, tackled me to the ground with a thunderous crash—

—oh God oh God oh God Dennis Connelly he's here he found me can't move can't breathe can't see can't scream—

"Tessa!"

I heaved a breathless sob, waiting for him to strike, to slice me open.

He lifted himself off me. "Tessa," he panted, "it's me."

Dennis Connelly sounded just like Tristan.

How was that possible?

"Tessa," he said again. "Hey. Clockwise."

A small handful of people called me Tessa—my family, Tristan, Dennis Connelly. But only one person called me Clockwise.

I forced myself to turn my head, peek open one eye.

Tristan's face was inches from mine. "I am so sorry." He was out of breath. "I got you out of the way in time, but I knocked you down pretty hard." He sucked in another deep lungful of air. "Does anything hurt? Your neck? Your head?"

Through the heavy fog that had settled over the woods, I saw a thick tree trunk lying behind us, where I'd been running just moments before. Scattered around us, whipping about in the wind, were hundreds of broken branches, twigs, dead leaves.

Stiffly, I turned over and sat up. Tristan swept the leaves and twigs from my jacket, lifted my hair off my face, and inspected my forehead. He pulled off my torn mittens, then pressed the cuffs of his hoodie on my scraped palms to blot off the speckles of blood. My left collarbone hurt a little. My jeans had ripped at the knees, revealing more scrapes and more blood. My hip bones hurt.

Tristan's hoodie was torn at the elbows. "You're bleeding," I said dully.

"I'm fine." He rotated his shoulders and winced. "Didn't you hear me shouting for you?"

I blinked at him.

"I called you too." He plucked the white phone from my waistband and read the display. "Two missed calls. Why is your phone on silent?"

I blinked at him again. My black phone was on the loudest setting. The phone Tristan gave me was on silent so my parents wouldn't hear it ring. "It's foggy," I said.

"That's not fog. It's snow." He cupped my chin in his hand. "Are you okay?"

"What happened?"

He pointed to some charred bark at the jagged end of the tree trunk lying across the path. "Looks like the tree was struck by lightning at some point, and today the wind knocked it down." He flicked the trunk with his finger and some burned bark chipped off. I followed it with my eyes as the wind carried it into a pile of broken branches and leaves. He pushed the trunk, and it didn't budge. "You would've been killed if this landed on you."

I nodded as if I understood.

Tristan gingerly helped me up, supporting me as we walked down the path. "Does it hurt to walk? Should I carry you?"

After a few seconds, I realized he was talking to me. "What?"

He frowned, then picked me up, one arm under my shoulders, the other under my knees. "I'm taking you to my house. My aunt is there. She's a nurse."

Tristan's aunt was a nurse. I knew that. She wore pink scrubs with Scooby-Doo on them.

Wait. Why would I need a nurse? "Am I hurt?"

"I tackled you really hard. I think you're confused."

That's right. Tristan knocked me down. Not Dennis Connelly. "I thought you were—" I stopped myself. Even in my foggy daze I knew I couldn't say his name.

But it wasn't Dennis Connelly trying to kill me. It was Tristan trying to save me.

Tristan had pushed me from the path of a falling tree.

Huh.

"Tristan? How did you know—"

"Shh. I need to get you to my aunt."

"Aunt Melissa!" Tristan called for his aunt the moment he got me inside his house, his voice cracking with alarm.

Through the haze, I looked down at myself. A few aches and scrapes, but nothing too bad. Why was he so scared?

Melissa rushed into the foyer. "What's wrong?"

I held out my hands, palms up, so she could see the scrapes. "Tristan saved me," I said. "See?"

She examined my palms. "Saved you from what?"

My first impulse was to answer *Dennis Connelly*. But I couldn't say that. So instead, I said, "A tree." My head began to clear, and I realized how ridiculous that sounded. I clamped my hands over my mouth and giggled until tears came to my eyes.

She sighed. "Tristan, why don't you explain?"

He pulled his hand through his hair. "She's right. A tree almost fell on her, and I pushed her out of the way. But she landed pretty hard, and I landed right on top of her."

"Well," she said, "come on in the kitchen, Sarah. Let's take a look at you."

"Tristan too," I insisted. "He's hurt too."

He sheepishly held up his elbows. "I'm fine." He took my arm and led me to the kitchen.

"Sit on the table," Melissa said. She helped me take off my coat, then asked me to follow her finger with my eyes as she moved it back and forth.

As I moved my eyes to the left, I saw Philip peeking in the kitchen. Sweet Philip. So worried about me. I gave him a goofy grin and a wave as Melissa gently pressed her hands on my head, feeling for bumps. "You didn't hit your head," she said with surprise.

"No, not my head. My hips and my collarbone…my Borderline," I said, and burst out laughing.

An embarrassed smile flashed across Tristan's lips. "Sarah. Stop. This is serious."

I bit my lips to keep the giggles corked as Melissa felt my hip bones. "You'll have some bruising here. Can you take off your shirt?" she asked. "I want to see your clavicle."

"Um…" If I took off my top, they'd see my scars. I stretched the neck of my sweater to expose my collarbone. "It's fine." I shifted my shoulder up and down and tried not to wince. "See?"

Perhaps mistaking my reluctance for modesty, she nodded. She lifted my arm up and down, then lightly touched her fingertips to my collarbone. Her touch was warm and comforting. I smiled at Tristan to show him I wasn't in any pain.

"You're right," she announced. "Nothing's broken." She brought me a bottle of Tylenol and a glass of water. "All you need is acetaminophen and rest. If anything starts to hurt, I want you to tell me right away."

I nodded dutifully and swallowed two pills. But when she came at me with a handful of Band-Aids, I jumped off the table. "Tristan needs those more than me."

Tristan rolled his eyes but humored me. He peeled off his hoodie, and I couldn't help staring at his strong, broad chest. I had to hold myself back from running my hands across it.

"It's almost dark," I told him. "My parents are expecting me home."

He looked at Melissa, who nodded as she applied antiseptic to the scrapes on his elbows. "She's fine," she said. "Stop worrying."

"I'm more than fine. I'm great." I twirled for him to prove it.

"Hold on a minute," he said. "I'll drive you."

"Um." I didn't want my parents to think I was lying to them, and they would find it suspicious to see me with Tristan after I'd told them I was at Vanessa's. And if they thought he had anything to do with my scrapes and bruises, our shaky truce would crumble completely, and they wouldn't let me see him anymore.

Also, there was something I needed to think about. Something I needed to figure out. "I should walk," I said.

"Sarah." He casually brought his finger to his lips, then took it away.

He didn't want my parents to know he'd saved me from the falling tree either.

I shook my head slightly, in a silent reply: *I won't tell.*

"I'll pick you up at six," he said.

Hands jammed deep in my coat pockets, I walked the two blocks home through the wind and snowflakes. Thinking. Remembering. No other trees had fallen to the ground, but I stepped over plenty of fallen branches. I sensed Tristan trailing me, making sure I made it home okay.

My mother noticed the rips in my jeans right away. I told her I'd tripped over a branch on my way home from Vanessa's. She smoothed antiseptic gel on my scrapes and chastised me to be more careful next time.

I ignored the almost audible *plink* of another weight being added to my scale of lies.

CHAPTER TWENTY-ONE

SINCE MELISSA WANTED me to take it easy that night, Tristan and I canceled our plans with Vanessa and Chad and hung out at his house instead. Melissa and Philip stayed home too, and ordered a pizza for the four of us. Melissa examined my collarbone and checked my bruises again, and asked me lots of questions to make sure I was no longer confused. I was in no pain, and my head was clear now—*perfectly* clear—but the three of them kept a casual eye on me all evening.

Later, after Melissa and Philip went to bed, Tristan set two mugs of hot chocolate on the coffee table. Giant marshmallows bobbed on top, and the mugs had smiling snowmen with green mittens painted on them.

We'd never finished *Say Anything* during our first date, so he brought it back up on Netflix. We snuggled on the couch under a heavy fleece blanket. I leaned into him and gave him a dozen tiny kisses. He returned my kisses with a dozen of his own, each one longer and more passionate than the one before, stopping only when I became breathless.

Curling up in his arms, I leaned my head on his shoulder. "You risked your life to save me today."

"I'd do it again, too. As many times as I need to." He stroked my arm as he turned his attention to the TV.

I pretended to watch the movie while gathering my courage. "Tristan?"

He stiffened, just the tiniest bit. "Hmm."

"What were you doing at the park today? You told me you were watching basketball at Chad's."

"I was. I just wanted to check on you and make sure you were okay."

He wasn't telling me the whole truth. I could hear it in his stilted voice.

I took my hot chocolate and blew on it. Tristan knew I had to lie, yet he never pressured me to tell him the truth. Was it fair if I pressured him?

No. It wasn't fair at all.

Accepting his answer with a nod, I turned back to the movie.

But I didn't have as much self-control as he did. "But I didn't tell you when I was leaving Vanessa's house."

He pointed to the TV. "Watch this part coming up. It's hilarious."

I slid off his lap and looked directly at him. "Tristan. How did you know I was in the park at that exact time?"

He shifted and cleared his throat.

"You knew that tree was going to fall today," I said. "Before it happened."

His gaze remained glued to the movie.

"Back when we first started jogging together, you stopped me before I ran into a woman on the other path."

His gaze darted to me, then back to the television.

"And when I was dicing that tomato on our first date, you pulled the knife from my hand and said I was going to cut myself."

My hands trembled, and he took the mug I was holding and put it back on the table. "You're going to spill."

I stared at the mug. The snowman smiled back at me. "I think you just did it again," I whispered.

He scraped his hand through his hair and stared hard at the TV.

"Tristan, please." I couldn't say it out loud. If I was wrong, he would think I was delusional. But it was the only thing that made sense. Could it be possible? Of all the people in the world… "Are you…can you…"

He met my eyes and held my gaze for a long time. Then, inch by inch, he leaned in close, putting his lips to my ear. His answer was so soft, I felt it more than heard it.

"…Yes."

CHAPTER TWENTY-TWO

GASPED AT Tristan's admission. "You can see the future." I had to say it to believe it.

"I know I should've told you," he said, looking guilty, "but I didn't want to scare you away."

I *was* easily spooked, but this was one thing that would not have frightened me. "This is wonderful!" Knowing Tristan had a secret similar to my parents' would finally make them trust him. Maybe his precognition was the reason my father's mobile eye didn't work on him.

He pulled back, eyes stern. "You can't tell anyone. Not even your brother or sister. Your parents are so strict, they'd never let you be with me if they found out."

"But—"

"Please, Tessa."

His plea was so similar to the request I'd made of him, to tell no one my family was in trouble. *Please don't tell,* I'd begged him, and he hadn't.

And maybe he was right about my parents. In addition to being strict, they were suspicious. If they knew he was anything other than a normal boy, they'd trust him even less. Maybe we'd even run again. "I won't tell anyone," I said. "I promise."

He exhaled slowly, then tucked me under his arm, my favorite place to be. "Can you see my future right now?" I asked. Could he see when Dennis Connelly would finally kill me?

"No. The premonitions just come to me. When I try to see the future, it doesn't work."

"Oh." I wasn't sure if his answer disappointed me or not.

"And they're always some kind of warning. They only come when something bad is about to happen."

"So you were at Chad's and had a vision of a tree falling on me."

"Well, yeah. But it's not like I go into some kind of trance," he said. "It's more like a thought or an image that forces its way into my mind, kind of the way you can see a daydream. Except I can't control it, the way you can control a daydream."

"What did you see?" I was almost too scared to hear the answer.

His words sounded tight, like it hurt to speak them. "I saw you lying on the path, crushed under that big tree trunk."

"Was I dead?"

He didn't answer, which was an answer in itself.

"I was supposed to die today." I whispered the words, but they seemed to echo around the room. I'd never considered my death being caused by anything other than Dennis Connelly. The thought was actually comforting.

"But you didn't die today. Most of the time I can change the course of events to prevent my vision from happening."

"So nothing bad ever happens to you," I said, almost accusingly.

He chuckled. "I've always avoided little things like paper cuts and big things like speeding tickets and car accidents. I've never spilled my hot chocolate." Grinning, he gestured to my snowman mug, now sitting securely on the coffee table.

Then his grin faded. "Bad things do happen to me, though. My visions come only a few minutes or even a few seconds before the actual event, and sometimes they come too late. Like when I told you I loved you at the party. As soon as I said it, I had a vision of you running off. But it was too late to change anything. I'd already said the words."

Tristan's warning premonitions made him invulnerable, yet I'd still managed to hurt him. "I'm so sorry." I caressed his cheek with my palm as if I could erase his pain.

He kissed the tip of my nose. "The weird thing is, I've never gotten premonitions about anyone else before. They've always been about things that would happen to *me*. My dad had a heart attack a few years ago, and I didn't get a warning about that. But now I get premonitions about *you*. On our first date, I had a premonition that you fainted at the restaurant."

I remembered how he had suddenly whisked me away.

"And today, I wasn't even with you when I had the premonition about the tree crushing you," he said.

We were silent for a few moments, feeling the weight of his statement.

"I was just sitting at Chad's watching the game when the premonition hit me. I bolted out of his house. I didn't think I'd make it in time, but I did," he said. "So now you can believe me when I say I can keep you safe. I know I will. I can prevent anything bad from happening to you."

Did I dare hope he was right? His premonitions, combined with my dad's mobile eye, would make it harder than ever for Dennis Connelly to kill us.

The fact that Tristan was blessed with a psychic talent meant more than just another line of defense against Dennis Connelly. That I should find someone who possessed the exact ability needed to protect me meant there were greater forces at work here. Tristan could see and change the future—proof that life wasn't just plodding along on a predetermined, linear path. Perhaps whatever force that sent those warnings to him—be it fate, destiny, or some kind of higher power—was the same force that had brought him to me.

We were meant to find each other, so he could keep me safe.

"You're a superhero," I laughed. "My own personal superhero."

Grinning, he gave a mock bow. "At your service."

I had a million more questions for him, but there was only a short time left before I had to go home for the night. So I grabbed him and brought him close, putting all my love and gratitude and relief into a kiss.

CHAPTER TWENTY-THREE

LEEP EVADED ME all night long. At least that kept my nightmare at bay. I kept time by the rumble of the snowplows as they cleared the streets every hour or so throughout the night. The sun was rising before I admitted to myself that sleep just wasn't going to happen, so I got up and went to the kitchen. I wanted—needed—to do something nice for my family.

I spent the next hour making cinnamon rolls, and the warm sugary scent of baking pastries soon filled the house. My mom came in as I was taking them out of the oven. "Need any help?"

"Nope. Thanks, though." I said, bracing myself for another round of her tight-lipped, silent disapproval of Tristan. Would that condemnation turn into commendation if I told my parents about his precognition? That his warning premonitions had saved my life yesterday?

It didn't matter. I promised Tristan I wouldn't tell them. He was keeping my secret, and I would keep his.

From her seat at the table, Mom helped me with breakfast anyway. Plates and glasses took themselves out of the cabinets and set themselves on the table. The refrigerator opened and the jug of orange juice floated over to the table and poured itself into the glasses.

I cut up a couple of grapefruits and placed them, along with the cinnamon rolls, on the table, then took my empty plate and put it back in the cupboard.

Mom frowned. "You're not eating with us?"

"Tristan's picking me up soon. I wanted to make breakfast so you didn't have to."

She said nothing for a moment. Then, "You're in love with him."

The air thickened, and I tensed, backed away. "Please don't be upset."

She sighed remorsefully, and with it, the air thinned again. "I'm not upset. Not anymore. Tristan…he's good to you. He's good *for* you. We trust him now, even without your father watching through him. He's proven himself."

Tristan had won my parents over. Despite his immunity to my dad's remote vision. Despite them not knowing about his warning premonitions. He'd won them over because he was kind and respectful and supportive and dependable. Because he was Tristan.

Mom rose and glided over to me. "Babydoll," she murmured, and kissed my forehead.

I crushed her with a hug. She accepted Tristan, and she called me Babydoll. "Thank you, Mom. Thank you so much."

She came to wait with me by the front window for him, and when he walked up the driveway, she opened the door. "Come on in for a minute, Tristan."

I shot him an alarmed look as he entered. My parents trusted him now, but this was the first time he'd have to talk to them since I'd told him we all had aliases. He could ruin it all by accidentally calling me Tessa.

I wondered if he'd had a premonition about this.

He gave me a wink—*Relax, I got this*—and said, "Hi, Sarah. Morning, Mrs. Spencer."

"Shelby mentioned she's going to a dance at school on Friday night," she said.

"Yep. Winterball."

I'd seen posters for the dance at school, but hadn't given it a thought, and Tristan had never mentioned it.

"I assume you and Sarah are going too?" my mom asked.

He shook his head. "Sarah doesn't like crowds. I thought we'd do something on our own instead."

Mom's hopeful smile fell, and she looked at me with such hurt and disappointment, I was sure she was about to cry.

"I—I want to go to the dance," I said before her tears could form, and forced my lips to curve up. "It'll be fun."

She nodded with a happy sigh.

We walked to Tristan's house, my mittened hand clasped in his gloved hand, my book bag slung over his shoulder. A few kids built snowmen and forts in their yards while their dads ran snow blowers down their driveways. The snow squeaked under our boots and little clouds puffed from our mouths with each breath.

"Tristan," I said, trying to sound casual, "can anyone else in your family...you know, do what you do?"

His steps lost their rhythm for a moment, then found it again. When he spoke, his voice was soft, almost under his breath. "My mom has dreams about the future sometimes."

I inhaled, unsure if his answer surprised me or not. "Do her dreams always happen?"

"Almost always. But the future is never definite, as my own premonitions prove. Sometimes she interprets her dream wrong, or something happens to change the course of events. But lots of things happen exactly as she dreamed them. She's had dreams about you."

He said that last part casually, like an afterthought, but it surprised me so much I stopped short. My only possible future was to be killed by Dennis Connelly. Had Tristan's mother seen my murder in her dreams? "Wh-what did she see?"

He gave my hand a reassuring squeeze. "Only good things. She had her first dream about you ten years ago. In the dream we were little kids, like nine or ten years old. We were playing up in the tree house in my backyard." As he said it, he looked out into the distance. "I wonder what happened to change the course of events and prevent that dream from happening."

I knew the answer: Dennis Connelly.

"She had one more dream about you, two years ago," Tristan said. "We were older in this one. She said I brought you home, and she gave you a hug and said, 'Welcome to the family.'"

"But why does she think that girl is me?"

"Because of your wildflower eyes."

I blinked. "My eyes?"

"A couple months ago, when we first started jogging together, I was talking to my mom on the phone. I guess she could tell I was upset about something. She wouldn't let up until I told her that I kind of liked this new girl who seemed to like me too, but then she would get scared and run away. My mom asked me to describe her eyes. I thought it was a weird thing to ask, but I told her how they were green with flecks of color. She got all quiet for a minute. Then she told me about her dreams. She said she's been waiting ten years for the girl with wildflower eyes to come into my life."

I sucked in air, and Tristan wiped a tear from my cheek with his gloved finger. "Why does that make you sad?" he asked.

"Because her dream won't come true. It can't."

"It will," he said. "She believes you're my future, Tessa. She knows it."

Maybe he was right. That dream confirmed the hope I felt last night. If I was his future, that meant I actually would *have* a future.

And I didn't want a future if Tristan wasn't in it.

He put his arm around my shoulder. "I've put all my faith into her dr—"

"My mom's psychokinetic." The words forced themselves out before I knew I was going to say them, like they'd been waiting for the slightest opportunity to be spoken. Now they hung heavily in the air.

He froze, then pulled away from me. His face was stone.

"That means," I whispered, "she can move things without touching them."

"Tessa…"

"Just this morning she set the table and poured the orange juice without ever leaving her chair. She can watch TV in the family room and switch channels without using the remote, all while folding the laundry upstairs and cutting up vegetables in the kitchen. She can lift furniture. She can crush cars. She doesn't even need to see the object she wants to move. She just pictures it in her mind, and it happens."

He kept his eyes on mine. "Are you sure you want to tell me this?"

I'd never been more certain of anything in my life. "If I'm your future," I said, "then you have to know my past."

After my revelation, Tristan took my hand, a strange, almost sorrowful expression on his face. He whisked me to his house and up to his room without a word. I was shivering with cold—or maybe it was apprehension and guilt.

He plugged his phone into his speakers, then sat with me on the bed. "Tell me."

"Where are Melissa and Philip?"

"Melissa's working her shift at the hospital. Philip should be back any second, but he'll probably go straight to his workshop. He won't hear you."

I took a deep breath, and the words poured from my mouth like water from a fire hose.

I told him about my father's remote vision.

About Jillian's psychokinesis and her new ability to piggyback on our father's mobile eye, and her failed attempt to develop one of her own.

About Logan's PK and his automatic learning power of hypercognition.

How my parents hadn't trusted Tristan until just this morning because he was one of the rare people immune to my father's remote vision.

How my dad used his mobile eye only a few times a day now because of his headaches and bloody noses, and how Jillian had started getting them too.

For over an hour, I told him everything about my family's powers, and then I stopped.

The following silence was broken only by the soft music from the speakers and a muffled whirring from Philip's workshop on the other side of the house.

Tristan had said nothing the entire time. In the silence his awed expression turned into one of anticipation. "And what about you? What powers do you have?"

Of course he would expect me to have a psychic power when everyone else in my family did. I gave him an apologetic smile. "I don't have any," I said, speaking around the lump in my throat. "None."

"None? Really?"

My eyes suddenly burned with tears. "You're disappointed."

"I'm surprised, not disappointed. I don't care that you're not psychic."

"I don't want you to feel sorry for me," I added. "I get enough of that from my family. They treat me like I'm this helpless, weak, breakable thing."

"I hope I've never treated you that way."

"No, and that's one of the reasons I like being with you," I said. "And I liked being equal with someone. But now, every single person I love is more powerful than I am. You're all members of a club I can never join."

He kissed my neck. "Now I wish I wasn't psychic."

"Don't say that." I chuckled. "Your warning premonition saved my life yesterday."

Tucking myself into him, I nestled my head on his shoulder. "Sometimes I stare at something and try to make it move, or try to see through someone else's eyes. But nothing ever works. Jillian and Logan's abilities first appeared when they were babies, but my mom said her own PK didn't show itself until she was thirteen. So I waited. I turned thirteen, fourteen, fifteen …and nothing."

Tristan rubbed my back.

"A few years ago I convinced myself I was adopted," I said. "But I'm not. My mom told me I'm just like her mother. She was four foot ten, same as me, and left-handed, just like me."

"Was? She's no longer alive?"

"She choked to death on a dried apricot when my mom was eighteen."

"Oh. That's horrible."

"My grandma wasn't psychic either," I added. "Only normal, like me."

"There's nothing wrong with being normal."

"In my family there is. Jillian and Logan used to call me the runt of the litter."

"Ouch."

"I try not to be jealous, but sometimes I am. Mostly, though, I just feel…useless."

He tucked my head under his chin, his breath stirring my hair. "I'm so sorry, Tessa. That sucks."

"It's Jillian and Logan you should feel sorry for, not me," I said, my lip trembling. "Jill wants to be a doctor and use her PK for heart surgeries. Logan wants to compose symphonies. But we won't live much longer, and she'll never be a surgeon. He'll never be a composer. They're the ones you should feel sorry for."

Tristan went rigid. "What did you say?"

"You should feel sorry for them, not me."

"Not that. The part after that."

"Oh, shoot. I used their real names, didn't I?"

"Tessa. You said 'we won't live much longer.' *That* part. What are you talking about?"

Oh no. Oh no! I'd gone too far, said too much. Even one word was too much. Oh God, what have I done?

In one fluid motion I slid out from his embrace. "I need to stop now." Then I ran from the room.

Tristan pounded after me as I raced down the stairs. "You can't tell me your entire family's not going to live much longer and then run off. Are you all sick?"

He caught my arm right before I made it to the bottom step. "But sickness doesn't explain the fake names, the leaving town without notice, the paranoia. Your family's not sick. You're running from something. Hiding from something." He drew me close. "Tessa. Tell me what it is."

I closed my eyes. Took a breath.

Licked my lips, swallowed.

Then I forced myself to tell him. "We're being hunted, Tristan."

His grip tightened on my arm. "What?"

"And when he finds us, he'll kill us."

"Who?"

"We've been running for eight years. My dad's mobile eye is the only thing keeping us alive."

He was frozen, stricken, silent, until he whispered, "Oh my God. It all makes sense now."

And then the sobs came, painful, dry, rasping sobs, so strong they brought me to my knees. He sank to the floor with me and only after my sobs lessened to tears, and my tears lessened to sniffles, did he release me.

He wiped my tears, then pulled his hands through his hair. "Tell me what's happening."

"Everyone we've gone to for help is dead," I said. "I won't do that to you. I can't risk—"

"Don't worry about me." He tapped his forehead. "I'll be fine. Now I need you to tell me everything."

Tell me everything. Three little words that spoken separately would be weightless, but together were heavy enough to sink the whole world.

I glanced across the foyer. Ten steps, I could be out the door. Two blocks, I'd be home. Five seconds to tell my parents I'd slipped up. And one minute after that, we'd be gone forever.

Instead, I took Tristan's hand and led him back upstairs.

CHAPTER TWENTY-FOUR

RISTAN SAT ME on his bed and wrapped a blanket around me like a cocoon. Then he sat behind me, drawing me against his chest. Whether he held me to comfort me or to keep me from running away again, I didn't care. I belonged there, in his arms.

He would keep me safe. I could tell him anything.

So I told him everything.

"My dad really is a writer," I said. "But he doesn't write books. He used to be an investigative journalist for a newspaper in Washington, D.C. He made a lot of enemies because he exposed politicians doing unethical things, so he used a pseudonym. Xander Xavier. You can probably find his articles on the internet. My mom was the head event planner at a fancy hotel. My parents invested in some businesses and stocks and made a lot of money. We lived in a big red brick house, and my brother and sister and I went to a private school. We went on vacations to the beach and to Disney World. I had friends. I went to birthday parties. I *had* birthday parties. We had a nice life. It was perfect. But it wasn't because of the big house or the private school or the vacations. We were just …happy."

I sniffled as homesickness hit me. It'd been years since I allowed myself to remember my life in Virginia, before Dennis Connelly took it all away.

Maybe I'd started shaking, or maybe my voice had quivered. Whatever the reason, Tristan tightened his arms around me, gently, protectively. "Tell me what happened."

My gaze landed on a tennis trophy across the room. His name was engraved on the bottom: *Tristan Walker.* I focused on his name, wrapped my emotions up in a blanket of fog, and the room became blurry and hazy.

From far away, I heard myself tell the story, easily remembered because I relived it in my dreams every night.

"One day when I was eight, Jillian and Logan and I were playing at a park down the block. I fell from the monkey bars and hurt my knee, so I came home. My mom gave me an ice pack and sent me back outside with a book, and I sat under one of the big trees we had in the front yard. I'd read a couple of chapters when a man came up to me. My parents taught me about stranger danger, and I knew I should get up and run, but I didn't. He didn't seem scary. His eyes were kind. I liked him."

"Who was he?" Tristan asked.

"He told me his name, and then he said I must be Tessa. Before I could answer, he put his finger to his lips and told me not to talk, that he could hear my answers in my head. So without speaking, I told him, yes, my name was Tessa. He said he'd heard I was eight years old, but that couldn't be right because I was much too small to be eight. To prove it to him, I thought about the cake my mom made for my eighth birthday. He said he'd never seen a cake shaped like the number eight before, and it looked like a very yummy cake."

Tristan chuckled, a tight, forced guffaw.

"He'd ask me questions, and I'd answer in my head," I said. "Then he'd repeat my answer out loud. I imagined silly things, like a purple elephant jumping on a pogo stick, and he'd laugh and tell me what I was thinking. He was right every time. It was fun. Then all of a sudden he went stiff, his eyes turned mean, and he held out his hand and told me to come with him. That's when I knew that he was bad, that I shouldn't have been talking to him, that I should have run away the moment he came into our yard. I tried to run away from him then, but I couldn't. I tried to call for my parents but he grabbed me and threw me in his car."

Tristan grabbed me too, wrapping his arms around me as if he was afraid the man would materialize right there and take me away again.

"He ran back to my house," I continued. "I tried to get out of the car. I pulled the handles, pounded on the windows, kicked at the doors, but they wouldn't open. I screamed, but no one heard me. There was a cigar somewhere up in front, and the car was smoky, and it smelled like, like burning cherries…"

"You're about to panic," Tristan whispered, bringing me away from the memory and back to his room, back to now, back to safety. "Breathe. You're okay. Breathe."

I obeyed and took a deep breath, realizing only then how my lungs burned for air.

"Again," he said, and I took another shaky breath. "Do you need a break? We can stop."

I couldn't stop now. "I want to tell you everything."

He tensed a little, bracing himself. "Okay, then. The man locked you in his car, then went back to your house. Why?"

"The politicians my dad exposed in his articles," I said. "One of them, or some of them, or all of them. They hired that man to kill us."

"Your whole family? Why?"

"Maybe they thought we all knew what my dad knew about them and they wanted to silence us," I said. "Or maybe they wanted revenge. Maybe they wanted to send a warning to other journalists. All three, probably."

"What did the man do when he went inside?" he asked.

"He attacked my parents," I said."He sliced my dad's chest and arm. My mom got cut down her back."

"He had a knife?"

I shook my head. "No."

Tristan was silent for a moment. Then, softly, "How did they get away?"

"My mom finally threw a table at him with her PK. It stunned him long enough that they were able to run out of the house."

Even now, years later, I clearly remembered my parents bursting outside, bloody and wild-eyed, as I cried for help from the back seat of Dennis Connelly's car.

"My dad used his mobile eye on me and found me in the car, just as the man ran out after them. He was limping, but he still came for them. My mom used her PK to throw him to the ground and hold him down while my dad tried to get me out of the car. But he couldn't get the doors open. He shouted to my mom for help, and she used her PK to shatter the windows, all of them at once, and my dad dragged me out. But the man, he…he…"

The words had been tumbling out of my mouth, so when I suddenly stopped talking, the silence was deafening.

"What did he do?" Tristan's words were whispered and laced with fear.

I closed my eyes. Took a breath.

Licked my lips, swallowed.

Then I forced myself to say it. "He cut me too."

"He *cut* you?" A fearful whisper no longer, his words boiled with possessive anger, and he resisted when I tried to pull away from him.

"Let me go," I said. "I'll show you."

He released me, and I stood. I turned to face him, then, shaking, lifted my sweater to reveal my stomach and the five thick, jagged scars that ran from my breastbone to my pelvis.

He drew in a breath. "That man did that to you?"

"Without even touching me," I said. "He was across the yard, on the ground. That's…that's how he kills people."

Gingerly, he ran his fingertips over the puckered, raised skin, tracing them one by one. "Oh, Tessa."

"My father still can't look at me without his eyes going to my stomach first." I pulled my sweater down and returned to his lap, then pulled his arms around me even tighter than before.

"Do you want to stop?" he asked.

"No." Showing my scars to Tristan was difficult, but before today, I felt like I'd been broken into a million pieces. Now, each word I spoke put one of those pieces back into place.

"Everything was a blur after that," I said. "My dad ran me to the garage and threw me in our car, then my mom jumped in and we raced away. The last I ever saw of our house was the man running after us. I don't remember stopping at the park to get Jillian and Logan, but I do remember Jillian screaming when she saw how bloody we were. I remember hearing a big explosion and seeing a ball of fire in the sky and bricks and rubble flying through the air. It was our house. That man blew up our house."

I told Tristan what else I remembered of that horrible day.

How my dad drove as fast as he could while my mom found Logan's old sweatshirt in the car and pressed it hard on my bleeding stomach, ignoring her own wounds.

How she couldn't stop crying, and I couldn't stop screaming.

How when we finally had to stop for gas at a truck stop, they bought all the first-aid kits gauze pads and elastic bandages they could find. How they had to peel the shredded, blood-soaked clothes from my skin before they could clean me and wrap me up.

How they made me drink an adult dose of that sleepy cold medicine, and when I woke up, it was nighttime and we were in a motel with my mom pacing the room, objects flying uncontrolled around her, and my dad standing guard by the door, rubbing his temples.

I continued, not really seeing the room around me, not really hearing myself speak, but still feeling Tristan's heart beating against my back, his shallow breath on my neck, and his arms around me, keeping me safe. "We drove around for weeks, buying food from gas stations and sleeping in a different motel every night. I started having nightmares and waking everyone up with my screams. One night my mom, she…um…"

"What?" Tristan breathed.

"She didn't mean to do it. And anyway it was my fault. She was so stressed, and she could never sleep because I woke up screaming all the time. She was exhausted. She just lost control."

"What did she do?"

I closed my eyes. Took a breath.

Licked my lips, swallowed.

Then I forced myself to tell him. "She flew me across the room and slammed me into the wall."

He hissed in a sharp breath.

"She said if I didn't stop screaming she would let that man get me. And even though I still have nightmares every night, I have never, ever screamed again."

"Jesus."

"She cried the whole next day," I said, scrambling to apologize on her behalf. "She promised she'd never hurt me again and said she would *never* let that man get me. She was so upset that I gave her flowers. They were just dandelions from the cracks in the parking lot, but she held those dandelions in her hand for three days before my dad finally threw them away." I inhaled a huge lungful of air. "And that was when my parents decided to stop running."

It took Tristan a long time to respond. "Where did you go?" he finally asked, his voice strained.

"My dad watched for the man almost constantly, and realized he could only see him when they were close to each other, within a few hours. We were in Utah, and my dad hadn't seen him in a few days, so my parents thought we might be safe if we stayed there."

I told Tristan how my parents took out as much cash as they could from their bank accounts and how they found someone to forge new IDs and birth certificates for us. We became the Perry family, and an old, rickety rental house became our new home. My mother hated that house. She'd taken such pride in our big red brick house in Kitteridge, Virginia, but this one was tiny, with peeling white paint and floors that creaked with every step. She said it reminded her of the trailer she grew up in.

But we were alive—and together—and that was all that mattered, and all that still mattered.

I told Tristan how the wounds my parents received during the attack had healed completely by then, but my own cuts were much deeper and took a lot longer to heal.

I told Tristan how, just as we'd gotten used to life in Utah, just as we thought we'd be okay, my parents pulled us from our beds and told us to get in the car. My dad had seen the man with his mobile eye. He found us, he knew where we were, and he was coming, getting close. A few days earlier my parents had gone to a local police detective for help, but the man tracked us down through the police report. As we sped away down a dark highway, my father watched, horrified, as the man cornered that detective and sliced him open.

I told Tristan how the same thing happened in Pennsylvania, when my parents asked an FBI agent for help. A few hours later my dad saw the man coming, and we ran. The next day my dad watched the man kill the agent in Pennsylvania as we refueled our getaway car in Ohio. After that, we stopped seeking help from others. We could do nothing but flee to another location, rent another house, and get new names.

"It's been eight years," I said. "We've lived in thirteen different places. We've had thirteen different names. He keeps managing to find us, and every time we escape he gets angrier. My dad is getting weaker. I'm scared his mobile eye will kill him before the man does. My mom's PK is strong, stronger than ever, but emotionally…she's falling apart. We all are. Every day, we fall apart a little bit more."

I stopped. I was done.

"What about your friends and neighbors?" Tristan whispered. "Didn't they wonder why your whole family just disappeared?"

"The police reports said they found our bodies in the rubble when our house exploded. That's how powerful that man is. My parents decided it's safer to let everyone believe we're dead. There was a memorial for us and everything." With a small sigh, I added, "My friends from Virginia…they were the only real friends I ever had. I twisted in his lap so I could look at him. "Until now. Until you."

He lifted my hair and planted a small kiss on my neck, right over my collarbone. "There has to be something else you can do," he said. "You can't just keep running and hiding your whole life."

"There's no other option. I had a plan, but it didn't work." I told him about emailing the college professor. "We check every day at school, but he's never put that red star on his website. Maybe he doesn't believe us. Or maybe he's too scared to help."

"You keep calling him 'the man,'" he said. "You know his name though. He introduced himself to you. What's his name?"

I'd told him everything else. I'd told him volumes. I could tell him two more words. Five syllables. I could say them. I could do it.

I closed my eyes. Took a breath.

Licked my lips, swallowed.

Then I forced myself to say it.

But nothing came out but a little squeak.

Exhaling with a sob, I shook my head. I told my parents his name that day eight years ago, and that was the first and last time I ever said it. Logically, I knew he couldn't hear me. My family said his name all the time. But I could not bring myself to force those two words from my vocal cords and out of my mouth, releasing them into the universe.

Saying his name wouldn't conjure him up and make him suddenly appear. But names were important. Nobody knew that better than me. Names were powerful. And Dennis Connelly already had too much power over me.

I simply couldn't, wouldn't, give him any more.

"You don't have to say it," Tristan murmured. He took a notebook and pen from the drawer on his nightstand. "Write it down."

"Why?"

"I just want to know his name."

"You can't look for him!" I cried. "My parents have been looking for information on him for eight years. They've never been able to find anything. If you Google him, he'll know it. He'll trace it somehow, and he'll come here. He's done it before. He'll kill us, he'll kill you—"

"I won't look for him. I just...I need to know the name of the man who is torturing you. Please. I have to know." His pleading eyes made him look so vulnerable, so helpless. It reminded me of Jillian and Logan eight years ago, when they'd begged our parents to tell them *who* had sliced me open, *who* had chased us from our home, *who* was hunting us. They had been at the park the day he came to our house. They didn't witness his attack. They didn't even know what he looked like. They needed something solid—something concrete—to fear, rather than a shapeless, nameless shadow.

Tristan needed the same thing.

With trembling fingers, I took the pen from him.

For a moment I considered writing a fake name, just to give him something tangible. But I didn't want to lie to him anymore. I opened the notebook to a random blank page. In tiny, shaky letters, I wrote:

Dennis Connelly

—and slammed the notebook shut.

"Don't look until tonight, after I've gone home," I said. "Then you have to burn it. Promise me you'll burn the page."

"I promise."

"Burn the whole notebook."

"I will."

"And then you can never say his name out loud."

He agreed, then opened a drawer on his nightstand and put the notebook inside. "Now I need you to promise me not to leave Twelve Lakes," he said. "Don't let your family know you told me anything. If there's any chance of my mom's dream coming true, you need to stay here with me."

I nodded. I never wanted to leave Twelve Lakes. I wanted to stay right here, with my family and with Tristan, forever.

"Can you think of anything else?" he asked. "Anything at all?"

"You know everything now. No more secrets. No more lies." My scale of lies was now completely empty on Tristan's side. I pictured the little weights rolling off the scale in a loud clatter and then disappearing into nothingness. My parents' side of the scale shot straight down, so heavy was it with my lies.

Tristan was reluctant to bring me home that night. "But I need to get home. If I'm late, my dad will send out his mobile eye to make sure I'm okay," I said, then smiled. "I love that I can tell you that now."

He returned my smile, but it didn't reach his eyes. He kissed me with a desperate urgency, as if he thought he'd never see me again. I had to reassure him I was safe until my father saw *the man* coming. I gave him the same assurances my parents gave me, assurances I never quite believed.

By the look in his eyes, I knew he didn't believe them either.

CHAPTER TWENTY-FIVE

HEN I WENT to my room to get ready for bed, feeling lighter and heavier at the same time, I was surprised to see something on my bed. A silver dress. A note in my mother's handwriting lay on top:

For Winterball

She must have purchased it for me just hours after accepting Tristan and calling me Babydoll, while I was betraying her by telling Tristan our family's secrets.

I ran my fingers over the material. The dress was strapless and fell to just above my knees. Several layers of crinoline hung from under the silver bodice and a wide silk ribbon tied around the waist in a bow. A gift box held a pair of silver heels and a little silver handbag. It was too extravagant for a simple school dance, but I didn't care. I loved it.

"I've already sewed a pocket under the skirt for your cell phone," my mom said from the doorway.

She loved me so much.

I tried not to think about all the secrets I was keeping from her now.

The dark shadows under Tristan's eyes were visible from twenty feet away as he paced at the corner the next morning. When he saw me, he almost collapsed in relief. He grabbed me and held me for a long time. He kept both arms around me as we headed toward school, making it difficult to walk.

"Did you tell anyone?" I asked him.

He shook his head wearily. "I need time to figure everything out anyway."

"I'm sorry to burden you with this."

"You're never a burden."

I told him about my Winterball dress, hoping to see his face brighten, first his eyes, then his smile. He did smile, but it only reached his lips.

The shadows under his eyes grew darker each day. I knew he wasn't sleeping at night and insisted he nap after school while I studied. I would lie on his bed, and he would climb in next to me, lifting my sweater to give each of my scars a gentle kiss. He used my stomach as a pillow. I loved the feeling of his head on my belly, right over my scars. It gave my stomach a new purpose, something other than a permanent reminder of Dennis Connelly's attack.

At lunch on Thursday, Tristan and I sat with our friends, as usual. He pretended to laugh along with their jokes, but his laughter was hollow and always a second late. He kept his arm tight around my shoulders, as if I would disappear if he let go.

He suddenly sat up straight, eyes wide, then murmured in my ear. "Your brother and sister are coming. They're going to take you away."

"What—" But before I could finish, Jillian and Logan rushed into the cafeteria and up to the table.

Her eyes were damp. "Sarah, you need to come with us."

"Did Mom call?" I didn't hear my phone ring. Did she call and I missed it? "Are we leaving? Now? We have to leave?" I grabbed Tristan.

"We're not leaving," Logan said. "Shelby needs to show us something." He raised his eyebrows meaningfully. "In the computer lab."

The professor. The red star!

Tristan said he only had premonitions when something bad was about to happen, but this wasn't bad at all! I scrambled to my feet, and he stood up with me. Jillian glared at him and swiped away a tear. "Not you, Tristan. Stay away." She seized my hand and tugged.

He gave me a tiny nod, a silent message: *I'll be right behind you.*

As Jillian pulled me from the lunchroom, I turned to give him an excited smile.

But his face was grim.

And Jillian was crying.

Something was horribly wrong.

Professor Fielding's portrait smiled at us as we huddled around the monitor in a private corner of the computer lab. His webpage had changed, but there was no red star. Instead two words hovered in a fancy bold font over his head.

~In Memoriam~

"Wh…" I swallowed hard. "What does that mean?"

"It means he's dead!" Jillian's voice was high with near-hysteria. "It means our email led Dennis Connelly straight to him." She covered her mouth with her hands and whimpered. "He's dead, and it's our fault."

No. "It's *my* fault." I was the one who'd seen that word, *parapsychology*, in the catalog. I was the one who wanted to contact the professor. I was the one who'd convinced Jillian and Logan to help me email him. Guilt swept through me like a fog, making me sway with dizziness.

Logan took my arm and placed me in a chair. "Hold on a minute. Don't jump to conclusions." He clicked on a link that led to the professor's obituary. "Look. It says here he had a brain aneurysm. He wasn't…" He eyed my stomach and made a swiping motion with his fingers.

My hands fluttered to my belly, the scent of cherry cigars filling my nose.

"The webpage was updated today, but he died three weeks ago," Logan said. "If Connelly had intercepted the email, he would've found us by now. I don't think he had anything to do with this." Settling the issue with a firm nod, he clicked back to the professor's portrait and stared at it with a disappointed sigh.

"What's going on?"

Jillian and Logan jumped, but I recognized Tristan's voice behind me. He pulled me from the chair and into his arms.

"Jeez, Tristan, possessive much? I told you to stay away," Jillian snapped, but her bark lost its bite when she sniffled.

"Just making sure everyone's okay." Tristan pointed to the smiling professor on the computer screen. "Who's that?"

Through damp eyes, Jillian sent me a distressed look, devastation snuffing her usual lightning-quick ability to make up lies.

"He was a friend of the family," Logan said."We just found out he passed away."

Turns out we didn't have to lie at all.

"Oh wow," Tristan said. "I'm so sorry." He gave me a squeeze, a silent question: *What really happened?*

I squeezed back: *Tell you later.*

The bell rang, and with a sniffle, Jillian wiped the makeup from under her eyes and padded from the room. I touched my fingertip to the professor's portrait in a wordless goodbye before Logan closed the browser.

As Tristan walked me to class, I hurriedly explained the man on the screen was the professor we had emailed for help. His face turned gray, but he said Logan was right. His death could not possibly be my fault.

I tried desperately to believe him.

CHAPTER TWENTY-SIX

E WERE QUIET at dinner that night. Not unusual for me, or really even for Logan, but it was for Jillian. She slouched in her chair and picked at her food. Claiming exhaustion, she floated her plate into the kitchen and shuffled up to bed.

Later I sat at the desk in my room, staring at my study guide but seeing Professor Fielding's portrait instead.

The image was shattered by an anguished howl.

I stumbled from my room. My sister knelt in the hallway, clutching her head.

The world grew hazy as Mom and Logan ran up the stairs. Our dad followed, slowly, his eyes dazed and unfocused.

"Jillian, what's wrong?" "Are you okay?""What happened?" all of us asked at once.

"I was…piggybacking…" she moaned, "and…" She choked on her sobs as blood, thick red blood, gushed from her nose.

Mom, jaw clenched, shook her head. "This is exactly what we were afraid of. We told you to stay out of your father's head!"

"I had to try, Mom. I need to know where he is." She blubbered through the blood on her lips as a fresh spurt poured from her nose. "I need to figure out how to stop him. I can't keep living like this." She moaned and gripped her head. "I can't."

"Mother, help her!" Logan cried.

But Mom remained motionless. The picture of the faded yellow flower vibrated against the wall, then the glass cracked and shattered.

"Wendy," Dad mumbled, blinking the daze from his eyes. "Calm down."

Logan shot his hand up to catch an ice pack as it zoomed up the stairs. "Press this to Jillian's head, Tessa."

Shaking, I took it and sank down next to Jillian. She gripped my hand, making it sticky with blood. Dizzy, woozy, I pressed the ice pack around her forehead, unable to take my eyes off the blood running from her nose, down her chin, dripping onto the carpet and soaking into the fibers.

I flinched when a vase flung itself against the wall. "What has gotten into you lately? All three of you?" Mom screeched. "Do you think we don't know about your training sessions with those Zener cards?" All the doors lining the hallway trembled violently in their hinges. She wasn't even trying to control herself now, and this time, she was more than upset. She was furious.

Her gray eyes seemed to flash silver as a table lamp bulleted through the air, and I shrieked as it slammed into the wall, barely missing Jillian and me as we huddled on the floor. Logan dove to shield us.

"Wendy!" True panic in his voice, my dad grabbed her hand and tugged, but she yanked away.

Her next words were growled. "If you think you got away with something by emailing that college professor, you are wrong."

My lungs turned to stone, and Jillian peeked up through swollen eyes. "How did you know?"

Lips in a straight line, Logan answered. "I told them. Tonight after dinner." He gave us an apologetic shrug. "They needed to know what we did. We took a stupid risk."

My sister hung her head, then flinched as another vase slammed itself into the wall. "It was incredibly stupid!" Mom screeched. "Do you not care at all about this family? Do you not realize what your father and I have sacrificed to keep us all together?"

"I'm sorry!" Jillian screamed, then whimpered. "I am so sorry."

"Get in your room. Now!"

Grimacing with pain, Jillian crawled to her room. My mom jerked her arm back and Jillian's door slammed itself shut, splintering the door frame.

"Wendy, that's enough." Dad inched toward her with his palms up like he was approaching a rabid dog. "Let's go downstairs and calm down." He took her hand, and this time she didn't pull away.

As he directed her to the stairs, he turned back to Logan and me. "You two also. Get in your rooms."

On trembling legs, I rose, and Logan and I shuffled to our rooms.

Our house became very quiet.

A few minutes later, after I stopped shaking, I crept to my window and peeked out. Tristan was there, standing in the shadows across the street, shivering against the cold.

I knew he'd be there. He had a premonition that I was distressed and had come to make sure I was okay.

I waved to him. *I'm okay,* my wave said. *Thank you for checking on me.*

He pulled his hand from his pocket and waved back.

After an hour or so, I snuck out of my room. My parents were still downstairs, their words muffled, Mom's high and fast, Dad's calm and soothing.

I brought a dampened washcloth, along with a glass of water and two Tylenol, into Jillian's room. She lay on the bed, curled on her side, stifling her sobs and moans of pain. I wiped the dried blood off her face and hands and carefully cleaned her gold bracelet. I supported her head as she took the pills, then held her hand until she fell asleep.

We were hurting, bleeding, even though Dennis Connelly wasn't close enough to slice us open. Was this part of his plan? To keep us running, hiding, terrorized? Maybe he was toying with us, the way a cat plays with a mouse, letting it scurry a few feet away and then catching it again, before growing tired of the game and finally pouncing on it and crushing it between its jaws.

He had to know we were suffering.

He had to know that even though he hadn't captured us, he was killing us anyway.

CHAPTER TWENTY-SEVEN

JILLIAN DIDN'T GO to school the next day. When I left in the morning, my parents were sitting on either side of her bed, Dad pressing an ice pack to her head and Mom quietly crying. When I got home Mom was on her hands and knees in the hallway, scrubbing Jillian's blood from the carpet.

The Winterball dance was starting in a few hours. I told my sister I'd stay home with her, but Mom insisted Logan and I go. She told Jillian she could go too, but Jillian just shook her head.

While I was trying to do my hair in the bathroom, Jillian shuffled in. Her eyes were red, but she didn't appear to be in as much pain. She curled my hair into dozens of loose spirals and applied my makeup.

I slipped into my silver dress and heels. The sparkles caught the light as I turned around for her, and she tied the ribbon in a bow around my waist. "It didn't work," she whispered. "Developing my own mobile eye. It's not going to happen." She raised a shaky hand to rub her temple. "I'm so sorry, Tessa. I really thought I could save us."

"Don't be sorry," I said. "You tried. I tried with the professor. We'll try something else."

"But what?" she asked. "What else can we do?"

"We can—" But I stopped. There was nothing else. "We can hope," I said.

She just shook her head.

We stared at each other for a long time, then she grabbed me in a fierce hug. "Have fun at the dance tonight, okay?" she said. "Have the most fun you've ever had in your entire life."

I hugged her back as tight as I could.

Downstairs in the kitchen, I modeled the dress for my mother. "You look like a snowflake, Babydoll," she said. "A tiny silver snowflake."

I gave her a small smile, and she returned it. "Why don't you take some extra time tonight with Tristan?" she said. "We can extend your curfew by a couple hours."

We both knew her offer was an apology for last night. I accepted it. I needed to apologize for something too. "I'm sorry about emailing the professor."

She sighed and rubbed her eyes. "I'm sure you were only doing what Jillian told you to do."

"It was my idea."

"*Your* idea?" Her head jerked up, and the air turned to ice. "Tessa, you know how dangerous Dennis Connelly is, more than anyone! How could you create trouble like that?"

A glass shattered behind me and I flinched, bracing myself to be flown into the wall. "Mom, I'm sorry! Please!"

The anger in her eyes was replaced with horror, then remorse. "I'm losing control," she said, high and helpless. A tear rolled down her cheek, and she covered her face. "I'm just so…tired. I'm so tired, Tessa."

She looked so small, hunched over like that, rocking back and forth. I put my arms around her. "Things will get better soon," I said, knowing my words were just another lie.

Logan got a ride to the dance with his friends from jazz band. While I waited for Tristan to pick me up, I found my dad slouched in his leather armchair, rubbing his temples. When he saw me, he straightened. "Hi, Tessa Blessa." As usual, his eyes went straight to my stomach before focusing on the total me. "You look adorable."

I perched on the armrest next to him. "Thanks."

"Pretty scary, last night," he said.

"Yeah."

"I've never seen your mother like that."

"She had a right to be angry," I said, and I meant it. "What we did was wrong."

He looked at me then with such guilt and despair, and for a few seconds he didn't breathe. "I'm so sorry, Tessa," he said, his voice tight. "For…" He gestured to the kitchen where my mom sat, up the stairs where my sister lay in her room, to my stomach, and finally threw both hands in the air. "For everything."

He looked so hopeless, so…broken. "Dad, no one blames you for anything."

He finally exhaled. "*I* blame myself. For everything."

The doorbell rang. "Go on," he said. "That's got to be Tristan."

I hesitated. "I should stay home."

"He's a good kid, that Tristan," Dad said. "Have a good time at the dance. That's an order."

"Okay, but no more headaches, Dad. That's an order."

He chuckled and closed his eyes.

Dozens of giant cardboard snowflakes dangled from the ceiling and strings of tiny white lights twinkled, transforming the school gymnasium into a winter wonderland. The music pulsated and the gym was packed with TLC students, but I entered the dance with confidence, certain Tristan would whisk me away before a panic attack hit.

As I slipped off my coat, I saw a sparkle of lust behind his tired eyes. I grinned and twirled around. "You like?"

He touched one of my curls, then slid his hand down to my bare shoulder, then to the silver ribbon around my waist. "I love."

"I love you too." I gave him a kiss. "Your turn." He imitated me by slipping off his sports jacket and spinning around. He wore a crisp white button-down shirt with a little pink horse embroidered above the pocket, showing off his broad chest. His wavy hair was tousled. His chin was scruffy, and his lips…

Suddenly ravenous for him, I slid my arms around his neck, drawing him close. He kissed me, tender and eager at the same time. The DJ played a series of romantic ballads, and Tristan and I swayed to each song. The crowd swirled around us, but I felt like we were alone on the dance floor.

When I saw a girl take out her cell phone and start taking pictures, I told Tristan I was thirsty. We went to get a drink in the front hall.

While we waited in line, Logan came over and pulled me into a quiet corner. "This is our first chance to talk," he said. "I just wanted to let you know that I'm sorry."

My whole family was a big bundle of apologies today. "For what?"

"For telling Mom and Dad about the professor. Well, I'm not sorry I told them, but I'm sorry if it got you in trouble."

"No, you did the right thing." Now I was the only one keeping secrets from our parents.

Logan leaned against the wall. "Mom's losing it. Big-time."

"Yeah." I leaned next to him. "Dad too. Jillian's given up."

But since neither of us knew what else to do, we said nothing more. Tristan broke through the crowd and headed over, holding three cups of punch.

And then I did know what to do.

CHAPTER TWENTY-EIGHT

I TOLD TRISTAN I wanted to skip the rest of the dance. I needed to go home, I explained, but first I needed to tell him something. With a slightly suspicious look, he suggested we go back to his house to talk.

When we got there, Melissa and Philip weren't home. Tristan was surprised, but I was glad. We had the whole house to ourselves. But really, I only wanted to be in one small part of it. We climbed the stairs to his room, then after Tristan turned on his speakers, we sat on his bed, facing each other. "Tristan," I started.

"Wait." He reached into his pocket and pulled something out. "Give me your hand."

I did, and he slid a circle of tiny pearls, set in a band of gold, on my forth finger. It fit perfectly, like it was made just for me. "It's like the ring in *Anne of Green Gables*," I exclaimed.

"I know."

"You read the book?"

"I skimmed it. I thought you'd like a ring like the one Gilbert gave Anne, so I found one. I've been carrying it around for weeks."

I held it up to the light. It was old, but clean and polished, and the gold shone. My parents never took off their wedding rings because their love would last forever. My sister never took off the gold bracelet from her Nebraska boyfriend because it reminded her that love was possible, even if it couldn't last.

Either way. "I'll never take this ring off. No matter what. I promise."

"Good. Because this is a promise ring," he said, taking my hand and kissing it. "A promise that every time I've told you that I love you, I meant it. I love you."

"I love you too."

"I don't want to lose you, Tessa. I wish…"

"Shh." He wouldn't lose me. Not if my plan worked. Locking my eyes on to his, I straddled his legs and ran my palms over his cheeks. My new ring sparkled. "Tristan."

"Hmm."

"I have an idea. A plan."

He tensed. "Okay…"

"You promised that you would keep me safe."

"Yeah." The suspicion didn't leave his voice. "And I will."

"But there's only one way you can keep me safe," I said. "And that's if I tell my parents."

Stiffening, his eyes flew open wide. "About what?"

"About how I told you everything. About your warning premonitions."

"What? No!" He slid me off his lap onto the bed, almost angrily. "You can't!" He stood, raking his hand through his hair. "You didn't tell your brother and sister already, did you?"

"Not yet. Tonight. When you take me home, we can tell them together."

"No. Absolutely not. They'll take you away. I'll lose you. You can't tell them, Tessa. You *can't*."

"My parents are so tired. My dad's headaches aren't getting better. And my mom—you know how upset she got last night. They won't be able to keep us safe much longer. But you can. You're the only one who can. You can warn us if something bad is about to happen." I swallowed hard. What I was about to say would sound desperate, but I *was* desperate. "…And when we run, maybe…maybe you can come with us."

He froze, his face a mask of horror.

"I'm asking you to go into hiding with us," I said. "That's huge, I know. We'll find a way for you to keep in contact with your family."

Why wasn't he saying anything? I drew my knees to my chin. "It's the only way we can stay together," I said. "Us. You and me."

He paced, frantic, scraping both hands through his hair. "I need to think. Let me *think!*"

"But Tristan," I whispered, "you promised you would keep me safe."

Pity and despair chased each other across his eyes as he sat on the bed and took my face between his hands. With an anguished, guttural groan, he pressed his lips on to mine. He slid one hand behind my head, his fingers tangling in my hair, the other hand sliding down my neck, my bare shoulder, stopping at the ribbon around my waist, and pulled me close.

I pressed into him, tasting him, inhaling his smell of soap and spice and masculinity. But this kiss was different from all the rest. So joyless, so…final.

With a gasp I pushed him away. "You're not going to help us," I said, pushing the words past the lump in my throat. He grabbed me before I could run away, because he knew I was about to do just that.

"Let me go." I tugged, but he held tight. "Let me go!"

"Tessa." He held on, staring hard at me until I met his eyes. "There's something I need to tell you."

I didn't want to hear it. I didn't want to hear how he thought my family's situation was hopeless, that there was no escape, that we were fated to be slain like animals. I didn't want to hear him say I was selfish for asking him to give up his family, his friends, his future.

I didn't want to hear him say he wasn't helping us because he didn't love me as much as I loved him.

But, chin trembling, I waited for him to tell me anyway. It would be easier to leave him if I heard him say it.

"I'm not who…" He stopped, took a deep breath, then let it out slowly. Closed his eyes. Then another deep breath. He opened his mouth to speak again, but before he could, his eyes flew open wide with terror.

"Get up." Tristan grabbed my arm and pulled me off the bed. "I have to get you out of here. Come on."

Heartbroken, confused, I stumbled behind him as he rushed me from the room. He peered down the stairway, then pulled me down the stairs and through the living room, to the front door. "Tristan, what were you saying? You're not who?"

"Shh." He reached for the knob, then drew his hand back. "He has a guard at the door to stop us."

And then, like an axe to the chest, the panic hit. There was only one *he.*

The living room, the entire world, spiraled as Tristan pulled me into the kitchen. "We might be able to sneak out through the patio—damn it."

A bald man with a red beard—my memory flashed an image of him sitting at the bar with two drinks when Tristan took me on our first date—stood by the patio door, blocking our exit. Two expressionless men in black jackets stood behind him.

A grin slid across his bearded face like a snake slithering in the grass. "Tessa Carson," he said. "At last. Our friend Dennis Connelly will be so happy we finally met."

This man knew my name. My real name. My last name.

I had never told Tristan my last name.

"Get out of our way, Kellan," Tristan growled. "I know what you want to do, and I won't let it happen."

Heart pounding in my ears, lungs frozen in my chest, I was unable to take my eyes off the man Tristan called Kellan. Tristan *knew* him?

Where was Dennis Connelly? I glanced around, every nerve prickling with panic. Was he in another room? Stealing in through the front door? Creeping up behind me?

"Dennis Connelly isn't here," Kellan said. "But don't worry, I'll take you to him." He snapped to the guards and pointed at me. They shoved Tristan aside and grabbed my arms.

"But this isn't the way we do things!" Tristan yelled, and lunged at Kellan. Kellan threw a punch, but Tristan darted away and Kellan swung into empty air. "You can't touch me," Tristan said. "I'll always see it coming."

Kellan chuckled. "But *she* won't."

Tristan's eyes widened. "Tessa, duck!"

But I couldn't. The guards held my arms, and Kellan swung, cuffing me hard in the face. I stifled a scream as my head jerked back, pain exploding in my cheekbone.

Tristan pounced at him. "You son of a bitch!"

"You want me to do it again, Junior?" Kellan roared, his fist flying back. "Because I will do this as many times as it takes to get you to back off."

Cheek throbbing, vision blurred by red-hot tears, I watched Tristan back away. "I'm sorry, Tessa," he mouthed.

Kellan turned to me. "Now. Just in case your father's watching…" He pinched my jaw in his fingers, forcing me to look up at him. "Good evening, Mr. Carson," he said into my eyes, my father's camera. "Connelly told me not to make this a personal thing, but it's about eight years too late for that. It's time to give yourselves up. I'm taking your daughter as insurance that you do. I'll send instructions soon." He took me from the guards and dragged me to the front door.

"Kellan! Wait!" Tristan shouted, chasing after us. "I'm going with you."

"Get rid of him," Kellan said to the guards, holding me easily as I tried to pull free. "Now, before he does something else to ruin this."

Snarling, they fell upon Tristan like hungry lions. Punching and pushing, Tristan fought them, ducking before each attempted hit. But as the blows came faster and from all directions, it became clear that his warning premonitions were only confusing him. Unable to distinguish premonition from present, he darted away from nothing, only to slam his face directly into a guard's fist. He whirled around, stumbling backwards as the other guard punched him in the gut.

Then he froze mid-punch, lips bloody, eyes wide. "No—don't—"

A millisecond later, a high-pitched whistle pierced the air. Tristan's head snapped back and his body crumpled to the tile floor with a dull thud. Heaving, the guards backed away, leaving Tristan lying motionless, eyes open, but empty.

Gripping my arm tightly with one hand, Kellan used the other to calmly slide a gun back into his jacket.

"Is he…" I whimpered. "You killed him?"

"Had to. Kid was ruining my mission." Twisting my arm up high behind my back, Kellan clamped his hand over my mouth, then half dragged, half carried me outside.

Tristan was dead.

The air, bitter and cold, stung my bare shoulders and legs. All the streetlights, shining brightly when we came here after the dance, were dark now. No neighbors would see. I tripped on my silver heels and they fell off my feet. Kellan kicked them aside into a pile of old snow.

Tristan was *dead.*

Sobbing behind the bald man's hand, I didn't resist as he propelled me, barefoot, to a black SUV in the driveway. The vehicle was identical to the car Dennis Connelly threw me in eight years ago. "Go on," Kellan said, "get in." He pushed me into the back seat.

Logan would fight. Jillian would fight. They had their psycho-kinesis. I had nothing.

But I could run.

So with my last ounce of sanity, I shifted and kicked Kellan as hard as I could with both feet, right in the chest. As he staggered back, I scrambled out of the car, then slipped past him and raced down the driveway.

Two blocks home. I could do it.

I shot myself forward, slicing through the wind like a knife. I imagined myself a racehorse, a cheetah. A falcon. A jet.

But I was used to running in daylight, breathing deep with easy rhythm, not in blackness, each breath constricted by panicked sobs. In weather-resistant jogging clothes, not a strapless silver cocktail dress. In running shoes on a clear paved path, not barefoot on a sidewalk covered with snow and puddles of icy water. With my boyfriend keeping pace at my side, smiling gently down at me, not a killer's hired hand and his guards pounding right behind me.

I was at least three steps ahead of them when I felt a tug around my middle and was jerked back, then hurled to the ground, my chin splicing open on the sidewalk.

It was the silver ribbon around my waist. They grabbed the ends and used it to rein me in.

I'd made it all the way to the end of the block. Halfway home.

A knee between my shoulder blades held me on my stomach, moaning and sobbing, cheek pressed in a puddle. Kellan pulled my hands behind my back, then snapped something cold and metal around my wrists. Handcuffs.

He hauled me up, and his hand went back over my mouth. "Connelly calls you tiny little Tessa, and he's right. You are tiny." He hoisted me under his arm, back to Tristan's house, where he shoved me into the SUV again. His hand was smeared with blood from my chin.

He jumped into the passenger seat, and the two guards sat on either side of me. I sobbed quietly, damp and shivering, as we drove away. I couldn't watch Tristan's house as it disappeared behind us. I watched the blood drip from my chin onto my dress instead.

We drove past my street. Why didn't we go to my house? Did another one of Dennis Connelly's colleagues already have my family? Or was Dennis Connelly there himself, slicing them open?

"Does she have a cell phone on her?" Kellan asked the guards. I thought about my black cell phone, hidden in the secret pocket of my dress. My white cell phone, the one that Tristan—my heart stabbed in confused pain at the memory of his lifeless body on the floor—had given me, was still in my silver handbag at his house.

Why hadn't I thought to use either of those phones while Tristan was dragging me down the stairs? I could have warned my family. This was all my fault. Dennis Connelly was killing them right now, and it was all my fault.

"Check in her dress," Kellan said.

"No," I begged.

He held up a roll of duct tape. "Not one word, or this goes over your mouth." He motioned to the guard. "Get the phone."

I shrank from the guard's touch as he lifted each layer of crinoline until he found my phone. He pulled it from the pocket and handed it to Kellan.

Except for the hum of the tires on the road and the pounding of my heart, the car was silent. I saw nothing but Tristan, lying dead on the floor, his eyes staring into nothing.

But…Tristan knew these people. He knew Kellan's name. He said, 'This isn't the way we do things.'

We.

Tristan wasn't who he said he was. Tristan was one of *them*.

Burning panic rose in my chest, nearly choking me. This was all my fault. I told Tristan everything, every secret, and he betrayed me. I groaned. Heaved.

"Kellan! She's gonna puke," the guard to my left said.

"Damn it," he sighed from the front seat. "Get a bag."

The guard opened a plastic bag under my mouth just before I vomited. The driver shouted in disgust. Unable to control myself, I retched a few more times.

"You done?" the guard asked.

Moaning and sniffling, I nodded, my head rolling back against the seat when he pushed me upright again. He opened the window and tossed the bag out, then dabbed my mouth and chin with a cloth. "I could tranquilize her."

"No," Kellan said. "If Carson can't see through her, he'll think we killed her already. We need to keep her awake until they surrender."

I closed my eyes, and tears squeezed past my lids and down my cheeks. I couldn't even wipe them away.

More silence.

Tristan was dead. Tristan betrayed me.

I forced myself to stop thinking about Tristan. He was dead. He was the past. I had to think about what was happening *now*.

My family wasn't dead. Not yet. Not if Kellan wanted them to surrender. My parents thought I was at the dance, then Tristan's house. My dad hadn't used his mobile eye on me in weeks, and the chances were slim he would do it before two in the morning, when I failed to come home.

But at least there was a chance. If he was watching through me right now, he would find a way to rescue me. I opened my eyes and glanced around to give him clues. I looked at the men in the front seat, and at the guards sitting on either side of me.

I turned my sight to the windows. The sky was dark, but the illuminated signs on the road showed me—and hopefully my father— that we'd already left Illinois and were heading north on I-90 in Wisconsin. We passed a town called Shanoka. Red Oak. Jeffersonville. Why were they taking me so far away?

Kellan turned around. "She's reading the road signs. Take that ribbon from her dress and tie it over her eyes."

Panic surged once again. "No. Please. I'll stop."

The guard blindfolded me anyway. Music, classical music, the kind Logan liked, started playing through the speakers. Kellan was playing music so my father would hear it. I was unable to show him anything through my eyes, but he would still hear what I was hearing, and know I was still alive.

"That's right, Miss Carson," Kellan said. "That's exactly what I'm doing."

Did Kellan know what I was just thinking? Could he read my mind?

Of course he could. He worked for Dennis Connelly. How could I possibly plot an escape if Kellan was telepathic?

"You can't," he said.

The fog that always held me prisoner during times of fear loomed. I surrendered to it.

Awareness returned like a slap when my cell phone rang from the front seat. It must be two in the morning. My parents knew I was gone.

CHAPTER TWENTY-NINE

KELLAN DIDN'T ANSWER my phone.

My dad would be sending out his mobile eye for me now, but because of the blindfold, he wouldn't be able to see anything. But he would still be able to hear me. "Dad!" I cried into the darkness. "Run!"

I heard a ripping noise, then felt pressure over my mouth. Duct tape. All my father would be able to hear now were my muffled sobs.

My phone stopped ringing, and a minute later, it rang once more.

It rang again, a few minutes after that.

Then it stopped. It didn't ring again.

Minutes or hours later, the SUV slowed, then stopped. I took hard, jagged breaths through my nose to get enough air. I flinched as I heard the car door open and I was pulled out. Icy wind whipped my bare skin. Was it snowing?

Stumbling, I was dragged, blind, over a sharp, cold ground. We entered a building, the sudden warmth like fire on my arms and legs. Kellan pulled me along, the patter of my bare feet barely audible over his boot-heeled strides. We might have been in an elevator at one point, going down, down, down, into an echoey place that stank of mildew and death. I staggered as he towed me behind him, barking out orders. I tried to memorize the twists and turns but quickly lost track. Men shouted. Footsteps pounded. Doors creaked open and slammed shut.

Kellan's hands gripped each of my shoulders, and he sat me on a hard chair. "Stay."

I stayed. Fear had broken me. Guilt had destroyed me.

He pulled the ribbon from my eyes, then grabbed my jaw. "I hope you're watching, Carson, because this is the only time I'll tell you," he growled, glaring into my eyes. "Follow the instructions I left in your mailbox. My men are following you. Any funny business and your daughter will pay the price. Now come and get your darling Tessa."

He peeled the tape from my lips and released my wrists from the handcuffs before pivoting on his heel and stomping away, slamming a door behind him. I collapsed into tears, head to my knees, stomach and sides aching with each sob.

Eventually I stopped. I had nothing left. Sniffling, I lifted my head and looked around. A tiny windowless room. A surveillance camera over the door. Unpainted cinderblock walls. A black metal cot. A thin sheetless mattress. A dim light bulb hanging by a wire cable from the low ceiling. A small bathroom at the back.

A cell.

I stood, supporting myself on the back of the chair until my head stopped swimming, then stumbled to the door. It had no knob. I tried to pry it open with my fingernails but the seam was airtight.

Giving up, I sank to my knees. I understood everything now.

Dennis Connelly had planned for this night for a long time. He worked with Kellan. He worked with Tristan. As soon as I told Tristan all of our secrets, he'd reported them to Dennis Connelly. And then, because my dad would see him if he came close, he had Kellan capture us.

Dennis Connelly won.

Dennis Connelly was a cruel man. A patient man.

Tristan lived in Twelve Lakes for five months before my family moved there. They'd somehow known we would come there long before we did. And then Tristan courted me for four more months. He gave me a tiny bit of hope. He made me believe he would rescue me.

But none of it was real. Tristan wasn't real. And now he was dead.

Mom, Dad, Jillian, Logan. We were going to die in a matter of hours. And it was all my fault.

Waves of dizziness and nausea crushed me. My cheekbone throbbed. I touched it lightly, feeling the tenderness and swelling. I touched my chin, and my fingers came back bloody and dirty from the eye makeup I'd cried off. My bare feet were filthy, and a little bloody. My dress, now missing the silver ribbon, was wrinkled, damp, and stained with blood and dirt. My entire body was cold.

Breath coming in rasping sobs, I crawled to the back of the cell and pressed myself into the corner. I drew my knees up, making myself a tight little ball. I stayed that way, stiff, shaking, not taking my eyes off the door.

"Dad?" He would be watching, listening. I was sure of it. "This is all my fault. It was all a trap. Tristan was a trap. You didn't trust him and I did. I told him all of our secrets. I told him *everything*. I am so sorry."

If Kellan heard me, via the surveillance camera or his telepathy, he didn't burst in to tell me to shut up. Maybe he knew there was nothing I could say to my father that would change anything now.

Except for this: "Don't come for me, Dad," I pleaded. "Tristan is dead. They killed Tristan, and they're going to kill me, whether you come or not. I can't let them kill you too. Take everyone and run. Don't come for me. Please. Don't come. Don't come. Don't come."

I grappled with the fog, begging it to stay far enough away so I could focus. I could not allow my family to come here.

Don't come, don't come, don't come.

I heard nothing but my whispered pleas.

I saw nothing but Tristan's eyes, staring blankly into mine. Empty. Dead.

Don't come. Don't come. Don't come.

CHAPTER THIRTY

*H*OURS PASSED.

I hadn't moved. The only sound was my desperate chanting. *Don't come, don't come, don't come.*

With a bang the door flew open. I cowered as Kellan and two guards strode into the cell. "It's time." He yanked me up, turned me around, and slapped handcuffs around my wrists again. "March."

I could not make my legs work. I wanted to be brave, but I could not walk myself to my own execution. Kellan grumbled and dragged me from the cell. Accompanied by the guards, he pulled me down long dim hallways, into an elevator, then another hallway. Their footsteps echoed. My bare feet made no sound, but my breath came in ragged gasps.

We reached the exit to the building and a guard opened the door. "Please," I begged Kellan. "Don't do this. Please."

He towed me outside without reply. The frigid air stole my breath. Partially hidden behind falling snow, the sun peeked over the horizon. Wind clawed at my skin, protected only by my short strapless dress, and whipped tiny snowflakes into my hair, on my shoulders, on my eyelashes. I struggled against the handcuffs in a fruitless attempt to shelter myself from the cold.

Kellan dragged me through a patch of trees, down a path of sharp white pebbles that cut my feet. The path ended at a parking lot. We waited, shivering, my feet so cold they were in flames. Men with black jackets and serious faces hovered along the perimeter of my vision, and in the trees. All of them had guns.

I heard a car approaching, and my heart sank when I saw a rusty maroon minivan. Our getaway car.

I was no longer cold. All I felt now was utter terror.

Kellan rumbled to the guards, "Get in position." He pushed me to my knees. Pressed the barrel of a gun to my head.

Two guards, guns at the ready, signaled for the car to stop. The headlights shone in my eyes, then turned off.

The guards opened the doors.

My mother sat behind the steering wheel. Her gaze traveled from my knees in the snow to my bruised and bloody face, then focused on the gun pressed against my head. "I'm sorry, Mom," I mouthed.

She glared, sharp enough to cut stone, at Kellan.

"Don't even try it, Mrs. Carson," he shouted. "I've got men stationed everywhere, and they've all got guns pointed at your daughter's head. You can take my gun, you can attack me, but if you do, you have my solemn vow that Tessa is dead."

She sobbed, then lowered her eyes in defeat.

I knew, then, my parents would surrender without a fight. Dennis Connelly's plan had worked perfectly.

"Get out of the car and put your hands on your head," Kellan commanded.

Shaking, my mother did as ordered.

"Your turn, Mr. Carson," Kellan said. My dad slumped on the passenger seat, chin to chest. A guard took him under his arm and dragged him out.

I shrieked when I saw him. Blood poured from his nose. It trickled from his mouth, dribbled from his ears, dripped from his eyes. His shirt was soaked with it.

I looked through the minivan windows for Jillian and Logan, but the car was empty.

The guards forced my parents to their knees. My mother knelt, trembling chin held high. My father collapsed with a groan, unable to lift his head, the white snow beneath him peppered with crimson.

The guards raised their guns, aimed them at my parents, held steady. An eternal second of silence, then Kellan whispered the command. One word. "Now."

The gunshots were quiet, not the loud bangs I'd expected.

But the results were the same.

Their heads jerked back, then they crumpled to the ground.

And now it was my turn.

I squeezed my eyes shut.

Kellan cocked the gun—

CHAPTER THIRTY-ONE

ND LIFTED IT from my head.

"Do it," I whispered.

No shot. No bang. No high-pitched whistle.

"Do it!"

Still no shot.

Footsteps. Running, pounding, going, coming.

Someone—tall, strong, male—pulled me to my feet. Pressed me to his chest. "It's over. You're safe."

I opened my eyes, peeked over my shoulder, peered through the fog.

Trees. Snow. Guards. Kellan.

Not over. *Not* safe.

Kellan stood over my parents' bodies, shouting orders at guards in black jackets. My mother's neck was angled obscenely; a mask of blood covered my father's face. Guards lifted their bodies onto gurneys, then wheeled them away, into the fog.

"They're dead," I informed the person holding me.

"They're not dead," he said.

"But I heard the shots. I saw them fall."

"They weren't shot with bullets. Just tranquilizers." He scooped me up, one arm under my shoulders and the other under my knees. "Let's get you inside and out of those handcuffs. Warm you up."

Through the fog, a guard with yellow spiked hair appeared. "Kellan wants the girl back underground."

"I'm taking her to the clinic."

The guard tapped his gun. "Kellan's orders."

He sighed, but following the guard, he carried me back inside and down the hallway, into an elevator. My head wobbled and fell back, and he used his shoulder to push it forward until it rested on his chest.

"He was going to kill me," I told him. "The man with the red beard. Kellan."

"He was never going to kill you. He just needed your parents to think that."

The elevator door opened, and we followed the guard down another long hallway. "Are Jillian and Logan here?" I asked.

"No. We don't know where they are."

They must be hiding. Hiding in the fog, where it was safe.

He carried me through a door and propped me on a cot. I recognized this little gray room. I'd huddled in that back corner all night.

The fog danced and swirled as he unlocked the handcuffs. From far away, I watched as he unbuttoned his shirt, then put it around my shoulders and pulled my arms through the sleeves.

Automatically drawing my hands up inside them, I looked down at the shirt and saw a little pink horse embroidered on the pocket. "My boyfriend had a shirt like this."

"I know," he said, his voice tight.

"He promised me he would keep me safe."

He paused. "I know."

"But he couldn't...he wasn't...real..."

He deflated, burying his face in my lap, layers of crinoline and silver billowing up around him. "I'm sorry, Tessa. I am so, so sorry."

I blinked, forced myself to focus through the fog.

Blue eyes, dark with guilt, stared up at me.

Tristan's eyes.

"Please, Tessa," he said. "Please forgive me. Please."

Dark and thick and rumbling, the fog swept me up and took me away.

"Tessa?"

I blinked, and the fog thinned a bit.

A woman with dark brown skin and a white lab coat knelt in front of me as I lay on the cot. Tristan stood above her, pulling his hands through his hair. The gray cinderblocks of the cell surrounded us.

"Hello, sweetheart," said the woman. "My name is Kendra Sheldon. I'm a physician. Mind if I take a look at you?"

I looked at Tristan. He nodded, so I nodded too.

She helped me sit up, then shone a light in my eyes, listened to my heart and lungs, felt my throat. Examined my cheek and chin. "I need to see what's in your mind. It won't hurt."

She placed one hand behind my neck and another hand on my forehead. "Don't move." Closing her eyes, she bowed her head. I relaxed into her gentle touch. Her hands were soft and warm, like my mom's, when she would feel my head for a fever.

But my mom was dead now.

The doctor opened her eyes. "She's not dead, sweetheart. Neither is your dad."

"Remember, Tessa?" Tristan said. "They were shot with tranquilizers. Like I was."

Tranquilizers. Not bullets. Tristan was alive, so maybe my parents were too.

I heard them talking but understood nothing. I flinched at an angry tone in Tristan's voice. "She's neutral," he was saying. "Totally defenseless. That's why Kellan could do this to her in the first place. Look for yourself."

The doctor placed her hands on my head again. So warm. A long minute of silence passed. I was about to slip away again when she spoke. "You're right. Completely neutral."

The doctor-woman talked calmly, and Tristan paced, saying angry words like *trap* and *punch* and *shot*. Then he said something that made the cell stop spinning: *Dennis Connelly*.

And I suddenly understood why we hadn't been killed yet, why my parents had been tranquilized instead of sliced open. "You're keeping us alive so he can kill us himself."

Tristan said something else, but his words disappeared into the fog. Dark and thick, it beckoned. It wanted me. I could feel it, trembling in its effort to hold itself back.

It would be easier this way anyway, if Dennis Connelly killed me while I was lost in the fog. I called it in, and let it swallow me up.

CHAPTER THIRTY-TWO

*N*OTHING.

Darkness.

Whimpering.

Sobbing.

Shrieking.

Screaming.

Screaming.

SCREEEEEEAAAAAAMING!

A prick in my arm.

Then nothing again.

CHAPTER THIRTY-THREE

HE FOG EBBED and flowed, bringing me along with it, sending me tumbling from the depths of unconscious nothingness to the edges of painful awareness and back again.

Eventually, slowly, the fog released me. Silently I protested, calling it back to me. I wanted to stay in the fog. The fog kept me safe.

But the fog retreated, leaving me alone.

Orphaned.

Deceived.

Betrayed.

I remembered.

He was lying with me. Holding me. Tristan Walker, the boy who handed me over to Dennis Connelly.

He tensed even before I did, his eyes shooting open. "Tessa, don't—"

With a shrieking gasp, I jerked out of his arms. Scrambled off the cot. I tripped and landed hard on the concrete floor, then clambered to my feet. Stumbled to the door.

He leaped off the cot and in two strides stood over me.

My fingers fumbled for the knob, but there *was* no knob, no way to open it. My eyes darted from wall to wall. No windows. No air. No escape. I was trapped, trapped in this tiny gray cell, a fly caught in a web.

The spider reached for the fly. "I'm not going to hurt you, Tessa. I love you."

At those words, the cold, hollow fear inside me faded, churned, curdled, spun and grew, spitting and howling, into a solid mass of rage that erupted in an explosive roar. *"Liar!"*

He flinched and backed away.

Teeth bared, I stormed over to him. "You used me. You made me fall in love with you. You made me tell you everything. And then you delivered us straight to Denn—" I couldn't say it, even now. "Straight to *him!*"

After each sentence I punched him. He bowed his head and put his hands behind his back, accepting my abuse.

"You can believe me when I say I can keep you safe. A lie!" I mocked his words. *"My mother had a dream about you.* Another lie!" I hit him, as hard as I could. *"Every time I've told you that I love you, I meant it.* All. A. Lie!" I yanked the pearl promise ring off my finger and whipped it at him. It ricocheted off his chest and flew across the cell.

The memory of pleading with him, of *begging* him, to go into hiding with my family to protect us, when all along he was plotting against us, made me sick. "Get out of here. Get out!"

He brought his eyes, red and pained, to mine. "No."

Dizzy with rage, I ran to the door and kicked it, pounded on it. "Let me out of here! Let me *out!*"

When no one came, I turned back to Tristan, hands in fists. "Tell them to open that door. Make them let me out of here!" I punched him again and again, unable to stop.

He stood there, taking each hit, barely even swaying. That angered me even more. I snarled. "Fight back!" I wanted to fight. I wanted him to hit me. I needed to feel physical pain, anything that would make me forget the memory of those men shooting my parents. Anything that would extinguish this agony, this guilt, this heartbreak.

"Hit me back!" I pounded on him, shrieking with each strike. "Hit me!" I shoved him hard, trying to provoke him, but he stood there, looking at me with wounded and guilty eyes.

I wailed and pulled my arm back, intent on slamming my fist into the cinderblock wall.

He grabbed my wrist before I could swing and held it tight. "I'm not going to hit you, Tessa," he said. "I'm not going to let you hurt yourself either. You were about to break every bone in your hand. If you don't calm down, they will come in and sedate you. I see it happening." He tapped his temple. "And you're going to kick me now, but it'll hurt you more than it hurts me."

I kicked him anyway, and howled in pain as my bare toes collided with his shin. "Stop it! Stop using your precognition on me!"

For the first time in my life I understood how my mother felt while caught in a fit of despair, and I drew up every ounce of will in my body and roared, picturing Tristan flying across the cell and slamming into the wall.

But he didn't move.

Because I was not psychokinetic.

Because I was nothing.

I sank to my knees, sobbing. "Let them come. Let them sedate me. Please."

He knelt next to me and smoothed my hair. "No."

"How could you do this to me, Tristan?" I buried my face in my hands.

He gathered me in his arms and carried me to the cot, then lay me down and held me against his chest until my breathing slowed.

I wanted to pull away, but I also wanted to stay in his arms. I tried to pretend we were lying in his bed in Twelve Lakes, that nothing in the past few hours had really happened, and he was just comforting me from a nightmare.

But I couldn't pretend.

"Please don't touch me," I said.

Slowly, he unwrapped his arms. Sat up. Put his head in his hands. I slid as far away from him as I could and drew my knees under my chin. I shivered. My arms and shoulders were bare. I had a vague memory of a white shirt—something about a little pink horse?—but all I wore now was my silver dress.

Tristan slid a duffle bag from under the cot and pulled out a bright blue hoodie. "Here. Put this on."

I slid it over my head. It was thick and soft and warm. The sleeves were longer than my fingertips. The soapy, fresh scent reminded me of the Tristan I knew in Twelve Lakes.

"If I ask you something," I said, "will you tell me the truth?"

"I swear to God, Tessa, I will never lie to you again."

"Are my parents really alive?"

"Yes."

"Where are they?"

"Down the hall in high security."

"Can I see them?"

"I don't know. Probably not."

"What about Jillian and Logan?"

"Nobody knows where they are. We think they slipped away on foot before your parents drove up here."

Good. At least two of us were safe. My parents should have escaped with them. But they came to save me and drove into an ambush.

I leaned my head against the wall. Anger, such an alien feeling for me anyway, was ineffective. I'd lost control. And fear just paralyzed me. That strange mental fog numbed me and made everything disappear. But if I could keep the fog at the level it was now, maybe I could figure out what was happening.

I'd always known Dennis Connelly would find us, but not like this. I had assumed he worked alone in his mission to eliminate my family. But he had precognitives, telepaths, and guards by the dozen under his command. An army. An empire.

We never had a chance.

"If you knew we were coming to Twelve Lakes," I said, "why didn't you just take us the day we moved in? Why did you wait so long?" I wanted to add, *Why did you make me fall in love with you first?* But I bit off the words before they left my mouth.

"You evaded us so many times before, and we never knew how you knew we were coming. We took it slow this time so we could learn exactly what you could do and what you couldn't. We had to figure out the best way to apprehend your parents so no one else would get hurt."

"*I* got hurt, Tristan."

With a guilty look, he reached for my cheek, but I swatted his hand away. Kellan punching me was not the kind of hurt I was talking about.

"So you coerced me into telling you exactly what you needed to know," I said. "What did you do, take a class called Advanced Interrogation Methods or something?"

He nodded, with pride. "I went through training, yes. Interrogation and trust-building techniques, things like that. You still took a lot longer to open up than we thought you would."

Was that supposed to make me feel better? "Where is he?"

"Kellan?" Tristan shrugged. "He's probably around here somewhere. Or maybe he went home. I don't really care, as long as he stays away from you."

"Not Kellan. Where is…" I closed my eyes. Took a breath.

Licked my lips, swallowed.

But I still couldn't say Dennis Connelly's name out loud. "Where is *he?*"

Tristan understood now. "*He* is probably at home. He came to check on you a couple times."

"He did? He was here? Right here?" I pictured him standing above my unconscious body, cackling with victory. "Why didn't he kill me?"

Tristan sighed, a long, slow, hopeless sigh. "Because we don't kill people, Tessa."

I shook my head. *Tristan* might not kill people, but the people he worked with did. He reached for me again, to comfort me perhaps, but I turned away.

Last night—was it just last night?—we were dancing at Winterball. We were in love.

But Tristan never loved me. He'd been lying the whole time. He'd been lying to me since the day we met.

"Did you know this was going to happen?" I asked him, gesturing around the cell.

"Not like this."

"But you knew my family was going to be captured."

"My assignment was to learn if anyone in your family had psychic abilities. That's all. I didn't know what was really going on until a few days ago, and even then, I didn't know that Kellan was so vindictive that he'd kidnap you."

"You still lied to me the entire time."

"I only lied when I had to. You, of all people, should understand why lies are necessary."

I huffed. "I lied to protect my family. You lied to destroy us."

He gave a slow, reluctant nod.

"Just leave, Tristan. Get out of here."

"I'm not leaving you."

Tears squeezed from my eyes, and I turned my head so he wouldn't see them. "Is that doctor coming back?" I asked.

"She came back a couple times already. Don't you remember screaming?"

I was screaming? I never, ever, *ever* screamed. That was a rule. But my voice was hoarse. My throat felt raw, like I'd swallowed razor blades.

I'd broken the rule: I screamed. And now, just like my mom said, Dennis Connelly was coming.

"We couldn't get you to stop," Tristan said. "Dr. Sheldon had to sedate you. She came back again to bring you some clothes. Amy and Heath came with her. Amy healed your cuts and bruises. You had some frostbite on your feet. She healed that too."

"Who are Amy and Heath?"

"Melissa and Philip."

"Your aunt and uncle?"

"They're not really my aunt and uncle."

I succumbed to sobs again.

CHAPTER THIRTY-FOUR

"WHAT TIME IS it?" I asked a while later. Neither of us had moved from the cot.

"It's about three in the morning."

I did a quick calculation. My parents had arrived just as the sun came up. I'd been asleep almost a whole day.

And not just sleeping. Apparently I'd been screaming, too.

I sniffled and rubbed my eyes. My fingers came back stained with dirt and makeup. My whole body felt dirty. Contaminated. Used. "Can I ...am I allowed to take a shower?"

"Of course." Tristan took my elbow to help me stand, but I jerked my arm away. He sighed and handed me a plastic bag from under the cot. "Here are the clothes from Dr. Sheldon. There's soap and stuff in the bathroom."

I took the bag and, without another glance at him, closed the bathroom door behind me. I shed his hoodie, then my dress, which was now more filthy gray than sparkly silver.

A dingy white curtain on a flimsy metal rod hid the minuscule shower. I turned the water hot, much hotter than comfortable, and forced myself to stand under the burning stream. A wire basket stocked with shower supplies hung from a hook. I washed myself, wishing the washcloth was sandpaper, scrubbing hard, in between my fingers and toes and every square inch of skin, even my cheekbone and chin. My bruises and cuts were completely healed.

The scars on my stomach were still there.

I turned the temperature all the way up, as hot as it could go. The scorching water, and the fog I had called in with it, almost kept my mind off the fact I was showering in the lair of the man who had given me those five jagged, twisting scars.

The fog receded when the door opened, and Tristan knocked on the door frame. "You okay?"

"Go away, Tristan," I said as icily as I could. The water, I realized, had become cold as ice too.

Enduring the freezing water, I called the fog in deeper, and deeper still. But that made the world spin and fade.

I sent it away, but that made everything too sharp, too clear, too painful.

I brought it back, just a little. Then a little more. Then a little less.

Perfect.

After turning off the water, I forced myself to stand in the cold air, wet and shivering, before drying off. Despite subjecting myself to the temperature extremes, I was able to keep the fog under control—just heavy enough to keep myself from feeling too deeply, but light enough so I wouldn't lose myself again.

Inside the bag from Dr. Sheldon were crisply laundered gray cotton pants and a loose top, white underwear, white socks, and white tennis shoes. A prison uniform.

I pulled the drawstring tight to keep the pants from falling, but I still had to cuff the bottoms so I wouldn't trip over them. I put on the socks, and even they turned gray on the bottom with my first steps on the concrete floor.

Over the gray top, I slid Tristan's blue hoodie back on. It was large enough to hide in. The logo on the front read *Lilybrook High School Tennis* in faded white letters.

Tristan was on the tennis team at his old school. Lilybrook High. That could be the first true thing I knew about him.

And now I had to learn the truth about everything else, so I could find my parents and get us out of here.

I stepped out into the cell. Tristan sat on the cot with his head in his hands.

"Tristan, what is this place?"

CHAPTER THIRTY-FIVE

RISTAN PATTED THE cot, inviting me to sit next to him. I sat, but as far away from him as I could. His arm wavered in the air for a moment, like he didn't know what to do with it if it wasn't around me. Finally he just let it drop.

"What is this place?" I asked again.

"Most people think we're a research facility called the Northern Wisconsin Science Laboratory," he said. "But really, we're the Agency for Psionic Research. The APR. We're funded by the federal government."

"What's 'psionic?'"

"That's what we call people with psychic abilities. We find them around the country and invite them to come here. There's a lab up on the ground floor where we study them."

"You want to study my family? Like, test us?" That couldn't be right. "You didn't *invite* us, Tristan. You hunted us. You forced us to come here."

"We also," he said, rubbing his eyes, "have a division called Investigations. That's where I work. I'm an agent. Well, a junior agent. This was my first case."

"So you're not really a high school student," I said.

"No."

I exhaled hard. Tristan wasn't even in high school. "How old are you?"

"Eighteen," he said. "I postponed college to stay on the case."

Only a year older than I thought. That wasn't too bad. "What's your real name?"

"My real name is Tristan. My alias was supposed to be Mason, but Amy messed up the first day. She introduced me as Tristan to the neighbors, so I had to stick with it."

I was glad his real name was Tristan. It comforted me, somehow. But it didn't change anything. He was still a liar, still working for Dennis Connelly.

That made me think of something else. "What's *his* real name?"

"You mean Dennis Connelly?"

I nodded.

"That is his real name. Recruiters didn't start using aliases until after they ran across your family."

Funny, that's when we started using aliases too. "Did your parents really move to Malaysia?"

"No."

"Do they know you're working for a killer?" I said it with a slight growl, hoping to rattle him and break his calm demeanor.

It didn't work. He sighed and hung his head. "Dennis Connelly is not a killer. He doesn't even work here anymore. He was on the recruitment team, then he was executive director. He retired last year."

"But he kills people, Tristan. You said this place is funded by the federal government. Someone from the government sent him to kill my family. My father saw him kill the people who tried to help us," I said. "You don't know as much about that man as you think you do."

"Tessa." He looked at me then, with eyes so filled with pity and sympathy it sucked all the air from my lungs. I was suddenly very, very sure that whatever he said next would shatter every truth I'd ever known.

My body grew numb.

And then he said it. "Dennis Connelly isn't the killer. Your parents are."

CHAPTER THIRTY-SIX

"ID YOU HEAR me, Tessa?" Tristan said.

I heard him. He'd just told me that Dennis Connelly wasn't the killer, my *parents* were.

I heard him say it, and I tried to tell him he was wrong, that he was lying, but shock and fury and disgust formed a block in my throat, choking off my words, cutting off my air.

"Some of what your parents told you is true," Tristan said. "Your father was a journalist. He used his press pass to meet politicians and businessmen. Your mom was the special events director at a hotel. She knew when politicians and important people were coming. Your dad used his press pass to meet them too. Then he'd watch all of them with his remote vision. If your dad saw them do something unethical, your parents would contact them anonymously and demand money from them. That's how they made so much money. Blackmail. Not writing a newspaper column and planning parties."

I blinked again, slid farther away from him. He was lying. He had to be.

And yet he continued. The putrid, rotten lies, each one worse than the last, came spewing from his mouth like vomit.

"If the victims refused to pay, if they called the police or started investigating who was blackmailing them, your mother would use her PK to give them heart attacks or brain aneurysms. She'd kill them and make it look like a car accident, or illness or suicide."

I stared at him and tried to let the words sink in.

But they wouldn't.

Because they were lies. All of them. Every single one.

"I'm so sorry." He reached for me, but I slapped him away and scrambled off the cot.

"You said you would never lie to me again," I seethed through clenched teeth. "And that is the most vicious lie I've ever heard."

"I'm not lying. I wish I were."

"That man came to our house to kill us," I said. "My father watched him slice open two people with his mind."

"Dennis Connelly has one psionic ability, and that's telepathy. He cannot slice people open with his mind," Tristan said. "Your parents built him up to be some kind of all-powerful, indestructible super-villain. They demonized him to keep you scared and obedient."

I cringed. That lie was the worst of all. "They would never do that to us."

"We have evidence."

"No, *I* have evidence." I yanked my shirt up. "That man, that monster, did this to me."

He touched his fingers to the scars and I flinched. "He didn't even know you were cut until I told him last week. He thinks you must have gotten cut on broken glass when your father pulled you from the car window."

"Does he deny trying to kidnap me too?" I tried to growl it, to sound strong and menacing, but my voice came out high and uncontrolled.

"He did put you in his car," he said. "But he wasn't kidnapping you."

"How is locking me in his car not kidnapping?"

"Eight years ago," he said, "one of our Sensors was in Washington, trying to find psionic people. Doing his job. He walked by your dad at a coffee shop and sensed he had some kind of psionic ability. So the APR sent Dennis and his recruitment team to your house to talk to him. If they found evidence of psionics, they planned to invite him to the APR for testing and possible employment. While Dennis was outside talking to you, his team went inside to talk to your parents. He put you in his car when he heard what was happening in your house."

I crossed my arms and narrowed my eyes. "And what, exactly, was happening in my house?"

"Your parents were killing his partners, Tessa. He was just trying to keep you safe. Then he went inside to help his team, but it was too late. Your parents attacked him, too. Your mom gave him a heart attack. He barely escaped alive."

The cell fell silent.

His words echoed in my mind, each one like a punch to the chest. I stumbled to the corner and sank to the floor as waves of dizziness brought back the fog. "Liar," I managed to squeak, before the fog took me away.

"Tessa?" Tristan's voice broke through the fog.

I didn't move. I wanted—needed—to stay in the fog for a while longer.

"I need to tell you something else."

"No more."

"I don't want you to think I'm holding anything back."

"I can't handle anything else right now. Please."

"Okay. When you're ready."

We hadn't moved in hours, it seemed. I remained huddled in a ball in the corner. Tristan sat on the edge of the cot, elbows on his knees, head hung low.

Finally he took a deep breath. "Tess—"

"Don't say it."

"I need to—"

"I know what you're going to say, and I don't want to hear it. Please don't say it."

But whether he said it or not, I already knew what he wanted to tell me. Forbidding him to say the words wasn't going to change it.

I gave a stuttery sigh of defeat. "He's your father, isn't he?"

Please, please tell me I'm wrong.

But he didn't. He just nodded. "Dennis Connelly is my father."

Perhaps knowing I was about to cry, he opened his arms in an offer of comfort. I shook my head and pulled myself into a tighter ball, and cried alone.

"How did you know?" Tristan asked from the cot when my tears had slowed to sniffles.

I sniffled one more time. "Back in your kitchen. Kellan called you

Junior."

"Ah."

I put my head on my knees. I just wanted to go back in time, back to Winterball. I wanted to go back to the running path. Back to lounging on his bed with his head on my stomach.

But there was no going back. I was here, locked in a cell with the son of Dennis Connelly.

Tristan was the son of the man who tried to kill me. The son of the man who'd chased my family out of thirteen homes in eight years. The son of the man who would soon come and finish the job he started.

I was in love with Tristan *Connelly*.

"Oh God…" Dennis Connelly's son leaped off the cot and scooped me up, rushing me to the bathroom and bending me over the toilet just in time. He knew I was going to throw up before I did.

He held my hair back as I vomited for the second time since Kellan kidnapped me.

No, the third. I had a flash of screaming, screaming so long and so hard I choked and threw up all over his white shirt with the pink embroidered horse, and started screaming again.

But now I was too tired, too broken, to scream anymore. I coughed the last of the vomit from my mouth, and he handed me a plastic cup of water from the sink. "Sip and spit."

I did, and he guided me back to the main cell. He tried to bring me to the cot, but I pulled away and slunk back to my corner. "Just leave, Tristan. I don't want you here."

He retreated, but only to sit on the cot again. "I'm not leaving you."

CHAPTER THIRTY-SEVEN

HE DOOR TO the cell slid open and I startled, lowering the fog, certain it was Dennis Connelly. But it was just a guard, holding a plastic tray. A gun hung in a holster on his belt. I'd seen him before somewhere; his yellow spiky hair looked familiar. I raised the fog again but kept it close.

Spiky Hair nodded to the tray. "Breakfast."

Breakfast. It was the next day. I'd been in this cell for over twenty-four hours.

Tristan took the tray and placed it on the cot. "Thanks."

"Congrats on the mission, Connelly," Spiky Hair said. "Nice job." His gaze flickered to me in the corner.

Tristan's face reddened. "Thanks," he mumbled.

The guard left, the door sealing itself shut behind him. Tristan held out a plate for me, but I shook my head. "How do I know it's not poisoned?" I was imprisoned by a killer, after all.

He took a large scoop of scrambled eggs from one plate and ate it, then did the same with the other. "Nope. Not poisoned."

I narrowed my eyes at him and moved from the floor up to the chair. He placed the plate on my lap. I looked with distaste at the eggs, toast, and orange slices. "Are my parents getting the same meal?" Mom would hate this breakfast. Rubbery yellow eggs and white bread. She would've used egg whites and whole grain.

"They're probably still unconscious. It takes a long time to neutralize someone."

"What does that mean?"

"Their psionic abilities are being taken away."

"You mean, so they can't escape?"

"And so they can't hurt anyone." He looked pointedly at me, as if silently adding, *So your mother can't fly you into a wall anymore.*

I blinked. "She didn't mean to hurt me, Tristan."

He swallowed his eggs. "I know."

"She would never hurt anyone. There's no way my parents did any of the things you said."

He said nothing to that.

In a display of loyalty to my mother, I pushed aside the eggs and toast, and ate only the orange slices. But because I was weak in both body and spirit, I betrayed her again by eating the eggs. "Does it hurt to be neutralized?"

"No. It's like blowing out a candle. In fact, your dad's headaches will probably stop."

That, at least, was a tiny bit comforting. But my mom's PK was as much a part of her life as me, or air. She couldn't survive without it, or want to.

Thank God Jillian and Logan weren't here. My parents were right to send them away before driving up here. They wouldn't want to live without their PK either.

The cell door opened again and I jolted, my fork clanging to the floor, and again I lowered the fog. A dark-skinned woman in a lab coat entered, a thick green binder in one arm. "Hello, Tessa. I'm Dr.

Sheldon. Do you remember me?"

"Yes, ma'am." She was the one who'd put her palm on my forehead and looked inside my mind. She was gentle. Warm. "Can I see my mom and dad now?"

She tilted her head. "Sweetheart, do you understand why your parents are here?"

"No." I didn't understand anything anymore.

"I told her," Tristan said. "But she won't believe me."

Dr. Sheldon clucked. "I wouldn't want to believe something like that about my parents either." She patted the binder. A series of letters and numbers was printed on the spine: CARS0520. "But we have evidence."

So Dr. Sheldon was a liar too.

"Any news about Tessa's brother and sister?" Tristan asked. "Did we find them yet?"

They were still looking for Jillian and Logan?

"Let's see." She opened the binder and flipped through the pages. "Their parents gave them all their cash before sending them away on foot. We have an agent watching the house in case they return, but so far no one knows where they are."

"We'll find them for you, Tessa," Tristan said. "I promise."

Impossible. Jillian and Logan were too smart to go back to our house. They knew better than to return to Twelve Lakes. With all our money, and without me to ruin everything, they could run forever.

"Poor kids," Dr. Sheldon said. "They must be very frightened."

Terrified, I was certain. Jillian was probably disguising her terror with anger. Logan was probably not bothering to hide it. But the important thing was they weren't imprisoned in this horrid APR place, being neutralized. As long as they weren't here, they would be okay.

Dr. Sheldon held up her palms. "Stand up for a minute. I need to examine you again." She placed one hand on my forehead and one on the back of my neck, then closed her eyes.

I tried to think about nothing. Just empty space. Fog. As nice as she was, I didn't want her inside my mind. Tristan was being nice too, and I couldn't trust him.

After a few minutes, she took my chin in her hand, a frown on her face and alarm in her eyes. "I don't know what it is that I'm seeing deep in that mind of yours, Tessa, but I don't like it. You have me very worried. I'm afraid you'll have to stay here for a while."

She made some notes in the file. "Completely neutral," she muttered with a pitiful shake of her head, then closed the binder and tucked it in the crook of her arm. With a warning to Tristan to watch me carefully, she left, taking the binder with her.

Hearing all those awful lies about my parents, and the guilt over causing all this misery to everyone I loved, made me despise myself. Before Tristan could even offer a comforting word, I went into the bathroom and shut the door behind me. It was the only place I could go to escape from him.

I shed my clothes and stepped behind the shower curtain, then started the water. I washed myself again, scrubbing as hard as I had last night.

When I was five and Jillian was six, we were on a softball team. The Dragonflies. We were the best team in the league, and my sister was the star player, no surprise. She hit every ball. It wasn't until *I* hit three home runs in a single game that our parents realized Jillian had been using her psychokinesis to control the ball the entire season. They made her stop. It wasn't fair, they said. It wasn't right.

My parents were ethical. Moral. Honest.

They had not blackmailed anyone. They had not murdered anyone.

They had not lied to us this whole time.

They had *not*.

I ran my fingers over the scars on my belly.

Shattered glass.

No.

CHAPTER THIRTY-EIGHT

RESSED IN MY gray prison uniform, I shuffled out to the cell. I stopped short at the sight of Melissa and Philip—no, Amy and Heath—standing with Tristan. Instantly on guard, I lowered the fog, just a bit. Amy and Heath had been in on Kellan's plot the whole time. Any kindness they'd shown me in Twelve Lakes was fake.

"Oh, Sarah," Amy said, wringing her hands. "We're so sorry."

"Her name is Tessa," Tristan said.

"That's right. Tessa." She brushed my cheek and I flinched. "I just want to check your injuries."

"I'm fine," I said, stepping away.

"I won't hurt you," she said. "I'm a healer. And Heath's a safeguard. He feels awful he couldn't protect you from Kellan. We both do. He sent us away Friday night and said he didn't need us anymore. Neither of us knew he was going to do what he did."

Heath, sighing regretfully, shook his head.

"What's a safeguard?" I asked.

"A safeguard is a bodyguard," Tristan said, "except he protects people from physical *and* psionic harm. That's why your dad couldn't see me with his remote vision."

So Tristan wasn't one of the five percent who were immune to my father's mobile eye after all. No wonder Heath was always around.

Heath clapped Tristan on the back.

"Hey, man. Thanks," Tristan said, shaking Heath's left hand with an awkward laugh. The knuckles on Heath's right hand were bruised and swollen.

After a few moments of uncomfortable silence, Amy said, "We'll leave you alone. We're just glad you're safe now, Sarah—I mean, Tessa."

I didn't reply, and they turned away. The door sealed shut behind them.

"That day, when I pushed you away from the falling tree?" Tristan said. "The tackle fractured your collarbone. Amy healed it."

I remembered how she ran her fingers over my collarbone as I sat on her kitchen table, and how the pain had disappeared. "Oh."

"And Heath was so upset about what Kellan did to you, he punched him."

"When?"

"While you were sleeping yesterday. He safeguarded his thoughts, then walked up to Kellan in the lunchroom and punched him in the face. Dislocated his jaw. The healers fixed Kellan right away, but Heath won't let anyone heal his hand, not even Amy. He's proud of those bruises."

Heath had never even spoken in my presence. The idea of that sweet, shy man punching Kellan in my defense filled me with vengeful glee.

Tristan's duffle bag lay open on the floor, another of his hoodies folded on top, a white one with royal blue lettering and a lightning bolt. On impulse, I slipped it over my gray prison top.

"You can make holes in the cuffs if you want," Tristan said. "You did on my other one."

"I did? Sorry." I looked down at the sleeves. I'd already started rubbing the fabric with my thumbnails.

"It's okay. I like it when you do that."

"Lilybrook High Lightning," I said, reading the sweatshirt.

"I went from the Lilybrook High Lightning to the TLC Thunderclouds."

"You told me you were from Milwaukee."

"Milwaukee is about four hours south of here."

I traced the blue letters with my fingertip. "Are all the kids in Lilybrook undercover agents?"

He laughed. "No. Most kids in Lilybrook are just regular kids. But the people who work here at the APR are all psionic, and usually their kids are too. We can work here as interns once we're in high school. I was interning in the lab back in March when Kellan asked me to help him out with his new case. He wouldn't tell me any details, just that I'd have to live in a town called Twelve Lakes and wait for a family to move in, then befriend the kids to find out if anyone in the family had psionic abilities. I accepted the job. Being an investigator for the APR was all I've ever wanted to do."

"What about school?"

"I was a senior just weeks away from graduation. I had straight A's and I already had enough credits to graduate. The APR arranged it so I could finish my senior year by correspondence. But I had to enroll as a junior at TLC because we didn't know how long we'd have to wait for your family. When you still didn't come by the end of summer, I had to postpone college and be a senior again." He sank to the cot, chin in hand. "Taking this job was the hardest thing I've ever done."

I refused to be impressed or to feel sorry for him. "I'm sure your father gave you lots of advice."

He shook his head. "He was against it, even though Kellan told him it was a basic fact-finding mission and he'd arranged for a safeguard and a healer to be my chaperones. Combined with my warning premonitions, I'd be perfectly safe. My dad was still against it, but I was eighteen, so ultimately it was my decision."

That's right—Tristan was eighteen. He'd graduated high school. "There's still so much I don't know about you," I said, "and you know everything about me."

"That's not completely true," he said. "I didn't know your last name until Friday night." He said my full name aloud. "Tessa Carson."

"Tessa Lynne Carson," I added.

"Really? Your initials are TLC? Like the school?"

"Yep. 'You'll find TLC at TLC'," I quoted Twelve Lakes Community High School's slogan. "I guess you really did."

He laughed. "TLC. That's amazing."

"Why?"

"My middle name is Lawrence."

"Tristan Lawrence… Oh. We have the same initials." I was quiet for a moment, and then I decided to be cruel, because for a moment I'd forgotten he was the enemy and his kindness was just another one of his tricks. "But I think for you, TLC stands for terrible, loathsome, and contemptible."

The light left his eyes, and he sank to the cot. "I hope one day you'll change your mind about that," he murmured.

I just shook my head. Never.

"You want me to believe my parents are criminals," I said to Tristan after sitting in silence for a while. "That they blackmailed and murdered people."

"Yes."

"You want me to believe that Denn—that *he* isn't going to kill us."

"Yes."

"You want me to believe the complete opposite of everything I've known for the last eight years."

"Yes."

"Even after everything Kellan did. Punching me, kidnapping me, holding me as bait. He made me watch his men shoot my parents. After all that, you still want me to believe that *my parents* are the bad guys."

Sighing, he ran his hand through his hair. "Yes."

"If I believe you," I said, "that means my parents were lying to me."

"They were," he said.

"If I believe my parents, that means *you're* lying to me."

"I'm not lying to you."

"But you did lie to me, Tristan *Walker*."

He winced. "Yes."

"So the only thing I can prove is that *you* are the liar."

He slowly nodded his head. "What can I do to make things better?"

Nothing he did now could ever make things better. He lied to me. Used me. Betrayed me. Tristan was the son of Dennis Connelly. Killer's blood coursed through his veins with every beat of his heart.

I studied him from the corner of my eye. Legs wide, shoulders slumped, elbows on knees. Head down. Dejected.

He turned his head to look at me, his eyes wide and sorrowful.

He was desperate as well.

I licked my lips. Tristan had used me; now I was going to use him. "There is something you can do."

"Anything."

"I need you to help me get that green binder Dr. Sheldon had."

"Why?"

"Whatever evidence you claim to have is in that binder. I want to see it." And then I would prove there *was* no evidence. Once I convinced him of that, I would get him to help my parents and me escape.

And then I would leave him behind forever.

He eyed me for a long moment, and I offered him a tiny smile.

"Okay," he said. "Tonight. After everyone has gone home."

CHAPTER THIRTY-NINE

THE ALARM ON Tristan's phone rang at exactly eleven o'clock that night. "Ready?"

Holding my breath, I nodded.

He rang the buzzer on the intercom, and a few moments later a low voice crackled through the speakers. "Yeah?"

"We need a guard down here."

"What's wrong?"

"Nothing. I just need a guard to let me out."

The intercom went silent, and Tristan buzzed it again. "I'm not a prisoner. I work here. I'm an agent."

"What's an agent doing locked up in the Underground?"

"That's classified."

No reply from the intercom.

Tristan sighed. "You don't know who I am, do you?"

"…No."

"I'm Tristan Connelly."

"So?"

Licking his lips, he glanced at me. "So, my dad is Dennis Connelly."

I tried not to show him how much that upset me as the intercom clicked off.

When a few minutes passed without it clicking back on, I said, "He's not coming."

Tristan gave me a knowing smirk. "He's coming."

A few minutes later, a guard with a thin, weasely face and a stubbly attempt at a mustache opened the door. Tristan took my hand and stepped into the doorway. "Whoa, not so fast," the guard said. "Warden says you can leave whenever you want." His eyes landed on me. "But the girl stays."

Tristan tightened his grip on my hand. "That's right. She stays with me."

Weasel Face widened his stance, folding his arms across his chest. "I can't let her out. Warden said it's Doc Sheldon's orders."

Tristan growled and fisted his hand, but I stepped in front of him. Intimidation wasn't going to get me that binder, not with this guard. I lowered my chin and looked up at him with doe eyes, attempting to appear as docile and meek as possible. "Please, sir?" I begged Weasel Face, who couldn't be more than three years older than me. "You're the only one who can help us."

He looked nervously down the hall and back to me. I made my lower lip tremble. With one more glance down the hall, he stepped back, waving us out. Tristan squeezed my hand, and we rushed from the cell before the guard could change his mind.

I'd been in the hallway three times before but had never seen it. I'd either been blindfolded, paralyzed by fear, or lost in the fog. This time I purposely raised the fog, enough to clear my mind and focus on every detail, planning an escape route.

The hallway was long, narrow, full of turns. Musty and damp. Gray metal doors, all sealed shut, lined the cinderblock walls.

My parents were behind one of those doors.

Strutting beside us, Weasel Face watched me with a suspicious frown. I blinked innocently at him.

We reached the elevator. "Wait for us here," Tristan told the guard.

He snorted and rested his hand on his tranq gun. "No way."

The elevator doors slid open silently, and the three of us entered. We rode up four floors and arrived at ground level.

We dashed close to the walls. This hallway was lined with closed doors as well, but instead of solid steel, they were made of heavy paneled wood and had brass knobs. Our shadows stretched before us as the hall disappeared into complete blackness at the far end. From somewhere came the faint tapping of booted footsteps—guards on patrol, perhaps. I tried to breathe slowly through my nose, sure they would be able to hear each exhale.

We neared a door illuminated in red from the word EXIT hanging above it. Tristan seized my arm, pulled me in tight. Weasel Face noticed and gripped his gun.

They were probably right to suspect I'd try to burst through that door and flee, but running hadn't even occurred to me. I needed that binder. I needed Tristan to know the truth, that my parents were innocent. I marched past the exit without a second glance.

Tristan stopped at the last door in the hall. "This is Dr. Sheldon's office," he whispered, and turned the knob. "Locked. Damn." He turned to Weasel Face. "Do you have the key?"

"Nope."

Before I could even begin to be disappointed, Weasel Face bent his fingers into a claw and stared hard at the knob. He swiveled his hand in the air, and a few seconds later I heard a tiny click.

"Nice," Tristan said. "You're psychokinetic?"

"Kinda. Ferrokinetic. I can manipulate metal." He pointed to his belt buckle, which was twisted into a big, stylized G. "I just made this tonight," he said. "It's for the Green Bay Packers."

I gave him a whispered, awed *ooooo*, like I was amazed by his handiwork. He beamed and pushed the door open.

Tristan ushered me inside. A computer monitor was on and gave the room an eerie blue glow. The monitor sat on a utilitarian desk, cluttered with papers, pens, and old cups of coffee. A garbage can stuffed to overflowing sat in the corner. Black filing cabinets lined the back wall. Stacked haphazardly on top of the filing cabinet was a pile of manila folders with papers sticking out, old date books, and a vase holding a dusty silk flower.

And balanced precariously on the very edge of the cabinets were four green binders. I could just make out the code running down the spine of the top one: CARS0520.

Tristan and I glanced at each other, then he turned to Weasel Face. "So, buddy, where you from? Who recruited you?"

"I'm from Sioux Falls," the guard said. "Ted Rigby found me. I was just working for a mechanic, doing oil changes and pretending to pound out dents. Now I'm here. Wild."

"Yeah, Rigby's great. How long have you been working here?"

While Tristan kept Weasel Face occupied, I grabbed the binder, then slipped it under my top, grateful I was wearing Tristan's huge sweatshirt. Dr. Sheldon's office was so messy, hopefully she would just assume she'd misplaced the binder. I put a confused look on my face. "I don't see it."

Tristan played along, pretending to look around the office. "I don't either."

"What are you looking for?" Weasel Face asked.

"Um, my Green Bay Packers sweatshirt," Tristan said. "It's lucky. Every time she wears it, they win."

Weasel Face pursed his lips as he scanned the office. "I don't see it.

Damn."

I swapped my confused expression for a disappointed one. "I hope the Packers can win without me."

"Hopefully," Tristan said, and smiled. *We work well together,* his smile seemed to say.

Yeah. We do, I smiled back.

Too bad for him this was the last time.

CHAPTER FORTY

EASEL FACE—WHO no longer seemed so weasely—escorted Tristan and me back through the hallways and down the elevator to the Underground. Tristan gave him a handshake and a promise to go out to watch the Green Bay Packers soon, then suggested it would be awesome if he would disable the surveillance camera over the door. With a conspiratorial grin, Weasel Face wiggled his index finger at it. Tristan quickly steered him out, the door sealing shut behind him.

I took the binder from under my sweatshirt and opened to a random page. A black and white surveillance photo of my parents. Young and serious, they were sitting at an outdoor cafe. Mom was absently fiddling with her wedding ring. Dad was looking at the menu. A completely bland photo, boring really, but it brought tears to my eyes.

I flipped through the pages. How odd to see our real names in print after all these years.

Andrew Carson. Gwendolyn Carson. Jillian. Tessa. Logan.

We'd wiped away our identities with each move, and this binder held the only proof of our existence.

Clips from my father's newspaper columns when he wrote as Xander

Xavier.

A picture of our big red brick house in Virginia, standing majestically over an expansive lawn.

My parents' old financial records. "See, Tristan? They really did make all that money," I said. "Paychecks. Business investments. Stocks. It's all right here. All legal."

"They wouldn't mark their blackmail payments as *blackmail*. They'd mark them as investments and stocks."

I glared at him for a full minute before returning to the binder.

Another photo of our house, this time reduced to rubble and ashes.

Pictures of some of the other houses and apartments we'd lived in.

Testimonies from our old neighbors.

A list of our aliases.

Phone records. My parents were right to get rid of our landline.

A list of websites we'd visited. My parents were right to get rid of our internet access too.

Reports from various precognitives and psychics, including a child's drawing of a dozen blue misshapen circles with wave symbols. "What's this?" I asked Tristan.

"Twelve lakes," he said. "That's how we knew you would go there."

In the binder, Dennis Connelly had written notes about where we'd been and where he guessed we might go next. We were always careful not to leave anything personal behind, but he still found a few items. Those items he brought back to the APR for psychometric readings, and he also flew psychics out to the homes we'd fled. Several times he noted his frustration that the psychics were never able to get a clear reading on our family through the objects or places we'd left behind.

I read every detail of a receipt from an electronics store near our hideout in Seattle, back when we were the Abbott family. My name was Amanda for about ten months. Jillian was Allison and Logan was

Alexander. The receipt showed that we'd paid cash for a DVD player and a stack of Disney movies.

One of the papers was a program from a dance recital. The name Renee Roberts was circled on the program—Jillian's alias in Oregon. My pseudonym was Rachel, and Logan's was Ryan. I'd wanted the name Rebecca, but my father said no. Jillian didn't appear in the class picture with the other little ballerinas, but my parents were upset that her name was in print. We fled to our next hideout soon after that.

Logan left behind one of the music scores he'd written when we lived in Florida. Another page was a scan of a painting I'd made in art class, probably when I was eleven. A single petal lying on the ground, broken off from the rest of the flower. What state were we living in then—maybe Missouri? North Carolina? The image on the page was black and white, but I remembered using shades of blue for the petal. It might have been the last painting I'd ever done. It was too painful to paint anyway, knowing my parents would ooh and ahh over it, tell me I was so talented, and then sometime before our next run, they would burn it. The canvases wouldn't fit in my getaway bag, and we could leave nothing personal behind.

Disney movies, dance recitals, art classes. It was nice to remember that a small part of our childhood had actually been normal. How odd to think that Dennis Connelly was the keeper of my childhood memories.

D. Connelly was written on the bottom of the earlier reports. Toward the back pages, his name was replaced by *J. Kellan*. Tristan's name appeared on some of the reports too.

My stomach clenched when I saw recent pictures of me. Jogging with Tristan. Walking happily to school, holding his hand. In one photo he was laughing as I whispered in his ear. An intimate, happy moment, captured by a long-range surveillance camera.

Another photo of the two of us sitting on a bench under a leafless tree. Ethan's backyard. That was the night Tristan told me he loved me, the night I told him my real name. The next photo, taken the same night, showed us talking in the back seat of his car. When I looked closely, Heath was in the background in almost every picture, either standing behind a tree or huddling in a car.

For someone constantly on the lookout for suspicious people, I'd been so blind. Blinded by love—I was a living cliché.

The binder held photos of the rest of my family too. Mom and Jillian shopping for Homecoming dresses. Logan looking under the hood of our getaway car in the pouring rain while our mother paced behind him. Jillian looking wistfully out my bedroom window, the morning after our dad's mobile eye almost blew out, and she'd volunteered to let him test it through her eyes. Only one picture of Dad—he stood on the driveway with his hands in his pockets. It was the one time he'd stepped outside the house in Twelve Lakes, as he waited for me to return home from jogging with Tristan, so he could shake his hand again.

With every turn of the page, my heart hurt a little bit more.

The hardest pages to see were the photos of the alleged victims, the people the APR accused my parents of blackmailing and murdering. Underneath each photo was their name, along with the location, date, and manner of death. Heart attack. Car accident. Heart attack. Fire. Falling down stairs. Heart attack.

Tristan sipped in a long breath when I turned the page to photos of two men. "My dad's partners," he said.

The location listed was Kitteridge, Virginia. My hometown.

The date was the day Dennis Connelly came to our house eight years ago.

Their manner of death: Stabbing.

Those were the only deaths that didn't match the rest, the only deaths that weren't accidents or illness.

A lump grew in my throat. Calling the fog in a bit closer, I dragged my sight from the words to the pictures of the two men. Both photos were simple headshots against a plain backdrop, perhaps taken by the APR for their ID badges. The men stared accusingly back at me, the elder man hefty and wizened, the younger man thin and determined.

"That guy?" Tristan said, pointing to the younger man. "He was Kellan's brother-in-law, but they were more like real brothers. I guess Kellan didn't want to just apprehend your parents. He wanted revenge." Hands curling into fists, he muttered, "So he took it out on you. Defenseless you."

My despair, and the fog, lifted as I realized I didn't recognize either of those men. I'd never seen them before.

"Ha!" I cried. "I would have remembered three men coming to my house that day. But there was just one. Your *father*." I shoved the binder off my lap and onto his, as if it was contaminated.

He licked his lips. "My dad was purposely distracting you."

Narrowing my eyes at him, I slid the binder back onto my legs and resumed flipping the pages. It didn't matter what Tristan said; I had absolutely no memory of three men in my yard. I remembered only one: the man who tried to kidnap me. The man who sliced me open.

I vaguely recognized a few of the people in the photos—was that the man who'd sold us our getaway car when we left Montana? The binder said he died when he cracked his head open after slipping on motor oil. And the hook-nosed waitress from a Georgia diner a few years ago. She died of a heart attack.

I had to stop this. I had to stop looking at these photos. There were too many, and they weren't helping me prove Tristan was lying. I thumbed through the rest of them as quickly as I could, barely glancing at them—

Wait.

Was that…

Yes. That last photo. The date in the corner showed it had been added to the binder this past Thursday night.

Dr. Fielding. The college professor who taught parapsychology.

I stared at his picture, the same portrait from his website. Even the words "In Memoriam" were printed on top. But it was the words printed on the bottom that made my breath catch.

I ripped the page from the file. Shoved the binder to the floor. Jumped to my feet and waved the page over my head like a trophy. "I knew it!" I said, my voice screechy and frantic. "You're lying. And I can prove it."

CHAPTER FORTY-ONE

"$\mathcal{I}$'M NOT LYING," Tristan said.

"Yes you are! This," I said, waving the photo in his face, "is Dr. Fielding."

"That professor?"

I stabbed the words under his portrait with my finger. "He died in Hebron, Iowa, on November twenty-third. My family moved to Twelve Lakes, Illinois, in August. We never went further than ten minutes away from our house. And Iowa was at least two hundred miles away. There's no way my mom could have killed him. She's not *that* powerful."

Tristan's face went white.

"I knew you were lying." I ran my finger down the professor's portrait. Dr. Fielding had rescued my family after all.

Tristan scrambled to gather the papers that had scattered on the floor and began to read them again. Elated, I held Dr. Fielding's photo in front of me. I could have kissed it. A hysterical giggle escaped from behind my lips.

They were innocent.

My parents were innocent.

They never blackmailed anyone.

They never killed anyone.

They never lied to me.

I turned to Tristan with my hands on my hips and snarled. "Now let my parents go, you disgusting, pathetic liar."

But instead of being intimidated, he just gave me another one of his sad, sympathetic looks. "You didn't read the notes on the next page. It says here that Dr. Fielding was in Twelve Lakes on November twenty-second."

"That can't be true. He didn't know who we were. We left all of our personal information out of that email, and Logan made it untraceable. How would he know to come to Twelve Lakes?"

He referenced the notes again. "Because your parents called him and told him to come."

"But…how would my parents know about him back then?"

He shrugged. "Maybe when Jillian was piggybacking he was able to see inside her mind. Or maybe your parents didn't trust her, so your father still watched her."

If that was true, then my parents had mistrusted the wrong daughter.

"It says here your mother arranged to meet him at the coffee shop in the town square," Tristan said. "The security cameras show him getting there at 10:54 a.m. He waited for two hours, and when no one showed up, he left."

"See? My parents never met him. So they couldn't have killed him."

He read the notes. "Your mom came in at 11:06, bought a small coffee to go, then went home. She never spoke to him, but she was close enough to plant an aneurysm in his brain. Aneurysms don't necessarily kill right away. She probably chose that method so he wouldn't die until he got home."

I stared at him for a long moment. "Don't talk about my mother that way."

"Sorry, Tessa. For a minute there, I really thought the APR might be wrong about your parents."

I sat down hard on the cot. "This file is fake. It has to be." I grabbed it from him and flipped through the pages, almost tearing them from the binder.

"My parents donated to charities," I said. "They gave money to anyone who needed it. Once when we were on the run, driving through Massachusetts, we were at a motel and the manager was kicking out a woman and her two little kids because she couldn't afford to pay. My parents gave her enough cash to stay in a different motel, a better motel, for a month. If they were killers, they wouldn't have done that. They wouldn't."

"That doesn't mean anything," Tristan said.

I tried again. "What about the police detective and the FBI agent we asked for help?" I said. "My dad watched your father kill them, he watched your father slice them right down the middle, and each time, I watched my dad. He could not have faked the horror in his eyes. My mother could not have faked her tears. She was hysterical, Tristan."

He only shook his head with a sorrowful sigh.

Memories. All I had were my memories of my parents' altruism and my father's horrified expression as he witnessed those murders. Those memories were enough evidence for me, but they wouldn't be enough for Tristan.

I was no longer happy that Jillian and Logan had escaped. Selfishly, I wanted them here, with me. They'd help me prove our parents were innocent.

But Jillian and Logan were gone. I'd have to find the proof myself.

Shaking off my despair, I studied the notes in the binder again. Kellan wrote how he would not use his telepathy to read our minds, in case one of us could sense his intrusion. He recorded his plans, from hiding a tiny camera under our front windowsill to record our comings and goings—it must have been Kellan's handprint on our window—to pulling the wires in our getaway car in an effort to provoke my mom or brother into using psionics to fix it. But with my mother standing watch and clearly ready to attack, and still not fully informed on all of our powers, he had decided not to move in.

The bulk of his strategy involved Tristan prying information from me. It was those notes that made my stomach churn.

A note written by Tristan, on the day we met for the first time: *Followed targets 4 and 5 as they left the house and went running in park. Made first contact with target 4. She resisted conversation. –T. Connelly*

A note written by Kellan, from the night of Ethan's party: *Instructed agent to tell target 4 he has fallen in love with her to prompt her to confess her own secrets. Partial success. –J. Kellan*

"Our whole relationship was set up," I said, my voice small. "You manipulated every moment of it."

"Tessa—" He took my hand.

I jerked it away. "I think you mean 'Target 4.'"

He grabbed my hand back. "No. I mean Tessa. I love you. That is not a lie. I wanted to tell you, but not because Kellan said to. I wanted to wait until you knew the real me."

I knew the real Tristan now, and he was a liar.

"Tell me, Tristan." I narrowed my eyes. "Was the tree almost falling on me part of the plan too?"

"God, no. We'd never purposely put you in danger like that."

"And what would you call this?" I waved my arms around the cell.

"This," he said as he copied my movements, "is the first time in your entire life you *haven't* been in danger."

I rolled my eyes.

He roared then, a frustrated, furious growl, and jumped up. "It terrified me when you told me some man was hunting you, Tessa! The first thing I did was call Kellan to demand an army of guards to protect your family until we found him. But before Kellan answered, I saw the name you wrote in my notebook. Dennis Connelly. My *father*."

He slapped the wall. "So I hung up on Kellan and called my dad. All missions are supposed to be confidential, but I told him everything. That's when he realized which case I was on, that I was on a criminal case, his old case. Kellan was lying to us all along, and your parents were lying to *you*."

His anger scared me a little, and I shrank back. He sank to the cot and raked his hands through his hair. His next words were gentle. "When I was ten, my dad went out of town with his team on a simple recruiting mission, something they did a couple times a month. But that afternoon, some guards came and brought my mom and sister and me to the APR. They told us that my dad had a heart attack and his partners were dead. Murdered. We were never told any details, except that they were interviewing a potential psionic subject, and something went wrong and the subject and his wife attacked them. They stabbed his partners to death, and they suspected they actually gave my dad that heart attack. The healers healed my dad, but he was weaker than before. He spent the rest of his career here trying to find your family and bring you and your siblings to safety, until my mom finally convinced him to retire so he could rest his heart."

I said nothing, trying to imagine a weak Dennis Connelly.

I couldn't do it.

"Then last week," Tristan said, "once I knew what was really going on, I did everything I could to protect you. I begged Kellan to let Heath safeguard you, but he said no. If your father tried to use his remote vision on you and couldn't, he'd know something was up. We couldn't use psionics on your family at all. We couldn't do anything that would make your parents suspicious until he had a plan."

Head down, he stared at the concrete floor. "It was the worst week of my life, Tessa. You kept looking up at me with those big hopeful eyes, but I'd never felt so helpless. I couldn't tell you the truth. I was afraid to let you go home, knowing what your mother could—"

With a strangled whimper I shoved the binder to the floor. I could not let him finish that sentence. How dare he even *think* that my mother would purposely hurt me, let alone say it out loud. "You're *still* trying to manipulate me. You want me to feel sorry for you, but it won't work. You strut around with that cocky smile and your stupid warning premonitions, knowing nothing bad will ever happen to you. But now, for the first time in your life, things didn't work out the way you wanted. And you don't know how to handle it."

He released a shaky sigh. "You're right. I don't."

"So stop trying to make me feel bad for you. I'm not your puppet anymore. I'm not your girlfriend anymore either."

It worked. He never finished the sentence. He stopped talking completely. He just stared at me, looking hurt.

Good.

The binder's rings opened when I pushed it to the floor, and the papers had scattered. With shaking hands, I bent to gather them up. One page caught my attention as I slipped it back in the file, a transcribed phone conversation between Tristan and Kellan, dated this past Thursday night:

J. Kellan: Now that we know what they can do, we have to figure out what they can't do. There's got to be a way to apprehend them without getting anyone else killed. They must have a weakness.

T. Connelly: I've been thinking about it for days. They don't have a weakness.

J. Kellan: You know that family better than anyone, Junior. There's got to be something you're not telling me.

T. Connelly: I'm telling you everything I know.

J. Kellan: I'm on my way over there right now, and I'll order Heath to remove your safeguard. I'll read your mind and find out what you're not telling me anyway.

T. Connelly: (unintelligible)

J. Kellan: Damn it, Connelly! Tell me! What else do you know? What is their weakness?

T. Connelly: (unintelligible) …They think she's breakable. They take care of her. They protect her. Their greatest weakness, their only weakness…is Tessa.

I couldn't speak. Couldn't even breathe. The only sound in the cell was the pounding of my heart. I read Tristan's words over and over again, then finally looked up at him.

His face was ashen. "Tessa, I am so sorry."

Pressing the heels of my hands to my eyes, I sank to the cot and tried to get air into my lungs. "You gave Kellan the idea to kidnap me."

"I didn't mean to. I begged him to leave you out of it, and he swore he would. He lied to me right up to the very end." He put his arm around me, rubbing my back. I couldn't even shake him off.

He was right.

I was my parents' greatest weakness.

My parents were locked up, neutralized, and unjustly accused of murder. All because I believed Tristan when he said he loved me. Because I believed him when he said he would keep me safe. Because I told him our secrets.

This was all my fault.

Exhaustion weighed me down like a blanket of lead, and the desire to call in the fog was so strong I couldn't fight it, or Tristan, any longer. "I want to go to sleep now, please."

"Okay." Relief was clear in his voice. "Go get ready for bed."

I slipped from under his arm and shuffled to the bathroom. Like a robot, I washed my face and brushed my teeth. Thank goodness there was no mirror over the sink. I wouldn't be able to stand looking at myself.

When I returned to the cell, Tristan had fallen asleep. He slouched against the wall, the binder open on his lap.

I stared at him, trying to decide whom I despised more at that moment: Tristan, or myself.

I declared a tie.

Leaving the bathroom light on and the door opened a crack, I snapped off the main light. I went to my familiar corner of the dim cell and curled up on the floor, using my forearms as a pillow. The chill from the cement seeped through my gray cotton pants and sweatshirt.

Good.

I stared at the darkness for a long time.

"Tessa?" Tristan's whisper broke the silence. "What are you doing over there? Come to bed."

I said nothing.

"I won't—I won't touch you. I promise. We'll just sleep."

Still I said nothing, just bent my knees up to my chest and shivered. The fog rumbled, and I imagined it surrounding me, taking me away. But it disappeared with a whoosh when Tristan's strong arms scooped me up. I shrieked and tried to bat him off, but he held tight.

Without a word, he deposited me on the cot. Then he took my place on the floor, stretched out on his back with his hands behind his head, and closed his eyes.

I glared at him for a few moments, then pulled the blanket up to my shoulders and turned to the wall.

CHAPTER FORTY-TWO

THE SMELL OF soap and masculinity woke me the next day. I opened my eyes to see Tristan pulling a hockey sweater over his freshly showered chest, a chest that once upon a time I'd associated with strength and safety.

He moved stiffly and rotated his shoulders with several crackling pops, but stopped when he saw me watching.

The cell door opened. A guard, stout and husky, trampled inside with black shoes that squeaked with every step. He carried a tray with two baskets of cheeseburgers and fries and two cartons of milk.

"You slept through breakfast," Tristan said to me. "It's almost noon."

Squeaky Shoes handed Tristan the tray and turned to leave.

"Hey, buddy, wait." Tristan gestured to me. "She's a vegetarian. Can you bring her something else?"

"This is a prison," the guard said. "Not a restaurant."

Tristan pulled his wallet from his duffle bag and handed him some money. "Send an intern to Hawthorne's for a veggie burger and one of those fruit platters. And three slices of blueberry pie," he added. "Keep one for yourself."

The guard pocketed the money and squeaked away.

Tristan grinned at me. "Hawthorne's is famous in Lilybrook for their pies. No one can resist them."

Without reply, I escaped to the bathroom, closing the door behind me. Tristan was only being nice to me in order to ease his own guilt. He still believed my parents were killers. He still believed his father was a good man.

When I returned from the shower, dressed in a new prison uniform, the cheeseburgers and fries still sat untouched in their baskets. Tristan waited for Squeaky Shoes to deliver my new lunch, then he ate both cheeseburgers while I ate my veggie burger and fruit.

He was right: the blueberry pie was irresistible. Warm and sweet and tart, and I ate the entire piece. Jillian and Logan would have loved it. What kind of food were they eating? Were they eating at all? They had enough money, but what if they were too frightened to leave their hideout, wherever it was, to go buy food?

"Is Kellan still looking for my brother and sister?" I asked.

Nodding, Tristan swallowed a bite. "He's assembling a new team. He did not ask me to be on it."

Jillian and Logan were out there, somewhere, frightened and confused and alone. I wanted them here, with me. But for now, it was best if they stayed hidden, as far away from the APR as possible. I needed to prove my parents were innocent. Not just for their freedom, but for Jillian and Logan's safety. What if Kellan neutralized them too?

With the side of my fork, I scraped the last crumbs from the plate. I chose my next words carefully. "Last night, when I found the information about the professor, you said you thought the APR might be wrong about my parents."

"Yeah, for a moment." He wiped his mouth with a paper napkin. "And then I read the rest of the facts."

"But there was a moment."

"Yes."

"So you're not completely convinced my parents are criminals."

He paused for a moment. "I guess not."

"Then let me go," I said. "Let my parents go."

"I can't do that. Not without absolute proof that the APR is wrong."

I lifted the binder onto my lap. "If I can find that proof, then will you get us out of here?"

He gazed at me, then nodded.

With the fog blanketing my emotions, I spent the afternoon and late into the evening poring over every page, every photo, every note. The few times I found something that could confirm my parents' innocence, Tristan found something else that proved me wrong.

"You're supposed to be helping me," I said crossly.

"I'm trying. I swear," he said. "I want your parents to be innocent as much as—" He stopped, his eyes growing wide, and he gripped my arm. "Don't be scared," he said. "Don't... Jesus. Don't faint."

"Why? What's…"

"My dad's about to walk in that door," he said. "Right—"

The door slid open.

"—now."

CHAPTER FORTY-THREE

TRIED TO jump up, but Tristan held me.

There he was. Standing in the doorway. Round wire-rimmed glasses and gray mustache and kind blue eyes. The man who tried to kidnap me eight years ago. The man who sliced me open. The man who had chased my family from countless homes and gave me nightmares every night, the man who had ruined my childhood and destroyed my family. The man who was going to kill me.

Dennis Connelly.

Nowhere to hide. Nowhere to run. No escape.

The oxygen evaporated from the cell and was replaced by fog. The world started fading away.

"Don't faint," I heard Tristan say. "Tessa? Hey. Hey, Clockwise, look at me."

I peered through the fog. Tristan was inches from me, holding my face between his hands. "Breathe." He inhaled, showing me how to do it.

I inhaled.

He exhaled, and I did too.

"Again." He inhaled, then exhaled, his eyes locked on to mine.

I inhaled, then exhaled. The fog gradually thinned, and Tristan came back into focus.

"Good," he said. "He won't hurt you. I promise. Tessa, I *promise*."

I shook my head, my hands fluttering to cover my stomach.

He stood, pulling me up with him. My body was frozen, but the room around me was swirling. He had to support me so I wouldn't collapse, or maybe he was holding me so I couldn't run.

Dennis Connelly stepped toward me. I imagined the fog slamming down between us, like a curtain. An iron gate. A brick wall.

"Dad, this is Tessa," Tristan said, pride clear in his voice.

My heart stopped as his father turned his attention to me. "Tiny little Tessa, all grown up." He held out his arms.

I braced myself, ready for the sharp pain of him piercing my stomach, slicing me open again.

"Dad, stop. No hugs. She's really scared," Tristan said.

A hug? That's what he wanted?

He held up his hands, palms open. "Of course. I'm sorry."

Was he sorry he'd cut me? Sorry he'd torn my family apart? Sorry my parents were locked up without cause?

I forced myself to look at him for the first time in eight years.

My nightly dreams of Dennis Connelly had morphed my memory of him into a monster, a demon, with wild rolling eyes and sharp yellowed nails. But one glance at him now and I remembered how he really looked that day eight years ago, when we chatted on my lawn. He looked the same now, a bit older. He wore the same round, wire-rimmed glasses, and he had the same mustache, just whiter.

He was, in fact, handsome. Bald on top now, his eyes a darker blue than Tristan's, but with the same bright, friendly quality. His face was open, and...youthful, jovial. Merry. How different from my own parents' faces, which had become tired, sunken, and troubled over the years.

How dare this man enjoy life for the past eight years, while he'd destroyed ours?

Dennis Connelly was the murderer. Not my parents.

But where was the sickly sweet, burned cherry scent? Why didn't he smell like cigars?

"My partner smoked those cigars," he said. "Not me. The smell always clung to my clothes. Tristan's mother hated that."

That's right; he was telepathic. And a liar. And a killer.

He looked around the cell. "This is no place for a reunion. I'm sure they won't mind if I take you upstairs. It's much nicer up there."

No. I did not want to leave my nice, safe cell.

Tristan put his arm tight around my shoulders and nudged me forward. Certain he would drag me or even carry me if I refused to walk, I brought the fog in even farther, then a tiny bit more, until nothing seemed real. On shaking legs, I walked with Tristan, and we followed his father into the hall and up to the main level. Two guards followed us.

Tristan had no idea what a horrible man his father was.

I concentrated on breathing and walking. In, out. Left, right.

One of the guards unlocked a room at the far end of the hallway. "We'll use the boardroom," Dennis Connelly said. "I may have retired, but I still have some pull around here."

The boardroom, with shiny hardwood floors and dark paneled walls, was dominated by a glossy wood table and wide padded leather chairs in the center of the room. At the far end was a more intimate sitting area, with a black leather sofa and two matching armchairs in front of a fireplace. Dennis Connelly gestured to the sofa. "Have a seat."

Still holding me tightly, Tristan led me over. "You okay?" he whispered in my ear.

I didn't know how to answer that. This wasn't how I'd expected to meet Dennis Connelly again.

He sat in an armchair and smiled at me. "Imagine my surprise when I heard my son had fallen in love with tiny little Tessa. Isn't it wonderful how things have turned out?"

"Did Dr. Sheldon tell you everything Kellan did to her?" Tristan said, eyes blazing. "He hit her. He made her watch as they shot her—"

I squeezed Tristan's hand: *Stop.* I did not want to relive that night.

He squeezed back: *Sorry.*

"John Kellan has always been driven and ruthless, as you know," his father said, "but he's never been violent before. One of the agents killed in the attack was his brother-in-law. He wanted vengeance. Regrettably, he took it out on Tessa."

"So they fired him, right?" Tristan asked.

"He was formally reprimanded for hitting Tessa. That's all. After the professor was murdered, the board gave him the green light to do whatever it took to apprehend the Carsons before they killed anyone else."

Tristan sat back with a growl of disgust.

"I'm as upset as you are, Tristan. Kellan traumatized Tessa, and he put your life in danger. If I'd known about his plan, I would have stopped him. And he knew it." Dennis Connelly turned back to me. "Tessa, I am truly sorry."

All these years, I'd thought he was angry, obsessed. Insane. But now I felt only earnest regret and sympathy and…paternal *affection* from him.

But it had to be fake. "You destroyed my family," I whispered. "You tried to kidnap me."

"No, honey. I was trying to keep you safe."

"You cut me."

"No. That was the shattered glass from the car windows."

I had an argument he could not twist around. "You hunted my family for eight years."

"Your parents did some very bad things. We had to stop them."

"You made it all up."

"We have proof, Tessa."

"What, that binder?" I spat. "That binder isn't proof. It's just a bunch of pictures and notes. There's no proof at all in there that my parents blackmailed or murdered anyone. The only think it proves is that you stalked us for eight years."

Tristan chuckled. "She's right, you know."

"That's true." His father nodded. "That file would not qualify as proof of guilt in a regular court of law. But this is the APR. We have our own laws, our own courts, and the full support of the federal government. We deal with extraordinary people, people who have special gifts that make them more powerful than most. That power shouldn't be used to hurt anyone. And that's what your parents did. We saw them do it through visions. We read your mother's mind. We don't need physical proof."

This was not going the way I wanted it to. "Do they even get a chance to defend themselves? What about a lawyer? Don't they get a trial?"

"There's no need for a trial," he said. "Trials are for people who can't read minds, who can't see the past or the future. Trials are for neutrals."

Neutral. I'd heard that term before. Dr. Sheldon used it when she looked inside my mind. Tristan had told me that my parents were being neutralized. "That's what you call people like me—neutral?"

"People who aren't psionic," Tristan said, "are neutral."

"So how do *I* know you're telling me the truth?" I asked, gaining strength and courage with each word I spoke. "I'm neutral. I need physical proof that they're guilty, and you don't have any."

"I suppose you're right," Dennis Connelly said. "We can't prove it to you."

"You can let me see my parents," I said. "They have no reason to lie to me now. If they really are guilty, they'll tell me." They would tell me the truth—that they're innocent. And then we could figure out how to get out of this place.

But Dennis Connelly shook his head. "I'll try, but your father is still unconscious, and they're having a hard time neutralizing your mother," he said. "Her psychokinesis keeps regenerating. Until she's completely neutralized, they won't let anyone see her. But I checked on them before I stopped in to see you." He tapped his temple.

"You read their minds?"

"I did."

"Are they okay?"

"Your mother is weak and groggy, but she knows where she is and why."

I hated thinking of my mother as weak and groggy. She was the strongest person I knew, and the smartest, too. "What about my dad?"

"I was unable to read his mind. All I felt was his pain. It's excruciating." He raised his hands to his temples, and his face contorted for a moment, as if he could still feel it. "It's blocked out thoughts of anything else."

"But you have healers! Tell them to fix him!"

"They're doing everything they can. It's fortunate that he's here. Those headaches and bloody noses would have killed him, and very soon, without our intervention."

No, my dad wasn't *fortunate* to be here. He wouldn't have had to use his mobile eye at all if he hadn't had to watch for Dennis Connelly for eight years. And when Kellan took me, he'd aggravated his condition to the breaking point by watching me from the minute he realized I was missing, even though he was bleeding from his nose, his ears, even his eyes, until he was shot hours later.

"Will he ever wake up?" I asked.

He was quiet for a moment. "I believe he will. And here's why. Your family always fled just a couple hours before I found you. I was constantly safeguarded, so I was never able to figure out how you knew I was coming. But when you told Tristan last week that your father was unable to see me except when I was close, I figured it out. My original safeguard died during the attack in your house eight years ago. The few minutes I was unguarded left me vulnerable to your father's remote vision whenever I was close to him, even though I'd gotten a new safeguard."

Before I could protest that no one was in my house that day eight years ago except for *him,* he held up his palm. "My point is, no one has ever been able to penetrate a safeguard's protection before. Your father is very strong. If anyone can wake up from this, he can."

Psionic strength was not the same as physical strength, and now my father had neither. But Mr. Connelly was trying to comfort me, and I needed to be comforted. "Thank you, sir."

"Please. Call me Dennis."

How strange that sounded. *Dennis Connelly* was evil. *Dennis* was…harmless.

Dennis leaned forward in the armchair, elbows on his knees. "Tessa, we need to discuss where you're going to live."

Beside me, Tristan tensed, sat up straight.

"What do you mean?" I asked. "You're letting me go?"

"I can't think of a reason to keep you here any longer. Now. You'll want to live with your brother and sister, of course. Until we find them, you have three options."

"What are they?" I asked.

"One, you can live with your aunt."

"I don't have an aunt," I said. "It was always just the five of us."

He furrowed his brow. "Your father has a sister. Rebecca. She lives in Delaware. You didn't know?"

"My dad never told us about her."

"Well, they were never close," Dennis said. "Early in our investigation we learned that he was ten years older than her, and when she was very young she was diagnosed with leukemia. She recovered years later, but by then he'd grown distant from the family. The last time they spoke was at their father's funeral, fifteen years ago."

"Does she have a mobile eye?" I asked.

"No. She's not psionic. Like everyone else, she believes you were all killed when your house exploded. She went to your memorial."

"Would she take Jillian and Logan too?"

"I'm sure she would. Would you like me to contact her for you? We can't tell her about the APR or where your parents are, but we can think of a good cover story about where you've been all these years."

I considered it. I suddenly had an aunt. Aunt Rebecca. She was neutral. It would be nice, living with someone like me.

But I knew my answer. I did not want to go live with an aunt I'd never heard of before. And I'd still have to lie.

I was so tired of lying.

"What are my other options?" I asked.

"We can place you in a foster home," his father said.

That was even worse than living with an unknown aunt. "What else?"

"The other option," he said, gesturing to Tristan and giving me a wide smile like he was presenting me with a precious gift, "is that you come live with us."

Tristan gave his knee a triumphant slap. "Thank you, Dad. That's what I was hoping for."

I blinked with disbelief. Then my throat closed up, panic rumbling in my blood like water about to boil. Dennis Connelly had lulled me into complacency with his kindness and his soft voice and his fake fatherly concern. But now I knew what he was doing.

"You finally captured us after eight years," I said, "and now you want to bring me home like a trophy to hang on your wall after a hunt."

His face paled, his eyes widened.

I rose and stepped toward him. "You may have Tristan fooled, you may have everyone else fooled, but you can't fool me."

He cringed and shrank back, and I took another step. "You kill people. My dad saw you do it. He watched, through your own eyes, as you sliced open that cop and the FBI agent. You probably killed everyone in that binder and framed my parents for it."

Another cringe, another step. "The only reason you haven't killed us is because you don't want Tristan to know the truth."

Standing directly in front of him now, I held my arms out wide, my stomach unprotected. "Show him," I hissed. "Slice me open again. Show your son what you really are."

Arms grabbed me from behind, wrapping around my torso and dragging me away. Tristan. I struggled as he pulled me from the room, but then I realized—he finally understood. He believed me! I raced with him as he stormed down the shadowed hall, the staccato tapping of the guards' boots echoing behind us.

When we reached a security door, Tristan gestured impatiently to the guards. "Open it!" he demanded. One of them scrambled to unlock it, and Tristan shoved it open with a bang. We rushed out onto a white pebbled path with snow piled high on each side, toward evergreens that stretched up to the onyx sky. Taking my hand, he strode with steps so fast and wide I could barely keep up.

"You saw it, didn't you?" I cried, victorious. "You had a premonition that he sliced me open. That's why you took me out of there."

"What? No," he said without slowing. "I took you out of there because I'm bringing you home. Maybe at my house you'll finally see that we're not lying to you."

I tripped over his words. Stumbled to a stop. "Nothing I say will ever convince you. You will *always* believe your father over me." I yanked my hand from his and marched back to the building.

"Tessa, what are you doing," he called. "Come back."

"I'm not leaving this place until I can leave with my parents, or until your father kills us. Whichever comes first."

Radiating anger hot enough to melt the snow, he strode over to me. "Then we're going to die in there of old age, because neither of those things are going to happen."

The night air went silent and still.

I shattered it with a whisper. "I'm not asking you to stay with me, Tristan."

He grabbed me then, pressed me to his chest. Sliding one hand behind my head and in my hair, he forced me to look into his blazing eyes. "I'll help you through your panic attacks. I'll let you use me as your punching bag. I'll break into offices and steal files for you. I'll even try to prove your parents are innocent. I'll do anything for you, Tessa. Except one thing. I. Will. Not. Leave. You."

Our gazes locked for one endless moment, each cloud of breath dancing between us, melting into each other, becoming one. Then he crushed his lips to mine. I struggled, pushed against him, but my muscles conspired against me and I found myself wrapping my arms around him, pressing into him, as I kissed him back with fierce desperation.

Even my own body was betraying me.

I pushed away with a sobbing gasp.

Tristan's arms fell to his sides. "Tessa. Please."

"You promised you would keep me safe," I said. "And you didn't. Go home, Tristan. I don't want you here." Turning my back to him, chin held high, I walked back inside the APR. My family needed me. I would not fail them again.

The guards followed me to the Underground and let me in my cell. I shut the door myself.

As big as Tristan was, the cell somehow seemed smaller without him. Darker. Silence screamed at me. Unable to warm up no matter how tightly I hugged myself, I slid under the blanket on the cot.

Shivering, I ran my fingers over my stomach. The scars were there, but I was still whole. Uncut. Instead of killing me, Dennis Connelly had offered me a home.

I hated him for it.

Eventually the fog came, rolling in like a storm cloud, and carried me off to sleep. As always, my nightmare visited me. But this time it was different. This time, my parents were the monsters.

And when I woke up, Tristan was sleeping on the floor.

CHAPTER FORTY-FOUR

HE WEEK PASSED in a murky haze of fog. I kept time by the meals delivered by the guards. Whenever they brought something with meat, Tristan would send them away with a command to get a vegetarian meal for me. Periodically I'd ask the guards for updates on my parents and on the search for my brother and sister.

The reports were the same, day after day: Mom disconsolate and defeated. Dad unconscious and in pain. No leads on Jillian and Logan.

Other than that, neither Tristan nor I spoke. I tried not to look at him. Every time I did, he was gazing at me with pleading eyes, and the faith I had in my parents' innocence faltered.

Everything the APR said about my parents made sense. I couldn't find a way around it. I spent a lot of time in the shower, hiding in the fog. Trying not to think. Thinking led me places I did not want to go.

Once I came back into the cell and discovered Tristan had replaced the wool brown blanket with a thick, soft one in periwinkle. Another time, a fuchsia backpack decorated with chartreuse peace symbols—so bright it hurt my eyes, which were accustomed to the cell's dim shadows—sat on the cot. Inside were clothes from his sister to replace my prison uniform.

I refused to acknowledge the blanket and, using my foot, slid the bag of clothes under the cot. My faith was starting to crack, but I couldn't allow it to shatter. I wouldn't. I was all my parents had left. If there was any chance, any at all, that they were innocent, it was up to me to prove it.

Tristan just watched me from the chair, elbows on knees, saying nothing. I tried to pretend he wasn't there.

When the guard with the spiky yellow hair brought breakfast one morning, I asked him to please bring me some paper and a pen. The APR wouldn't let me see my parents, but maybe they'd deliver a letter to them.

After Spiky Hair brought the paper, all I could do was stare at it. I'd start writing a few lines, sometimes a whole page, then cross off my words. The floor became littered with the letters I'd started and rejected, all crumpled into balls.

By lunchtime, I was down to my last sheet of paper. But I finally knew what to write. There were really only three things to say, an affirmation to them as well as to myself.

Mom, Dad,
I know you're innocent.
This is all my fault.
I am so sorry.
~Tessa

How strange it was to write my real name. It'd been years. I took a sheet of paper from the floor, smoothed it out, and wrote *Tessa Carson* dozens of times until it felt natural.

I buzzed for the guard again and asked him to deliver the letter to my mother. He plucked the paper from my hand and left without reply.

"Hey, Clockwise," Tristan said, "Watch this."

He picked up some of the crumpled papers from the ground and juggled them in one hand. "I can do this, too." He kicked a paper ball around like a Hacky Sack, his hair bouncing up and down, turning gold in the light.

He'd changed tactics. From pleading to playful. And it was working. I missed this. I missed this Tristan, the one I knew in Twelve Lakes. Carefree and confident. I felt myself about to smile, so I covered my mouth with my hands.

"I'm really good at soccer," he said, "but my parents never let me play contact sports because my warning premonitions give me an unfair advantage. I'd know if I was going to get charged or tackled and prevent it from happening. That's why I play tennis and run cross-country. I ski and play golf too. And I coach. I volunteer at the Park District, coaching soccer and base—" His eyes opened wide, and he flew to my side. "Kellan's coming," he said, just as the door slid open.

John Kellan stormed into the cell with two guards. Tristan pushed me behind him into the corner, shielding me, his stance wide. The fog whooshed in to shield me too, thick and dark, enveloping me.

Kellan thrust a thin stack of papers at Tristan. He spoke behind his red beard. "I need you to sign off on this report so we can close the Carson investigation."

"I'm not signing anything that implies I approve of how you handled this case," Tristan said.

Kellan's eyes flickered to me for a moment and returned to Tristan. I wasn't worthy of a second glance, a second thought. I was simply the tool he used to capture my parents. To Kellan, I was scum, the daughter of a thief and a murderer. I was weak. Meek.

Neutral.

"My actions were justified," Kellan said. "The Carsons were all packed up and sitting in their car that night, ready to run. If I didn't act when I did, we would have lost them again. And what if your little girlfriend decided to contact another professor? She would've gotten him killed too. But I don't have to defend myself to you."

Get out! I screamed. But only in my head. I couldn't speak.

Kellan heard me anyway. He looked straight at me, the disinterest in his eyes turning into disgust. "And you. How can you defend your parents? Do you know how many people your father blackmailed? How much money he stole? And that's nothing compared to the number of people your mother killed."

No.

"Yes. We learned so much when we were finally able to read her mind. She killed more people than we even suspected."

Stop.

"You know those headaches your sister was getting? The bloody noses? Your mother gave those to her. She wanted her to stay out of your father's head so she wouldn't figure out what they were doing."

No. Stop it.

"Your father's a killer too. He delivered the final blows to one of our agents that day in your house. Stabbed him in the back as he tried to crawl away."

You're lying.

"I'm not lying. That agent had a wife and two sons. He was a safeguard who died trying to protect his team from your mother's heart attacks. But he couldn't protect them from her knives."

Stop.

"My brother-in-law was the other agent," he said. "He was a precog. He predicted a peaceful outcome that day at your house, but he missed something. He didn't predict *you.* You weren't supposed to be there.

You kept Connelly from going inside and reading your parents' minds. If he had, those agents would be alive today, and my sister wouldn't be struggling to raise her daughter all alone. And here's something else—"

"No," I whispered. "No more. Please."

"Shut up, Kellan!" Tristan pulled his arm back, fingers curled into a fist. "You've tortured her enough."

Kellan laughed. "You're staying down here with your little girlfriend. Fine. You broke into an office and stole confidential files. Fine. But if you hit me, I'll haul your ass out of here so fast your head will spin."

I gripped Tristan's shirt. *Don't leave me don't leave me don't leave me…*

Shoulders still tight, fingers still clenched, Tristan slowly lowered his arm. Kellan smirked and thrust the papers at him. "I don't need your approval. Just your signature."

Tristan grabbed the pen and scrawled something on the paper. "Signature Refused," he said. "That's all you'll get from me. Now leave."

"Good enough." Kellan pivoted on his heel and left, followed by the guards.

The door slammed, then sealed shut. Tristan sank against the wall.

"He made it all up," I said, thrusting out my chin to stop it from trembling. "He wants a promotion, so he made his report look better by making up all that stuff about my parents."

"Will you please let me take you out of here now?" Tristan said. "Even if you don't come home with me. You can't stay in this place. Not with Kellan here. He'll just keep taking his vengeance out on you."

The air was too thin in here. I couldn't take a deep enough breath. I pushed past Tristan and into the bathroom. "I need to take a shower."

"All you ever do is take showers. You don't need another one."

"Yes I do." I slammed the door, shed my clothes, and turned on the water as hot as it would go.

I needed that visit from Kellan. I'd allowed Tristan to cheer me up with his juggling and dribbling and showing off, and I didn't deserve to be cheered up. Kellan reminded me *I* was the one at fault here.

Weak. Too weak to keep my family's secrets from Tristan.

Neutral. No powers to stop Kellan from taking me, or to stop him from shooting my parents.

Scum. The daughter of thieves and murderers.

No. I couldn't let myself think that. Not even once. Not even for a second.

Mom. Dad. Jillian and Logan. Professor Fielding. Tristan. Dennis Connelly. My thoughts raced from one problem to another and couldn't find a peaceful place to rest.

So I called in the fog. I imagined it nestling inside every crevice of my brain, preventing all those horrible thoughts from surfacing and becoming whole. Only one thought was able to penetrate the fog—*all my fault, all my fault, all my fault.* No matter how close and thick and dark I made the fog, I couldn't block out those three words.

All my fault, all my fault.

This was good. As long as I concentrated on those three words, I wouldn't have to think about anything else. Like a robot, I shampooed my hair.

All my fault. All my fault.

I heard the bathroom door open, and, from the doorway, Tristan's voice echoed through the fog. "You can't keep escaping into the shower, Tessa."

I rinsed the shampoo and applied conditioner. *All my fault, all my fault.*

"You'd rather blame yourself for what happened than accept the truth."

All my fault! All my fault! I scrubbed myself with a washcloth.

"You don't need physical evidence to prove your parents are guilty. All you need is logic."

I scrubbed my arms and legs. *All! My! Fault!*

I returned the soap to the basket when something twinkled. The blades on Tristan's razor, catching the light. Silver blades. Sparkly blades.

I took the razor, touched the blades with the tip of my finger. Ran the razor up and down my arm. Grazed the thin skin on my wrist.

Running to the shower was just a temporary escape.

But escape by these little silver blades…that escape would be permanent.

How hard would I have to press—

Tristan yanked open the shower curtain.

"Hey!" I shrieked. The fog vanishing at the rush of cold air, I whipped my towel from the rod and held it against myself. Tristan had insisted on that prudish Borderline when I was his girlfriend, but now that I was his prisoner he thought he could watch me take a shower? "Get out!"

But his eyes weren't focused on my body. They were staring with horror at my hand, the one not holding the towel.

Clutched in my fist was a razor.

Did he have a premonition? Was I about to cut myself?

The blades glimmered, just once, like a wink.

Dr. Sheldon had looked deep into my mind. She'd known something was wrong, but she didn't know what.

This was it. This was what she had seen. My despair. My devastation. My guilt.

But she was unable to see the silver blade through the fog.

"Give me the razor," Tristan said.

Frozen, my fingers gripped the handle. He pried it from my hand, then turned my wrist up, looking for blood.

I looked too. The skin was smooth and unbroken.

Was I relieved, or disappointed?

I settled on shamed. I'd spent the past eight years running from death. I couldn't purposely bring it upon myself now.

"I'm sorry," I said, not to Tristan, but to my parents and Jillian and Logan. I couldn't put our family back together if I was dead.

"I'm sorry too," he said. "I'll stop pushing you so hard. It's just making you run further and further away."

Staring at my toes, I nodded.

He sighed hard. "Maybe seeing your parents will help."

"Yes," I said, my heart riding up into my throat. "Please."

"I'll do whatever I can to make it happen." Giving me his now almost-permanent look of helpless pity, he slid the curtain back and left the bathroom. He took the razor with him.

The next morning, the guard delivered a clean prison uniform for me, the same shapeless gray top and pants as the others. When I slipped on the pants, they fell down my hips a little. I looked for the drawstring but couldn't find it.

It wasn't until they replaced my tennis shoes that I realized what was happening. The new shoes were exactly like the ones I had before, but the laces had been taken out.

I was on suicide watch.

CHAPTER FORTY-FIVE

Y MOTHER PACED back and forth across her cell. It was identical to mine, except hers didn't have a separate bathroom. A half wall partially hid the shower, sink, and toilet in the back corner. She wobbled, then steadied herself against the cinderblock wall. Staring hard at the knobless steel door, hands fisted, neck tendons straining, she howled when it didn't fly open. She sank to the cot, sobbing, then looked up, staring right at me. "Please," she cried soundlessly.

Blinking away tears that blurred my vision, I watched it all from the warden's office, through the monitor hooked up to the cameras in her cell.

Tristan tried to make arrangements for me to visit my parents, but because my mother's psychokinesis kept regenerating, watching them via security cam was all the head warden would allow. Not as good as in person, but we'd been here for almost two weeks now. I'd take any opportunity I could get to see my parents, even if it was through a security cam.

Tristan stood behind me, so close I could feel his heat. He hadn't taken his eyes off me since my razor blade incident a few days ago. He'd even removed a pair of scissors from the warden's desk.

The warden, Mr. Milbourne, stood in the corner. The massive block of pure muscle watched me, the daughter of killers, with the same disgust Kellan had. I almost preferred his icy glower over Tristan's longing, overprotective gazes.

Another monitor showed my father in his cell, which looked more like a hospital room. Eyes closed, he lay withered and motionless on a railed bed. Dr. Sheldon stood over him, making notes in a chart. Machines lined the perimeter of the room.

I squinted at the monitors, absorbing every detail. An IV needle pierced my father's arm, and a breathing tube ran under his nose. His chest rose and fell with slow rhythm. I'd never seen him sleep so peacefully.

My mother's hair was ratted. She wore a uniform like mine. Her shoes had no laces either. As she rocked on the cot, she absently twisted her hands together, rubbing the fourth finger of her left hand. "She's not wearing her wedding rings," I said, and looked closely at my father's hand. "His ring is gone too. Where are they?"

Mr. Milbourne grunted. "Evidence room."

"I want them."

The warden shook his head and grunted again.

Before I could plead my case, Tristan pulled out his cell phone and dialed. "Dad?" He murmured my request.

A minute later, the phone on the warden's desk rang.

And a few minutes after that, I held a clear plastic bag that contained my parents' wedding rings.

They had an evidence room, and it was close by. I tucked that knowledge away for later.

After flashing Tristan a reluctant thank-you smile for getting the rings, I shook them from the bag: an engagement ring with a minuscule diamond and two thin gold bands. Nothing fancy. My parents got married almost immediately after they met, when Dad was a reporter at a small town newspaper and Mom was a housekeeper at a motel. But no matter how wealthy they eventually became, no matter how many other jewels my mother acquired, they never took off their original wedding rings.

One by one, I slid them on my finger.

Guilt overwhelmed me, cutting off my air, and I pulled them off. I had no right to wear them when it was my fault they couldn't.

"If they don't fit," Tristan said, "I'll get you a chain so you can wear them around your neck."

I tossed them back in the bag. "If my parents can't wear them, no one should wear them."

As Mr. Milbourne led me away, I gave one last glance at my parents, sending them a silent apology.

When Tristan stretched out on the floor that night to go to sleep, I told him it wasn't bedtime just yet. I pressed the buzzer on the intercom.

"Yeah?" The crackly voice belonged to Weasel Face. Perfect.

"Can you come, sir?" I asked in my most helpless tone. "We need you again."

Tristan cocked one eyebrow when the intercom clicked off. "More breaking and entering?"

"I want to see what's in that evidence room."

"Tampering with evidence is illegal, Tessa."

"So is locking up my parents without physical proof," I said. "But I won't tamper. I just want to look."

The disapproving frown on Tristan's face didn't go away.

"I'm going, with or without you," I said with a shrug.

Sighing, he stood up. "I'm not leaving you."

Ha. I knew he would say that.

All it took to convince Weasel Face to lead us to the evidence room and unlock it was a few pleading eyelash bats from me and a friendly discussion about the Green Bay Packers from Tristan. With a waggle of his finger, he even disabled the surveillance camera hanging in the corner.

I snuffed my guilt that Weasel Face could lose his job if he was caught. He shouldn't be working for such an evil place anyway. Once I got my parents released, they would gratefully—and generously— reward him.

Aisles of stacked beige lockers, each about three feet square, filled the evidence room. The rows were separated by narrow stainless steel tables. We wandered the aisles until we found a locker marked CARS0520 near the back. Weasel Face opened the lock with a few wiggles of his fingers, then Tristan sent him to guard the door.

Taking a deep breath, I swung open the locker door to see what was inside.

Almost nothing.

I was torn between disappointment that there were few items to help me prove my parents' innocence, and pride that we'd left so little behind for Dennis Connelly to find.

I raised the fog as high as I dared. I needed to think clearly. Tristan and I took out each item and placed them on the table. Each one was in a separate plastic bag with a form printed on the front, referencing where the item was found, the initials of the psychic who'd read it, and the information they were able to obtain from it.

On almost every form, that last line was left blank.

The silver ribbon from my Winterball dress was in one bag, coiled up like a snake. On the form, Kellan reported how he used it to catch me when I ran from him in Twelve Lakes, and then to blindfold me. Quite a useful tool, that silver ribbon.

Three bags contained the originals of the papers that had been copied into the green binder: the receipt for the Disney movies, Jillian's dance recital program and one of Logan's old compositions. Dennis Connelly had retrieved those items from our various hideouts and brought them back here, as evidence, and for psychometric readings. The psychic couldn't tell much from the receipt, but from the others he was able to tell that both of my siblings were psionic. He said the dancer was rebellious and resentful. The musician was cautious and protective. He predicted we'd go to Arkansas next.

He was wrong. About Arkansas, anyway.

Inside another large bag was an eight-by-ten inch canvas: the blue petal I'd painted in school when I was eleven. My alias *Nicki Nelson* was scrawled in the bottom right corner. The form said I made it when we lived in Missouri. I remembered now why I hadn't brought it home— my teacher, Mrs. Dixon, thought it was so good that she hung it in the hallway for everyone in the entire school to see. I knew my parents would be upset at the attention, but I wanted to wait just one day before asking Mrs. Dixon to take it down. We fled to our next hideout that night.

The psychic who read the painting hadn't been able to learn anything from it, other than she suspected my real name started with the letter T. She'd also written the word *guilt* and circled it several times.

She was right.

Inside another bag was one of my old copies of *Anne of Green Gables.* The copy Tristan gave me was in my getaway bag. That bag wasn't in the locker, which probably meant Jillian and Logan had it. As soon as I found them, I would toss out Tristan's copy. Maybe burn it.

I inspected the rest of the items.

A tiny SD card. "What's this from?" I asked.

"It was in my phone," Tristan said.

Before I could ask why *his* SD card was considered evidence, I realized it probably was a bug. He always plugged his phone into speakers when I disclosed my secrets.

"I recorded you," he confirmed.

My black cell phone, the one from my parents. Kellan's guard had fished it out of the secret pocket in my silver dress.

The handbag I used at Winterball. Inside was the sleek white cell phone Tristan had given me. "And that had a tracking device in it," he said. I remembered what he said when he gave me that phone, so clearly it was like he was speaking the words aloud right now: *I will not let you just disappear into the night.*

Pushing the electronics and my guilt aside, I moved on to the next items.

Miscellaneous items from homes and motels. Textbooks and worksheets from various schools. The charred pages of a cookbook from our stay in Florida. Strands of Jillian's blond hair and Mom's graying hair. A toothbrush, a napkin, a coffee mug. I recognized the mug from a truck stop in Georgia a few years ago. A passing waitress, her tray heavy and unbalanced, had spilled hot coffee down my shoulder and arm. I bit my lips bloody to keep from screaming. But my mother sure screamed. My dad dragged us away as the waitress fell to her knees, unable to speak she felt so bad for burning me. And then we raced out of the state. The burn stopped hurting once Dad put some ointment on it, so I'd completely forgotten the whole incident until I saw the mug just now.

That—that wasn't the hook-nosed waitress whose photo was in the green binder, the one who died of a heart attack, was it?

"Tessa." Tristan's caress on my cheek woke me from the memory.

I cleared my throat and shoved the mug back in its bag.

My Civics notebook, Logan's reeds, Jillian's scarf. The rhinestone clips she lost at Homecoming. The hockey puck Logan had pulled from our bushes. Of course.

In the next bag was the spoon Jillian tried to bend with her mind at Ethan's party. I remembered Tristan scooping the spoon up from the floor, but now I realized he never put it in the sink. He must have slipped it into his pocket. On the attached form, the psychic had scrawled five words: *Defiant. Reckless. Desperate. Inebriated. Psychokinetic.*

A set of twisted car keys was next. The form said they were from the getaway car we'd used in Nebraska. A psychic with the initials BL had read them, and had drawn a picture of twelve lakes.

Only one bag left. The object inside was heavy and flat and wrapped in bubble wrap and tape. The old tape peeled off easily, then I unwound the bubble wrap.

A butcher knife.

Shiny. Long. Silver. The form said it was from the kitchen of our house in Virginia, from the set my mother kept on the granite counter.

Kellan said my father had stabbed an APR recruiting agent. Delivered the final blows. I'd never seen my dad be violent or even heard him raise his voice. Could he really have stabbed someone to death? I pictured my dad slamming this knife into the agent's back, again and again and again, as the agent crawled through a puddle of blood on our marble floor.

"Tessa. Let go of the knife. Now."

Tristan's sharp command penetrated the image, and it disappeared. He'd grabbed my wrist and was trying to pry my fingers open. They were wrapped around the knife's handle so tightly they hurt. I released my grip, and a tinny clang echoed around the room as the knife fell to the table.

How dare I even *imagine* my father using that knife?

I yanked my wrist from Tristan's hand and threw everything back into the locker as he glowered accusingly at me. He put the knife back himself.

Before he shut the locker door, I snatched my black cell phone out. Like a child finding her lost security blanket, I hooked it to my waistband and tapped it with my fingertips. I thrust my chin at Tristan, silently daring him to order me to put it back.

He didn't. He just gave me a solemn nod of understanding.

CHAPTER FORTY-SIX

M Y NIGHTMARE, NOW even worse than before with images of bloody silver knives and pleading waitresses, woke me with a start the next morning. As soon as my heart stopped pounding, I reached under the cot to the far back corner. My fingers brushed past Dr. Sheldon's green binder and the plastic bag that held my parents' rings, and I pulled out my black cell phone.

"I'm calling Jillian and Logan," I told Tristan in response to his curious glance from his makeshift bed on the floor. My siblings were still safer out there than they would be in here, but now that I had my phone back, the need to hear their voices was crushing.

Tristan sat up straight. "Great idea."

His enthusiasm made me suspicious. "I won't let them tell me where they are," I said with a glare, "so don't even think about sending an investigator after them. I just want them to know we're okay." I swallowed and decided to rephrase that. "Well...that we're still alive, anyway."

I flipped the phone open, heart sinking when it didn't light up. "The battery ran out."

"That phone probably wouldn't get a signal down here anyway." He held out his phone. "Use mine. Standard APR issue. It gets a signal down here."

"No way. You'll just track the call."

His guilty look showed me I was right.

"I can't use your phone anyway," I said. "Logan programmed ours so they would only accept calls from each other."

He hopped up. "Then let's go to the Lab. I know someone who can charge your phone for you."

We quickly dressed, then rang the buzzer for the guard. Spiky Hair opened the cell door a few minutes later. Before we could even start to convince him to let me leave the cell, he waved us out. His lips twisted in a snarl, he informed us that Dennis Connelly had made arrangements for me to go to any public area of the building, as long as a guard escorted me. He was fortunate, he said, to have that pleasure this morning.

He accompanied us up to the ground floor, now brightly lit and bustling with APR employees, many of whom greeted Tristan cheerfully and welcomed him home while giving me curious looks.

On the left side of the hall was a small open room with a microwave and a refrigerator. The lunchroom. Smiling to myself, I imagined Kellan flying back against the fridge, perhaps breaking the coffee maker, as Heath punched him in the jaw.

Across from the lunchroom was a door decorated with crayon drawings. Red, blue, and yellow cubbies lined the walls on either side of it.

"That's my mom's classroom," Tristan said. "She runs a preschool for psionic kids who haven't learned to control their abilities yet. They're on winter break now."

A stray knit mitten, royal blue with a brown teddy bear design, peeked from one of the cubbies. The bear's eyes were made from tiny black buttons. I pictured a towheaded, rosy-cheeked little boy, so excited to get home to bake cookies with his grandma that he didn't notice he'd dropped his mitten.

I stared at the colorful artwork on the door, then stuffed the mitten into a cubby and rushed away.

Closely followed by Spiky Hair, we walked to the very end of the hall, which opened into a big room with smaller offices along the perimeter. "This is the Lab," Tristan said, "where we test potential psionic subjects."

The room didn't look like the science lab I'd expected. Bright and open, it was more like a lounge, with round tables and comfortable chairs scattered about and large glass windows showing the snowy forest beyond. No unpainted cinderblock walls here.

But I could see a tall, electrified fence just beyond the trees.

Tristan led me to one of the small offices lining the lab and knocked on the door frame. "Mr. Halloran?"

"That's me." An older gentleman with a large nose sat at a desk strewn with piles of gadgets, USB cords, and computer chips. He peered through a magnifying glass at a tiny circuit board on his fingertip.

"I don't know if you remember me," Tristan said. "I'm Tristan Connelly. I used to work in the Lab as an intern, and now I'm in Investigations."

"Oh. Yes," he said. "You're Dennis's son. What can I do for you?"

"We were hoping you could charge my girlfriend's phone and make it get a signal in the Underground."

I glared at him to remind him I was *not* his girlfriend.

Mr. Halloran held out his wrinkled hand. I gave him the phone, and he pressed it tightly between his palms.

"Mr. Halloran is technokinetic. He can manipulate technology,"

Tristan explained.

A minute later Mr. Halloran opened his palms. "You're good to go. What's a lovely young girl like you doing in the Underground anyway?"

"Oh, just proving that the APR is an evil organization and should be destroyed," I said with an innocent smile, leaving him speechless as I took my phone back. "Thank you so much, Mr. Halloran."

Half sighing, half laughing, Tristan thanked him for his help and pulled me from the room.

Spiky Hair followed us from the Lab, but just before we reached the hallway a short man with a smiling reindeer on his sweater stopped us. "Tristan, hello! How long have you been back? Who's your friend?"

"Hi, Mr. Rigby," Tristan said. "I got back a few days ago. This is my...this is Tessa." He shot me a glance: *Better?*

I was too astounded to reply. He introduced me using my real name. How liberating. I could tell everyone my real name now. No more aliases, ever.

"Mr. Rigby is a Sensor," Tristan said. "He goes around the country looking for psionic people. When he senses one, he calls in a recruiting team. That's how we find most of our test subjects and employees."

The way Mr. Rigby was looking at me with his head cocked made me squirm. "Tessa, I'm having trouble reading you," he said."Tell me, what is your ability?"

"My ability?"

"Oh, she's not psionic," Tristan said.

"Hmm." Mr. Rigby pursed his lips. "I thought I sensed something, but it's gone. May I look deeper?"

I agreed. He could look as deep as he wanted; he wouldn't find anything. He placed both hands on my shoulders for a minute, then let go. "You're right." He patted my shoulder sympathetically. "Neutral."

I supposed every psionic person felt sorry for us neutrals.

"But I know why I sensed something from you," he said. "You must have family members who are psionic."

"Yes, sir," I mumbled.

Mr. Rigby rubbed his hands together. "Have you kids heard the news?"

Tristan shook his head. "What news?"

He leaned in conspiratorially. "They finally captured the Kitteridge Killers. They won't give us any details, as usual, but word is they surrendered right outside this building to one of the investigators. Your father must be thrilled, Tristan. What a relief."

Tristan gave him a curt nod as I froze. Kitteridge. My hometown.

"We really have to go. Nice seeing you, Mr. Rigby." Tristan pulled me into the hallway. "Sorry," he muttered. "Most people up here don't know who your parents are."

Good. I didn't want anyone to know my parents were the Kitteridge Killers.

Spiky Hair gave me a knowing smirk.

Spiky Hair had barely locked Tristan and me back in our cell when I slid open my phone. It lit up right away, signal stronger than ever. But then I hesitated. I'd never used my phone to make calls, just receive them. How had Logan always programmed our phones?

That's right: he programmed our speed dials going from oldest to youngest. Our parents were one and two. Jillian was three, I was four, and Logan was five. Just like the target numbers assigned to us by the APR.

I hit pound-three, and the phone automatically dialed Jillian's number.

Answer on the first ring: that was the rule. In one moment, I would hear Jillian's voice.

One ring.

She didn't answer.

Another ring.

No answer.

And another.

Why wasn't she answering her phone?

After another ring, a chipper, animated voice told me to leave a message.

I froze for a moment, unsure what to say. Then the message tumbled out of my mouth. "Oh my God, Jillian, Logan, it's Tessa. I'm alive. Mom and Dad are alive. We're in Wisconsin in a town called Lilybrook. They have us locked up in this place called the Agency for Psionic Research. But don't come for us. Stay as far away as you can. They're saying terrible things about Mom and Dad, they're calling them the Kitteridge Killers..."

I sucked in a lungful of air. "I'm trying so hard to prove them wrong. But they have a preschool here. A preschool! How could a place with a preschool be bad? I should tell you to run, to run and never stop, but I need you to come, even if you don't want me anymore after what I did. Please, come. I need you. Because I—oh God...I..."

No. I couldn't say it. I wouldn't say it. I bit my lips to keep from saying it.

But the words came anyway. Soft, barely a whisper, but they came. "I think they might be telling the truth."

My voice, my heart, the air—they all shattered as I heard myself say those words. With a sob, I sank to the cot. From far away I felt Tristan take the phone from my hand, heard the tiny click as he closed it.

Which is harder: To refuse to believe something, or to believe something and not want to?

I hated that I knew the answer.

CHAPTER FORTY-SEVEN

W E SAT IN heavy silence. Timidly, Tristan slid his hand over the periwinkle blanket so his pinky touched mine. "So you believe me now about your parents?" he whispered.

Unable to speak, I nodded. I drew my hands into my sleeves, hugged my knees to my chin.

"You okay?"

No. I was definitely not okay. Faith that my parents were innocent was all I had before. Now I had nothing.

Even the fog wouldn't come when I called it. Now there was nowhere to hide from the truth.

The guard with squeaky shoes delivered dinner to our cell that night. Tuna casserole and green beans. Tristan automatically sent the guard to Hawthorne's to get a meatless meal for me. I asked him to get one for my mom too. She could never eat the tuna. Even the smell of it would make her sick.

By losing faith in my parents, I'd betrayed them yet again. Maybe all I needed to get my faith back and take the jackhammer out of my heart was to do something nice for my mom.

An hour later Squeaky Shoes returned with two Styrofoam containers of vegetable lasagna and blueberry pie, and a grunted promise to deliver one of them to my mother.

It didn't work. My faith didn't return. The jackhammer kept hammering away.

My parents were guilty.

As we ate, I tried calling my brother and sister again. My eighth call that day, and they hadn't answered yet. I tried Logan first this time. After four rings that stupid robotic voice requested I leave a message. With a sigh, I slid the phone shut and tried Jillian next.

Her phone rang and rang, and I closed my eyes and pictured them, weary and frightened, hiding in a dingy motel room somewhere and wondering why we hadn't come for them yet. And now, just as they feared the worst, Jillian's phone would ring, and with trembling fingers she would flip it open, her gold bracelet sliding down her arm, the heart charm catching the dim light. "Mom? Dad? Tessa?" she would cry, so relieved she could barely speak—

I shot up straight. "Tristan! I know where Jillian and Logan are!"

"Jillian had a boyfriend who gave her a gold bracelet," I told Tristan. "She was in love with him. I bet they went to find him." My leg bounced up and down, shaking the Styrofoam container on my lap and even the cot.

"Where were you living then?" he asked.

"Um…" Should I tell him? Now that I knew their location, any telepath in this place could just pluck the information from my mind anyway. "Nebraska," I said. "Union, Nebraska."

"What's his name?"

"Gavin. Gavin… He was quiet. Smart. But his last name…" Finally I gave up. "I don't think I ever learned his last name."

"Let's do a search for all the Gavins in Union," Tristan said. "We can use a computer in the Lab." He pressed the buzzer and looked over his shoulder. "You're going to sp—"

Too anxious to wait patiently for the guard, I jumped up. Vegetable lasagna and blueberry pie spilled down the Lilybrook Lightning hoodie I was wearing, and a bit got on my gray prison pants.

Tristan chuckled and tapped his temple. "You're going to *spill,* I was about to say." He went to the bathroom for a towel as I grabbed the fuchsia and chartreuse backpack from under the cot. Now I needed those clothes from Tristan's sister.

I shed my messy outfit and pulled on a pair of jeans. Tristan's sister was two years younger than me, but her jeans were still too long. Even worse, they had five glittery, sequined butterflies appliquéd down one of the legs. "Are all of your sister's clothes like this?" I asked Tristan, showing him the butterflies. Jillian and Logan would crack up, seeing me wear something so outrageous.

He grinned. "That's tame for her."

"She dyed her hair purple too." I pulled her indigo sweater over my head, then slid into my sneakers and pressed the buzzer again. "Bright purple with streaks of lavender."

"It was pink last time I saw her," Tristan said, then his smile faded. "Wait. How do you know her hair is purple?"

I blinked. "I…I don't know. I just do." I searched for a loose strand of purple hair on the jeans or sweater. I must have seen one.

But no, the clothes were clean.

Tristan stared at me. "Tess…"

I saw him walking to me, but I saw his sister too. Amber. No—her name was Ember. Wearing a pair of jeans with sequined butterflies. Hair shiny, straight, and purple. Rehearsing with her band, strumming an electric guitar and singing into a microphone. A white sheet hung behind them, displaying the band's name in gold spray paint.

"Lyre," I said.

"Tessa, I swear I'm not lying to you."

"No. Your sister's band is named Lyre." My whole body grew hot, then cold.

"How did you… it's the clothes," Tristan whispered. "You're wearing her clothes."

I shrieked and pulled them off as if they burned. The vision disappeared. Tristan pulled a new sweatshirt over me, and I put my gray pants back on. In a daze, I sank onto the chair. "What was that?"

"I think you might be—Oh God." He bounded to the door, then pounded on the buzzer and yelled for help.

The fog was coming back, and I pushed it away. The Styrofoam container was still on the floor where I'd dropped it, and automatically I leaned down to pick it up. It slipped from my hands as an image blasted into my consciousness of the young woman who'd put my dinner in the carton—she'd just discovered she was pregnant and was worried she didn't make enough money working at Hawthorne's. Patricia Garrity. That was her name.

The chair I was sitting on—it used to be in the prison's visiting room. It looked just like all the other chairs, but I knew it was *this exact* chair, and then it sat in a supply closet for a couple of years before it was moved in here. Faces of all the people who once sat in it flashed in my mind like a rapid slide show. I knew all their names. I knew if they were prisoners or visitors. I knew the name of the maintenance man who'd bolted the chair to the floor of this cell back in 1995: Jerry Herrington. He could change his hair and eye color at will.

I shot up from the chair, and the visions faded a bit. Shaking, I clutched the wall for support. But touching the wall made it worse; more images exploded, sharp and vibrant images of everyone who'd ever been in this cell.

Dennis Connelly: so relieved his son was back home safe.

John Kellan: too good to be just an investigator. Closing the Carson case should earn him that promotion.

Dr. Sheldon: she doesn't care what Kellan says, Tristan can stay with that poor neutral girl in the Underground as long as he wants.

The guards: Weasel Face was Warren Fontanini. He was awed that someone like Tristan Connelly wanted to be friends with him. Sam Santiago was the heavy evening guard with the squeaky shoes. He planned to apply to be an investigator as soon as he lost a little weight. The day guard with the spiky yellow hair was Shawn Harris. He'd laughed at the note I'd written to my parents, and instead of delivering it, he crumpled it up and threw it away.

And the people who'd been held under observation in this cell over the years—men, women, even children…some psionic, some neutral, all frightened.

Tristan's hoodie forced images into me too: Tristan stuffing it into his duffle bag, realizing he shouldn't have brought it to Twelve Lakes in case I saw it. Buying it from the Lilybrook High School bookstore with money he'd made from his first APR paycheck when he was fifteen. Wearing it last March when Kellan pulled him aside: *Hey, Junior, how'd you like to jump-start your career and go on your first investigation?*

All these images swirled around me, making me dizzy. Faces. Names. Ages. Dates. Talking, thinking, chattering, clattering, becoming louder, faster, detonating one after another, forcing the real world down a long tunnel.

Clutching my head, I squeezed my eyes shut, trying to block the visions.

But they wouldn't stop. They were suffocating me.

So I did the only thing I could do. I opened myself up to the fog and called it in, called it all in, and it came swiftly, rushing to me, darker than ever before and so thick it was almost solid.

tristanhelpme

I had just enough time to see the breathless panic in his eyes before the fog slammed into me like a brick wall.

And then there was nothing.

CHAPTER FORTY-EIGHT

Heavy.

Dark.

Silent.

Numb.

And then…a whisper.
"Tessa."
Tristan.
"Wake up, Tessa."
So far away. So heavy.
"Please, Clockwise. Open your eyes."
More voices. Low, mumbled.
Tristan was gripping my hand.
Then I heard other people around me. Doctors, nurses, guards.
Each of them brought visions, and when they placed their hands on me, the visions became vibrant and razor sharp. They ebbed and flowed nonsensically through my consciousness, twisting together like snakes.

With a whimper, I surrendered to the fog again.

"Stop touching her!" Tristan's voice whipped through the fog. "You're making it worse." Each word became harder to hear, the last part just an echo, and then they all disappeared.

Only Tristan touched me now, but I went deeper into the fog until I no longer felt his hand on mine.

If I wanted to, I could keep going, deeper and deeper, until I felt nothing at all.

The fog never lied to me. The fog never betrayed me.

In the fog there were no visions. No blood. No pain, no guilt, no *all my fault.*

They could take away the shoelaces and drawstrings. They could take away the razor blades. But no one could take away the fog.

And if I went deep enough, I could stay in the fog forever.

But…

Jillian. Logan. Mom and Dad.

They needed me.

So I clawed my way back from the blackness, lifting the fog, making it thin and thick, close and far, dark and light.

There. Perfect.

I held the fog steady.

No more images appeared. No more visions emerged.

Whatever was happening to me, I could control it.

I opened my eyes.

He was there, staring down at me.

"Tristan."

My voice was so soft I barely heard it, but he collapsed with a heavy sigh, his head burrowing to my stomach. "Thank God."

The guards left the cell, leaving Tristan and me with Dr. Sheldon.

Dennis Connelly was there too, near the door. He watched me for a moment, brows knit with worry, then slipped out before I remembered to be afraid of him.

Dr. Sheldon approached, palms out. Tristan immediately shifted to block her access to me, throwing his arms wide. *"No one* touches her."

Twisting her lips, the doctor retreated. "I will have to examine you soon, Tessa. But for now, let's try to figure out what happened without me touching you. Tristan said you put on his sister's clothes and had a vision of her, and then you fainted. Is that right? You had a vision?"

I decided to cooperate, as long as she didn't try to touch me. Being careful to keep the fog balanced, I sat up and drew my hands safely into the sleeves of Tristan's hoodie. "I had more than one vision. A lot more." I recounted my visions, giving her names, dates, details. "It's almost like I was—"

Tristan listened breathlessly until he stopped me with a single whispered word. "Retrocognitive."

I blinked at him. "Yeah, but I'm…I'm neutral."

"Retrocognition is psychically knowing the history of a person or object," Dr. Sheldon said. "That's what you did."

"You're psionic, Tessa," Tristan said.

I said nothing, letting the word sink in.

Retrocognitive.

I was psychic after all.

I was psionic.

Me. The runt of the litter. Tiny little Tessa.

Earlier today I'd imagined the little boy losing his mitten, and Kellan breaking the coffee maker and flying into the fridge when Heath punched him. Were those images really visions?

"But I don't like that the visions made you pass out," Tristan said. "Is that going to happen every time?"

"The visions didn't make me faint," I said. "The fog did."

"What fog?" The question came from both of them.

"The fog," I said with a shrug. "It's always been in the background, but I've noticed it a lot more since I've been here. I bring it in when I'm upset and lift it when I need to think clearly."

When their confused expressions didn't change, I explained further. "The visions wouldn't stop. I tried closing my eyes, but they still came. Touching things made it worse, but even when I touched nothing, they still came. Faster and faster, dozens, hundreds, one after another. The only way to make them stop was to call in the fog. And it came in so fast and so heavy that I passed out."

"I bet that's why you get sick in crowded places," Tristan said, getting excited. "The fog has trouble containing the visions from all those people. And I bet that's why our psychics could never get a clear reading on anything your family left behind. That fog was obscuring their visions."

Could that be true? *I* was the reason Dennis Connelly couldn't find us? I'd been *protecting* my family all these years?

But I was also the one who betrayed them.

"You had your ability extremely well-hidden," Dr. Sheldon said. "I've examined you several times, twice specifically looking for psionics, and I never saw anything. This fog of yours must be very strong. It's probably been stifling your retrocognition your whole life." She slid her pen in her lab coat pocket and stood. "I'd like to see it in action. Let's go up to the Lab."

I stiffened. "No. If I lift the fog I'll lose control again."

"You'll be perfectly safe." She held out her hand.

Tristan immediately sprang up to shield me. "She. Said. No."

Dr. Sheldon tucked her clipboard under her arm and sighed. "I won't test an unwilling subject. Maybe later this week?"

I shook my head. I had no intention of having another vision, ever again.

I only needed to do it one last time.

As soon as Dr. Sheldon left, I shot up and dug under the cot.

"What are you doing?" Suspicion was clear in Tristan's tone.

I withdrew the plastic bag I'd been searching for. "I'm going to read my parents' wedding rings."

"Why?"

I almost laughed at him. "So I can prove the APR is wrong about them."

"But you already know they're guilty."

"I was wrong about them too," I said, and this time I did laugh, and it came out light and fluttery and gleeful. How could I not laugh? I was practically floating with joy. I was psionic! And now I had a way to prove my parents were innocent. How ridiculous of me to ever doubt them, to ever lose faith.

Tristan knelt in front of me with a sigh. "Just…be careful. Promise you won't run into the fog if you don't like what you see."

No need to promise that. I wouldn't see anything I didn't want to. I'd never been more certain of anything in my life.

I pulled the wedding rings from the bag and closed my palm around them. Then I closed my eyes, took a deep breath, and lifted the fog.

CHAPTER FORTY-NINE

HE VISIONS EXPLODED into my consciousness, as if they'd been trapped inside the rings and couldn't wait to be released. Secrets imprisoned in darkness suddenly freed, bursting into the light. The big bang.

Jumbled, twisted, so bright they were almost fluorescent, the visions blurred together and swirled around me. Only the occasional flash, snippets of my parents' past, made it through—Logan plunking the keys of our grand piano with chubby toddler fingers, Jillian pouting at the sight of her private school uniform, my father taking my mother's hand and whispering her name—as the snarl of visions became denser, tighter, closer, squeezing the air from my lungs.

Gasping for breath, I yanked the fog in. The visions disappeared and were replaced by gray cinderblock walls and Tristan's worried face.

I blinked at him. "I'm going back in."

I lifted the fog before he could tell me to stop. Once again the visions rushed at me. I adjusted the fog, using it to corral them. They quivered, trembled, hissed, but I held the fog steady.

Vaguely aware that I was now lying with my head on Tristan's lap, I lifted the fog, just a teeny tiny bit, allowing one vision through. The first one.

This is not quite a surprise; she's been expecting a proposal but she didn't know it would happen today. Andy had brought her to a field of wildflowers, spread a blanket on the ground, and opened a cheap bottle of champagne. He reaches into his pocket and pulls out a ring. The diamond is minuscule, no bigger than a speck of dust, but it's the most beautiful diamond in the world. She cannot suppress her elation, and hundreds of flowers pluck themselves from the ground and float around them as Andy slips the ring on her finger. They kiss as they are showered with thousands of petals.

No. That was beautiful, but it wasn't what I needed to see. *Give me proof my parents are innocent*, I commanded the visions, and lifted the fog again. *Show me what I need to see.*

And they did.

He opens his eyes with a disgusted groan, then turns to his computer and starts writing his article about the politician he'd just watched with his mobile eye. With the help of his remote vision, he exposed the malfeasance of more than a few politicians during his short tenure as a reporter, and this guy, Representative Harold Applebaum, was next. He was returning from an all-expense-paid vacation to the Cayman Islands, courtesy of the tobacco lobbyists. And the young, bikini-clad woman he'd brought on that trip was definitely not his wife.

He lifts his fingers from the keyboard.

Exposing Applebaum in his column probably wouldn't even get the guy kicked out of office. And it certainly wouldn't help the victims of the tobacco industry.

There must be a better way to take advantage of this secret.

Maybe he can follow Applebaum around for a few weeks with his mobile eye, learn his habits, figure out where to plant cameras...

"Wendy!" he shouts. "How'd you like to take a few pictures without touching the camera?"

She makes a phone call, anonymous and untraceable, to Harold Applebaum. *"I know what you did."* She demands a large sum of money, impossibly large, to keep his wife from seeing the pictures of him in bed with his little blond mistress.

Neither she nor Andy are surprised when Applebaum pays, quickly and without question.

They use the money to pay off their bills, then anonymously donate half of the rest to a politician sponsoring a program to keep kids from smoking, and the other half to a hospital specializing in lung cancer.

They are modern-day Robin Hoods.

He flips through his mental database of all the wealthy people he's met. He and Wendy choose one of the wealthiest, an auto tycoon. He'd shaken the man's hand once at a press conference. He concentrates on the tycoon and sends out his mobile eye. Within a few days, he learns all his secrets, any of which would destroy him if they were leaked to the public. Then he makes the phone call.

She sits in a French restaurant in Washington with her girlfriends, nibbling nervously on a *petit four*. Her friends comment that she'd picked a beautiful place for lunch.

She glances across the elegant room at their latest victim, an auto tycoon, eating a filet and talking with his mouth full into his cell phone. He has only two days left to pay to keep her from sending proof of his embezzlement to his partners.

As she watches him inhale the filet, she decides this time they'll donate the money–some of it, anyway–to hunger relief.

The tycoon looks over at her.

"I think you have an admirer, Wendy," her friend Savannah says with a giggle.

She smiles weakly and looks back at the man.

He takes a last bite, then wipes his mouth with a cloth napkin. He stands up, a curious, knowing sneer on his face.

A cold sweat forms at the back of her neck. Is he coming to flirt with her, or does he know who she is?

He's coming closer. Has he seen her following him?

Panic skitters, then stampedes, down her spine, and she realizes what she must do.

The tycoon stops, grabs his throat with both hands, and his face turns red. Despite repeated attempts by the waiter to perform the Heimlich maneuver, he is dead within minutes. It was just a small piece of steak, but the waiter was not able to dislodge it from his windpipe.

Her friends cry at witnessing such a horrible tragedy, but she weeps inconsolably. She'd never used her PK to kill anyone before. Not on purpose.

They have to stop doing this. But it's so easy, it's become routine. Almost boring. The newspaper sends him to press conferences, or Wendy tells him which important and wealthy people have made reservations at the hotel. He shows his press pass, shakes their hands. Later he sends out his mobile eye to see what they have to hide. Then he and Wendy gather the evidence. They make contact. They collect the money.

They have to stop doing this. It's so easy, but now people are dead. Four, so far. All because Wendy panics. And then she's a hysterical mess for days, barely able to function. If he didn't have to take care of her, he'd be a mess too.

They have to stop doing this. But when he watches Wendy through her eyes, her gaze lands for minutes at a time on the big brick houses in the nice neighborhoods, so sturdy and safe. He watches through her eyes as she stares at the pregnant women and the families in the park.

They have to stop doing this. And they will, after this next job. This time they'll keep all the money. And then they won't ever do it again.

One more job. Maybe two.

He squeezes his eyes shut and rubs his temples.

She leans her head on Andy's shoulder and sighs contentedly. The floundering beat reporter is now a respected journalist at a prestigious paper in D.C., and the trailer-trash motel maid is now the director of special events at an elegant hotel in the city. They live in an elite neighborhood in Kitteridge, in the most impressive house on the block. Their children attend the most exclusive school.

"Look at our babies," she purrs as the children play in the pool in their large backyard. Jillian dives off the diving board, and Logan slides down the twisty slide. Tessa watches them contentedly from the steps in the shallow end, which is as deep as she will ever go.

Jillian, seven years old, bold and confident and beautiful, showed signs of psychokinesis before she could walk. Logan's PK was evident before he could crawl, and he's hypercognetic, too. An automatic learner. Only four years old, reading high-school level books with a swipe of his palm. Just last week he sat down on the bench in front of their new grand piano, feet not even reaching the floor, and he played the instrument like he'd been playing for years.

And then there's Tessa. Nothing makes her happier than seeing Tessa's big green eyes light up with joy. She'd never admit this to anyone, but she loves Tessa the most. Tessa needs the most love. Her lack of psychic ability, while surrounded by a family that has total control of the world, has made her timid and insecure. But maybe her psychic talent will develop later. Her own power didn't become apparent until she was almost thirteen. Tessa's only six. There's plenty of time for her ability to develop.

Her children are perfect. The love she shares with her husband is deep and passionate and perfect. Her home is perfect.

Her life, quite simply, is perfect.

A knock at the door.

Jillian and Logan are at the park, and Tessa's outside reading a book after she hurt herself at the playground. Wendy's on the computer. He's free for the moment, so he answers the door.

Two men. One about his age, tall and lean. The other a bit older and shorter. Both wearing ties and sport coats. One is holding a stack of flyers. The other holds a large manila envelope. Collecting money for something.

He decides to donate generously, whatever the cause. They show him a flyer with the picture of a little girl. Her name, Rebecca Lukas, is printed underneath the photo. "This little girl has leukemia," the shorter man says. "Her parents don't have medical insurance, so we're raising the money for her treatment through donations."

He takes the flyer. "Poor kid. My sister had leukemia. Come on in. I'll get the checkbook."

He leads the men to the kitchen and takes his wallet from the drawer. What an odd coincidence. His sister's name is Rebecca too. He decides to be especially charitable to the girl on the flyer. "You fellows know who Xander Xavier is?"

The shorter one clears his throat. "He's a journalist at the DC Daily. I enjoy his columns."

"Xander's a close friend of mine," he says. "I'll ask him to mention this girl in his column. Maybe some media attention will bring in more donations."

He notices the two men glance at each other, then back at him. The short man smiles. "That'd be wonderful."

He writes the check. "A thousand bucks okay?"

"You're extremely generous, sir."

"I just want to help little Rebecca make a full recovery."

"Well, your sister recovered, and there've been even more medical advances since then," the younger, taller man adds. "Your donation will go a long way to helping this girl's family afford the best treatment."

Hmmm."That's funny," he says softly. "I don't recall mentioning that my sister recovered."

The taller man licks his lips. "I—I just assumed..."

The house is silent.

Same illness. Same name. Maybe that coincidence is *too* odd to be plausible. "You're not collecting donations, are you?" He tries to sound imposing while his heart pounds.

"No, sir, we're not," the shorter one says. "We're from a department of the federal government. We'd like to ask how you learned so much about the politicians in your columns."

Ah. Nothing to worry about after all. He could handle this. "Then you must have figured out that Xander Xavier is my pseudonym."

"Yes, we did," the taller man says, then lowers his voice. "We'd also like to ask about your special...ability."

He exhales slowly. They know about his mobile eye.

They must know about the blackmail. The murders.

They must know everything.

"You've been watching us?" He stumbles backwards, blindly.

"Mr. Carson, please." The shorter man steps toward him, palms open. "Don't be alarmed."

From the office, she listens to Andy's conversation with the men who'd come to the door. Did he say a thousand dollars? Sweet Andy. Always so generous.

But wait. His voice sounds different now–apprehensive. Frightened.

Something is wrong.

One of the men says something about his special ability.

Terror surges through her body like an electric current, charging every muscle with panic. They know. They know! They're going to take everything away. Her home. Her Andy. Her children.

No. She can*not* let that happen.

On silent feet she darts to the living room and peeks in the kitchen. She pictures the men's hearts and imagines them stopping. They should be clutching their chests in a moment.

But they don't.

She tries again, this time picturing blood clots traveling through their bloodstream and lodging in their brains.

They don't keel over.

She imagines their lungs shriveling up, their tracheas crushing, their kidneys exploding, their brains melting, their bodies bursting into flames.

They don't ignite. They don't collapse.

They stand. They breathe. They live.

She can't let them take Andy and the kids from her. She can't. She can't lose them.

On the counter is a butcher block with six knives, their shiny black handles sticking out from the smooth wood.

Those men may be immune to her PK, but they can't possibly be immune to knives.

A half-second later, the largest knife flies through the air, silver blade merrily reflecting the sun, and silently embeds itself between the shoulder blades of the shorter, older man. He exhales with a surprised "Oof!" and falls to his knees.

The taller man sees the knife, cries out, pulls a gun from his coat. He turns around, swings the gun madly, and fires.

She stops the bullet in mid-air. It drops to the floor.

The other five knives pull themselves out of the butcher block and fly, silver tips gleaming and glowing, toward the taller man. He stands and watches, unable to move, as if he knows this is it for him, something has gone horribly wrong and he has no chance, he is going to die...right...now.

The blades entrench themselves in his shoulder, his stomach, his leg. His chest. His neck. He collapses to the floor, a look of dismayed bewilderment on his face.

But it's not over.

The front door bursts open, and a third man runs in, gun drawn, wire-rimmed glasses askew.

Frozen, he watches as Wendy battles with the two men, and now a third. From the corner of his eye he sees movement. The older man is still alive. He's on his hands and knees, crawling through the blood, trying to reach the knife in his back, trying to get away.

With a panicked shriek, he yanks the knife from the wounded

man's back, and plunges it back in.

Again.

And again.

And again, until the man finally collapses into the puddle of blood on the marble floor.

Andy has turned his attention to the third man. They scuffle, both men locked in a desperate fight to the death. She will not let her husband die. She mentally pushes on the third man's heart, willing it to stop beating.

The man inhales a shallow breath. Clutches his chest. Strains, gurgles, groans. Then he collapses, his glasses falling off completely.

She squeezes his heart one more time. If he's not dead yet, he will be soon.

"Wendy, wait!" He stops short as they run from the house into the front yard. "Where's Tessa?"

Tessa's book and the ice pack are under the tree. But Tessa's not there.

"She didn't go back inside the house, did she?" Wendy asks. "Tell me she didn't go back inside the house!"

Did she see what happened inside? Did she witness the murders? Dear Lord—Wendy lit the gas to destroy the evidence and burn the bodies. The house is going to blow any second!

"Find her!" Wendy screeches.

Quickly, quickly—he concentrates on Tessa and sends out his mobile eye.

He finds her immediately. She's not in the house. Thank God. She's in a car, the back seat of a car. She's crying and pounding at the windows. Did those men *take* her?

But the car is still here. Through Tessa's eyes, he can see their house. The car is parked on the street.

He runs over to the black SUV. The windows are tinted black, but he can hear the pounding of her little fists. He can hear her cries. He frantically tugs on the door handle, but it won't open. Tessa is locked inside.

Inconceivably, the third man stumbles from the house, his hand on his chest, dragging one of his legs.

Who *are* these people? Don't they ever die?

With a flick of her fingers, she hurls him to the ground and pins him there, then turns her attention back to Andy. He's trying to get Tessa out of the car, but she's locked in. She imagines the car windows exploding, and they do. With a loud shatter, glass sprays everywhere, and Andy drags Tessa out.

"My daughter was in your car," she rumbles to the man cowering on the ground. "You tried to take her."

"No," he croaks breathlessly. "I was keeping her safe. I didn't want her to see this."

Her blood boils at the thought of this man touching her daughter. Putting his slimy hands on her. A heart attack is too good for him. He needs to bleed.

Her eyes narrow, and she raises her hand into the air. She curls her fingers into a claw.

The man begs for his life. "Please..."

She imagines five razor-sharp blades slicing through the man's stomach, and swipes the air. Through her fury, she hears Tessa cry, and she glances at her.

And instead of cutting the man, she cuts her daughter.

They are safe, safe for now at least, at this rundown backwater motel. Jillian and Logan have been crying since they picked them up at the park and raced away, and now the two of them are huddled together on one bed. Tessa, finally awake from the overdose of Nyquil, is on the other. The blood from her wounds has soaked through the bandages and even the sheets. He cleans her up and wraps new dressings around her stomach.

Wendy can't even watch. She paces the room instead and questions her again. "Are you sure you didn't see anyone besides the man with the glasses?"

A sob. "It was only h-h-him."

"What else can you remember about him, Babydoll?"

"He could hear me, but I didn't say anything."

"He could hear your thoughts?"

"Uh-huh." A hiccup.

"Did he tell you his name?"

"Uh-huh." A whimper.

"What is it? What's the bad man's name?"

"Den-Dennis Connelly."

He sees a flicker of guilt in Wendy's eyes before she turns her back. "Dennis Connelly did this to you, Tessa. Dennis Connelly cut you."

He frowns at Wendy but says nothing. It's better if Tessa never knows the slices down her stomach were made by her own mother.

"Why?" Logan, small and haunted, asks from the bed. "Why would he do that?"

Wendy paces the room, and when she stops, determination has settled in her eyes. "Your father wrote some articles for his job at the newspaper," she said. "He did the right thing, but those articles made some people very angry, and they sent Dennis Connelly to kill us. Dennis Connelly does very bad things to very good people, and he wants to do those bad things to us."

"Wendy..." What is she saying? Those men came to their house to investigate them. Possibly, probably, to arrest them. But they definitely did not come to kill them. He and Wendy were the aggressors in the attack, not them. He and Wendy are the criminals. He and Wendy are the killers.

But they can't tell the kids that. Ever. The kids can never know.

Shaking, he turns to comfort his three traumatized children. "Dennis Connelly is a very bad man. But Mommy and I will keep you safe. We'll keep all of us safe."

What has she done, what has she done, oh dear Lord, what has she done?

She didn't mean to fly Tessa into the wall. She didn't mean to threaten to give her back to the bad man. She didn't mean to terrorize her own daughter.

She is just so tired of the screaming.

He doesn't need to fake his horror as he tells the kids he's watching Dennis Connelly slice open the Pennsylvania FBI agent. He hadn't faked his horror in Utah either, when he narrated the murder of the Utah police detective.

His horror is real.

But the FBI agent isn't real. There never was a Utah cop.

Tessa kept asking why the police aren't helping them. Jillian kept declaring they should contact the FBI, the NSA, the CIA.

So he and Wendy had to lie, again. They have to keep the kids from going to the authorities. They told the kids they'd already asked the police for help. They'd tried again with the FBI. But seeking aid from law enforcement would not only lead Dennis Connelly straight to their hideout, it would also get the lawmen killed.

Now, as they huddle in their getaway car at a gas station in Ohio, he's proving it to them again. He closes his eyes and describes the fabricated murder of a fictitious FBI agent to his terrified children.

His horror is most definitely real. He's horrified that he let greed convert him from Robin Hood into a killer. He's horrified about what he's doing to his kids. He's horrified by the whole situation.

But he can't find a way out of it.

She yells to the kids to get in the car: Dennis Connelly found them, and he's coming.

Andy hasn't seen him in months, but that woman in the mall today has been following her. She's sure of it. She's seen the same woman at the supermarket, at the drug store, riding her bicycle around their block. She must be working for Connelly. Even if she's not, they can't take the chance.

It's time to run.

There he is. Dennis Connelly. In the passenger seat of a black SUV, looking at a GPS. Heading west on I-80, straight toward them. It'd been so long, he was beginning to think that Connelly had given up the search. Now they have to run again. They only have two, three hours at the most before Connelly reaches them.

He focuses his remote vision on Wendy. She's at the store, buying groceries. He calls her cell phone. "He's close," he says. Wendy wails, then tells him she'll be right home. They'll need to burn and destroy all their personal things before they can leave. Once that's done, they'll call the kids at school.

Damn.

How the hell does Connelly keep finding them?

She shakes with fury as Andy tries to calm her down. How *dare* Jillian continue to piggyback on Andy's remote vision, when they expressly forbade it? And how dare she try to develop a mobile eye her own? The tiny headaches and bloody noses she gave Jillian had stopped her rebellion for a while, but then Andy caught her emailing that college professor, just before she turned off the monitor. Thank God he checked in on Jillian sometimes. They were right not to trust her. She'd cleaned up that mess by luring the professor to Twelve Lakes and planting the aneurysm in his brain. Foolishly, they thought that would be the end of it.

But tonight, Jillian piggybacked on Andy's mobile eye again.

Maybe she'd gone too far this time, giving Jillian such a debilitating headache and bloody nose. But how dare that girl disobey them *again!* How *dare* she?

1:58 a.m. He's sitting with Jillian and Logan in the getaway car in the garage, ready to go. He and Wendy woke Jillian and Logan up two hours ago and told them that Dennis Connelly had found them and was on his way. They burned everything they'd brought into the house—clothes, books, papers, sheets, towels—in the bathtub, then washed the ashes down the drain. The house was clean now, with no sign they'd ever lived here.

Dennis Connelly hadn't found them. That was a lie, one of thousands they've told the kids over the past eight years. But it's time to leave Twelve Lakes. Everything has fallen apart here. They need a fresh start in a new place.

Wendy is in the house, standing in the foyer, waiting for Tessa to come home from the school dance. The moment she walks in the door, Wendy will put their plan into action and then they will all leave town. But now it's exactly 2 a.m. and Tessa isn't home. Where is she? She's never been late before, not even by a minute.

Wendy calls Tessa on her cell phone, but she doesn't answer.

He concentrates on Tessa and sends out his mobile eye, but he can't see anything. He can hear music, and maybe...muffled crying?

He feels the first fluttering of alarm.

Jillian comes back from Tristan's house, sobbing and holding Tessa's silver heels. She found them in a pile of snow. Jillian says she knocked, then pounded on the front door, and when no one answered, she used her PK to open the door. No one was in the house. Tristan was gone. Tessa was gone.

Someone took Tessa. Not Dennis Connelly. Whoever he is, he already has her locked up in a cell, hundreds of miles away.

He and Wendy give Jillian and Logan three large bags that hold all the cash they have on hand, about 30,000 hundred-dollar bills. Jillian is crying. Logan is trying not to.

"Don't tell us where you're going," he instructs the kids. "It's safer that way. After we get Tessa back, I'll see where you are and we'll come get you."

After one last, ferocious hug, they push their children out into the cold night.

It wasn't supposed to end this way.

As she drives faster and faster toward northern Wisconsin, Andy groans with pain. Blood is pouring from his nose. It's trickling from his ears now too. But he will not stop watching Tessa. He narrates in a tight, stilted voice what he sees through her eyes.

Tessa, aware that Andy is watching, confesses she told Tristan all their secrets. And in turn, Tristan told the man with the red beard.

Tristan is dead now, Tessa says. The man with the red beard

killed him.

She didn't believe his threat at first, but that man killed Tristan, his own colleague. She's certain he'll kill Tessa too, if they don't come.

It wasn't supposed to end this way.

Jillian is piggybacking. He can sense her. He can feel her panic, he can hear her crying.

Through a veil of red, he and Jillian watch through Tessa's eyes as Wendy stumbles from the car, her hands in the air.

They watch through Tessa's eyes as a guard in a black jacket drags him from the car too.

They watch through Tessa's eyes as the guards aim their guns.

They watch through Tessa's eyes as the guards pull the trig—

And then he and Jillian see nothing at all.

CHAPTER FIFTY

ESSA. THAT'S ENOUGH."

Tristan's voice, faint and echoed, broke through the visions.

"Open your hand. Let go of the rings."

He pried my fingers open and pulled the rings from my hand, and the vision/memory of my parents collapsing into the snow disappeared.

"Breathe."

I gasped in air and opened my eyes. I was still lying with my head in his lap, but every muscle in my body was stiff, and my lungs burned. The fog waited anxiously for me to pull it in and escape into its dark nothingness. I called it in, but not all the way.

"They did it." I listened to my voice say the words. It sounded alien. Old. "They're guilty."

Tristan whisked me to the bathroom a moment before I threw up.

The tears came next, fierce and violent. I buried my head in Tristan's chest and sobbed.

My parents were criminals. They stole money. They stole lives.

My parents lied to us. They made us live in fear of a man who only wanted to rescue us.

My parents were killers.

Tristan stood outside the doorway to my father's cell, far enough to give us some privacy but close enough to rush in to prevent either the fog or the visions from attacking me. The warden, Mr. Milbourne, stood next to him with an angry frown, resentful that Dennis Connelly had gone over his head and convinced the board of directors to allow me this ten-minute visit.

Now that I knew, with absolute certainty, that my parents were guilty, I needed to see them more than ever.

The cell was silent except for the occasional beeping of machines that monitored his comatose body. He was relaxed, his breath deep and even. But an almost imperceptible strain on his face, a tightness right between his eyebrows, showed me his unconscious slumber was far from peaceful.

I knew what that tightness was: guilt. The healers had been able to relieve his pain, but they would never be able to cure it, because it wasn't caused by anything physical. It was caused by guilt.

If this were a movie, I'd be overcome with forgiveness and lean down to give him a kiss on his cheek. But this wasn't a movie; this was my life. I had no forgiveness for him.

Pity, yes. I had endless pity for this man who got caught in an ever-growing firestorm of secrets and lies. But he was the one who lit the match.

I had love for him too. He was my dad. Regardless of the crimes he committed, he loved me. I was his Tessa Blessa. I could never forgive him, but I would always love him.

Whether he ever woke up or not, he'd spend the rest of his life here. I brought my lips close to his ear. "I'm sorry your life ended up this way,

Dad. I know you only wanted us to be happy."

He didn't respond, or even move. He had no idea I was there.

Would I be like him, should I ever choose to escape forever into the fog? Mindless, yet tormented?

I gave my dad one last look, then left his cell.

Now it was my mother's turn.

Criminals with secret psychic powers incarcerated in a secret prison run by a secret government task force rarely have visitors. Still, as I sat on a metal chair in the Underground's cold, small visiting room, I kept the fog close to keep out any visions of those who'd been here before me. I didn't want to know.

I couldn't see him through the closed door, but Tristan was hovering in the hallway, again prepared to rush in if I lost control of the visions or the fog.

After a long, silent wait, my mother shuffled in.

Gray disheveled hair, gray sunken eyes, gray wrinkled uniform.

Mr. Milbourne himself escorted her, holding her arm just above the elbow. Her wrists and ankles were shackled. Her PK had not regenerated in several days, so after numerous tests, she'd been declared completely neutralized. She was harmless, but restraining prisoners when they had visitors was protocol.

Mr. Milbourne sat her in a chair across the table from me, then stood in the corner with his massive hands on his hips, a tranq gun nestled in a holster around his shoulders. It was also protocol that all guards escorting prisoners outside their cell, even those who'd been restrained and neutralized, carry a tranq gun.

My mother's eyes cleared when she saw me, and she made a high, desperate whiny sound. "Oh, Tessa. Are you all right? Did they hurt you? Did they touch you?"

So many emotions—despair, betrayal, disbelief—built a lump in my throat. "I'm fine," was all I could manage to squeak, and that was a lie.

"Have you seen your dad? They told me he's not bleeding anymore. How is he?"

"I saw him a few minutes ago. He's…resting." That was another lie, but I didn't think she could handle the full truth right now. But I added something I was certain was true. "He wants you to know he loves you."

She wrung her hands together and spoke in a tiny voice. "They took my psychokinesis away."

"I know. I'm sorry." That was true too. I knew how it was to feel so powerless.

"What are we going to do?" She started crying. "How are we going to get out of here?"

When my only reply was a cold stare, she gasped. "What did they tell you? Oh, Babydoll, you don't believe them, do you? You can't believe anything they say."

"I didn't believe it," I said with a shrug. "I refused to believe you could have stolen all that money and killed all those people. Even after I couldn't deny the truth anymore, I tried one last time to prove them wrong."

Her lips trembled in a half smile of hope.

I didn't return it. "But I ended up proving them right."

Her smile wilted. "How?"

"Maybe it's being in this building, around so many psionic people," I said. "Or maybe it was the trauma of being kidnapped and held as bait." I touched my cheekbone where Kellan had punched me. "Whatever it was, it woke up something in me that's been hiding all these years."

"What?" Her voice was a whisper.

"Retrocognition. I can see the history of people or objects around me." I drew the wedding rings from my pocket and stacked them on my finger, then spun them around. "A fog, a mental fog, has been blocking the visions from me. But now I'm learning to control it, so I can bring the visions to me or send them away."

She exhaled deeply as she sat back in the chair. "That makes sense."

"Did you know about this?"

"No," she said, "But when you were a baby, you cried all the time. The doctors said it was the worst case of colic they'd ever seen. We tried everything, but you kept crying."

I concentrated on the wedding rings, and they showed me another vision—my mother, pacing while holding a tiny, screaming baby. Me. I was crying because of the visions. They came from every object in the room, unfiltered, assaulting me with piercing vibrancy and deafening furor.

"And then one day," she said, "you just…stopped." She drew her hands out into a shrug but stopped short because of her restraints. "You went into a daze. You didn't respond to anything. We fed you, and you ate, but you just stared off into the distance. You didn't cry, you didn't smile. You looked so vacant and lost."

That was the fog, coming to shield me from the visions. The rings showed me another image: my parents standing over me, clapping, doing a silly dance. A teddy bear cartwheeled above their heads. I wouldn't respond. I couldn't respond. The fog held me too tightly.

"Then one morning I came into the nursery, and you smiled at me," she said. "Your eyes were bright and you gurgled and you kicked your tiny feet. After that you were a normal, joyful little baby."

The fog had lifted enough so I could come out of the daze, staying at just the right distance to suppress the visions. It had balanced itself so I could function, and it adjusted itself as necessary throughout my life. Until now. Now the fog was allowing me to control it.

"So, this fog," Mom said, "it protects you."

"Yes," I said, "but it also hid the truth from me. The truth about you and Dad."

"Babydoll, I—"

"All the running, all the lies, of the past eight years never would have happened if it wasn't for the fog. The APR couldn't track us down because of the fog. The two investigators, the waitress, the professor…so many innocent people died, Mom, because your secrets were hidden in the fog."

I flicked the wedding rings onto the table. One of them spun on its radius a few times before stopping.

Then I stood and lifted Tristan's sweatshirt to expose my stomach. In eight years, I realized, she'd never looked at the scars, or at my stomach, even while I was wearing clothes. My father couldn't look away, but my mother had never even seen them.

I wanted her to see them now.

Her gaze flickered to my belly, then darted away. "That was an accident."

"But nothing else was." I lowered the sweatshirt and sat back on the chair.

She hung her head and wrung her hands together. "All I wanted was to give you a better childhood than I had."

A muted, fuzzy vision of her childhood floated in the fog. A pink flowered blanket, heavy panting, the stench of fish and sweat, a sense of powerlessness.

I lifted the fog a bit and placed my hand on hers, and the vision zoomed into focus with knife-sharp clarity.

Her stepfather slithers under her covers, still reeking from his job at the fish market, pawing her with clammy fish-hands, his fish-breath wet and slimy on her neck. He'd barely waited for her mother to leave for her shift before creeping into her room tonight.

She lies as still as she can. She can feel his heart pounding, and she squeezes her eyes tight and wishes it would just stop beating, that it would explode in his chest, that he would drop dead and leave her alone forever.

Stop. Stop. Stopstopstopstop STOP!

And…he stops. Stops squirming on top of her, stops panting in her ear.

He slides to the floor, clawing at his chest, his fish-lips opening and closing soundlessly.

She peeks over the edge of her mattress, watching him until he stops breathing and his eyes stare up at nothing. His mouth gapes open. She gulps, and imagines her pink flowered blanket floating off the bed to cover his face, to cover his body.

And it does.

Wow.

"No touching," Mr. Milbourne rumbled from the corner, and the vision disappeared.

I gave Mom's hand a squeeze before I let it go. "I didn't know you had a stepfather."

She sipped in a sharp breath. "How did you…"

"I'm sorry that happened to you, Mom. He deserved what you did to him."

She froze for a moment, then she slumped in the chair. "You really are psychic."

We should have been celebrating my new ability. She should've been beaming with pride. But now she was only threatened. Disappointed.

"You told me your mother choked to death on a dried apricot," I said. "Did you do that too?"

"I met a boy at the food pantry, and he asked me to his prom. I saved and saved for a dress, but my mother got laid off and asked me for the money to pay the rent." Her voice was small, almost childlike, and she started rocking back and forth. "I got mad and pictured her throat closing around the apricot. I didn't mean to do it."

She sobbed, and I slid my hands into the sleeves of Tristan's hoodie to keep myself from running around the table to throw my arms around her. I reminded myself that she had stolen money, stolen lives, stolen my childhood.

"Jillian piggybacked on Dad's mobile eye while you were driving up here," I said. "She saw everything, right up until Dad was shot. Now he doesn't have his mobile eye. Jillian and Logan probably think we're all dead."

She said nothing, just rocked back and forth.

"I'm telling them the truth about you when I find them," I said. "The APR is still looking for leads, but I think they went to Nebraska, to look for her old boyfriend, Gavin."

But when Mom stiffened, I knew the only place Jillian and Logan would find Gavin was in a cemetery.

I collapsed back against the chair. "You killed him. Why?"

"Jillian was in love with him," she said. "She's so rebellious. We knew she'd tell him something sooner or later. Or she'd find a way to contact him one day. I gave him an aneurysm when he brought her home after a date. We left town that night."

My mother killed Gavin, a high school boy, simply because my sister was in love with him.

Oh God. Oh no.

With a garbled shriek I bounded across the table. Grabbed her shoulders. Lifted the fog. Frantically filtered through the visions. Prayed I wouldn't see it.

But I did.

She waits in the dark. 1:55am. Everything's ready to go. Andy and the kids are waiting in the car. Their bags are packed. They've destroyed all the other personal items.

Only one thing left to do.

She hates to do it. Really. Tessa is in love with that boy. She's never seen a love so strong between two people; it rivals the love she shares with Andy. But that's exactly why she has to do it. Nothing in the world, except death, would keep her from Andy. And nothing in the world, except death, would keep Tessa from Tristan.

So Tristan has to die.

When he brings Tessa home in five minutes, she will plant an aneurysm in his brain.

By the time the sun rises, her family will be halfway to their new hideout, and Tristan will be dead.

The vision disappeared when Mr. Milbourne peeled me off my mother. He returned with a grunt to his place in the corner as I, weary and crushed, sank back to the chair. "You were going to kill Tristan." I listened to myself say the words, but they still didn't seem real.

She spoke to her wringing hands. "I should have done it the week before, the morning you got up early to make breakfast for us and I invited him inside to talk about Winterball. But I didn't. I kept him alive for *you,* Babydoll. I wanted you to go to just one dance with him."

Dark and thick, the fog rumbled in the distance. I allowed it to creep in a bit closer. "How long were you going to keep it up?" I asked. "Were you going to kill everyone we loved for the rest of our lives?"

She rocked back and forth, back and forth. "We always knew it would end one day. But not like this. We thought Jillian would do something to get us caught, or Logan would figure it out."

She stopped rocking, stopped wringing her hands, and became statue-still, eyes closed, not even breathing. Then her hands clenched into tight fists, and she slowly raised her head. Her gray eyes, blazing with silver fury, and her next words, growled from behind clenched teeth, chilled and burned me at the same time. "We never thought it would be *you.*"

Externally I was frozen, but internally all I felt was a draining—the draining of blood from my face, the draining of air from my lungs, the draining of hope from my soul. My mother blamed me for luring her here, for taking my father and her PK away from her, for destroying our family.

She blamed me for everything. To my mother, this was all my fault.

Mr. Milbourne crumpled to the floor with a heavy thud.

Before I could blink, before my next heartbeat, the door flung open and Tristan burst in, shouting for me. My mother pounced with a frantic screech, shaking off her chains as if they were made of smoke. With a small flick of her hand, she sent Tristan and me tumbling backwards over the warden.

Trembling, panting with raspy sobs, she stood over us. "But I can forgive you, Babydoll. You're usually such a good girl. I know Tristan tricked you." She reached a shaky hand out to me. "Now let's go. No one can stop us. Let's get your father and leave."

Her gaze darted between the doorway and me. Her desperation hung in the air like a black cloud.

It was that desperation that turned her into a killer.

If guilt was my father's greatest weakness, then desperation was my mother's.

But it wasn't me. I was *never* their greatest weakness.

"Get up, Tessa. Now," she rumbled. I felt a strong tug, like an invisible rope, urging me up toward her and the open doorway. I wasn't sure if the tug was the force of her PK or my own compulsion to run, to escape, to mask the truth with fog and hide forever in denial.

The only thing keeping me from running was Tristan. Straining with effort, he anchored me against his chest. His muscular arms and broad shoulders, however, were no match against my mother's power, or her fury.

But he was holding me with something stronger than any of that.

I followed my mother's gaze to the open doorway. And then I betrayed her one more time. "Mom, I'm not going with you. I'm not running anymore."

She howled, her outstretched hand curling into a claw. She raised it in the air, and I braced myself, already feeling my stomach slicing open.

When her sight slid from me to Tristan, I realized her vengeance wasn't directed at me. "Tristan, watch out!" I shrieked, but he pushed me away with one arm.

With the other, he drew the gun from the warden's holster. Aimed.

Fired.

As the tranquilizer pierced my mother's neck, her eyes glinted with remorse for the tiniest of moments before she collapsed to the floor.

CHAPTER FIFTY-ONE

RISTAN STUFFED THE last of his clothes into his duffle bag while I leaned against the open doorway to our cell. I didn't need a bag. Everything I owned in the world, I was already wearing: the blue tennis hoodie from Tristan, the butterfly jeans from his sister, and a pair of laceless sneakers. My black cell phone, useless yet indispensable, was hooked to my waistband.

Weasel Face—no, Warren Fontanini—waited down the hall to escort us upstairs. He'd been among the guards who rushed in moments after Tristan shot my mother. Half of them took her away. The other half whisked Mr. Milbourne, Tristan, and me to the clinic. Tristan and I were thoroughly examined and declared unharmed. The healers repaired Mr. Milbourne's heart, but they were keeping him in the clinic until he returned to full strength. He hoped to be back on duty next week.

Dr. Sheldon wanted to keep me under observation for a few more days, but I convinced her that I was ready to leave.

My mother, still unconscious, was being neutralized again.

Tristan zipped his bag shut and stood to leave. "So, once we get home, we'll get you set up in our guest room. We have extra toothbrushes and all that kind of stuff. You can borrow clothes from Ember until we can get you your own things."

I blinked at him. "Just like that?"

"What do you mean?"

"I've accepted that my parents are guilty, so you assume I'll go back to being your girlfriend, just like that? And you assume I'll come *live* with you?"

His duffle bag dropped to the floor. "I…you're not?"

"Tristan, you lied to me. You betrayed me. You made promises that you didn't keep," I said. "I can't pretend that never happened."

"But I did it to help you. To rescue you. To save you."

"You aren't the person you said you were. Even after I told you the truth about myself, you continued to lie to me." I raised the fog as high as I dared. My head was clear, my mind made up. "Our entire relationship is built on lies."

"But…" he floundered in disbelief, scraping his hands through his hair. "If you don't come home with me, where will you go?"

"To stay with my aunt Rebecca," I said. "At least until they find Jillian and Logan. After that, I don't know. The three of us will decide together."

"But your aunt lives in Delaware," Tristan said. "My house is just a mile down the road from the APR. You can keep up with the investigation better if you're close." He strode over and took both my hands. "And what if I get a warning premonition about you? I can't keep you safe if you're so far away."

"You couldn't keep me safe in Twelve Lakes, and you were right next to me."

He pressed my hands to his chest, right over his heart. "I will never forgive myself for failing you in Twelve Lakes. And I will spend the rest of my life making it up to you," he said. "But I can't do it if you're half a country away."

"You want me to come home with you because it's close to the APR. Because you want to make amends for your broken promises," I said, pulling my hands from his. "Neither of those are good enough reasons for me to go home with you."

"That's not why," Tristan said. "I want you to come home with me because I love you."

Unable to meet his pleading blue eyes, I lowered my gaze. Stared at my shoes. Shuffled my feet. "I want to believe you, but I can't. There've been too many lies."

"I deceived you. I betrayed you. I didn't keep you safe," he said. "But Tessa, I love you. If you never believe anything else I say, please believe that." He reached into his pocket and held something out. "I found this under the cot while I was packing up."

The band of pearls. My promise ring.

"Take it," he said. "Lift the fog and read it. Like you did with your parents' wedding rings."

Ah. He wanted me to have a vision about his past that would prove his love for me was genuine. But my mind was made up. Tristan lied to get me to trust him, and those deceptions got me kidnapped, beaten, and terrorized. "I'm not going to read that ring, Tristan."

He staggered back as if I'd shot him with words made from bullets. "So that's it," he said, sitting down hard on the cot. "We're over. Us. You and me."

"There is no us," I said. "There is no you and me."

He stared at the pearl ring in his fingertips, looking like I'd just wrung all the hope from his heart like water from a sponge.

I opened my mouth to say goodbye, but nothing came out. So after one last glance at him, I turned away.

And left.

Fog raised, head clear, I walked up the dim hallway of the Underground. Warren Fontanini escorted me without a word, past the locked, windowless cell doors. When we reached the elevator, I pressed the button. I was leaving this place behind. Forever. The Underground, my parents, Tristan.

I would never see Tristan again.

Silently, the elevator doors slid open.

I would never see Tristan again.

I tried to step inside, but my feet wouldn't move.

The doors started sliding closed, and Warren stuck out his hand to stop them. "You getting in?"

I nodded and commanded myself to get into that elevator. To *leave*.

But I didn't move.

I would never see Tristan again.

Why couldn't I get on that elevator? Why couldn't I tell him goodbye?

Because if I got on that elevator, I would never see him again.

And I didn't want to say goodbye.

I spun around and ran.

I ran. Dashed. Sprinted. Flew. Faster and faster with each step.

I ran back down the hall, back to our cell.

I ran to him. I ran to Tristan.

He was sitting on the cot, elbows on knees, pearl ring in his hand. "Tristan!" I cried.

He shot up, eyes widening with cautious hope as I plucked the ring from his fingers.

"You came back to read the ring?" he asked.

"No," I said. "I told you, I'm not going to read the ring."

"Then why—"

"I don't need a vision to prove you love me. You didn't have to stay down here with me, but you did. You never left me. Not for one second. *That's* how you proved you love me."

"And that's why you came back?" he asked, heartbroken and hopeful at the same time.

"I came back," I said, "because when Kellan shot you, I thought you were dead. Because that last night in Twelve Lakes, my mother was going to plant an aneurysm in your brain. Because just a few hours ago in the visiting room, she almost sliced you open." I reached up and brushed his cheek, rough with stubble. "I almost lost you. So many times. I don't want to lose you again. I love you, Tristan."

I slipped the ring onto the fourth finger of my left hand, back where it belonged. Then I said the same words he'd said to me countless times: "I'm not leaving you."

He lit up from the inside out, first his eyes, then his smile. He picked me up, and I slid my arms back around his neck, tight, tighter. "Us," he said. "You and me."

And my heart echoed in rhythm: *Thump. Thump-th-thump.*

He kissed me hard, harder, and I kissed him back, until we both melted into it, into each other.

CHAPTER FIFTY-TWO

HE SOFT WIND blew fluffy snowflakes onto my cheeks as we stood on the front porch of Tristan's house. He squeezed my hand. "Ready, Clockwise?"

No, I wasn't. I nodded anyway.

He opened the door. "We're home!"

We stepped into a large foyer. A mammoth ball of golden fur bounded over with an excited bark. "Mac!" Tristan knelt to give the dog a vigorous rub as he panted and whipped his tail side to side. His head came up past my waist. "You're not afraid of dogs, are you?" Tristan asked me.

My first instinct was to say yes; I was afraid of everything.

But that didn't have to be true anymore. To prove it, I gave Mac a few pats. His fur was soft, and he licked my cheek.

Spilling into the foyer on all four walls were dozens of cheery family photos, mostly candids. I lifted the fog, just a little, to witness visions of a home filled with laughter and friends.

A flash of purple whirled into the room: Ember, looking exactly as she had in my vision, with shiny purple hair and a sprinkle of freckles across her nose. Another dog, as tiny as Mac was large, wagged its tail from the crook of her arm. A fluffy white cat rubbed at her heels.

"This," Tristan said, "is Ember, my annoying little sister." He messed her hair with the same vigorous rub he'd given Mac, then picked her up and swung her around. "Missed ya, sis."

"Glad you're home," she mumbled into his shoulder, then ended the tender reunion by shoving him away. She smoothed her hair and turned to me. "Hi."

"Hi," I said back, and we exchanged a smile. Ember could be my sister until I reunited with Jillian and Logan.

"Tristan?" A pale, plump, copper-haired woman with the same freckles as Ember rushed over to him. She reached up and hugged him tight, crying a little and patting him to make sure he was really home safe, the way a mother would greet her soldier son returning from war.

"Tessa, this is my mom, Deirdre," Tristan said when she finally released him.

She wiped her tears, then took my chin in her hand and tilted my head up. "Let's see those wildflower eyes."

I opened my eyes as wide as possible while blinking back my own tears.

"Beautiful," she sighed, then enveloped me in another hug. "Welcome to the family." I was unable to speak as she crushed me in her arms. "Oh!" She gave a tinkling laugh. "That was it! That was my dream!"

Tristan took me from his mom and put his own arm around me. He kissed me, as if to say *We made it, Tessa.*

Dennis Connelly stood in the entrance of the foyer, watching us from behind his round glasses, smelling nothing at all like cherry cigars.

I was standing in the home of the man I'd feared for eight years. And all along, I'd been in more danger with my own parents. I remembered my vision of him trembling on the ground under my mother's murderous glare, clutching his chest, begging for his life. My parents tried to kill him, and now he was welcoming me into his home, into his family.

I stumbled over to him. There was something I needed to say.

So I closed my eyes. Took a breath.

Licked my lips, swallowed.

And when I said it, the words came easily, loud and clear. "Thank you, Dennis Connelly."

The Connellys' guest room felt cavernous, the queen-size bed colossal, after sleeping on a narrow cot in a tiny cell for the past three weeks. Where were Jillian and Logan sleeping tonight? In a dirty motel, most likely, on beds with thin mattresses that smelled like cigarettes. Certainly not in cozy bedrooms in a safe, love-filled home.

I looked around the darkened guest room and saw visions of dozens of people who'd slept in this room over the years, most of them Tristan and Ember's friends, but also many from decades past. I pulled the fog in closer.

I missed our little cell.

I missed Tristan.

Was he craving me as much as I was craving him?

My question was answered a few seconds later. My door creaked open, and for the first time in eight years, I didn't jump. I smiled instead. "Come to kiss me good-night?"

"More than that." Tristan crept under the covers and took me in his arms. "Every night while I was lying on that concrete floor, all I wanted to do was crawl into bed with you and sleep with you in my arms," he said.

I lay my head on his broad shoulder, ran my hand over his chest. "Won't your parents be upset?"

"My telepathic father already warned me that he'll know if we do something we shouldn't. This is still the Borderline," he said, tracing my collarbone with his finger. "Well. I think we can lower it now." I tingled as he ran his fingers slowly down to my waist, then a bit lower.

He pulled me close, caressing me gently.

Tessa.

Hmm.

You can hear me?

Mmm hmm.

We aren't speaking out loud.

Oh. …Oh!

I think we've been doing this for a while now.

Can you do this with anyone else?

Nope. Only you.

Another power. Wow. *I love you, Tristan,* I said silently, just to test it, to make sure it was real.

"I love you too," he said aloud. *So happy you're here with me.*

It was real, and so was our love.

His breathing slowed, but I couldn't calm my mind down enough to follow him into sleep. I couldn't get used to the idea that until we found Jillian and Logan, this house was my home.

For the past eight years, all I wanted was to go back to the way things used to be, in our big red brick house in Virginia. But even when we lived in Virginia, my parents had been blackmailing and killing people. I couldn't wish for the way things used to be back then, or at any point in my life.

I couldn't look to the past for comfort.

I still wasn't used to believing I had a future.

My only option was to live for the present. And the present was living here, with Tristan and his family. There would be no more running. Ever.

I snuggled into Tristan, so tired my bones ached. I had a long journey to get here, but it wasn't over yet. I needed to mourn the loss of my parents, or at least, the parents I thought I had, but never really did.

I had to learn how to balance my newfound psionic ability and the fog.

I had to adjust to life in Lilybrook, with the Connellys.

I had to stop thinking every day could be my last day alive.

Most importantly, I had to find my brother and sister.

I didn't know what tomorrow held for me. What I did know was for tonight, for this moment, I was safe in the arms of the boy I loved.

ACKNOWLEDGMENTS

Writing can be a solitary endeavor, and when I first wrote *Deception So Deadly*, that's exactly what it was. I wrote the story for myself, and I never intended to show it to anyone. But thanks to my friend Mary Wasmer Kay, you are now holding this book in your hands. I will be forever grateful to Mary for encouraging me to let go of my fears and follow my dream. The girl with wildflower eyes is thankful too.

Upon my very first step along my journey from hobbyist writer to published author, my solitary activity became exactly the opposite. Joining Chicago-North RWA was the best thing I could have ever done for my writing career (and for my social life). Sonali Dev, Lynne Hartzer, Heather Marshall, Melonie Johnson, Melanie Bruce, Bethany Robison, Erica O'Rourke, Eliza Evans, Ryann Murphy, and the Aphrodite Writers are more than my writing-mates and critique partners. They are true friends.

Maya Rock's astute observations and keen editorial eye made this book shine. My rock star agent, Laura Bradford, continually blows me away with her savvy brilliance. And eternal gratitude to Tashya Wilson. She knows why.

My parents—all four of them—Judi and Richard, and Chuck and Bonnie, have always given me unwavering love and support.

My biggest supporters, my husband Glen, son Jack, and daughter

Kellyanne, put up with my long hours in the writing cave with good humor, and they don't care that the house is always messy and that all of my dinner recipes are the five-ingredients-or-less kind. I love them more than my heart can hold.

And finally, my deepest gratitude goes to you, my lovely readers. I adore each and every one of you.

Q&A WITH AUTHOR CLARA KENSIE

What inspired you to write the *DECEPTION SO* series?

I was pulling out of a parking spot at a grocery store when a series of "what ifs" hit me, one-two-three: *What if a girl was the only member of her family without a psychic ability? And what if they were being hunted by a telepathic killer? And what if they moved from place to place and had different identities in each one?* Thus Tessa was born. I gave her Tristan, the boyfriend I wanted to have when I was in high school—someone supportive and smart and charismatic, with maaaayyyybe a little bit of a dangerous side to make him exciting. And then I wrote their story. It was so much fun that I wrote a sequel, and then another…

Are your characters based on anyone you know?

My husband likes to think he is the inspiration for Tristan. They both play tennis, and they both have blue eyes and brown hair that turns gold in the sun. I can see where he gets that idea, and I'm not going to tell him otherwise.

Tessa is me, when I was in high school. Though I didn't like to cook or jog (still don't), I do like to paint, and I gave Tessa my habit of sliding my hands into my sleeves when I'm nervous or scared. We both hate green peppers, and we have the same hair—not quite blonde, not quite brown, not quite curly, not quite straight. When I was in high school, I was a lot like Tessa in that I may have had talents, but I didn't recognize them. I craved confidence but didn't have any. And like Tessa, I eventually found strength in myself that I never knew I had.

Ember, Tristan's little sister, is based on my daughter. Ember only has a tiny part in *Deception So Deadly*, but you'll see a lot more of her in the rest of the series.

Do you have a secret favorite character?

Oh, boy. Tough one. Tessa and Tristan are my ultimate favorites, but of the other characters in *Deadly*…I'd have to say Andy, Tessa's dad. He cherishes his wife and children. He's flawed. I love the relationship he has with Tessa.

Do you have any psychic abilities?

Not on a regular basis, but like Tristan's mom, Deirdre, sometimes I have precognitive dreams. An example: In the town where I grew up, there was a big empty field with a retention pond. One night in middle school I had a dream that I lived in a blue house on the edge of that retention pond. When I was a high school sophomore, a new subdivision was built on that field, with a blue house on the edge of that retention pond. You guessed it—we moved into that blue house. Pretty cool, right?

And a few years ago, I had a premonition while I was awake. Late one night, I was driving home down a dark road when I had a flash of a car careening behind me, headlights on high-beam, and crashing into me. When I looked in my rearview mirror there was nothing there— just solid darkness—but I just *knew* that I should pull over. A few seconds later, a car did come careening down the road, headlights on high-beam, out of control. It would have slammed right into me if I hadn't pulled over. That incident was my inspiration for Tristan's warning premonitions.

But if I could have any psychic power, it would most definitely be time travel.

What was it like to win the RITA® Award for *Deception So Deadly*?

One of the highlights of my career, if not my life! The RITAs are to romance novels as the Oscars are to movies, so it's a huge honor. Nora Roberts presented me with the trophy. We were in a fancy ballroom in Times Square in New York City. I gave an acceptance speech to a crowd of 2000 people. I still can't believe it happened.

Where would you hide if you were on the run like Tessa's family?

If I told you that, they would find me!

PLAYLIST FOR DECEPTION SO DEADLY

Listen on Spotify: spoti.fi/DeceptionSoDeadly

"Wildflowers" – Tom Petty and the Heartbreakers

"Closer" – Tegan and Sara

"Heavy Feet" – Local Natives

"High Above a Grey Green Sea" – Colin Stetson

"Heart in Your Heartbreak" – The Pains of Being Pure at Heart

"In Your Eyes" – Peter Gabriel

"Run" – Ellen and the Escapades

"Things that Scare Me" – Neko Case

"Demons" – Guster

"Porcelain" – Moby

"Secrets" – OneRepublic

"Dance With the Devil" – Breaking Benjamin

"Pretty Girl (The Way)" – Sugarcult

"Sweet Dreams (Are Made of This)" – Marilyn Manson (cover)

"Undisclosed Desires" – Muse

"Wicked Game" – Gemma Hayes (cover)

ALSO BY CLARA KENSIE

The Deception So Series

Book Two: Deception So Dark
(coming February 2018)

Book Three: Deception So Dangerous
(coming August 2018)

Other Novels

Aftermath

ABOUT THE AUTHOR

Clara Kensie grew up near Chicago, reading every book she could find and using her diary to write stories about a girl with psychic powers who solved mysteries. She purposely did not hide her diary, hoping someone would read it and assume she was writing about herself. Since then, she's swapped her diary for a computer and admits her characters are fictional, but otherwise she hasn't changed one bit.

Today, Clara is an award-winning author of dark fiction for young adults. Her novel *Aftermath* (S&S/Simon Pulse), a dark, ripped-from-the-headlines contemporary in the tradition of *Room* and *The Lovely Bones*, is on Goodreads' list of Most Popular Books Published in November 2016, and Young Adult Books Central declared it a Top Ten Book of 2016. The first two books in her super-romantic psychic thriller Deception So series were an RT Book Review Editors' Pick for Best Books of 2014, and the first book in the series, *Deception So Deadly*, was a 2015 RITA® Award finalist for Best Young Adult Romance and the 2015 RITA® Award Winner for Best First Book. Clara is re-releasing the first two Deception So books and continuing the series with Snowy Wings Publishing.

Her favorite foods are guacamole and cookie dough. But not together. That would be gross.

Visit Clara online at www.clarakensie.com.

www.ingramcontent.com/pod-product-compliance
Lightning Source LLC
Chambersburg PA
CBHW030525190726
48283CB00006B/1768